REDEMPTION GROUND

BOOK 3

THE NEWLAND TRILOGY

E.M. CARTER

Published by Resolute Books
www.resolutebooks.co.uk

"Darkness cannot drive out darkness:
Only light can do that.
Hate cannot drive out hate:
Only love can do that."

Martin Luther King

Previously…

REPRESSION GROUND

Carys, Amy, and Jacob have escaped the indoctrination of Ashton Training House, broken out of jail and found a way out of the heavily barricaded Midlands Compound, hotly pursued by NForce and their Trainers, after discovering an explosive secret that could blow up the whole of Newland: the truth about the Home, where Unproductive people are supposedly sent to live out their days in comfort.

The sickening truth is hidden away behind a veil of secrecy and an oppressive regime: no one questions the New Day Party, who claim to have saved the nation and set them on a better path. The three teenagers and Jacob's sick grandfather, Aiden, who was almost murdered in the Compound jail due to his perceived Unproductivity, are now fugitives on the run, wanted for treason and heading for the ruins of an old city on the Outside named Birmingham, hoping they might find shelter, safety – and more answers.

REBELLION GROUND

Carys, Amy and Jacob find refuge in the Subversives Community camp in the Birmingham ruins, where they learn about a new way of life where people are treated as equal and valued. But after finding Lora Dancer, the *S Word* judge, beaten and half-dead on the outskirts of a lonely forest, they take her back to the Centre along with Raza, a spiky girl from the community who just wants revenge on a Trainer who abused her. Still wanted for their crimes, they are almost killed but then rescued by Lora, who persuades Commander Anson to pardon them.

They are asked to appear on *The S Word* to publicly repent of their crimes and lies, but Carys breaks down and reveals the truth about Newland's murderous regime live to the nation then runs away. Jacob and Amy stay, knowing that Carys has more chance of escape if they remain in the game, but when they are forced to become presenters on the show they realise they are political pawns and in a very fragile position.

Carys is captured along with Amy's parents who have been living in an old airport community, and the story ends with them in the Centre Think as Commander Anson announces that Carys is now to be executed on December the fifth at Winter Festival.

FROM REBELLION GROUND

ℭARYS

EVERYONE IN THE cell is looking at us. At me.

Raza stands up. Walks to the side of the cell where the screen was lit moments ago and plants herself in front of it, arms crossed in her familiar stance. But this time, it's a fighting posture, not a defensive one.

'Carys will not die,' she states, and the faces gape at her. 'And neither will we. We will not let them do this.'

People begin to nod their heads, to murmur assent.

'We will be the means of change,' Raza continues, her voice hard and her eyes sparkling. 'Jacob Trader and Amy Plumber may have sold out, but we haven't and we won't. If there are enough of us, we can fight this. We can overcome them. We can escape from here and we can do this.'

They look to me for my reaction. I disentangle myself from Lois and go to Raza. I stand with her, mirroring her stance with my arms crossed, and I nod.

The cell breaks out in a clamour of voices. Some are cheering, some chanting our new slogan, 'Power to the Weak! Justice for All!' and some are quiet, their faces veiled with unease and, in some cases, disdain.

An older man with a white beard and a heavily lined face speaks up. 'It's all very well saying that,' he says, his face a mask of scorn. 'But let's be realistic. We are in here for good. Until the end, if she—'

he points at me, '—is to be believed, we all end up dead. In a furnace. I, for one, think that is probably true. But there is no way out of here. No way.'

Voices quieten and people break off their excited conversation as hope leaves the room as though air is sucked from its vents. I look at Raza, who gives me an almost imperceptible nod. I take a deep breath.

'Once upon a time,' I say, swallowing over a great lump in my throat and projecting my voice so that everyone is listening, 'I had a good friend. I used to tell him exactly what you said, that there was no way. That there was no hope. But you know what he used to say to me?'

The old man shakes his head. Regards me from faded grey eyes. I wonder what those eyes have seen.

'He said that he doesn't do impossible.'

On the wall the NScreen suddenly flickers on. It's a blurry scene outside Party HQ, where a few dozen people hold cardboard placards high and chant our slogan. One of them looks right at the camera, a tall woman who seems strangely familiar but whom I can't place through the pixellated haze, and she raises both hands high. One by one, the others in the crowd join hands and raise theirs with her at the camera, and they stand silent, a mass of beautiful rebellion, claiming the ground lost for so many years.

A guard runs into the room and flicks the screen off, his face hardened with anger, but something strange is happening in the cell. The hope that fled with the old man's words is flying back in like a hundred butterflies, their vibrant colours punctuating the gloom and lighting up every weary face.

We stand together, resolute, and raise our joined hands at the blank NScreen.

THE RESISTANCE

Party HQ Square, October

THE TALL MAN watches from behind the pretentious marble fountain as the small crowd whips into a turmoil of chaos before him. Rubbing his hand over his face, he turns to his companion. 'It's already happening.'

'Yes. But we're not ready.' The woman crouching next to him scans the area, her brow creased tightly, her body quivering.

'But it means it's all changing. Public opinion.'

'And we know why that is.'

The man sighs. 'Girl Clerk.'

The woman's eyes narrow. 'She may have set our cause back. The NForce will be super vigilant now. Stupid girl.' But she gazes out at the crowd with a strange light crossing her eyes, a mix of disapproval and longing.

'But we are strong. Years of work—'

'Half of it dashed to the ground with those Outsider camps.'

He shrugs. 'But the plans we've made… we could actually use this, you know?' He hunkers down and gazes at her. 'Your hard work won't be without result.'

The woman raises her hand. 'Wait.' She scouts the crowd. 'This is going pear-shaped.'

A ripple runs through the square.

NForce.

'There aren't enough of them. They need to get out of here,' the woman says, scrambling to her feet.

The man grabs her wrist. 'Don't risk yourself now!'

She shakes him off and rushes into the crowd. He watches as she pulls their arms, screeches at them to get out of there. But they stand steadfast, jeering at the NBC cameras shoved into their faces, brandishing their makeshift banners and placards. He shakes his head as she pushes right into the middle of the straggly crowd, her jaw all tight. The four silken banners in homage to the Newland Commanders flutter behind her, demanding a response these people will not give. When they don't run, she doesn't, either. When they don't bow, neither does she. Instead, she stands stock still and glares at one of the cameras. Then slowly, deliberately, she raises both arms in the air, head held high, in a mockery of the bent-over, cross-armed bow she is forced to do every day in her work. One by one the others join in, clasping raised hands together, faces set like flint, their shouts fading to silence.

He curses. Does she want to lose everything? To ruin all they've done?

That's when the first shot rings out.

A shout roars through the space. 'More of them. Run!'

The man stays in hiding, watching as confusion turns to terror. 'Get back here!' he yells at his companion. As she stumbles towards him, some of the crowd are slammed to the ground.

'You will not beat us down.' A short, weary-looking man, holding his trembling placard high, the spidery writing proclaiming "Power to the Weak. Justice for All". 'You will NOT beat us down.'

More of them now, rolling out their posters, holding their banners high, mouths agape in red faces as they are sucked into the anger. The thirst. The rage.

'*Stop.*'

This time the voice is stronger. Magnified. A bullhorn, echoing through the square. 'Any more, and we will shoot again. Come quietly, and you will be dealt with justly.'

The woman scrambles through the carnage, crashes to the ground behind the fountain, breathless and dishevelled yet glowing with something new. 'Couldn't stop them.'

'You shouldn't've gone out there. What if you're seen? Or arrested? You *fool*.'

She rolls her eyes. 'Just got caught up in it.'

'You have to bide your time.'

'It's too manic out there. No one would recognise me here anyway.'

He closes his eyes.

The crowd is frantic. People rush in different directions, screaming, banners bloodied and torn. Shrieks cut through the air, and then the mass of them press in as one against the line of officers.

They have no chance. There are just not enough of them. The NForce shoot, and cuff, and shove, and thump, until every last rebel is incapacitated.

Or dead.

The woman turns her face away.

'You couldn't have done anything.'

She bunches her fists. 'You know what'll happen to them now, though. What they're facing.'

'Of course. That's why we're doing what we're doing.' He takes hold of her arm. 'We just need to wait for the right time. There will be casualties.'

She looks at him. 'You're so cold sometimes.'

He curves his lips into a tiny, sardonic smile. 'Says *you*?'

'Neither of us has much to be proud of. Granted.'

They watch as a motley band of bloody and beaten rebels are marched from the square, hunched under the shadow of the great curved Party HQ building, the mirrored facade reflecting the blood-red umbers of the dusky autumn sky.

PART I

CAPTIVITY

1

THE CENTRE

*A*MY

SHE'D HOPED THIS day would never come.

It was supposed to happen at Ashton, surrounded by fellow trainees, with cheap fake bubbly and toasts from the Trainers, who would tell her they were proud of her for reaching this day at last. She'd have worn a new dress and flowers in her hair.

Back in the bunker, she'd rejoiced that it wasn't going to happen after all. But she'd never guessed, back then, that she'd be sold out to the system and standing here in a blue silk dress chosen by Coran, next to Jacob in a tux, his face as long as the night sky outside Lora's glass doors.

Instead of their Trainers it's the Commander himself here, pouring out expensive champagne and offering it around. His face is shiny with triumph. 'What a privilege for me... and you, of course! It's not often I get to attend Productivity Ceremonies. It's wonderful to see how far you two have come.'

Jacob shifts beside her, and she elbows him softly. This is just another thing for them to get through. She finds herself almost breathing a sigh of relief that Carys isn't here – what on earth would she do if she was? – but then remembers where she is and closes her eyes.

Lora stands at Anson's side, her arm tucked in his, her face made up so impeccably you wouldn't think there were bruises there unless you already knew. She forces a wide, bright scarlet smile that doesn't reach her eyes. 'You have your vows?'

'Mmm,' Amy says.

'Good. Good. Now, I know if you were at Ashton you'd be doing this in front of all your co-trainees, but this is different, of course. We decided that, to mark the occasion, we'd bring in a film crew.'

Jacob gasps; Amy kicks his foot.

Lora ruffles her hair. 'This is a very important event to the nation. They need to see this, of course, so your vows will be broadcast live for all to see the new *S Word* presenters attaining Productivity in an… um… exclusive manner.'

Amy clears her throat. 'Thank you.'

Lora inclines her head. 'And of course, there's the matter of your brand new Productivity names. You can't be *S Word* presenters without your legal names, can you?'

Amy twists a smile onto her face and pokes Jacob again; he can't quite manage more than a grimace. Not a fun birthday for him today, really; not like her seventeenth back in the bunker.

She won't allow herself to reflect on that for too long.

'But time enough for that. Let's get your speeches done, shall we? You just need to pretend you're on the stage in your Assembly Hall back at Ashton.'

I'd rather imagine anything else, Amy thinks.

Lora coughs. 'Commander, if you would do the honour of reading the Ceremony pledges for Girl P and Boy T?'

Anson's lips curl in an amused smile, as if all of this is some kind of elaborate joke to him. 'Of course. Is the crew ready?'

'Coran!' Lora calls, going to the door and peeping her head into the hallway. She's limping a little, Amy notices. 'It's time.'

Amy hears a commotion outside the door, voices and laughter and, above it all, Coran's command, barked in a much grumpier voice than usual. 'It's on. Go in.'

A silky-blonde woman and a thin cameraman enter the room and bow to the Commander, the man shoving his camera aside to cross his hands and lower his head. Amy recognises the woman as Elva Anchor, the much-loved NBC newsreader. 'So wonderful to be here!' she says, her blue eyes sparkling, spreading her hands wide and gazing around the room. 'Lora, your home... it's too divine.'

Lora smiles. 'Thank you, Elva. Now, let's get on with this; once it's done we can all have that cake and some more champagne.'

Elva signals to her camera guy and he starts setting everything up. 'Where will they be standing?'

'I think by the windows,' Lora says. 'I don't really want the nation feasting their eyes on my kitchen. Can you get a good shot with them there? The Commander will be next to them—' she points, '—there.'

'Fine,' the cameraman mutters, gathering up his stuff.

Amy fiddles with the folded piece of paper in the tiny pocket of her dress. Last night, she and Jacob had sat in the apartment they didn't deserve and scribbled out vows they didn't want to write. It'd been hard to get Jacob to write anything down at all.

'Ready?' Lora says when everything is set up with the camera and the lighting.

Amy swallows. 'Think so.'

'Don't be nervous,' Anson says, but his voice is all slime. 'You look perfect. That dress is very alluring on you, my dear.'

Lora stiffens by his side. 'Let's get started.' She ushers them over to the large bi-fold doors, the October night sky all black velvet outside. 'There. You there, Girl P, and Boy T – here. Commander, you stand there... is that okay for you?'

The Commander is still gazing at Amy. 'It's perfect for me.'

Amy contains a shudder and plucks the paper out of her pocket. Jacob stands next to her, smoothing his own paper out and staring at the words with his face crumpled up, like he can't believe what they say.

'I'll just sort out your mics,' the tech guy says, grabbing clip microphones and fitting them all up.

'The flag,' Lora says, slamming her hand against her forehead. 'I nearly forgot. Coran?'

Coran hovers in the doorway, watching them all with a face like a shrivelled lemon. 'It's there.' He slumps into the room and grabs the large Newland flag from the table. 'I'll get it ready.' He spreads it out and secures it to the glass door behind Amy and Jacob, whispering to Amy as he does so, 'Go get 'em, gal. You'll be super.'

She smiles at him, and he gives her arm a squeeze before he walks away, his face falling again. *What's wrong with him?*

The flag takes up most of the space behind them, the white silk with its design of cogs and gears like a backdrop in a law court. Amy almost feels like she's on trial and is taken back for a moment to the last time she was in a courtroom, when her parents were banished to the Outside and her soul child – her brother, as she knows the word now, Lewis – was taken for execution.

Because of her.

She grips Jacob's hand. 'Let's do this.'

He drops his head, stares at the ground.

The cameraman lifts his hand and counts down on his fingers, and the room falls into silence.

2

CENTRE THINK

CARYS

THE CELL DOOR crashes open.

'Get in.' A harsh voice cuts through the uneasy space, and the sound of shuffling chains breaks through my doom-laden thoughts. I look up as they are shoved into the room like cattle, the space filling too quickly. There are already too many of us.

Where did all these people come from? I think about the pixellated scenes we saw on the NScreen only hours ago. The resistant few in Party HQ Square, linking hands. I think of how glorious they looked.

A woman is bent double, a wound on her scalp bleeding. She gasps and presses her fist into her stomach.

And they keep coming. Like a tide rolling in, until the space is jammed with them. Gasping, wheezing, weeping, shouting.

I glance at Raza, slumped against the wall in the corner, her arms folded in her familiar stance, still bent low by the scenes of the Subs Community bombing we saw a few days back. She shuffles over to the woman with the head wound and touches her arm. 'What happened?'

The woman shakes her head, blood leaking from her nose.

A man near the door speaks up. 'It was peaceful... I mean, we weren't hurting no one. Just asking the Party to reconsider their... ideology.' A pained smile pinches his lips. 'But the NForce got to us, and well... that was it. They shot on the crowd.'

Someone starts to sob.

I stare at him. 'They killed people?' Although I'm not really surprised. I think about the scenes of carnage we've seen played across NBC the past few days. About how they chased me down and bombed the old school. About the destruction of the airport we narrowly escaped. About the Subs Community, the children dancing in the rain and welcoming us in. All gone now.

The man slouches against the door. 'Yup.'

'I'm... I'm sorry.'

The man shrugs. 'You're the one who gave us the strength to protest.'

I look down. 'And look where that got you.'

'Better than saying nothing.' His blue eyes pierce the gloom and pin me down. 'Not gonna stop now, either. I know plenty more where we came from.'

I help Raza and Lois tend to the sick. Some of them are dying in here, their lifeblood leaking out over the cold stone, their cries of pain ignored by the guards. We do our best to make them comfortable, but for some there is nothing we can do. The toilet and the buckets in the corner are overflowing and the stench rises, its tendrils wrapping round us all in choking waves.

I did this.

My thoughts flit to Jacob and Amy, the ones who betrayed me, living in luxury and abandoning me. I push them out of my head, sickened. But turns out I can't keep them away for long. The huge screen on the cell wall flickers on, showing a darkened room and three silhouettes framed against glass doors and a backdrop of a slightly wonky Newland flag, the Newland anthem playing in the background. Is that Lora's kitchen? My pulse speeds against my throat. *No.* Not them again, surely?

But it is, of course. I can tell who they are even in shadow. Amy's slight figure and Jacob's tall one, both standing straight, both faces lit with smiles as the lighting adjusts and the camera focuses in on them. And then next to them, standing solidly with feet planted wide: the Commander. Anson himself.

What now?

The cell falls into silence as people catch on to what is happening on the screen. 'They're doing their Ceremony,' one woman mumbles.

Raza spits on the ground.

I don't know how to feel. I pick at the skin around my nails, already so shredded it's raw. I search their faces for regret, for sorrow, for grief, but find nothing. They are blank, vacant, like there is no emotion at all left in there. I look down; Lois has grabbed my hand and stares at the screen, her mouth wobbling.

'Welcome to the Productivity Ceremony for Girl Plumber and Boy Trader, our new *S Word* presenters,' a bubbly voice says as the camera sweeps around to Elva Anchor, impeccably dressed as ever. 'We at NBC are delighted to be bringing you their Ceremony live today from Lora Dancer's own mansion, with our beloved Commander presiding. Please join with me in a sign of homage.' She crosses her arms across her belly and bows low, and the camera pans to show first Lora and then Jacob and Amy bowing with her.

No one in our cell moves a muscle.

'It's a short ceremony, but vital, of course, to our nation. All of you Productives out there will have fond memories of your own, and now you are privileged to watch these young people take the biggest step they will ever take on their Productivity journey. Please enjoy the occasion and join us by raising a glass at the end.' Elva smiles warmly and nods to Anson, who has stood through the proceedings so far with a sardonic grin twisting the corner of his mouth.

He stares at Amy, his eyes lingering too long, and I remember the night he pinned me against a tree and want to throw up.

'It is my joy to be here with you, dear trainees Girl P and Boy T, in front of our good nation. We will start with the pledges, then you will share your own vows. Finally, we will have the honour of sharing your brand new Productivity names with you and the nation.'

Amy and Jacob stand there, smiling and nodding. Not a tremble.

Anson takes out an old-fashioned scroll and unrolls it, clearing his throat. 'We are gathered here today on this solemn occasion to witness the Productivity Ceremony of Girl Plumber and Boy Trader. They stand before me here willingly, in love for Newland and for me, ready to take their new places as Productives in our land, ready to work for the good of us all. Power to the Strong. Justice to the Good.' He pauses, staring at Amy again. 'We'll start with you, then, Girl P. Please step forward.' She takes a step and he grabs her arm, pulling her towards him. 'Now kneel.'

On the ground, her stature is so tiny, so fragile under Anson's looming shadow, I wonder if she might break. But she kneels well, head bowed, hands clutching a piece of paper in her lap. By her side Jacob stands, as relaxed as I've ever seen him. The dimple in his cheek… I will not look.

Anson places his hands on Amy's shoulders. 'Please respond to the Productivity pledges, Miss Plumber. Are you ready?'

'Yes,' she says, her voice clear as a bell.

He smiles and grips her shoulders harder. 'Today, the tenth of October in the year N121, you, Girl Plumber of the Midlands Compound, will swear your allegiance to Newland and all our adages. Will you, Girl Plumber, promise to work towards ever-greater Productivity in our land?'

October tenth, I think. Jacob's seventeenth birthday. Of course.

She looks up at him. 'I will.'

'And will you, Girl Plumber, swear to uphold our mighty laws and always work for the good of this nation?'

'I will.'

Anson smiles; it's more like a smirk. 'And will you, Girl Plumber, honour the great Illumen and me, your Commander, for now and as long as you live?'

A very slight pause. 'I will.'

I search her face, but some of her hair, grown longer these past weeks, has fallen over her eyes as she bows her head.

'Well, good,' Anson says, squeezing her arms. 'Glad to hear it.' He breaks into a loud guffaw, and Amy smiles with him. Jacob looks down at the paper in his hands. 'Now to Boy T, then we will hear your vows; the good bit, of course. I'm all agog to hear what you have for us, my dear children.'

Amy gets up and backs away slowly, allowing Jacob to take her place, kneeling before Anson. This time, Anson doesn't take hold of Jacob's shoulders, but rushes through the pledges with less grace. Jacob replies with a firm 'I will' to each, standing and smiling wide as he finishes.

'Girl Plumber, then,' Anson says, taking her hand and pulling her closer again. 'You have your vows?'

She nods.

'Please,' Anson says, patting her shoulder. 'Go ahead.'

I watch her face closely as she slowly smooths out her paper and takes a deep breath. I wonder if that is a quiver at the corner of her mouth, but I can't tell; the screen is so big the image is fuzzy.

The silence in here presses down on me as we wait. Beside me, Lois stifles a sob.

Amy clears her throat. 'I, Girl Plumber of the Midlands Compound and Ashton Training House, declare to you today my promise to uphold my great nation of Newland.' Her paper crackles against her microphone as she shifts her hands; there's a tiny tremor in her fingers. 'I promise that I shall strive to Productivity every day, that I will work hard and that I will always tell the truth. I am leaving behind the girl I once was, when I made up pernicious lies, and, in warmly accepting the generous pardon of the Commander and the wonderful hospitality of Lora Dancer, I declare once again today that I will be an upright Productive. Newland is good and the Commander is great. Power to the Strong, Justice to the Good.'

I stand frozen, my body trembling. The words spill out of her mouth quickly and slightly robotically as she bends over her paper, but sincerely enough. She smiles as she says the last words and then bows her head at Anson, who regards her with a predatory glint in his ice-blue eyes.

I huddle closer to Lois, who stares at the screen with brown eyes wide. 'I'm sorry,' I whisper, but she says nothing.

Anson begins to clap, and a polite smattering of applause patters through Lora's kitchen as the crew join in and the camera pans to Elva Anchor, smiling as she claps delicately. 'And now Boy T's vows,' she says, gesturing at Jacob.

There's a twitch in his jaw; I can see it. I'm sure of it. But his body is relaxed as he takes out his paper and then smiles at Anson. 'Thank you for the opportunity, Commander.'

Raza puffs out her cheeks.

Anson sneers, then quickly twists it into a grin. 'Go ahead.'

Jacob coughs. 'Umm. I… I, Boy Trader of the Midlands Compound and Ashton Training House, give you my solemn promise today that I will always work for the good of our nation.' He pauses, looks at Anson then directly at the camera. 'I will always work for truth and justice.'

My heart skips a beat.

Anson clears his throat.

'I… I will become an upright Productive, exemplary in every way, an example to other trainees after me. I renounce the lies I so maliciously joined in with, and I… um… I state today that Newland is good and the Commander is great.' I feel my shoulders slump as he lowers his paper. 'Power to the Strong. Justice to the Good.'

This time Anson's applause is slower, more deliberate. 'Wonderful. Wonderful. What a shining example our young trainees – no, *Productives* – have given us today.' He beckons to someone further into the room, and Lora rushes to stand by his side, her face flushed and her eyes made up so thickly they lie in great shadows. 'Without further ado, we will assign these youngsters their new Productivity names, all ready for their first airing on our flagship show. I know how delighted they will be with these names, which I have undertaken to choose personally.' His grin is wide now, splitting his face in two, his thick lips wet and his teeth over-white in the bright lighting. 'Lora, dear, will you do the honour of carrying out the Naming Ceremony?'

Lora nods. 'It would be my pleasure.' She signals to someone and is handed two glasses of champagne, which she gives to Jacob and Amy, then two more: one each for her and Anson. She raises hers slowly and stares earnestly into the camera, where I know there must be autocues for her to read from. 'Today, in the glorious presence of our revered Commander, I offer these two brand new Productives their Newland names. Please be upstanding and raise your glasses, and all you who are watching, too.' She pauses, and there is shuffling around her as unseen crew move around. Anson holds his glass to his chest as Lora raises hers further. 'As you all know, names are important in Newland. Each trainee is usually given a name chosen by their Trainers – something that describes who they are. Take my name, for instance, taken from the Old English for laurel tree, meaning honour and victory, because my Trainers saw something in me.' She smiles up at Anson, who remains impassive. 'Our dear Commander here, of course, is named for greatness; his name means he is the son of the Illumen. Which all Commanders are.'

She pauses and bows; Anson gives her a slight nod.

'Names are given when we reach seventeen years of age, because that is the age where Productivity kicks in after many years of our exceptional training system. So today, which is the day Boy Trader reaches seventeen – Girl Plumber is already there – I am delighted to bestow on these two their new names. Their surnames will remain the same for now; they are temporary presenters but will receive permanent surnames when they attain their final

Productivity positions, of course. So: Boy Trader, please kneel before the Commander once again.'

I watch closely as Jacob, slouched over slightly, gives his glass to Amy and kneels, bowing his head.

Lora holds her glass higher. 'I declare you as Oswall Trader.'

Jacob shifts slightly.

She touches his shoulder. 'You may rise and drink to your name: it means that you are the servant of the Illumen.'

I screw up my nose; Jacob's face stays in shadow as he slowly gets up and Amy presses the champagne into his hands. He sips it slowly, his swiftly-stifled grimace a reaction to the name or the drink – I do not know. I do not care.

Raza snorts next to me. 'Oswall?'

I can't find the tiniest smile.

On the screen, Lora beckons to Amy, and Lois stiffens. 'My daughter is Amy. My daughter is Amy.'

I have no words, but Raza nods at her. 'And she always will be.'

Amy kneels, her face flushed. Lora waits a few seconds, then says, 'And you, I declare as Esla Plumber.'

Amy stays still.

'Now rise and drink to your new name: Esla, meaning truth. You are now a truth-teller, despite your history of lies. Your new name displays the mercy of the Commander and his willingness to allow new starts when deserved.'

Amy stumbles as she gets to her feet, and Anson grabs her arm and helps her, his face close to hers. 'Here.' He hands her the champagne. 'Drink with me.' He stays close as she sips, draining his own glass in one.

Lora snaps her fingers, and someone hands her two pieces of thick card: the name certificates. She shows them to the camera, one after the other; the gold-embossed names are large against the cream background. *Oswall. Esla.*

I look at Lois and Alwin. Alwin is hunched over, a shadow of a man. Lois is pale, her eyes darker than ever. 'Truth?' she says.

Truth. Is this really Amy's truth now? Has she left behind real truth forever? She is a servant of lies and Jacob the servant of the Illumen. For a moment back there, when he talked about working for truth and justice, I thought he might mean it. That he was telling me something.

Now I know that he has bowed to Newland's version of truth and justice.

But still: I will never, ever say their new, fake names out loud.

As the Newland anthem strikes up again and Jacob and Amy, holding certificates aloft, join in full voiced with Lora and Anson, I slump to the ground, sinking my head into my hands and trying to drown out the images and sounds that so invade my soul.

LATER, I LISTEN to guards mumbling outside the cell, their low tones echoing through the grating in the door. 'We'll have to open up the old cells.'

'On it. At least three, I'd say, or we'll have the Scourge back before we know it.'

'Maybe that's not a bad thing? Not enough manpower for this lot. The nurses are well behind schedule, and I can't see that changing.'

'No. Only getting worse, actually. This demo today – I reckon it's the tip of the iceberg. There'll be more where this miserable lot came from. We'll be overrun with Unproductive scum.'

'Yeah, and I guess if Scourge hits then we'll be hit. Hmm.'

'We get the other cells prepared, and we separate 'em off. Then hopefully someone'll come to a solution soon for the rest.'

'Mmm.'

I squirm, bile rising in my gut. I turn to Raza, who is stroking the greying hair of a thin woman, her face lost in shadow. 'Did you hear that?'

She flicks a glare at me. 'Who didn't?'

'We always knew they'd be getting rid of us. Looks like they're struggling, though.'

'Small mercies.'

I bite my lip. 'I suppose.'

'Look at it this way,' she says, clearing a strand of hair from the woman's ruined face, 'it buys us some time. To make a plan to break out of this hellhole.'

'I wish I could believe that's possible.'

'Of course it is.' Raza's voice drips with scorn. 'You were the one who literally just told us that earlier. Like what Jacob said. Impossible's not our thing, right?'

I shrug. 'Yeah, and you heard what he had to say earlier.'

'You can't lose hope, Carys.'

But I can.

3

THE CENTRE

AMY

AMY PLUMBER SHIVERS as she perches on the edge of an ancient uncomfortable sofa in the cramped, airless room behind the stage. 'Not exactly judge standard, is it?'

Jacob drums his fingers on the table. She knows his mind is heavy with the scenes they saw only the other day and what's happening with Carys, not to mention that sham of a ceremony. 'Whatever,' he says. 'Who cares anyway?'

Amy looks at her gold-tipped nails, recently painted by Coran. 'We have to keep up the pretence.'

He says nothing.

The door opens and a harried-looking producer pushes into the room, straightening stray hairs and scraping out one of the chairs. 'Right. Few changes for tonight's programme.'

It's only their second time as presenters on *The S Word*, but Amy wishes it were their last. 'Changes?'

The guy shifts in his seat. 'Well, um, it's kind of like a special, I guess. Bit like when… well, the other week.'

Images of Carys screaming at the audience flicker through Amy's mind. *Carys telling the truth.*

Jacob slumps in his chair and closes his eyes.

'We've got two special guests. They're going to tell their story, and then we've got a couple more entertainment acts than usual as well. The judges have been discussing things… we're ripe for change. For better entertainment. It'll be an amazing show.' The producer sounds like he's trying to convince himself.

'What special guests?' Amy says, dread snaking through her stomach. Special guests mean Commander Anson. Or Principal and Gardener.

'Just go with the autocues, no time to go through the whole thing.' He scratches his neck. 'Bit of a last minute decision, see. Now, are you ready? Did they give you something to eat yet?'

Amy shakes her head.

'Ah. Well, I'm sure you can grab something later. You look good, by the way, both of you. Look the part. You'll be introduced with your new names tonight.'

Jacob rolls his eyes.

'Time to go on and get sound checked. You with me?'

Amy breathes out. 'Yes.'

'Present and correct,' Jacob says.

AMY AND JACOB hold it together as they run onstage to a drumrolled announcement, thunderous applause and a hundred shouts of the names they will never want: 'Oswall! Esla! Oswall! Esla!'

The judges look weary tonight. Even Lora is worn around the edges, as if her patience is wearing thin, and she bickers with Raulf as the four of them enter to the usual souped-up acclaim and take their place in the huge plush purple chairs. Amy and Jacob paste on their smiles as they follow the cues above the stage, welcoming each of the judges and stumbling through some fake banter. 'Make it real,' a voice squeaks through Amy's earpiece, almost deafening her. 'You're not on form. Get back on it now.'

She forces her mouth into an upturn and spreads out her hands. 'So, tonight, we have a great treat and surprise for you all here in *The S Word* studio.'

Jacob takes up the reins. 'Yes, as… Esla says, we have something different for you tonight. We're proud to welcome some guests you may recognise from past editions of *The S Word*.' Amy watches as he screws up his face then smooths it over just as quickly. 'As you know, here on *The S Word* we refute all the treasonous lies that have been… spread around the nation. We reject the damaging stories spun by Girl Clerk, who is… who is now to be executed in the Commander Lucan Arena at Midwinter Festival.' He swallows and looks away from the camera for a second then turns back and gazes straight into its eye. 'To prove that these are nothing but malicious lies, we are thrilled to welcome Garrett House and… and Audrey Retail to the show tonight.'

Something ripples through the far west side of the auditorium. Amy stares, trying to make out what's going on, but she is blinded by the autocue and what Jacob just said. *Audrey Retail*? Could it be? The same woman they saw collapsing on the show two years ago when she was branded a Skiver? But surely… No. Must be another with the same name.

Jacob nudges her, and she clears her throat. 'Yes, that's right! We are pleased to welcome Garrett and Audrey back to *The S Word*. Of course, they were judged as Skivers by our fair and balanced panel here—' she pauses, gulps, '—but we do not hold that against them. They are here to tell their stories and, of course, to throw light on the truth that is so important to us here on Newland's flagship show.'

The audience wait in silent expectation as two Productives – or are they Unproductives? – are ushered onto the stage. The judges are stony-faced, but a scattering of applause welcomes them. A broad-shouldered man and a petite woman. Amy gazes at them, taking them in. The man she doesn't recognise; she doesn't remember the episode that featured him. She stares more closely at the woman – Audrey. She thinks back to the time she sat out in the auditorium, squashed next to Miss Trainer One, afraid and bewildered as she watched Audrey tell her story of a back injury. She pictures that Audrey in her mind, thinking of her stooped stance, the pain written across her pale face, and she cannot superimpose that image over this cool, collected woman. *It can't be the same one.*

Jacob steps forward and lays his hand on the man's arm, beaming out at the crowd, who cheer him on. 'Garrett. Welcome. Four years ago, you were judged a Skiver, right here on this stage. How do you feel about that now?'

Garrett grins. 'Well, Oswall—' Amy can feel Jacob's flinch, '—all I can say is it taught me a great lesson. My time in the Think – it was educational, you know? I'm thrilled to say I'm more Productive than ever before now. In fact, just last week I was rewarded with a Gold on my Productivity Points card.'

A smatter of applause, then another ripple over to Amy's right. A Trainer hissing at a kid.

Jacob nods. 'So, let's see your story from four years ago.' He inclines his head towards the giant NScreen behind them, which lights up with rather fuzzy-looking footage of an old show. Amy squints to try and make out the man, but his features aren't clear. He looks similar to this guy, though. Could easily be him – same height, same hair.

They wait through a familiar *S Word* story. Garrett House is an estate agent, and in the original footage he told the story of an accident that left him unable to work for four months. The judges had been mean that night, Amy thinks, watching Raulf now as he roars with laughter at his past self passing sentence with less compassion than a spider toying with a fly. They'd written him off quickly, told him he was a disgrace to Newland and would be sent to the Think for re-education there and then. He'd hung his head, beaten, but now he stands tall, grinning away at the judges.

Jacob moves them on quickly to Audrey, who is vivacious and energetic. 'And you, Audrey? We're going to see your story now, of course, but tell us what *The S Word* did for you.' Amy can almost taste the bile soaking his words.

Audrey takes a few dainty steps forward so she's facing the judges. 'What can I say?' She smiles at Portia. 'You gave me a new path. A better one. I know now that I was lazy, but you taught me that hard work always pays. And here I am, two years later, twenty pounds lighter and now a manager at my store!'

The auditorium breaks into applause, but as they trail off a lone jeer echoes through the space. Another rustle over to the west of the auditorium stops Audrey in her tracks for a moment, but Jacob breaks in. 'That's perfect, Audrey! Or should I call you Audreee, as our wonderful Cadman did?'

Amy shudders.

'Of course,' he continues, 'Esla here and I were privileged enough to be right here for that particular show. We saw you, Audrey, and we're lucky enough to see you again tonight!'

On the screen the story plays out, the footage grimy and hazy, bringing it all back. The beat-up supermarket, the ladder, the accident, the slipped discs. Raulf's scorn and Lora's kindness, Portia making it all about her once again. The video stops short as her sentence is proclaimed – her collapse, so clear in Amy's memory, is cut out.

Amy gathers herself together. 'Your story was powerful, Audrey,' she says to the woman in front of her who bears no relation to Audrey Retail other than being of similar height and hair colour. She clenches her teeth hard. 'And you've obviously changed your life as a result.'

The woman's smile is smug. 'I've achieved so much more than I ever did as that… creature I once was on there.' Her lip curling, she waves a hand at the screen, frozen on the image of Audrey's stricken face. 'I don't even recognise her now.'

Raulf Singer is up from his chair and clapping. 'You're an inspiration, Audrey. A true Newlander. And you have shown us once and for all that these lies are just that: ugly, disgusting *lies*.'

The woman preens. 'Indeed.'

Jacob's forehead glistens with sweat. He takes a breath, staring at the autocue, but before he can say anything a lone word rings through the auditorium.

LIARS.

Amy looks up, gazes around the audience, glances back at Jacob, whose mouth is open, frozen. 'Um…' she begins, cold fear beginning to coil through her body.

'LIARS.' Again it comes. One high-pitched voice. This time followed by a commotion; the angry shout of a Trainer, a whoosh of something. A flail?

Raulf strides to the edge of the stage and peers out, his hand sheltering his eyes against the floodlights. 'You,' he yells, pointing in the general direction of the hubbub, 'account for yourself. I'll not have groundless accusations made on my show. Once was quite enough.'

A hush falls on the crowd.

'Well?' he says, his voice thundering through the heavy silence.

Through the darkness Amy sees a Trainer standing up awkwardly, dragging a skinny boy to his feet. 'It was this child, Mr Singer. I'm very sorry. He will be punished, I assure you.'

Raulf considers the Trainer and the boy, his face lost in shadow. Then, 'Bring him up here, Miss Trainer. He can account for himself here. We will address lies like this at their root. Zero tolerance of this kind of thing, right, Oswall?' He gives Jacob a sideways glance loaded with meaning.

Jacob coughs. 'Um… of course, no… yes, I mean.'

Trainees throughout the crowd whisper and shuffle as the Trainer drags the lad forward into the light and up the steps to the stage. Spotlights follow their progress, and Raulf turns to meet them, throwing a snide grin at Lora. 'Well, who do we have here? A little surprise guest?'

The Trainer, a sharp-faced woman barely in her twenties, shoves the child forward. 'This is Boy H, sir… I mean, Mr Singer. Boy House.'

Amy watches the screen, zoomed in on Raulf's face. His eyes light up. '*House*? Who were you calling a liar, Boy House?'

The boy is small and frightened looking, yet there's something staunch about him; the way he stands, maybe. He clasps his hands together and stares straight back at Raulf.

Lora clambers to her feet and skitters her chair back. 'Raulf—' she shoves at his shoulder with a light touch, '—Raulf. He's just a little one. Barely a trainee! Leave him alone.'

Raulf guffaws. 'No.'

Lora frowns and looks to Portia and Edwin for support. Neither of them budge from their chairs, both of them waiting with expectant faces. She huffs. 'You lot are mean.'

Raulf sneers. 'Turned her head, these lot did,' he says, gesturing at Amy and Jacob in turn. 'Made her even softer.' He laughs harshly, and a few trainees in the audience join in. 'Now, Boy H. Do tell us, who do you believe to be lying?'

The boy pushes a messy brown curl from his face and looks straight at Amy. 'Garrett House was my father,' he says in a low voice. 'This man—' he points at Garrett, his finger quaking, '—is not Garrett House. Not my father.'

A surge of gasps and shouts swells through the audience. Lora pales and frowns at Raulf, drawing her eyebrows into a question. Raulf's face is unreadable for a second, and then he grabs the boy's arm and marches him over to Garrett. 'You would disown your own father?'

'No! I—'

Raulf cuts him off. 'Garrett, this is your son?'

The man shifts. 'Yes, of course. My son. Boy H.'

The boy wriggles out of Raulf's grip. 'He's not, he's not,' he shrieks, the crowd hanging on his every word. 'You're liars. He's not my father. My father is dead. You killed him, just like Girl Clerk said…' He breaks off, glancing wildly around as if suddenly realising the gravity of the situation. Then he runs, ducking to evade his Trainer and the stage staff, stumbling down the steps into the arms of a beefy security guard.

Raulf brushes himself down, the anger burning in his eyes. 'I believe some time in the Think would help you, boy, just as it helped these two tonight. The proper Think here in the Centre, not the one at your training house, of course. Guards. Take him.'

Amy can only watch as the boy is dragged away to the side and through the exit in the east wing. She can hear his sobs as he is taken, his desperate shouts echoing through to the stage. 'He's not. He's *not*.'

4

CENTRE THINK

𝒞ARYS

THE KID REMINDS me of Sim.

We watch on the NScreen as he is dragged offstage, his little fists pounding helplessly at the guard's chest. Even his hair is similar, all messy curls, but brown rather than red, and his eyes are a light brown rather than Sim's bright blue. But he snaps something inside me. How can Amy and Jacob stand there on stage and not say a word? How can they let this boy be carried off to the fate they know well awaits him? How can they not say a word about that obviously fake Audrey Retail? It's like the *S Word* producers are laughing at us; they didn't even bother to get someone who looked much like the original, let alone someone who acted like her. They know they'll be seen through, and they don't care.

I think for a moment about the real Audrey and her fate, and I shudder, looking at Lois and Alwin as they keep their eyes pinned on the screen. On Amy. How must they feel, with her yielding to the Party narrative yet again? With her using this new name? They're in denial.

Later on, the boy is shoved into our cell along with four or five other rebels. He stands stock still in his too-large training uniform, eyes wide and staring, fists bunched by his sides. I scramble up from my place on the floor. 'You're Boy House, right? We saw you.'

He gazes at me, his eyes unfocused, then glances around the cell, then back at me, his forehead crumpling. 'You're…'

I nod. 'Girl Clerk. Yes. But you can call me Carys.'

He frowns. 'You have a name?'

'Well, no, not officially. But I do, yes. It's the name my parents gave me.'

He stares at me with a light that looks like wonder crossing his eyes.

'I'm sorry you had to go through all that, with that actor saying he was your father,' I say.

He scuffs a foot on the dirty stone floor. 'My father was killed.'

'I know. Mine too.'

He stares at the ground.

'You were brave,' I say gently, putting a hand on his arm.

He lifts his shoulders. 'I s'pose we're dead now, right?'

I look at him, then at the blank NScreen, then at Raza, skulking in her corner. 'Not if I can help it.'

THERE ARE MORE of us. Too many for this cramped cell; the guards barge in and grab hold of prisoners, shuffling them out a few at a time, shoving them in the smalls of their backs. Taking them into the other cells, I guess, the ones that haven't been opened up for years because there's never been need for them. I feel like I can breathe again. But later, more prisoners are brought in and the space fills up again and the air seeps out of the room.

Lois hunkers down with me and the boy. 'There are so many. We can have hope, dear child. You have started a fire, and it's not going to go out.'

My mouth is too dry. 'What if it does? If everyone who protests is just put in here until… until…'

She strokes my knee. 'Amy will be working behind the scenes. I know it.'

'Whatever.'

She draws back from me. 'You have to believe, Carys. Without you...'

I look at the kid next to me again. My heart tugs wide at his light brown gaze, at the ravages of what he's experienced written across his face. 'You should have a name.'

'It's Boy H.' His little face is so serious, so tender. Different to Sim's; he doesn't exude mischief but something else. Something like deep intelligence and kindness all at the same time.

'That's not enough. You are more than that. Did you ever have any other kind of name? Did your parents call you anything?'

He shakes his head. 'My father wouldn't dare, and then... then when he was taken to the Think, well, I never saw him again, and my mother, she... she went to the Home when I was born.'

'I'm so sorry.'

He blinks. 'No one's allowed a name till Productivity anyway.'

I smile at him. 'None of that stuff matters anymore. Do you have a favourite name? One you'd like if you could pick? How about Garrett, for your father?'

He pushes his lip out. 'Dunno. No. I couldn't be Garrett 'cos it would just be like a reminder all the time, like when I saw him go down on *The S Word* and I reckon I knew, knew right then what would happen. I can't think about him.'

'I get it. Any of the other Newland names?'

'Don't like any of 'em, really. They all suck.'

I laugh. 'Not much choice, right?' I pause for a few moments, staring up at the grimy ceiling. 'Listen, I have an idea for a name for you. I read a book from the Before with a lad about your age who had a name that starts with H. He was super brave. Not on the Newland names list, of course.'

He stops picking at his nails and fixes his gaze on me. 'What was his name?'

'Harry.'

'Harry.' He says the name slowly, carefully, as if turning it over, weighing it up. *'Harry.'*

'Suits you.' Raza, from the shadows in the corner. 'You look like how I pictured him. I read it too.'

His mouth curves at the corners in a tiny, tentative smile.

Lois takes his hand and squeezes it. 'I think it's perfect. You are Harry!'

'You don't need to be Boy H anymore,' I say. 'And I bet your father and mother would love it.'

Tears gather in the corners of his eyes. 'Will you tell me that story sometime?'

I nod. 'I'll try and remember it all.'

He nods slowly. 'Then yes. Yeah. I'm Harry.'

'You're one of us now, Harry,' I say. 'You can help us get out of here.'

Harry smiles through shimmering eyes. 'I'm not good at much stuff.'

'That's okay. We kind of excel in not being good at stuff round here. My Trainers used to tell me I was rubbish at everything. We are Unproductives, and we own it.'

A clang, and the door is open once again, another few people shoved into the cell. One of the guys squares up to the guard. 'There are too many in here.'

The guard smirks. 'Suck it up.' The door bangs shut behind him.

'The other cells must be full,' I mumble to Lois. The rotten stench of the place weaves through my nostrils and I close my eyes. How much more of this can we take?

Raza shuffles over to our little group. 'We have to spread the word with all the new inmates. Everyone must know what's planned for them so we can join together and come up with something to break out.'

'But how?' I say.

'We could—'

She's interrupted by a loud commotion in the middle of the cell. The crowd parts to reveal two guys ripping into each other, punching and shoving and kicking. Blood streams from the first guy's nose and the other holds his arm awkwardly, prowling round his opponent looking for a weakness. The first man slams his fist into the other's chest, and he goes down, moaning.

'What are they fighting about?' Lois says.

No one answers. Another man weighs in and tries to separate them and gets thumped for his trouble, and then the door is crashed open and two guards are on them, pulling them apart and shoving them against the wall, cuffing them. The second guy collapses once again, holding his chest. 'What now?' one of the guards, a grim-faced, squat brute, says to the other.

His colleague spits. 'Take that one to Cell 2. Keep 'em apart. Nothing else for it for now, until...' He trails off, taking us all in, quiet and wide-eyed as we watch.

Grim-face drags the first guy out of the cell, and the other guard kicks the second guy hard, his hobnailed boots leaving great sore welts on his upper arm. 'Any more of this and you're toast,' he shouts as he leaves, gesturing to the handgun on his belt. The man groans, writhing on the ground.

The cell hangs in heavy silence, punctuated by the moaning of the guy on the floor. Lois crouches with him and asks if he is okay. 'Get some water,' she says to Alwin. 'I can clean his wounds, at least.'

The tap in the corner belches out rusty-looking water none of us dare drink. Alwin grabs a deserted plastic cup and fills it. 'Here.'

Lois ministers to the man, soothing him and whispering to him. She is so like Amy, with her natural flair for healing and her sincere compassion. My heart twists suddenly, and I turn back to Raza. 'You were saying?'

She sits with her head tilted to one side, her eyes flicking from side to side as she ponders the room. 'That's given me a bit of an idea.'

'What has? What idea?'

'Them fighting.'

'What?'

'If we could get separated, we could get the word out easier. If not to every cell at least to another, and then it'd get out more anyway, right?'

'He said he'd shoot if there was any more fighting.'

'Doubt he meant it. They haven't got the resources for all this, it's obvious. We could probably storm them right now and get out—'

'That's a stupid idea,' Alwin interrupts. 'This is not some provincial Think, you know. There are dozens of guards strutting round out there with their guns.'

'Then why don't they just finish us all off here and now?' Raza says, drawing her heavy eyebrows close.

Alwin lifts his shoulders. 'No clue.'

'They must have a reason for keeping us here,' Lois says. 'But Alwin's right. We can't just storm our way out of here. Think of Harry here and the other kids.'

Raza bites on some loose skin by her fingernail. 'Hmm. But if we could get me and Carys in different cells, at least we could start getting our plan in order.'

I stare at her. 'What plan? And how are we supposed to communicate when we're separate?'

She shrugs.

I think on her words for a few moments. She's right. The only way we're going to beat this is if everyone in these cells is aware of what's going on and we can somehow mobilise them together.

Raza pulls me to my feet. 'Make like you're laying into me.'

'What?'

She grins. 'It's not that hard. You don't like me, right? We're hardly best buddies. Get some of that fire in you we all saw the other night. Hit me.'

I stand frozen, my hands by my sides.

She grabs my hair. Starts screaming, spinning me round. 'Act it, Carys. Come on.'

I don't want to be separated from the others. From Lois and Alwin. From Harry. From Raza, even. I don't want to be on my own again. I don't want to do this.

The crowd around us catch on and take up the cause, chanting our names. My scalp prickles as she yanks at it and I snap, slapping her in the face. She recoils, staring at me, then grins wider. 'Well, who'd have thought?'

I brush my hands together, heat creeping through my face. A flush of embarrassment. A flush of fear. A flush of red hot anger, against Raza, against the Centre Think, against Jacob and Amy, against everything that has led to this moment. I grab her hair in return.

The guards are on us quickly, Grim-face scowling and tugging us apart, the other sweating heavily as he grabs hold of my arms, my flesh crawling at his touch. The stink of him hits me in the face and I screw up my nose. He is almost purple with rage as he drags me to the door. *No. Not me. Don't take me.*

5

THE RESISTANCE

THE ROOM IS so dark the man can barely make out faces in the shadows. A clutter of cobbled-together stations and ancient NCom equipment takes up most of the space, wires running everywhere, a mess of posters he cannot read pinned on disintegrating cork notice boards. The air hangs musty and weary, as though this place has been left untouched for a hundred years.

'We've had intelligence through from Wales, sir,' one of the women says after clearing her throat and breaking into the uneasy silence. 'It's… um, it's not good news.'

He sighs. Why would it be? Nothing is going as planned so far. The idiot Ashton kids have caused chaos: one in the Think after running her mouth off, two on *The S Word*, of all things. The Party HQ protests are squashed as quickly as they start, all the rebels in the Think by now, probably disposed of. He rubs his neck, his chest tight with anger and something else. Something he will not allow himself to feel.

'What happened?' he barks at the woman with the printout trembling in her hands.

She swallows. 'There's nothing there.'

'What do you mean, nothing there? Nothing where?'

'In Wales.'

He snorts. 'There's nothing in Wales?'

'Yes, sir. They broke through the old barriers and over the bridge. Scoured the countryside. It's all burned, like ours, but there aren't even any Compounds left now.'

His number two squirms next to him. 'So there will be no support from that quarter. What happened to the Welsh Compound? The main one in the north?'

The messenger shakes her head. 'We don't know. It's all in ruins like everything else. The barriers are wrecked, all in great big pieces like a wrecking ball got to them or a bomb blew them up. See here.' She shows them the email printed with a few words and images. 'No sign of civilisation. It's like a ghost town out there, they say.'

'And Outsiders?' his companion asks.

'None. Not that our groups found, anyway. They travelled as far as they could and found nothing but wild sheep and goats.'

'Damn it.' He slams his hands on the arms of his chair. 'Nothing left out there at all? That's why we never see planes out that way anymore. The Party finished the whole lot of them, for reasons we'll never know, I guess. No wonder no one ever comes to help.' He sinks his head into his hands. 'Ireland's gone, we know that. Will Scotland be the same? Do we have *any* communication with anyone up there?'

Number Two nods. 'There's that one Outsider camp. The big one near the old Glasgow ruins. They escaped the raids.'

'Good.'

'They're willing to get involved, but they have conditions.'

'Of course.'

'I'll try and reach them again. Organise a meeting…' she breaks off, avoiding his eye.

'Is there something wrong? Something else wrong, that is?'

She shakes her head. 'It's all in hand. It's just—'

'Just what, woman?'

She rolls her eyes. 'Don't take that tone with me, Ed. You'd not be here without me.'

He raises his eyebrows at her.

'It's just that most of the radio equipment was destroyed in the raids. The southwestern camp has gone, and the Birmingham camp, as well as the airport camp, of course. And our side... we are compromised. We can't really use NTech anymore.'

'Why?' He frowns. 'We had a way in before. Coder got us in under the radar, didn't she?'

'Coder is dead.'

'What?'

'Or, at best, rotting in the Centre Think with Girl Clerk and a hundred others. She was at that protest we saw in the Centre, only she didn't get out in time, unlike us. Don't know what she was thinking.'

'Shit!'

His companion pauses. Takes a breath. 'I know. So we have lost our way in through the network, and we must use old technology again. We could do with Boy Trader, you know. Sorry, I mean Oswall Trader now, of course.'

He frowns. 'Well, he's made his choice. But... don't call him by that name.'

She sniffs. 'Hmm. But has he really? Chosen, I mean?'

'Seems like it to me.' He drums his fingers on his lap. 'We'll get a system sorted out. Let's move on.'

'We are so few. Can we really make a difference now?'

He stares at her. 'We've come too far to give up. Look at all the work Reia and her crew did with smuggling kids out of Thinks and to the Outside. There are still pockets of that group in action in the Centre at least. And think of all the small subgroups all over the nation. More are rising up every day – that tax bill is doing our work for us, right? Everyone who was just about keeping their heads above water before are screwed with that raise. They're waking up.'

Murmurs of agreement ripple through the space.

A woman in the corner raises a hand. 'And don't forget all those Outsiders roaming wild. The ones who got out of the camps, that is. We've heard from some of them, but no idea how many there are.'

He nods. 'We just have to find a way of getting everyone in one place and on one page. We've lost Coder – so be it. But there will be a way. Now is the time, like never before, with Clerk having set all this in motion, misguided though she was.'

Number Two ponders her long red fingernails. 'I often wonder how it all got out, with her and the others, I mean. How the media got hold of their findings. It wasn't like they went to NBC as soon as they discovered the truth about the Home, was it? They were skulking out in the Birmingham ruins by then.'

A hush falls. The man glances around at the faces, all shadowed by the gloomy lighting in the room; some earnest, some worried, some sparkling with something. 'Yeah. The media spun it, for sure; but where did it all come from in the first place?'

A hefty man clears his throat. 'Um… there might have been some… intelligence leaking, shall we say, from the Midlands Think.'

He stares at him. 'Intelligence leaking?'

The man shifts in his seat. 'You know I worked there—' he looks down, '—to my shame.'

Number Two crosses her arms. 'You… *you* told the media what they'd found?'

Number One frowns. 'Why?'

The hefty man rubs his chin. 'They were all over the news as it was, as wanted fugitives. That was when I snapped, when I walked out of the place. I… I just had to tell the truth about what was really going on. Anonymously, of course, but NBC were all over it. A… and, after all, I thought it would help any resistance rather than hurt it; and that's happened, right? With all that stuff getting people thinking, and then the tax bill, and Clerk on *The S Word…*' He trails off, twisting his hands.

Number One shrugs. 'It was Clerk's actions that really got the fire started, no doubt about that.'

'And now Anson is having her executed at Festival,' Number Two says.

He opens his mouth then closes it, looking around the room, searching each face more closely. All of them here representing other groups, some tiny in number and some larger. All of them committed to seeing this thing through. He thinks about Benedict and Sarah (or Ora, her Productivity name she only kept in public) Clerk, how they got all this going in the first place. The compromising files Benedict got hold of but never got to deliver, instead mown down by the NForce in the Midlands Compound sixteen years ago. He thinks about the day Benedict approached him in a shadowy corner of a crusty old inn, how he tentatively sounded him out, said he'd heard so much about him and all his dealings but knew he was something more than all that, how they'd found common ground straight away and bonded over smoky prohibition single malt and their hopes for the future. He still misses Benedict now; he was a good man, so full of fire and courage it got him slaughtered but got everyone else going after far too long in slumber. A great raw lump forms in his throat for the best friend he ever had, and for a moment he thinks about the other people he has lost along the way.

'Ed?' His companion touches his arm, her face crumpled in concern.

He will not cry. 'Yes. So. The execution… seems to me that might be our opportunity.'

A man across the room sits up straighter. 'That's just what I was thinking. Everyone will be there – all the Party elite, all the Centre NForce, everyone who matters. Every single high-up Productive in the Commander Lucan Arena at one time.'

'And so?' Number Two says, leaning forward.

'And so we'll have them penned in one place. Even more than usual Festivals – all the other Compound heads will be down in the Centre for this one. They're making a huge deal out of it, have basically issued a three-line-whip to all Party members and hangers-on.'

'Hmm,' another man says, pressing his fingertips together under his chin. 'So we take action – I mean, forceful action. It's going to be the only way, and our only chance.'

Number One pauses. 'That seems possible, Dale. Yes.'

Number Two gets up from her seat and paces the room. 'But we get the girl out first, of course. And the others, if they are present.'

'Suddenly have a soft spot for our young trainees, do you?' He grins slightly, but it is forced through gritted teeth.

She shakes her head at him. 'Ed...'

He breathes out slowly. 'I think we will have to leave them be. Any kind of rescue attempt will compromise the mission—'

'But—'

Dale interrupts, 'I know. I know. But we must think about the future here. We're going to take casualties. The truth is that Girl Clerk will be a distraction, a spectacle if you like, and this will go in our favour. We will blow up the whole thing.'

Silence hangs as heavy as the stale air.

Number One spreads his hands. 'Does anyone have another idea?'

Number Two pauses in her pacing. 'But Girl Clerk... think about her parents. Think about what we owe them. And the other two? What about them?'

He shakes his head. 'They made their decision. I've been clear on that.'

'And you don't care?'

He says nothing.

She turns away from him and faces the others in the room. 'Even if we go ahead, do we have the fire power for this? We'd need a Copter, but how can we get one? What if it goes wrong – do we have enough in our arsenal to defend ourselves?'

Another man clears his throat. 'We're building it up all the time. We scavenged some from destroyed camps and others we've been stockpiling for years. Some of our people escaped from Outsider camps when they got communications through about the Party attacks; they got some of their stuff out with them. The vault in the Centre is looking good.'

'But what about manpower? Do we have enough people?'

Silence.

'Ed?'

He closes his eyes. 'Even if not, we must go ahead, mustn't we? The question I ask you all—' he pauses, gazing into each face, '—is this: how far are you willing to take this?'

6

CENTRE THINK

CARYS

THEY'RE CAGEY IN here. They believe me – most of them are here because of me, after all – but they won't tell me anything or commit to anything. They are beaten down, dazed and pale in the gloom of the cell. It's smaller than next door and just as cramped, and just as before we can hear the guards mumbling outside if we're quiet enough. 'Shh,' I whisper, finger to lips at a couple of kids shoving each other in the corner, 'they're saying something.' I crouch down, put my ear to the door, down near the grille at the bottom; the floor is slimy with stinking mud from dozens of shoes.

'… make an example of 'em.'

I lean in further, trying to make out their words.

'… easier to get rid of them now.'

'It's orders from the top, sir. Put more buckets and more water in there. Blankets. No more nurses for now, keep feeding 'em, don't let Scourge take hold.'

'No stopping that if it turns up.'

'Just do your best.'

'Too many of 'em.'

The guard mutters something unintelligible.

A sigh. 'I'm not being held responsible if everything goes wrong in here. It's inhuman, them living like this.'

'Who cares? They're Unproductive scum.'

A few more mutters and some whispers, then footsteps clattering away from the door. I lean back on my haunches, thinking.

'What were they saying?' a man asks.

'I'm not completely sure. It looks like they're trying to keep us alive for now, which is a good thing, I suppose.'

'And?'

'It sounded like they're planning on something with us… I mean, you. Making an example, or something.'

'So killing us off—'

'Blake!' A woman nearby cuts him off. 'The children…'

Blake shakes his head. 'Yeah. Sorry.'

Another woman weaves her way through the cell. 'Did you hear any more details? When are they planning this… this…'

I shake my head. 'No. Nothing. Are… are you okay?' I notice the perspiration trickling down her face, the sickly pallor of her skin.

She waves a hand. 'I'm fine. A bit tired. I didn't introduce myself before—' she breaks off, wheezing, '—but it's time I did. My name is Ava. Ava Coder.'

'Hey, Ava. You know who I am.'

She smiles softly. 'Of course. I got caught over by Party HQ, holding a banner a bit too high for their liking. I was stupid.'

'I think I was the stupid one.'

'You gave us all a bit of a kick up the backside, to be honest.' She leans in towards me, starts whispering, 'There are more of us out there than you know. We've got something going.' Her eyes slide around the room. 'Don't know if we can trust everyone here.'

'Don't think we have a lot of choice,' I say.

She frowns. 'Yes. Well. I'm confident my colleagues are working to get us out of here.'

'Colleagues?'

She purses her lips. 'Resistance workers,' she hisses in my ear. 'You might know… no. I can't say more.'

I search her face, mystified. Resistance workers? Suddenly my chest warms, my limbs loosening. 'They can save us? Save me?'

She looks at the ground. 'I hope so. We don't have much chance otherwise.'

'You're an IT specialist?' I say, thinking about her name.

She smiles, and it lights up her face, pinking the paleness. 'I set up a network. But the less you know, the better.'

'You sound like Jacob… um… Boy Trader,' I say, unwilling to voice the other name, my stomach wrenching at the picture of him that flies through my head. Him at the NCom in Arthur Waste's house; the set of his shoulders, his lopsided smile as he brought the old computer into willing compliance. But then him making vile vows to the Commander and celebrating his Productivity Ceremony.

'I know he's called Jacob really,' she says softly. 'I know you're Carys, too.'

I stare at her. 'What… how?'

She blushes and turns her head away. 'Just something I heard.'

She has cropped brown hair and intelligent blue eyes behind large, black-framed glasses. I want to hear more of her story, to know everything she knows, to hear about the network and the Resistance and what is really going on out there. I think about Wade, the man I met in the Midlands Think, and wonder if he was working with them. Then I think about the Queen, lying dead under a pile of rubble in the Birmingham ruins, and the work she did with a group of rebels who were helping kids escape. I grab Ava's arm. 'Do you have people smuggling kids out?'

Her lips curve in a weary smile. 'You mean Reia's crew.'

'Reia?'

'She got the whole system going nationwide, then she got chased down. Escaped, though, but she was in the Birmingham camp—' she stops, looks square at me, '—oh. You three were there, of course.'

'I don't know the name.'

'She got called the Queen there.' She laughs softly, and there is something in her eyes, something like pining. 'Wasn't much into being called that, but she was a hero. I never heard from her, though; I don't think they had much communication stuff out there. It was only intelligence from E… from the Resistance, where I heard where she was and what she was up to. She never knew about us, though.'

'She was a bit scary, but she was awesome,' I say, squeezing her hand as tears form in her eyes. 'I'm so glad I know her name.'

'It means "queen",' Ava says quietly. 'She found it in some old Before book. She dropped her Productivity name because it meant "foreigner".' Her mouth trembles. 'She was so brave.'

I smile, thinking of Reia and her stern welcome, of her noble conduct on Remembrance Night, the story she told us and the lights on the boats on the lake as dawn painted the sky with gold.

'Still going, though,' Ava says, her voice husky with sadness.

'Still going?'

'I mean her underground thing. There are pockets of it here in the Centre and other Compounds too. Kids still making it out because of her.' Ava's face is glowing. 'I wish she knew what she'd started.'

The door opens once again, and I prepare myself for another stream of rebels and less space to breathe. But only one comes this time, a kid. 'Harry!'

He pushes his way over to me, his solemn little face cracking into a tiny smile. 'Carys.'

I put my arm around his shoulder and draw him in, feeling his body relax against me. 'It's okay. It's okay. What happened? Get into a fight with Raza?' I grin down at him.

He shakes his head. 'Nah. Just with some other kid. He was laying into Lois about Amy, and I told him to shove it.'

'Ah.' I stiffen. We don't need all these fights in here; we don't need people turning against one another. Amy may have deserted us, but Lois doesn't deserve that. 'And you got separated.'

He shrugs. 'Yeah, but I'm glad. 'Cos I'm with you now, and Raza is boring.'

I laugh. 'She's not so bad.'

'She just sits there all the time with a face on her.'

I hug him. 'Well, you're here now.'

'She said to say to you to get down by the wall at night if you was in the next door cell. And you are. She says there's a grate there. You can talk through it.'

'Oh!' How did I miss that?

'It's kind of behind the toilet bit in our other cell. So, like, behind all the disgusting stuff.'

'Ah. I see.' I make my way to the right side of the cell, not far from where one of the kinder guards helped us hitch up a couple of blankets to give the toilet area some privacy. It's so dark in the corner I can barely see the filthy brickwork, but as I bend down I see it: a tiny grate right at the bottom under a rusty tap, looks like part of some kind of drainage system. I crouch down and try to see through it but it's too small and too murky down there. I recoil at the stench and place my hand over my nose and mouth as I bend my ear to the grate. I can hear them in there, the general noise and chatter, the occasional sob. 'Raza?' I hiss, with no response. 'Raza!'

Harry skulks behind me. 'She said at night,' he says plaintively. 'When it's quieter.'

I sink back onto the floor in the other corner, away from the stink, hugging my knees to me and thinking about everything Ava has said. Harry sits next to me, a quiet presence, a kindness I never thought I'd receive here in the darkest of places.

7

THE CENTRE

JACOB

JACOB TRADER CAN'T get the kid out of his head. The look on his face as the guards hustled him off stage, the sound of his wavering voice as he dared shout out the truth and brand them all – including him, Jacob – liars. Liars. He knows he's colluding and he's sick of it; he can't even imagine what Carys might be thinking of him right now. If she's even giving him a second thought – he wouldn't blame her if she never thought of him again. His gut twists at the memory of her on the stage that fateful night, a beautiful explosion of fire and fury. He balls his hands into fists as he stands in the same place now, right in the middle of the next show, Amy over to the right of him all done up in green silk and feathers in her hair. He laughed at those backstage, and she shoved his shoulder, rolling her eyes. She can't stand how they doll her all up, even when Coran does it.

'It's judgement time,' he hears Amy saying and snaps back to himself. *Get with it, man.* He pastes on a stupid grin as the judges go through their big fake rigmarole once again. Some poor woman stands between him and Amy, shaking her socks off. She's got no chance with them lot; she's toast. She told them this whole thing about how she'd been ill since she had some virus or other, and Jacob found himself getting unaccountably mad at her, wishing she'd stop talking, that she'd make something up to make herself sound better, anything to get out of her fate. But she was honest and true to herself.

Unlike him.

'Raulf?' Amy says, sweeping a hand out towards Singer and getting a huge cheer from all those idiot trainees on the edges of their seats. Hell, Jacob is bitter tonight. Raulf spews on and on about work ethic and Productivity and being a good citizen and bringing glory to the Commander. Jacob glazes over as the other judges follow, only Lora giving the poor woman some wriggle room, but not a whole lot. Lora is harder round the edges tonight; she is wearing this whole angular power suit get-up, not at all like her usual floaty stuff. He wonders if Coran approves.

He catches Amy's eye as the judges come to the end of their spiels, and 'SKIVER' blazes across each sign high above the stage. Remembers what they talked about earlier, what they'd agreed to do. To try, at least. He clears his throat and pins his gaze on Lora. 'We have a great idea,' he says, his voice magnified through the microphone, booming back at him. 'Esla and I, that is.'

Lora sits up straighter but does not smile. She brushes down the front of her red jacket and raises her eyebrows. 'Oh?'

Amy walks around in front of her, grabbing the contestant's hand as she goes and leading her along. The woman stumbles, her blonde hair all askew. She looks like she should be in a hospital bed somewhere. 'We think it's time for a little change on the show. Cadman Showman was keen to tell us he's all for change and all for us forging new ways forward. The Commander himself—' someone in the audience gasps, and is immediately quashed, '—told us to bring some new life to the show. So…' Amy trails off, looks at Jacob. *Cheers.*

He coughs. 'So we wondered if Skivers shouldn't go to the Think anymore. There are better places to help them… think.'

A titter in the audience.

Lora tilts her head. 'Really?'

He tries not to get flustered. 'We wondered if they might be banished, instead. To the Outside.' He crosses his fingers behind his back. 'After all, they'd have to really take control out there, right? In the Think they get treated well. They get food and… and warmth. All the comfort Newland kindly gives its Think inmates.' He screws up his nose, wondering if Carys is watching.

Lora opens her mouth to speak but Raulf butts in. 'Interesting. Yes, you're right, we do need to take the show in some new directions. In fact, Portia and I have been discussing some… progressive ideas, but they are not ready to share as yet.' He turns, grins out at the audience. 'You're going to love them.' The crowd whoop and holler his name. Lora stares at him, her brow all crinkled, then at Edwin, who looks like he couldn't be less interested.

Jacob smiles. 'Well… good. But for now, what about sending Skivers to the Outside for… for a real taste of what it means to be self-sufficient? To learn better Productivity?'

When he and Amy discussed the idea earlier, they both had misgivings. To send someone to the Outside – especially a sick person – could be sending them to their death. But at least they'd have some chance, unlike their fate when sent to the Think. Many Outsiders found tribes and flourished, as they found out when they ended up there themselves. Amy asked if they might think of somewhere else altogether to send them, a different plan, but they both know the Commander won't settle for a lesser sentence; that it would not look strong. And they agreed they would present their idea live on the show, in order to pressure change then and there. It was the only way.

Amy speaks up. 'How about it, Lora?'

Lora frowns. 'I'm not sure—'

'It wouldn't work,' Raulf says, getting up and opening his arms to the crowd. 'We all know about lawless Outsiders and how they have grown too much. I will not contribute towards them becoming even more of a danger to good Newland citizens. Thank you for the thought, though,' he adds with a saccharine grin. 'It was… novel.'

Lora still looks uncertain. 'I think it could work.'

Jacob wonders if she's thinking about everything Carys said. Maybe something of it has permeated the layers of lies that bind themselves around her. Maybe she has started to believe them after all.

But then he looks at her outfit, at her hardened face. Even her make-up is more severe than usual, jet-black kohl in harsh lines sweeping from the corners of her eyes. Something has changed in her.

'It's not workable. We don't want to build up another Outsider force,' Raulf says.

Portia snorts, waving a hand at the contestant. 'What, with this pathetic specimen?' The woman recoils, and Amy grips hold of her arm. 'I don't think she's going to be a revolutionary force, Raulf.' Some kids in the audience laugh, and Jacob wants to punch someone.

Later on, he leaves the stage with a sinking stone in his gut, Amy trailing behind him with a thunderous expression. 'They didn't buy it.'

She sighs. 'Of course they didn't.'

He pushes the door to their backstage lounge open and sprawls on one of the hard sofas. 'I'm about done with all this.'

She rubs her face. 'We have to keep it up.'

'Huh.'

The door creaks open again and Raulf Singer strolls in, hands in his pockets, immaculate, every hair in place. What's he doing in here, in the plebs lounge when he has his own posh suite? He stands in the doorway, staring them down from head to toe. Amy squirms under his gaze. 'What?' Jacob says, knowing he sounds off but not caring.

'Oswall. Esla.' He speaks the words pointedly, deliberately, spacing them out, his tone heavy with spite. 'Much as I admire your tenacity—' he pauses, smirks, '—there must be no more straying from the script. Do you understand what I am saying to you?'

Jacob stares right back at him and keeps his lips buttoned. Amy fiddles with a stray thread on a battered old cushion.

Raulf's jaw tightens. 'It's not for you to… ad lib, as it were, live on air. You have perfectly good autocues, and you needn't go far off those.'

Amy begins, 'We—'

'You are temporary guests. Politically useful, nothing more.' He twists his mouth into a sneer. 'Don't get ideas above your station. If you make any more suggestions or any trouble at all, the Commander will have no issue with bringing the execution date forward.'

Jacob feels the shiver go through him, like it's slicing him in two.

'I take it you understand?'

'Yeah.'

'And you?'

Amy twists her ring violently. 'Yes.'

CARYS

NIGHTS IN HERE blend into days. The noise level goes down, but the atmosphere is almost thicker with dark fears skittering through corners, nightmares that scream their terror and the sour scent of sleeplessness. We have more water now, and blankets to huddle in, but the room is choked with sweat and terror.

I talk with Raza through the grate in the darkest hours when most people are sleeping. 'You there?' I say now, crouching down and tilting my head towards the ground. 'Raza?'

'Yeah.' Her voice is husky, sour as ever.

'Anything new?'

'Few more folk squeezed in, but there's no more room.'

'Lois and Alwin okay?'

'Mmm.'

I wish she would talk more, that we could share secrets through the cold watches of the night, but she is sullen and monosyllabic. 'Are you okay?'

'I'm super.'

I sigh. 'Alright. Look, we should talk more about getting out of here.'

Silence.

'You were all for it the other day, when you told everyone we're breaking out.'

A shuffling sound. 'Yeah, well. You got a plan?'

I feel a warmth at my back and turn around. Harry is next to me, nestling into me. I drape my arm around his shoulder and pull my blanket over him.

'Well?' Raza hisses.

I rack my brains. 'I… no.'

The silence falls again, even heavier this time, then Raza says, 'I think there are enough of us to overpower the guards.'

'But they will shoot.'

'So some of us will get shot.'

I shake my head. 'Too risky.'

'You want to die?'

I stroke Harry's matted curls. 'No. Of course not. But…'

She says nothing, and I sit up slightly, resting back against the wall. I think about her plan and how it's not really a plan at all. The stillness presses in on me, Harry's tiny snores the only respite, and I close my eyes.

'I found my mother,' Raza says suddenly, making me sit bolt upright and Harry jump. I thought she'd gone, that she didn't want to talk.

'Your mother?'

'Yeah. You know, the woman who gave birth to me.'

I find my lips curving at her snarky tone; she never changes. 'When?'

'Oh, around eighteen years ago or so.'

I laugh out loud. 'You know what I meant.'

A pause. 'A couple of weeks ago. Out in the Centre. I was looking for… you know. Dr Chemist.'

Dr Chemist. The Trainer who raped her and allowed her baby girl to be murdered at birth.

'But you didn't find him.'

'I saw him. Went and checked out my old training house. Still a dump. Saw him in his car. But I couldn't get to him; the gates were guarded. Almost like they knew I was coming.'

'They were searching for you. Lora was in trouble with Anson for letting you go.'

'Huh.'

I shuffle forwards, wishing I could take her hand through the grate. But she'd probably snatch it away. 'So… your mother?'

She pauses. 'Yeah. So I thought… I dunno. I thought she might want to see me. Knew my father wouldn't, he made no bones of the fact he was ashamed of me for bringing shame on our family. Hated how I dress, too.' There's a catch in her voice.

I stay quiet, waiting.

'So I get to the street with her house. My house, I guess, though I was barely ever there. You know, Festivals and all that.' Her voice is bitter. 'Saw her, going in. Had a baby in a pram.'

'A baby?'

'Yeah, you know, one of those squalling things.' Raza shuffles behind the grate.

'But… how? She had you already… how?'

Silence.

Then, 'Replaced me. Guessing she got some kind of permission, given I'm Unproductive and all that, given I don't exist to them, right?'

I think about it. Would the Party really allow that?

'Didn't stop around to find out. She looked… happy.' Raza's voice cracks.

'I'm sorry.'

Raza says nothing, but through the quiet I think I hear the tiniest sniffle, the ghost of a sob, and I want to reach out to her, but instead I let the silence wrap itself around us and I think it's a little bit warmer than before.

LATER, I'M WOKEN by another low voice through the grate. 'Psst. Carys, are you awake?'

I prop myself up, allowing Harry's sleep-warm body to slump over my knees. Ava Coder is huddled up with us and she looks at me, a question in her eyes.

'It's Lois. Amy's mother,' I whisper.

She nods slowly. 'The one thrown out of the Compound? With her husband?'

I nod back, wondering how she knows so much about Amy. About all of us.

'Carys?' Lois hisses, her voice urgent.

I bend my head towards the grate. 'I'm here. Are you okay?'

She sighs. 'Alwin is… sad. He can't see a way out. But when you and Raza… the other day… there was something strong in your words. I believed them. And Amy…' She trails off.

I slump. 'Yeah.'

'Didn't you see them on earlier though? They were challenging the judges. Didn't you think—'

'I didn't think anything except that they were trying to justify themselves. They'd feel better if losers went to the Outside instead of the Think. They'd not feel so guilty that way.' I cross my arms over my chest.

'I think it was more than that,' Lois says softly. 'I think they're trying to bring change.'

A snort from behind her: Raza, probably.

Ava shuffles nearer. 'I think Lois is right.'

'Who's that?' Lois says, her voice on alert.

'Sorry,' Ava says, 'Name's Ava Coder. Got sent here for demonstrating at Party HQ. I'm… I'm with the Resistance.'

Lois is quiet.

'I've heard your story,' Ava says gently. 'I know how you raised Amy. I… I believe you, that she's trying to do something.'

I look at the floor. I don't want to hear their words, their justifications, their false hopes. I scrape my fingers over the cold, damp concrete and flinch.

Lois whispers, 'I've heard about your groups. I didn't know they were still going. We had some connections back at the airport.'

Ava pauses. 'I'm so sorry about what happened there.'

Silence falls once again.

Then, 'Can you still contact them?' Lois says. 'Your groups?'

Ava looks at me, shakes her head slightly. 'No. Not in here. No way to get anything through.'

'But we have each other, at least,' Lois says. 'We can't give up now. And they'll be working for our freedom, won't they?'

Ava fiddles with her shoelaces. 'I don't know.'

I look down at Harry, still fast asleep through our whispered conversation, his brown hair tumbling over his warm brow, and hope that someone, somewhere out there is working to rescue him. To get us all out of here.

And my stomach clenches hard as I face up to the probability that they are not and it is all down to us, a weak, motley band of prisoners, losing strength by the day in body and soul. I gaze at the curve of Harry's cheek and stroke it softly.

8

THE CENTRE

AMY

AMY STANDS AT the mirror in the hallway of their flat and smooths down her dark hair. It's growing at last, falling across her brow where it stood in messy tufts not long ago after Mercia's attack. Just three months ago, but it feels like years since they escaped from the Midlands Compound, even since they left the Birmingham camp. Her heart twists at the thought of it, and she swallows over the pain that is so large it might explode out of her chest.

'You look good,' Jacob says, making her jump. 'We should go. Stop your preening, we're only going to Lora's.'

She shoves him with her shoulder. 'Not preening, thanks. Wonder what she wants?'

'Who knows? Probably has Anson round to taunt us again.'

Amy shivers.

As they clatter down the stairs, Jacob shakes his head. 'I just wish we could do something.'

'We tried, on *The S Word*.'

'And look how that went. No, listen, I mean something more. We're just letting time slip by, and it's only weeks now until Festival… until… I can't let that happen.'

Amy stops at the foot of the stairs and lays her hand on his shoulder. 'I know.'

'I just feel like I've failed everything so far. I can't see a way out.'

Amy gazes at him, thinking about how far they've come. She doesn't feel like a success story either; she wakes up every morning with a great big stone sinking in the pit of her belly, thinking about what Carys must be feeling now, about the next show, about the upcoming Winter Festival and all that will mean. She is sickened by what they are doing yet can't see another way. 'We've got this far,' she says, pulling the door open and going out to the street where their driver, Crea, is waiting in the little red car. 'Something'll come up. You'll see.'

Jacob lifts his shoulders. 'I think we have to make sure it does.'

At Lora's house they are ushered into their old den and left alone with the NScreen on the wall playing NCasts of Party officials discussing the tax bill. Jacob snaps his fingers to stop it and sinks into one of the sofas. 'Home sweet home.'

Amy curves her mouth into a tiny smile. 'Mmm.'

The door creaks open. 'Darlings!'

Amy finds her body untensing. 'Coran.'

He sashays over, bearing a tray with a pot of tea and delicate china cups. 'Drinks?' He pours them out, his face wreathed in smiles. 'Delightful to see you, as always.'

Amy sees Coran at the studios, but only in brief bursts as he throws outfits at her and snappily oversees makeup artists. But here he sheds his professional skin; here he is just Coran again, and there's something about him that always comforts her in a world where that doesn't happen much. She wants to lean into him, to feel his arms around her, to sob everything out to someone she somehow feels safe with even though she knows she shouldn't.

Jacob takes some tea and sips at it. 'What are we here for?'

Coran shakes his head. 'I have no idea. Dear Lora arranged it all; I didn't even know you were here until Ash told me. He's our new gardener. He's… a good person.'

'Not like our Mr Gardener, then,' Amy says.

Coran smiles, lighting his whole face. 'Not a little bit. He's a bit nerdy, actually. Likes trains, has this whole thing about getting the old railway lines up and running again.' He clears his throat. 'Anyway, he told me, and I just had to come and see you. I—' he breaks off, glancing around the room.

Amy takes his hand. 'What?'

Coran smiles again, nervously this time. 'Oh, nothing. It's just wonderful to see you here again. I miss you, you know. And… Girl C, of course.'

Amy looks down at her tea; the cup is trembling.

'And of course I must call you Esla now, and Oswall. I always forget.'

'Don't worry about that,' Jacob says. 'We really don't mind.'

Coran stares at him, then at Amy, then at the blank wall above the fireplace where the NScreen lights when it's on. 'I wanted to ask—'

The door opens again and Lora walks in clad in a simple navy shift dress and, incongruously, a large straw sunhat that shades most of her face and sunglasses covering her eyes. It's not even sunny outside, Amy thinks, and then looks closer at Lora's face. More bruises, she is sure; covered with makeup but she sees their outlines in stark purple and yellowing edges.

'Good morning, Esla. Oswall.'

'Hello,' Amy says.

Jacob raises his chin.

'I invited you here with some good news.'

Jacob shifts beside her, and she glances at him. What is it this time? Lora's good news has been anything but for them so far.

Lora sinks gracefully into one of the large white chairs and begins to remove her sunglasses but just as quickly puts them back on, moving her hand to fiddle with an earring instead. 'The Commander is pleased with your progress, generally.' She pauses as Coran gives her a cup of tea. 'Of course, he wasn't so impressed with the way you behaved last time on *The S Word*, but I know Raulf has set you right on that.'

Jacob rolls his eyes at Amy, and she nudges him with her ankle.

'Anyway. As you are now seen as such great patrons of Newland – good citizens who refused to collude in lies – it's been decided that you will undertake a tour of the Compounds.'

Amy looks at Jacob. He scrunches his brow. 'What do you mean, a tour?'

Lora takes a sip of her tea. 'Now more than ever, the Commander sees the need to get people on side, as it were, and especially the youngsters of the nation. You will give talks at training houses, telling trainees about your experiences and about the goodness at the heart of the Party and the Commander himself of course. It will be a great honour for you.'

Amy swallows: she daren't look at Jacob again.

'And to kick it all off we thought you could start at Ashton. We know how much you miss your friends there, and we thought it would be a positive start for the tour. There will be press there, of course, to record the occasion and help things along.'

Jacob clears his throat. 'Of course.'

Coran sits in the other corner, and Amy notices his feet are jiggling. He catches her glance and smiles softly at her.

Lora points her cup at them. 'And you will also represent *The S Word* across the Compounds. You see, we have great plans for some fresh content on the show. You picked that up, didn't you, when you made your… um… suggestion the other night, but we already had plans.'

'Plans?' Jacob says.

Lora smiles wider now and takes her sunglasses off again, this time oblivious of them. Amy tries not to stare at the black ring around her left eye. 'Well, I wasn't going to tell you yet, but no harm, is there, Coran?'

Coran nods. 'Not at all, darling. It's all so exciting!'

'We plan to get more involvement from our audience. From trainees. You see, the Commander believes we should be showcasing their talents as well as those of Productive groups. This way, our young people will come back on board with us. Over the next few weeks, we're going to give them a chance to take part in live auditions for an *S Word* special at Winter Festival where they will perform in the Commander Lucan Arena—' she stops, clears her throat, '—the Commander wishes to make it a day of celebration, you see. As well as… other things. It would be a great honour to be chosen.'

Amy stares at her. Celebration? With Carys executed in full view of hundreds of thousands in the arena and across the nation? She catches Jacob's eye and flinches at the hardness gripping his jaw. 'What do you mean by auditions?' she says, trying to scrub the images of Carys from her mind.

Lora gets up and strolls over to the fireplace, where she picks up an ornamental cat. 'We want to hear trainees singing. See them dancing. See magic shows and acrobatics. We want to showcase them to the nation, to bring a new life to the show and to the country as a whole – to show that we care about their progression. So often trainees are kept silent until they become Productive, but now is the time for a new season where they will know how valued they are.'

The talented ones, at least, Amy thinks but doesn't say.

'Any trainee can apply, and you will announce it at Ashton with the press present so it's spread through the country. It'll start this next Saturday night – we already have several trainees lined up for that show.'

Jacob shakes his head. 'And this will help stop unrest, right?' Amy can tell what he's really thinking: this is all for political gain – young performers in the arena at Festival will give a new feel to the event and leave the audience with positive vibes, which will only be reinforced by the execution narrative – Newland loves its talents and its triers but does not love its rebels and revolutionaries. Take note, all Newlanders: be a striver, not a skiver…

Lora looks at him, her face lined with uncertainty. 'Well… yes, we do hope so, as I'm sure you do.'

Jacob stares at her for a moment, then at Amy. 'Sounds… good.'

Lora grins and holds the ornament aloft. 'I knew you'd like it. Now, you're going to Ashton tomorrow. It's all arranged; in fact, I shall be travelling there too. And more than that – guess who else is coming?'

Amy feels her shoulders slump. 'The Commander,' she says dully.

Lora doesn't seem to notice. 'The Commander himself, yes. He's very keen to visit the training houses with you; some of them, anyway, those his schedule will allow for. He will address Assembly at Ashton in person, with you by his side. You will be our representatives and give a speech, then give the opportunity for questions too in smaller class groups. Your purpose will be to stir up excitement about the new *S Word* format, but more than that, to renew faith in our nation and Party.'

'Great,' Jacob says, his jaw so tight Amy wonders if the veins might pop apart.

Lora beams. 'I knew you'd be pleased.'

In the corner, Coran stays unusually quiet. Amy wonders what he was about to ask them and if he'll get another chance.

The road to Ashton is swarming with bad memories. Amy stares out at the driving rain and thinks about their last trip up that way and what they found at the end of it. Her thoughts drift to Reia and the four girls, then to Will and his family. Are they safe in their secluded little hamlet in the Birmingham ruins? Are they happy? Is Esther coping with the loss of her mother? Amy finds herself gripped with a kind of grinding longing. Outside, the rain batters the windows and blankets the desolate landscape and it feels a little bit like her soul.

When they pull up to the Midlands Compound border gates, Amy sits stiffly, taken over by more memories; this time of explosions and desperate running, of Copters chasing them down and Aiden stumbling along with them. She glances at Jacob; his face is inscrutable as he stares out of his window, and she knows he, too is thinking of the last day they saw this place. She squeezes her eyes shut as they stop at the gates and the guards verify them. They are on their own in their car with just Crea driving; the Commander and Lora are travelling by Copter and will arrive later. Amy knows there won't be a problem, but her body tenses anyway. Jacob grabs her hand and squeezes then leans over to her. 'I've got a couple of ideas.'

'What?' Amy whispers, her eyes on Crea and the guards.

Jacob exhales slowly. 'I've been thinking, since last night when this landed on us. We could make use of it.'

'Make use?'

'Yeah, I mean like take the opportunity to try and… I don't know. Recruit people, I guess.'

Amy gazes at him. 'That's a dangerous game.'

Jacob frowns. 'Honestly, I feel like we've got nothing left to lose. We have to do something – we've been slumbering too long. Still can't believe we went through with that wretched ceremony.'

'I know.'

Crea has taken their border passes back and a guard waves them through.

'So we do the whole good patron thing on the surface, bigging up *The S Word* and the talent thing for Festival – but then we find ways of getting groups together. I have some ideas about a network—'

'Network?'

'Like a forum thing, a way for rebels to collaborate and see what's going on. I think I can get it into a back end somewhere. Get into an NCom.'

'Didn't go so well before.'

'We got the files, didn't we?'

Amy nods slowly. 'And how do you plan to… recruit people? We can't just go round saying hey, look at us and the wonderful *S Word*, and by the way, do you want to join the rebels?'

Jacob chuckles.

'What you two whispering and giggling about back there?' Crea says, turning onto the forest road towards the west of the Compound.

Amy looks at Jacob, and he shakes his head, mouths, 'Later.'

For the first time in weeks, Amy feels a spark of something like hope. Could they really do something? Could they find people who might be sympathetic?

But, even if those people are around, how can they find them while under such a burden of expectation and publicity? She sneaks Jacob another look and finds him staring out of the window again, his dark eyes sparkling with the reflection of a newly rain-washed sky. She'd barely noticed, but the rain had stopped the moment they entered the Midlands Compound.

9

THE CENTRE

RAZA

RAZA NEVER THOUGHT she'd confide in Carys Clerk, of all people.

She'd interrupted their peace back in the Community. Jacob and Amy were okay, really, but somehow Carys pressed all her buttons. She was too loose with her tongue, too taken up with herself, too recently indoctrinated to face any kind of reality.

And she had the same name as Raza's baby girl, who had been murdered by the Party.

On Remembrance Night she'd locked eyes with her for a moment and something had passed between them, but Raza wasn't going to let a moment come and make her all syrupy and fake-sweet; Carys was still bloody irritating and she, Raza, was still herself; cold, empty, all the prickles on the inside as well as the out, spiking at her as much as everyone around her. All she wanted to do was watch over the girls and keep the Community safe.

And then they went and rescued Lora Dancer, of all people, and Raza saw it as a sign. She had to go find Chemist; to finish him. He didn't deserve to live. She'd find him or die trying.

She'd not wanted the baby, of course, when she realised she was pregnant, months in. She'd been disgusted at the thought of his child, forcibly there, but now she had no choice. Something shifted in her though as the baby began to flutter and then kick, something that felt like connection. She'd not known love, really, not like she saw with other kids, but this was different. This baby was all hers.

She'd learned the name Carys from her mother, who'd told her it was an old Before name in their family; she'd remembered her own grandmother telling her about a great grandparent, how the name meant something like beloved. Raza kind of liked that, even though it was a bit lame. Knew the baby couldn't really have a name, but she'd never been one to care much about rules. Couldn't give a stuff. She'd be Carys to her, always and forever.

But then she was born too early. She was a dot of a thing but still had a head full of dark, downy hair Raza wanted to stroke and smell and kiss. But they whipped her away. 'Unproductive,' the nurse had said, and that was it. She never saw her again. She thinks back now to that hospital room; the cracked ceiling tiles, the beeping machines, the other mothers' labour screams echoing through dark hallways. The feel of her, light as a puff of air in her arms, dark, filmy blue eyes locked on hers. She was real. She was breathing. She was *hers*.

But Chemist… she wasn't his. Not really. He didn't deserve to know her name. He'd signed her off as Unproductive without a backwards glance, and it was his word that counted, naturally.

But she couldn't get to him. She spent her first week in the Centre dodging anyone who looked like NForce and skulking in alleys near her old training house. She saw him there, in his car, his face doughier than before, his jowls looser. She was repulsed all over again. She stalked the perimeter but it was heavily guarded, too many of them for her to sneak through, and she couldn't find out where he lived.

She's not giving up, though. She might be here in this rotten, stinking cell, but she will get him. She will kill him.

The next few days she'd spent tracking down her mother and plotting chaos on *The S Word*. She'd seen the news on various screens around the Centre, the ones in the shopping district where she hung out ducking in and out of stores to keep warm and sneaking into storerooms to sleep at night. She'd seen that Carys, Amy and Jacob would be featured, that they'd be pardoned, so she got this crazy idea bashing round her head. It started as a stupid joke, really, just a distraction for her, but once she stole the crossbow (just strolled into the NForce goods store and grabbed it from the unmanned counter, quarrels and all, and walked straight out again, with no one clocking her – luck or fate? Whatever), she knew she was gonna go do it; she was down for shooting everyone on that stage apart from her three… friends, she guessed, though figured they didn't think of her that way. But the judges – Cadman – they could all go down. It'd be carnage, and she'd probably get caught, but she didn't give a damn by then. Not after she'd stuffed up getting to Chemist and wussed out on seeing her mother. Had nothing left. So she went for it, went with Carys's bonkers outburst (she'd been pretty impressed with that) and managed one shot before everything went to shit. But what a shot it was – the shot that got Carys free.

She mulls over it all now, arms tight around her knees, shivering despite the blanket wrapped around her. She grins at the memory of that night, the one night she felt some sense of control and something like justice.

As for her mother, she tries not to think about her too much, so when she let slip to Carys she was mad at herself. What'd she tell *her* for? Not like she could help her with anything, let alone ease the strange grating pain at the centre of her that had only grown since she saw her mother with the new baby. She'd almost called out to her then, almost run to her, but stopped herself in time. She was kidding herself; her mother wouldn't be less interested, especially with a new kid in tow. She'd just grass on her and she'd end up… oh. She's here anyway.

She rocks in the corner, stuffing her hand into her mouth to stop the great raw sobs that push at her aching throat. *Get yourself together, Raza. Stop being so pathetic. You're strong. No more shooting your mouth off at Carys or anyone else. Keep moving on and get some actual plans together to break out of this hellhole.*

10

ASHTON

ᴊACOB

ᴊACOB Tʀᴀᴅᴇʀ ɪs *not* Oswall Trader.

It's the first thing Principal says to him when she greets them at the front doors, waiting with barbed poise for them to bow to the banners first. 'Oswall,' she says, and her voice is sickly-sweet with a hard edge. He flinches at it, his mind twisting him back for a moment to his grandfather's voice; to the way he said his true name. *Jacob. My dear Jacob.* The sound of his voice is almost real, right here in this moment, strong and gentle all at the same time, and with it Jacob catches the ghost of Baba's scent. Strawberries and wood shavings. He clenches his hands together, snaps himself back to now. To the other voice, the one he didn't want to ever hear again. 'Esla. So wonderful to welcome you back to Ashton. I must admit, I never thought I'd see you back here, but here you are. And I understand you are to address Assembly tomorrow with the Commander himself.'

Amy shifts next to him; he steadies her with a light hand on her back. *It's okay*, he wants to whisper. *We'll be okay.*

Principal's on her feet this time, no sign of the wheelchair or the great huge leg plaster she'd made so much of just days ago on *The S*

Word. She's clad in her usual stilettos and a harsh black suit with super pointed lapels, her hatchet face white against the blackness.

Her mouth twists till she looks like a disapproving crab. 'You'll be delighted with your accommodation. No Pods for you this time; you're in the house with the rest of us. Miss Warden will sort you out.'

She turns on her heel and struts away, leaving Amy and Jacob standing there, bags in hand. Jacob gazes around the entrance hall, memories crowding in then speeding round his head, wrapping him up too tight. The large stairway with the carved banisters. The sturdy oak door to the Think. He wonders if some poor kid is down there now, perched on the stone floor, shivering. Wonders how long it took them to get that wall sealed up again.

Warden looks older, more wan somehow, but gives them a shaky smile. 'It's good to see you.'

Jacob reckons she might mean it.

'I'm to show you to your rooms, then you'll join us all for supper in the dining room.'

'You mean with all the trainees?' Amy says, frowning.

'Mmm. Now, come on.' Warden hustles off up the stairs. Jacob looks at Amy, catches the doubt on her face, and the pain as well; this wasn't a happy place for her, either. He catches her hand and squeezes it.

Their rooms are at the front of the house overlooking the sweeping lawn and flowerbeds. *Gardener's domain,* Jacob thinks with a stab to his gut. No doubt Lora and Anson will get the best guest room in the place, but these are good. No night alarm to shock them awake in here.

They sit on Jacob's bed. 'Feels strange,' he says.

Amy stares up at the ceiling; a deep crack runs over its length. 'Yeah. It's… odd. But look, now we're here, we're going to need to make some decisions. See if we can do any of the stuff we talked about doing. Whether any of it's actually possible in reality.'

'Mmm.'

'We can't exactly call a meeting of possible rebels.'

'Nope.'

Amy pauses, contemplating her nails, still metallic silver after her last stint on *The S Word*. 'Did wonder, while we're up this way, if we should sneak out… go and see Reia and the girls.'

Jacob thinks about it. 'I don't know.'

'I just want to know they're okay.'

He shakes his head. 'We'd have to get border passes and have a good reason. Then there's Stephen to think about; he didn't exactly hold back about how he never wanted us to visit again.'

Amy's shoulders slump. 'I suppose.'

'We should leave them all in peace,' Jacob says. 'Reia and the girls might at last be finding some healing there. Don't want to go charging in and reminding them of everything they've lost.'

'I just… I need to know they haven't been…'

'Subdued?'

She nods slowly, her eyes shining with tears.

'I think they'll be fine. I get the feeling.'

Amy gets up and goes to the window. 'Everything looks the same, doesn't it. I mean, it's like everything's changed for us, like the world's split in two, but here it all goes on as normal and no one cares about the evil at the heart of it all.' Her back stiffens. 'We're not going to let this go, right, Jacob?'

'How d'you mean?'

'I mean… it'd be too easy to just keep doing what we're being asked to do. Makes an easy life for us, right? Gives us good Productivity prospects and all that.'

'You know I don't want any of that stuff,' he says quietly. 'And I know you don't. We're gonna do this – somehow.' He pulls himself up and goes over to her, lays his hand on her shoulder. 'For Carys.'

They stare out of the window at the sweeping grounds of Ashton, and Jacob thinks about what this place could be, if one day everything came tumbling down. His gut twists in a mixture of fear and hope, and he hugs Amy tight to him, his mind spinning with ideas and crazy schemes.

AMY

THE DINING HALL looks just the same. The arched roof soaring over the octagonal space, the long bench tables for each year group, the different hatches serving different food: better for each year older. It smells the same, too; overboiled cabbage, burned meat. Amy remembers her first day in year one and her stomach curls inside her; it wasn't only the indeterminable pile of mush she was served that had her running for the bathroom that day. It was the too-fresh memory of her brother, Lewis, her soul-child as she called him back then, being led through the hush of the courtroom in ankle irons and sentenced to death. It was seeing her mother and father rushed out of the room, sentenced to life on the Outside, her mum calling her name as she went. It was her upside-down life, all new and all unwanted. She'd wrapped herself up in the good memories and kept her mouth shut for months on end. It was only Carys and Jacob who got her talking at last.

Carys. She should be there with them now.

She follows Jacob and Miss Warden to the staff table at one end of the room. This table has no hatch; superior food is served to them by specially picked out trainees. It's served on china plates rather than plastic trays, and glasses of wine and sparkling water are brought to them by scurrying fourth formers who look at Amy and Jacob with great big round eyes.

A hush falls in the hall as Miss Principal stands. She bows slightly as she leads everyone in the Newland canon. This is new. They didn't do this when Amy was here. Are they doubling down on what it is to believe in this nation? The trainees join in with full voices, pride hovering in the air between their words, eyes staring straight ahead. 'We believe in a new nation of equality and justice. We believe every man should provide for himself, that each should prove his worth and productivity through hard work and striving for better. We believe in Commander Anson, commissioned by the Illumen to bring peace and fair rule to Newland. We believe in giving power to the strong and justice to the good.'

Amy joins in, forcing the words and feeling them fight from her like knives stabbing her throat from the inside. She glances at Jacob; his mouth forms the words but no sound follows.

'You may sit,' Principal says, and there's an immediate squeal of chairs scraping and then a growing hubbub of voices rising and cutlery clattering.

Amy looks around the table, taking in the Trainers. Trainer Three is in the corner, her eyes shifting away from the two of them. Gardener sits by Principal, and Amy avoids his gaze altogether, though senses it too often on her, the spike of his beady eyes like an inner pain, jabbing at her, taking bits of her she doesn't give. She screws up her nose then flattens out her face as Warden turns to her.

'I really am pleased to see you,' she says, her voice at a lower level than the rest. She bends closer to Amy. 'I was sorry for what happened to you.' Her gaze shifts to Principal, then back again, her eyebrows drawing together. 'I... I...' She trails off; takes a great gulp of her wine.

Amy smiles at her. 'You were saying?'

Warden shakes her head. 'Oh… nothing. I just wanted to let you know that you are welcome here, in some quarters. M… more than you might realise.'

Amy raises her shoulders in a question. 'What do you mean?' She throws a glance back at Jacob for a moment, but he's locked in conversation with Trainer Two.

Warden sits up slightly and grips her cutlery hard. 'Time and place.' She gives Amy a look loaded with meaning, but Amy can't decipher it. She can see it's no good pressing her now, though, so she changes the subject.

'Where's Miss Trainer One?'

Miss Warden pauses. 'She left.'

Amy is shocked. Trainers don't leave their posts; not until they become Unproductive. That's not how it's done. 'She left?'

Warden nods, lowers her voice again. 'Few weeks ago now. Moved on to another training house in the Centre, we think, but no one really knows.'

'Why'd she leave here?'

Warden shakes her head. 'Her and Miss Principal weren't always… in agreement, shall we say.'

'Oh.'

'Yes. Well, anyway, it's not my place to ask.' Miss Warden raises a forkful of roast potato to her mouth. 'We have a replacement, anyway. Over there.' She gestures the laden fork at a small woman at the other end of the table, deep in conversation with Trainer Three. 'She's a bit harsh on the kids.' Warden screws up her face. 'Not how I'd do it.'

Amy smiles to herself. Miss Warden was always one of the good ones. As far as there are any good ones in this place.

She eats quietly for the remainder of the meal, Miss Warden seemingly deep in thought and Jacob chatting away to those on his other side, always good at that stuff, unlike her. She wants to get out of this place, to box up the memories and throw them into the Think and leave it all behind her once again. She looks around the room, recognising so many faces; some come with happier memories than others. She scans the year five table. That's where she'd be sitting right now if all this hadn't happened. But while she's glad she's not, she can't help thinking about how much simpler life would be. Carys wouldn't be set to be killed in December, for one thing. She and Jacob wouldn't be forced *S Word* presenters for another. She doesn't want to be where she is, but she doesn't want to be back here either.

Her eyes take in all the trainees she knows so well. There's Boy L, that snitch from Jacob's Pod, whispering with Boy M and some of the others. There's Aida, for once not sitting with Mercia, who sits on her own at one corner, her eyes on her food. Aida sits with a few of the other girls, giggling and shooting the occasional glance at her and Jacob, quickly tearing her eyes away as soon as they meet her gaze. But Mercia is strangely silent and still, picking at her meal.

Amy shrugs. It's nothing to do with her anymore. Her last memory of Mercia, in the coach at the barrier, went some way to easing the pain of the years of bullying, but not far enough.

As dinner comes to an end, some of the fifth years come by the staff table. Amy feels a sharp bump against her shoulder and whips her head around; it was Aida, she's sure. Aida, now flouncing away with some of the others with Mercia trailing in their wake, her feet shuffling, her head down. She glances up at Amy as she passes, gives a half-smile. 'Hey,' Amy says, not knowing what else to say.

Mercia nods, then pauses next to her. Looks over at Warden, who smiles at her. 'Want to come to our common room for a bit?'

Amy begins to shake her head. 'Oh, no, we're a bit tired—'

'We'd love to,' Jacob interrupts, his hand on her arm, his eyes widening at her.

Amy sighs. 'Oh, well, okay. For a little while.'

'You know where we are. Oh, you've not been to the year five room, have you?' Mercia says.

Jacob raises a brow. 'We know where it is. We were here four years, you know.'

Principal catches the tail end of his words. 'You didn't have much to show for it, until now, I suppose. Go, then.' She snaps her fingers, and other trainees appear from the shadows to clear up after them.

Jacob

He knows Amy doesn't want to go anywhere near Mercia and co, and he doesn't blame her, but they must do something. They have to try. As he follows Mercia out to the long, oak-floored hallway and through the house, waves of lavender polish hitting his nose, he sets his determination in tune with his stride: one, two, one, two, do this, do this, come on.

The common room is charged; packed with energy and curiosity, all eyes on him and Amy as they enter, whispers and cackles and quiet, strange looks. He struts in, fakes confidence, slumps into one of the sofas. More of those in here; more luxury for fifth years, closer to Productivity. He remembers he *is* Productive now, and grimaces.

'So, Oswall, right?' Boy Lawyer says, slouching over and sinking into the chair opposite. 'Oswall Trader. Has a nice ring.'

Jacob takes a deep breath. 'Yeah.'

The others seem to lose interest quickly and drift back to their groups. Jacob remembers how he was never popular when he was here, either.

Boy L scratches his head. 'Um. Glad you're… okay.'

Jacob stares at him. 'Sure.'

'No, I really… I mean, it's good you're doing… what you're doing.'

Jacob sighs inside.

'So don't you want to know how we all are here? Don't you miss your old Podmates?' Boy L leans forward, punches Jacob's arm. 'Not the same without you.'

Jacob looks at him, wonders if he might actually mean it, if there is any truth behind his words. Something strange hangs in the air, something new and untraceable. It's like it's a taste on his tongue, something almost familiar but out of reach. He feels the warm rise of hope, bubbling through his body, but presses it right down; no place for that here. Keep on guard, Jacob. Say nothing. Sound it all out.

Mercia's here now, sitting next to Boy L, twisting her hands. There's something odd about her, too. Her face is thinner, but it's not that. She looks different. She leans over to Amy, whispers something in her ear. Amy frowns, leans back, says nothing.

'Alright?' Jacob says to Mercia.

She glances around her. Conversations have started up again; trainees giggle in packs, largely ignoring them now the novelty's gone, now they've provided no further interest for them.

'Is it really true?' she whispers.

'What?'

Boy L leans in with her, his hand on hers. Snatches it away quickly, his glance flicking round the room. Are these two a thing? Jacob never saw that one coming.

'You saying what you said.'

Amy clears her throat. 'We said sorry for all that.'

Boy L holds Jacob's gaze. 'You didn't mean it though, right?'

Jacob shifts, his body suddenly at odds with itself, his limbs weighty and uncomfortable.

Mercia whispers, louder this time, 'There are some of us here who kind of… might want to know more.' She glances over at Aida, lost in her pack in another corner.

'Are you and Aida okay?' Amy says.

Mercia just shakes her head.

Jacob feels it again: that bubbling up. Could Mercia and Lawyer have seen through his and Amy's *S Word* fakery? Could they be for real? No. No. Not them. They're the worst of them, the bullies, the sneaks, the ones who'd have the most to lose. They're probably a plant by Principal or Gardener, probably snickering inside as they put on this show. So he keeps quiet and wills Amy to keep it bottled.

'I know you don't trust me,' Mercia says. 'And I don't blame you. But… can you meet us? Tomorrow, early, before Assembly? In that room in the back of the basement. There will be a few.'

'What do you mean?' Amy says. 'Meet you for what?'

Mercia presses her lips together, gives a slight shake of her head. 'Seven o'clock. We'll be waiting.' She looks up as some of the other trainees drift over. 'So, Amy, what's it like to be on the show?'

Jacob sits back, swallowing down the bitter taste of distrust. Smiles round at the others as Mercia and Lawyer begin to bombard him and Amy with questions about *The S Word* and the judges. Puts his Presenter voice on. His Productive voice. His Oswall voice.

And hates every second.

Amy

SEVEN O'CLOCK SHARP they're tiptoeing down the main stairs. Hardly anyone's around; some kitchen staff are in and out of the dining room further down the hallway, but no one sees them. Amy feels her pulse speeding, sweat beading on her forehead. She barely slept; the bed was comfortable enough, but her mind wasn't. Should they be doing this? What if it's a trap? Jacob looks troubled. They discussed it for hours last night, throwing it back and forth, wondering if this was some kind of divine gift – after all, it's everything they've wanted, to get others on side – or a slippery slope to the Centre Think and Carys's fate. She grips the banister hard as they descend the stairs to the basement.

The low hum of sombre whispering greets her as she tentatively pushes the door. She peeks her head around and pulls up short, gaping. There are about twenty of them in there, all trainees… no, wait. There's a Productive there in the shadows at the back – Warden! Amy gulps, turns to Jacob. 'Should we scarper now?'

Jacob shakes his head. 'I've got a feeling about this.'

'A good one?'

He grimaces. 'Not sure.'

She sighs. A not-sure feeling? Not much to go on. Not much to stake their lives on.

Jacob pushes through the door in front of her. 'Come on.'

The room falls silent.

Amy doesn't know what to do with her hands, her feet. The room lies in shadows, dusty piles of old books and obsolete NSlates lining ancient wooden shelves, a musty smell hanging in the air. She tries to avoid people's eyes, to look away, to pretend she is not there. Any moment now Principal will walk in, probably with Gardener, probably with NForce—

Mercia steps forward, clearing her throat. 'Thank you for coming.'

Jacob nods. 'What's this about?'

Amy notes Boy L, next to Mercia, his arm linked with hers. A few other familiar faces, too, some from year five, some from year four and some even younger. Aida is not here, nor any of her and Mercia's old gang.

Mercia lowers her voice. 'We are risking a lot. We can't be seen. So please keep as quiet as you can.'

'Okay,' Jacob says.

'Listen. We've been… meeting, for a while now. We believe you, you see. I mean, we believe Carys, and we think you're putting on a show. Right?'

So she's come right out with it, Amy thinks. How do they reply? Do they deny it?

But Jacob weighs in. 'Of course.'

Amy's heart flips over. What is he doing?

Mercia's shoulders slump and she smiles at Boy L. 'Well, good.'

The crowd seem to relax as one. 'We thought so,' one of the girls says. 'But we were worried… that you might have been for real. And then where would we be?' She points accusing eyes at Mercia, then laughs.

Amy stares at them. Mercia? Is Mercia on their side? Is this real? Is Warden really here? She remembers Warden's cryptic words from last night, her uncertainty, and then she knows. This is true. These people are here with them, and they are ready to fight. She can see it in their stance, in their shining eyes, in the courage that brought them to this dingy storeroom.

Mercia folds her arms. 'We're guessing you have a plan.'

Amy looks at Jacob, and he looks down. 'Not really. Sort of. We're giving it a lot of thought.'

'But you're not leaving Carys to die there at Festival, are you?'

Amy shakes her head. 'Of course not.'

'We have to go carefully,' Jacob says. 'We don't know who we can trust. How do we know we can trust all of you?' He pins eyes on Warden in the corner. 'How about you?'

She steps forward slowly. 'I've been with you for a while. Since before all this happened. I suspected… I mean, I knew really… about the Think. What happens there. I just kept my head down and shoved it out of my mind. Couldn't afford to do anything else. If I got caught with these opinions… well, you know.'

Amy nods. 'Thank you for being here. All of you.'

Warden and the small crowd of trainees give half-smiles back at her.

'So what now?' Mercia says.

Amy rubs the back of her neck. Slick with sweat. 'Well, what have you been doing in your meetings?'

'Recruiting this lot, for one. We have our eye on others, more than a few. We just have to be so slow about it all. Can't let the cat out of the bag… if Principal were to find out…'

'Mmm,' Jacob says. 'So what if, while I'm here, one of you could get me into the IT room? To the main NCom? I've got some ideas I want to try out.'

Boy L frowns. 'You can't do anything on those. NComs are closely monitored, even more now if anything.'

'I can get a way through the back end. I can set up a forum to bring together groups like this.'

'Groups? You think there are more of us?' Mercia says.

'I think so. I hope so. The signs are there – the demos in the Centre, the fallout from the Outsider camps. There are thousands of disaffected people out there. We just need to find a way… and training houses are a good start.' He scratches his chin, thinking. 'See, me and Amy have to go and do this tour thing. You'll see why at Assembly. Anyway, so if I can get something going in the training houses we visit, get you linked up, and then find a way to get those links out to Outsiders and others in the Compounds…'

Mercia shakes her head. 'It all sounds impossible.'

Miss Warden raises a shaky hand. 'I think I know of some people who are like a version of us. Maybe. This guy I knew… I still have his contact. But I don't dare say anything on my NPhone. If you could do what you do to get me in touch… maybe that might help.'

Jacob perks up, and Amy feels a lessening of tension, a fluttering of hope. 'I think I can do that,' he says. 'Get me his details later. We shouldn't stay here for long… look. Mercia. You find a way of getting me NCom access today while I'm here, and give me the details of everyone here too, and I'll add you. But just… please, be careful.'

Amy looks at him. Looks at Mercia, at Boy L, and the rest of the group, all staring at her and Jacob with hope in their eyes, with something like trust. But can they really trust these people? And even if they can, what if she and Jacob can't pull this thing off? What if they let them all down?

11

THE RESISTANCE

THE MAN IS dog tired.

There are more of them every day. More channels have been opened up. More Outsiders finding their way to them, through word of mouth. But that's the thing. Word of mouth isn't always a good plan... word of mouth could mean extermination.

He scratches his ear, turns to his number two. 'How are the plans coming together your end?'

She sighs. 'Well, you know I don't have much clout where I am. Have to lay low. But there are good signs. Just yesterday we made contact with one of the northern camps, and they're left untouched. They have weapons, provisions... they are ready to go. Eager. The leader there has a child in one of the Centre training houses; she's desperate to make contact. Thinks her son will be on our side and get others rallied too.'

'Can we trust her?'

'Her, yes. Her son? I don't know. But all we can do is try at this stage.' She looks down at her hands, twisting together in her lap.

'Are you okay?' he asks.

'I... there are times I regret things.'

'We all do.'

'Hmm. But lately I've been heavy with it all. It's just made me more determined, though. We'll see this through.'

He nods firmly. 'We will. And thank you.'

'For what?'

'For being here. By my side in all this. I haven't said it much, but I... thank you.'

She blushes, an unusual look on her; usually so cold, so stern.

'Anyway.' He moves on, his face hot with confusion. 'We have a path ahead. Or several. Now to just co-ordinate everything – and everyone.'

'If only we hadn't lost Coder.'

His face falls. 'A great loss. I can only hope she's still alive in the Think. I've heard rumours there are crowds of them in there now, that the usual... eh... disposal system isn't being used. We've reason to hope.'

'Maybe. Anyway. Onwards.'

'Onwards.'

Jacob

JACOB IS HYPED after the unexpected gathering. He feels it in his body; his muscles quiver with tension and something like excitement. Amy's feeling it too, he can see; she's quiet and collected as ever but there's something about her – her head held just a little higher, maybe. He follows her into breakfast, keeping his eyes away from Mercia, Lawyer and the others.

The room falls into silence as Commander Anson and Lora Dancer stroll in, arm-in-arm, all smiles and waves. They didn't arrive before dinner last night; they must have arrived late and gone straight to bed. Anson stands tall and robust, his face red with vigour and pride, and Lora is made up more heavily than ever.

The trainees are on their feet, led by their Trainers at the staff table, crossing their arms over their bellies and bowing low. Jacob forces his body to bend, gritting his teeth. Anson laughs out loud. 'Good to see the Newland spirit alive and well. You may sit.'

At the table, Anson squashes in between Jacob and Amy, shoving himself up too close to her. Jacob feels the anger zinging in his fingertips and keeps his hands clasped under the table. 'All ready for Assembly, then?' Anson says to Amy. She flinches; his mouth, full of bacon, is too near her face.

'We're ready,' Jacob says.

'You've been told what to say?' Anson ignores Jacob and focuses on Amy. 'I'll be doing most of the talking, of course, but you'll introduce me. You'll then help whip up excitement about our project, just as you do live on the show.'

'Of course,' Amy says quietly.

'We believe all of this will help squash any remaining unrest. Especially in training houses. You are here to lead the way in your allegiance to Newland and to me.'

'Yes.'

Lora, on Jacob's other side, picks at her food. He turns to her. 'Are you okay?'

She smiles brightly, her eyes not on him but on Anson behind him. 'Yes, yes, I'm grand. I'm so excited for all this, aren't you?'

Jacob nods, trying to inject some enthusiasm into it. 'Yeah. Of course.'

She smiles again, looks down at her food, chases a mushroom around the plate, spearing it over and over again. She lays her fork down, pushes her sleeve further down her arm, glancing at Jacob then away quickly. Jacob looks closer. Sees the purple bruise blooming from under the sleeve, sees her eyes sparkling too much. He lays a hand on hers with a light touch. 'Listen, Lora, if you ever need to talk—'

Anson clears his throat. 'I'm not enjoying this food,' he says loudly, getting the attention of one of the Trainers. 'Get your chef to bring me and Lora better food in our room. Promptly. I have a lot to do today and need energy.'

The Trainer nods deeply, bustles off to the kitchen, and Anson yanks Lora up without care and strides out of the room, dragging her by the arm. 'What got his goat?' Amy says.

Jacob shakes his head. 'Let's just get this done.'

IN THE ASSEMBLY Hall, staff and trainees are waiting in silence as Jacob and Amy enter. Some of the younger kids start to clap, one of them to whoop, but the Trainers are on them quickly: not appropriate. Not here, in this hallowed hall.

Jacob stares round the space, wincing at the hated familiarity of it, at the way it makes his insides feel like they're all mixed up. The four banners with the images of the Commanders, the huge NScreen with scrolling pictures of the Scourge and the riots. Rain batters at the long windows, the sky outside whirling with troubled greys.

When Anson and Lora process in, everyone does the usual and Jacob finds it tough to keep the disgust from curling his mouth. For a second he's taken back to the last Festival, just months ago on a cloudless day, and his grandfather, bowing low at Parade; the grit in the set of his mouth and the hunched stoop in his wasted body. *Baba*.

He gets himself together and pulls in the words he has to say with a great deep breath. 'Trainees, Trainers, please welcome your Commander.'

That's when the kids are allowed to express some emotion, some applause, but it's more muted than usual. Jacob sneaks a glance at Amy, who stares resolutely at the back of the hall.

'Commander Anson and Lora Dancer have kindly cleared their schedule to be with you here today because we have an announcement to make about *The S Word*.' He pauses, swallows; he can feel Anson's gaze, his judgement: *Put more enthusiasm into this, boy.* 'You're going to be amazed. Thrilled. A... Esla and I can't wait for this next season. So, over to you, Commander.' He bows slightly, gestures at Anson and retreats behind him to stand with Amy.

He can barely be bothered to listen to Anson as he spouts all the stuff about the show, about how it'll be showcasing trainees now as well as Productives, how much they care about trainees and recognising the great talents that lie even in this room, blah blah blah. He stifles a yawn. The audience are more into it, though. They're loving the idea. They sit up straighter, eyes brighter, indrawn breaths, big smiles. Jacob goes cold. What if they lose some of their fragile newbies to this crap? He looks at Mercia: she was always the drama queen. Can sing, too. She'd love an opportunity like this. Will she pack it all in for this? Even if she is for real?

Probably.

AMY

ONE MORE THING to get through until they can get out of here: Principal has invited them to an 'afternoon tea' in her study – Amy, Jacob, Anson and Lora. Anson declined, not too politely; 'I have a country to run and subversives to subdue. I don't have time for scones and tea in some provincial training house. Lora, get our luggage; the Copter is waiting.'

Principal's face was a picture.

But she and Jacob must go; Anson made that clear, too. 'Remember what you are now: representatives. Go and sip tea with your dear leader here and then get yourselves ready for your tour. You won't let me down.'

Jacob was okay with it as he wanted to set up this forum he'd been planning. Boy L had somehow made it happen; he'd persuaded the IT Trainer to take the first years down to the basement storeroom to 'study' the old tech systems stored there. Said he, Boy L, would give them a lesson; he was into that stuff. 'He bought it,' he said to them at lunch, 'said it'd work for their history of computing module. Really I could just tell he was glad to get out of leading a session.'

Jacob had sniffed. 'As if they do anything like the actual history of computing here.' But he'd accepted the key card Boy L had somehow purloined and went off after lunch to do his stuff. Amy sat in the IT room next to him, keeping an eye out of the window into the corridor, listening to him clack and bang at the keys, spinning words in her head like prayers.

He murmured to himself as he worked, glancing at the clock on the wall every so often. 'How long we got?'

'Couple of hours,' she said. 'How's it going?'

He sighed. 'Slow. It's a good thing I set up this background routine before.'

'What's that?'

He scratched his neck. 'Ah, you know, I used to mess with all this stuff. I set up this routine back then, and I can use it to send data without them clocking us. Piggyback off it to set up this forum. Should work.'

'Isn't that the Ashton website?' she said, peering over his shoulder.

He laughed. 'Yup. I'm going to run this through their policies page. They haven't updated this in like forever.'

'But won't someone get notified if you do that?'

'No way. Have you seen this website? It's archaic. As is the IT Trainer. And the Party don't bother themselves with training house websites, as long as the prospectus pages are all shiny and boasty.'

'Hmm.' Amy hoped that was true.

He tapped a few keys. 'I need some way for people to access this. Can't just put it in a direct link.' He leant back, rubbing his chin. 'Could use a combo of keyboard inputs. Give people a passkey.'

'How can we get that out to people, though?'

He shrugged. 'Word of mouth, I guess.'

'This thing could blow anytime.'

'Yup. But we have to try.'

He worked for a little longer, and Amy noticed the sweat beads bubbling on his forehead. 'You okay?'

'Yup. Just got to insert a function into the main script that'll check for the passkeys.'

'Right.'

'And need to check encryption so anyone spying on traffic won't notice something's amiss. Immediately, anyway…' He trailed off, lost in thought.

She watched his fingers fly over the keys.

'Don't have time to make this properly,' he said, his voice raw with frustration. 'Just using some template code. Can't use styling.'

'None of that matters,' she said. 'People just need to get in and message on the forum.'

'It'll be bare bones. Like a load of hyperlinks with a message box.'

'And how will people identify themselves? I mean, we can't use names.'

'Just user IDs. String of numbers.'

Amy squirmed on her chair, then got up, peered out of the window. 'We should go.'

He nodded, skated his chair back, slammed his hand on the desk. 'Yeah. Good. I'll hook this into that routine, and it'll be good to go. I've sent passkeys to everyone on Mercia's list.' He paused. Rubbed his face. 'Just give me a few more minutes. Going to back this whole thing up to my phone.'

Amy hopped on the spot, waiting by the door. 'Hurry.'

He clicked some keys, shoved his phone in his pocket. 'It has to work, Amy.' His eyes had darkened. 'We have to get more help so we can get Carys out.'

Now they traipse up the old stairway together, treading the path to Principal's study, the worn carpeted treads creaking under their feet. Amy steels herself, thinking about the last time she was here, when she, Carys and Jacob were trying to find their friend, Girl S. She swallows over the great spikes in her throat. 'I don't want to go in there.'

'I know.'

Jacob knocks at the hefty oak door.

'Enter.'

He smirks at Amy. *'Enter.'*

She takes a deep breath and pushes the door open. She'd expected it to be hot in here, like always, but it's worse than ever. Cloying waves of incense from jars all over the room. A fire roaring in the grate, red velvet curtains shut tight against the rainy day, candles on the mantel, flickering against the gilt frame surrounding Commander Lucan's stern visage.

In the centre, by Principal's desk, a table has been set up with the trappings of afternoon tea: a cake stand with scones and tiny delicacies, a pot of tea and china cups and saucers. It all seems so incongruous, so out of place. Like a memory of summer on a dark winter night. A tablecloth with Newland flag patterns flutters slightly in the breath from the fire.

And there's Gardener.

Amy feels herself slump like wet cardboard. She wants to sink into the floor, to be somewhere else, to disappear. Instead she looks away, feeling the power of his gaze and trying to gather it up, to pack it up tight, to fling it into the fire.

Principal gestures at some chairs. 'Do sit. Mr Gardener will do the honours.' She nods at him, and he lumbers over and picks up the teapot. *Ignore ignore ignore.* 'I've called this select gathering to make known to you my gratitude,' Principal says, a spiky smile spreading over her thin red lips. 'I'm… delighted that you've repented, and I'm proud of you for standing up for what we all believe in. And especially for turning away from the traitor Girl Clerk.'

Amy can feel Jacob's body tensing next to her. She nudges him with her foot, and he closes his eyes for a moment.

'And I just want to make you aware that, once Cadman is well and you are no longer needed on *The S Word*, Ashton will be waiting with open arms for you to resume your studies and achieve your N levels.'

'Thank you,' Amy murmurs. In her head, in her deepest hopes, that will never happen. All of this will be gone. Something better will be here.

But, in reality, she knows it's not going to change. 'We will look forward to it.'

Jacob takes a sip of tea and winces. 'Something wrong?' Gardener says, and Amy looks at him for the first time. At the smirk crossing his face, creasing his features so much his tiny eyes almost disappear. She sees it then: the glint in his eye as he looks at Jacob's cup then at Jacob. She sees it and knows it.

'How's the gardens coming on?' she says brightly, calling Gardener's attention, pushing an edge into her voice; a warning. Will Jacob sense it?

Jacob takes another sip. *No.* She nudges him again, harder this time, and he looks at her, one eyebrow a question mark. She directs her gaze to the cup, then to Gardener, then back to Jacob, trying to make her eyes speak. 'How did the sunflowers do?'

Gardener smirks harder. 'They were the tallest yet this year. And my gardens have been entered into a Pride of Newland award.'

She twists her lips into a smile. 'That's great.'

Principal simpers. 'Garrett… I mean Mr Gardener… is an asset to Ashton. It's a very good thing he got over his… injuries.' She stares hard at Amy then, pinpricked pupils pinning her down. 'He was in shock for a long time, though. I hope you do realise the toll your actions took.'

Amy suppresses a grin as a picture of Gardener caught up in a mess of wire, leaves and nettles scampers through her mind. 'Of course. We're sorry, right, er, Oswall?'

Jacob stops, the cup halfway to his mouth, nods. 'Mmm.' She glares at the cup again. *Come on.*

'Are you going to drink your tea?' Gardener says to Amy.

'And a scone, perhaps?' Principal says, pushing a plate at her.

She takes one, spreads some jam and cream, but leaves her drink untouched. 'You must be pleased about the *S Word* news,' she says, trying to keep the conversation going, trying to keep the desperation from her voice while willing Jacob to understand. 'What trainees will you enter?'

Principal and Gardener are taken up with this, throwing around names, laughing at some, giggling with one another about possibilities. 'We could enter Girl Baker in year three,' Principal says, a mischievous note hugging her words.

Gardener guffaws. 'Well, the aim is to entertain the nation.'

Principal bends close to him; whispers in his ear, and they fall together, laughing. Now, Amy thinks, and, quick as a flash, swaps Jacob's cup with Gardener's. Jacob stares, frowns, then closes his eyes slowly, exhaling.

What should she do with hers? The jar of joss sticks on the table nearby. She slugs the liquid into it quickly, thankful the cups are so tiny, then raises the cup to her mouth as Gardener turns back, tears of mirth gleaming in his eyes. 'Nice cup of tea,' she says, then regrets it. Too obvious?

But he doesn't seem to notice. He slurps his back, all at once, and she watches him.

Jacob yawns. 'A little weary?' Gardener says, his mouth coiled up like a snake. 'Need a little lie down?'

Amy hopes Jacob didn't drink too much of the liquid. He yawns again, twitches, shifts his body so he can lean against the back of the chair. His eyelids sink, heavy.

But it hits Gardener more quickly. She sees the change in him; the moment of recognition, the malice crawling over his face then morphing to mush as he drops his plate and collapses to the floor.

Principal is on her feet. 'Garrett? Garrett?' She turns to Jacob. 'Get Miss Warden.' But Jacob is fast asleep, his eyes tightly shut. 'What the… Girl P! I mean, Esla…' she stops, flustered, '…get Warden. What is this?'

'He tried to poison us,' Amy says simply. 'I swapped the cups back.'

Principal stares. 'You've poisoned him?'

'No! I was trying to protect us!'

Principal grabs her NPhone from her desk, bellows into it, summoning Warden. Then she turns back to Amy. 'That's a dangerous accusation. If you have brought poison here… after all we have done for you…' She breaks off, striding back and forth over her fringed rug. 'Get out. Take him with you. I never want to see you again, do you understand?' She runs her hands through her hair, bends down to Gardener, supine on the floor. 'He's breathing. He's okay. He's okay.' She yanks at Jacob's arm. 'Wake up. Leave now. And you will say nothing about this, to anyone. Understand?'

Jacob stirs. 'Wha's happening?'

Amy nods at Principal. 'We understand.' And she does understand all right. She understands that Principal knows exactly what Gardener has done, and she understands that Gardener is still sending his nasty little messages, just as he did when he almost ran them down in the Centre. That he doesn't buy their act. And she understands that Principal wants – needs – them to keep it quiet.

That Principal needs Gardener more than she'd ever realised.

PART II

The Countdown

12

CENTRE THINK

Two weeks later

CARYS

I CAN'T REMEMBER what day it is. I've tried to count them, to keep track in my mind, to know when my fate awaits me, but days and nights merge together and leave my mind spinning with thoughts and fears and schemes that will come to nothing. I know time has moved on; too quickly, too maliciously. Maybe I have five weeks left. Maybe.

'Your group,' I say to Ava Coder, 'did they have any plans? Before you got caught?'

She shakes her head. 'We were always coming up with them, but nothing concrete. Our leader had some crazy ideas, full on blow up Party HQ kind of stuff, but we don't have the manpower. And not sure what that would achieve; too many Party reps across the nation. If we got rid of the Commander, there'd be another in his place in a day.'

'Who is your leader?'

She bites her bottom lip. 'I… don't think you'd know him.' She looks down at her hands for a moment and picks at a flap of loose skin. 'Anyway, best not to use names in here.' She glances round the room at the crowd of slumbering people. 'You never know.'

I shrug. It doesn't really matter anyway. Nothing does.

'Carys?'

Raza's voice, hissed through the grate, low and harsh. She's been quiet lately, unwilling to engage, refusing to reply when I call in the dead of night, and barely saying anything when she does. It's like her old shell is back; grown tougher, more prickly, and folded her deeper in than ever.

I squat down and bend my head. 'You okay?'

'We've been thinking.'

'We?'

'Me and Lois, mostly. Some of the others. Alwin's like a dead man, you know that.'

I pull my arms around myself, trying to keep out the cold. 'It… it's good to hear your voice.'

Silence.

'So, what have you been thinking?'

'We're fed up of just going through the motions here. Existing in these shitty conditions. We have to plan.'

'Yeah.'

'But we can't think of any other plan apart from that one I mentioned. Us overpowering the guards.'

I trail my hand over the filthy concrete floor. 'But they'll just shoot.'

'No. Listen.' She pauses, scrabbles closer to the grate. Her whisper echoes through and bounces off the wall, grabbing a different kind of energy. 'On the day of Festival, everyone will be there. I heard the guards talking about it.'

'How d'you mean?'

'So basically Anson has issued a demand that everyone be there, apart from a skeleton staff to keep us ticking over here.'

'And?'

She puffs a breath of air. 'And so it's obvious. We rush that skeleton staff. It'll be like two guards. Yeah, there'll be shooting, but they won't stand a chance.'

I muse on her words. On Festival Day, she says. On the day I'll already be out of here, in the Commander Lucan Arena, being executed. I won't be here to rush the guards. This plan does not involve me.

'You don't think they've thought of that?' I say out loud. 'They wouldn't leave so few.'

'Look, it's what they said. It's our only chance, so we're planning for it. I'm getting them mustered in here, and you can do it in there, so we have a strategy of sorts. Keeping our fitness is vital in all this, so we need to get some more regular group exercise going. I can see folk wasting away…' She trails off, goes silent for a few seconds. Then she lowers her voice even further. 'Look, I know… I mean, I just can't see a way we can do it before that day without mass murder.'

'I know.' I hear the crack in my voice and feel it in my head.

'I'm sorry. I just… we have to think of everyone here.'

'Right,' I say. 'Right. Yes. So, tell me more. Give me an outline.' I grip my knees, my fingers straining hard. 'I'll get everyone here up for it. I can do that. Ava, we can do that, right?'

Ava stares at me, her eyes too full of compassion for me to look at for long; I want to wrap myself up in them for a moment, to lie down and sleep in them and dream for one night that everything will be okay.

I curl my hand around my name stone, still deep in my pocket after all this time, and then I hold onto it harder, gritting my teeth, and glance over at Harry, asleep on a bench with his brown hair tumbling over his face, so peaceful in slumber. I think about him running out of here, free in the world again, the laughter I would see in his eyes, the sunshine in his smile. 'Yes,' I whisper. 'We can do that.'

13

THE CENTRE

Five weeks till Festival

ᴊACOB

I N THE STUDIO there's a new kind of energy. A buzzing in the air. Jacob waits in the wings as the official Party band perform Newland classics, whipping up the audience to new heights. Everyone here is on edge and excited all at the same time, kids barely able to sit as they wait.

Jacob thinks about the trainees they've met over the past couple of weeks. The groups they found already formed and the kids who were looking for groups to be part of: Jacob quickly learned the signs, the small indications that they wanted change. But always, ever, the hulking cloud of what ifs: What if these groups couldn't be trusted? What if they were caught? What if Gardener pulled another 'afternoon tea'?

He closes his eyes for a moment and exhales. The tour has gone better than they ever imagined, and the forum has new IDs added every day, spreading like wildfire, bursting with life and hope. No sign of any dissent there, but the NForce could find it any day now. Jacob's anonymous on there, of course, but that doesn't mean they can't hack the original code and figure it all out; that he was at Ashton that particular day, that it all bloomed from there. They're living on borrowed time, but while it lasts he will fan the flame as much as he can. The NComs in *The S Word* studio have turned out to be surprisingly easy to use; he'd never have expected to be able to just walk in there and send multiple messages to subversives and even Unproductive Outsiders who have somehow managed to join up from wherever they are. He grins at the thought of it; Newland's flagship show having the most ill-protected coms.

He wonders how many of those subversives are out there in this audience right now. Searches their faces for clues, but most of them seem caught up in the music, the anticipation, the newness of it all. Something falls down hard inside him; what if some are here but then swayed by all this?

He gathers himself and strides out on the stage as the band close, joining Amy from the other side. 'Well, what can I say? What a treat. Show your appreciation to the Party band!'

He waits as the audience cheer, catching Amy's eye and rolling his own slightly, stopping himself as he spots one of the camera crew sweeping in. 'Now,' Amy says, following the autocue on the screen ahead, 'is the time for our new slot on *The S Word*: trainees of Newland. As you know, one of you will be chosen to perform in front of the Commander at Winter Festival – an unbelievable privilege – and so now, for the next four weeks we will be holding auditions.'

The audience scream and holler, and Jacob takes up the story. 'Yeah, yeah, we're all just as excited! Trainers from each house have entered two trainees or groups of trainees, so we have a lot to get through. Tonight we welcome acts from the Centre Compound, the Southwestern Compound and the Southeastern Compound to kick us off. Esla, tell us about the first act!'

He listens to Amy and watches the judges, who sit in their purple chairs, smiles plastered all over their faces. Lora is whiter than usual;

thinner, even, but the others seem as robust as always, quipping and larking and playing to the cameras.

A girl who looks around Jacob's own age dances onto the stage, all confidence and swagger, and goes quickly into a ballet routine to background music. Jacob watches her with his feelings all mixed up: admiration and sorrow. Here she is, this beautiful, talented girl, giving her all for Newland, when all he wants is freedom for her and everyone like her. He wants to run in, to stop the music, to tell her the truth.

After the judges express high praise for her act, with Portia joining the girl on stage and dancing with her for a few moments, Amy welcomes the next act, from the same Centre training house: this time a younger kid, a boy with large ears and red hair. A ripple runs through the audience and Jacob's heart sinks. Are they laughing at this kid already? He joins him next to the mic, lays his hand on his shoulder. 'Boy G, then? It's so great to have you here with us! What do you have for us tonight?'

The boy looks at him and there is terror in his eyes. 'I have… a song,' he mumbles.

Jacob squeezes his shoulder. 'Great, Boy G! In your own time. It's okay. Relax,' he adds, whispering into the kid's ear.

The boy cannot sing. He stutters out the song, a well-known classic usually sung by Raulf Singer, and all his notes are flat. Why the hell did his Trainers send him? Why put him up here when he's clearly miserable?

Jacob gets it. Entertainment. Or so their star gets through without any competition within their house.

The judges are brutal and the audience worse. Jacob watches Amy's face drain as Raulf laughs loudly, slow clapping the kid. 'Look, I admire you putting yourself forward and all that, but boy, you sound like a herd of half-dead cats.'

The audience laugh; the boy shrinks.

'You just about murdered my song,' Raulf continues, laughter turning to scowls, 'I thought we were supposed to be judging talent here tonight.'

'Go easy on him, Raulf,' Lora pipes up, her white face lined with weariness and something like faded anger. 'He was brave enough to come on stage. Besides, some of his notes were sweet.'

Portia laughs at her. 'You always were the soft one, Nation's Sweetheart.' She spits the last words. 'I think I can speak for most of us here when I say No to this one. Edwin, is it a No from you?'

'It's a No from me,' Edwin says, snickering.

'And you, Raulf?'

'A thousand times No. Go home, kid, and try finding another talent.'

The boy is beet-red. Amy puts an arm around him, whispers to him.

'So, three Nos. You, Lora?' Raulf says, his voice laced with boredom. 'You going rogue on us?'

She pauses.

'Oh, get on with it,' he snaps. 'We have some talent to judge.'

She shrugs. 'I guess it's a No.'

The signs over the screen buzz harshly with four big Nos where the word 'Skiver' would usually go. At least they're not using that judgement for this, Jacob thinks. At least they're not sending kids they think to be without talent to the Think. He wouldn't put anything past them, though.

The kid scampers off stage, the tips of his ears glowing, away to join his training house in the audience. They jeer and mock, giving him thumbs down gestures and worse, drunk on crowd craziness. He sinks into his seat and puts his head in his hands.

Jacob doesn't know if he can do this anymore.

AMY

BACK IN THE flat they are quiet, crushed by the events of the evening after living high on hope for the past two weeks. They push past each other getting food, snapping at one another and getting in the other's way. Amy wants to scream. She thinks about the red-headed kid, the shame on his face, and another couple of acts the judges were less than kind with, and how the audience lapped it all up as if they loved every second of the crowd-shaming. She bangs mugs on the kitchen counter, disgusted at herself. Jacob swigs milk from the fridge. 'Will you pack that in? It's not hygienic,' she shouts.

He raises his eyebrows, puts it back. 'Sorry for breathing.'

She takes a long breath. 'Sorry. It's just…'

'I know.'

'That poor kid, he—' She stops as her NPhone beeps. She sweeps it up and opens the message. 'What the—?'

Jacob looks over her shoulder. 'What is it?'

'No name. No number.' Just words.

> I know about you

A second later, another beep; another message:

> You're dead. Both of you

Amy lets the phone slip out of her fingers and onto the counter, clattering against one of the mugs and ringing through the silence between them.

'Gardener,' Jacob says. 'Has to be.'

Amy's uncertain. 'Could be, I guess.'

'It's his style. And he hates us even more after we gave him his own medicine.'

Amy scowls. 'Hmm. Shame he survived.'

Jacob laughs out loud. 'Ooh, get you. Not like you! Anyway, he was never out to kill us with that stuff, not in front of his precious Augusta. He just wanted to 'play with us', like he did in the car.'

'Hmm.'

The phone beeps once more. 'You look,' Amy says, her chest aching with it all.

Jacob reads it out: '"You will die with Girl Clerk."'

Amy shakes her head. 'What does that even mean?'

Jacob purses his lips. 'I don't know. Ignore it. It's Gardener, and he's not worth it.'

But it has rattled Amy, and now she can't stop the words going round her head. *You're dead. You will die with Girl Clerk. I know about you.*

In just over a month she will know what that means.

14

CENTRE THINK

Four weeks till Festival

CARYS

THERE ARE PEOPLE in here enjoying this new S Word.

A group of them stand together near the back of the cell, gazing up at the giant screen entranced, cackling at the kids brought to the stage to make fools of themselves and clapping and cheering the ones the judges love. I look at Ava, see the disgust stamped on her face. I feel the old rush rising in me, the flame that burns my toes and flicks through my body, stealing my breath and pushing out my anger. No good. I'm already overheated from tonight's show, seeing a group of young dancers heckled and shamed and sent off in disgrace. I watch as Jacob and Amy stand by, saying nothing, joining the applause for the ones deemed as talented, and feel sick all over again. My anger is a fire, and I'm pushing through the crowd to this group before I can stop myself, shoving at one of them, a young guy who should know better. 'Why are you going along with this crap?' I bawl in his face, and my voice sounds ugly even to me.

He leans back away from me, raises his eyebrows and his hands, palms outwards as if I am a threat, looks round at the others then starts laughing. 'What's it to you? Just enjoying a bit of Saturday night entertainment.'

A woman next to him says, 'We don't get much of that in here. Got to pass the time somehow. Got a problem with that?' She squares up to me, her face in mine; hardened features and weathered skin. 'Just 'cos you're the golden child round here, doesn't mean we all have to worship you.'

I feel the rage in my fingertips, my knuckles, my—

Ava is by my side. 'Carys. Leave them be.'

'Yeah, leave us be,' the woman parrots, laughing harshly. The three or four others in the group join in.

I scrunch my hands into fists.

Ava places her hand on my arm. 'Not worth it.'

I shrug her off, turn to the first man. 'I don't understand why you're enjoying this when you're here in the Think, and you know exactly what they do here?' My words spill out too fast, too loud, spittle flying with them, and he flinches.

'Not everyone believes you, you know.'

'But it's obvious!'

He shrugs, maddeningly, and my temper is a throbbing pain in my temples.

'Some of us love our country,' he says, and the others murmur an agreement. 'Some of us think you're a traitor.'

Ava is a presence by my side, a gentleness in the storm.

'But…' I trail off. Can't think of anything to say, of anything to convince them if they're not already convinced. Then, 'But wait, why are you in here then? Weren't you at the demos?'

The woman laughs harshly. 'Hah. We were there, alright, but we weren't a part of it. Just going about our day, walking down the street, then this lot—' she sweeps her arm around the room, sneering, '—started shouting and protesting, and we were caught up in it. NForce wouldn't even listen to us when we said it was nothing to do with us.'

'So, you can see they're corrupt, then?' Ava says quietly.

The woman frowns. 'Just doing their job.'

I bristle. 'And so if them "just doing their job"—' I curl my fingers into quotes, '—means death for you, you're good with that, then?'

She screws up her nose. 'You're not going to get us believing your conspiracy nonsense. We'll be out of here soon. My husband is a lawyer.'

I move closer to her. 'It's not a conspiracy! Look, I understand why you might think that; what we've found out is horrific. But I promise it's true.' I suddenly remember Amy's book back at the bunker. 'We even found out the Party started the Scourge themselves.'

Ava's face drops, and I know I've gone too far – these people already think I'm a conspiracy nut. 'What idiocy is this?' an older man with them says. 'You sound bonkers.'

I push my hands to my head. 'No, look, I'm not. Most people in here know what's going on. They tried to kill us, right here in the Think, when we brought Lora back from her attack – they had syringes. They murder Unproductives. You are not safe in here…' I stop, shaking my head. My words are bouncing off them; they are brick walls, faces wreathed in cynicism. But others are crowding round us now.

'It's true then,' one of them says, 'about the Scourge? The start of all this?'

I can only nod. I feel beaten.

'I knew it,' says this new guy. 'I always knew it.'

Nods and murmurs of agreement, but not from this small, resistant group. Everyone else, though, they are as wound up as me, their anger roaring through the cell. *Good.* We need that.

I look at the group and breathe out slowly. Try to gather up the fire and push it away. I allow Ava to lead me away, back to Harry on the other side of the cell. I sink to the ground, head in hands. Ava squats next to me. 'It's okay. Can't please everyone.'

I exhale slowly. 'I know. I just… what if they tell the guards about our plans?'

'Well, they haven't yet, have they? Everyone here knows about the Festival Day plan now. I'd bet they secretly believe you, or at least have enough doubt to keep their mouths shut, to save their own skin.'

'I hope so.'

∽

'HELLO?'

I've been trying for weeks to get hold of someone in the cell on the other side, as we don't have anyone in there. There's another drainage grate that side, and every night we whisper through, not wanting to make too much noise. But nothing – until now.

'Is anyone there?'

A weary low voice, hollow through the grate. 'Hello?'

I turn to Ava, give her a thumbs up. 'Can you hear me?'

'Yes.'

'Are there many of you in there?'

'A few. I kind of just got landed in here today.'

The voice is young. 'Are you okay?' I whisper.

A pause.

'My name is… well, Girl Clerk, but actually Carys.'

A sharp intake of breath. 'Oh! You're the one…'

'Yes, I suppose I am.'

His voice is higher. Panicky now. 'So, how long do they keep people in here before they off them? I mean, I know you're being… um… done at Festival… er… sorry. But, I mean, the rest of the people here?'

He is scared. 'They're not doing that at the moment. They have bigger plans, I think. Listen, I'm going to tell you about a plan we are forming in the other two cells. I'm going to need you to communicate it to yours, and you to be here at nights at certain times so we can talk. What's your name? Where are you from?'

He pauses again. 'My name is Boy Farmer. I'm not... er... Productive yet. I am from here in the Centre. Listen, there's—'

'Okay. Thanks. It's nice to meet you, well kind of.' I bite my tongue. None of my words are coming out well. 'Look, as there's no one out there willing to help us, we have to help oursel—'

'But that's just it. I got arrested because I was fighting at my training house. It got... out of hand. There's a whole group of us there; we call ourselves subversives.'

I stop short. Like the Subs Community. The memories crowd in, choke my throat. 'A group?'

'Yeah.' His voice is raspy. 'Quite a few of us. We got into a big argument with some of the other trainees, and it escalated, and people got hurt. I got blamed and sent here.' He stops, and I hear him gulp. I wish I could hold his hand. Tell him everything will be okay. 'But listen, it's not just us. Can... can anyone else hear us?'

I glance around. 'No. Most people are asleep. Just keep it low. They're all good in here anyway—' I break off, glance at the group from earlier, all curled up sleeping on the floor, '—mostly.' I look at Ava, crouching with me, her eyes wide.

The boy shifts, his body scraping against the grate. 'So just lately there's been this whole new forum thing set up, and it's getting more and more views and people joining. No one can find it unless someone else gives them a password. We can get it on our phones and slates, but I don't think the Party can see it. For now.'

'A forum?'

'Yeah, so like we can post and stuff, and people are organising protests on there and also like sharing stuff about resources and ideas for... well, for doing something, I guess. And, well, there's this action plan to get you out of here.'

My heart slows, my pulse whumping in my ears. 'Me?'

He coughs. 'Well, everyone here. This forum thing has a load of trainees – we think it was started up in training houses – but there are others on it now.'

'Like who?'

'Well, Outsiders, for one. But Productives too. Everyone is anonymous, of course, no one asks who anyone is. Too dangerous. We just have numbers.'

I clear my throat. 'And this… plan?'

'I dunno much. They were just throwing out ideas on the board before I got nicked. They were all like, they're just going to walk in here and set you free.' He laughs softly. 'But… I have an inkling who's behind it.'

My mouth is dry. 'You do?'

'Well, I reckon it might be your friends. Oswall and Esla.'

I look at Ava; the hope in her face is too raw, too much. I close my eyes. 'That's not their real names. But even so, it's not them. Have you seen them on *The S Word?* They're sold out.'

He's quiet for a few seconds. 'They've been going round training houses, and this thing's been spreading round training houses. Doesn't that tell you something?'

I shake my head, even though he can't see me. 'No. No.' I don't believe him. I don't. I can't.

Ava takes my hand. 'You're shaking. You okay?'

I snatch it away. 'Just cold.'

'You know, it could be them. You know Lois thinks—'

'Lois is Amy's mother. Of course she's going to think like that.'

Ava lifts her shoulders. 'You trusted them once upon a time, didn't you?'

I clutch my trembling hand. 'That was then.'

'So maybe you can again. Maybe someone is looking out for you.'

I shake my head again. It's too much. Boy Farmer is wrong. I'm glad to hear there are groups forming out there, glad they are planning to help, but I can't begin to dare to believe Jacob and Amy might have anything to do with it.

Because if I do, the fall will be so much harder when I find out they really have forgotten all about me.

15

THE CENTRE

Three weeks till Festival

JACOB

IT'S SPREADING FASTER than his wildest dreams. Every day there are more of them: Trainees. Productives. Outsiders. The messages on the forum have gone bonkers, with too many for him and Amy to keep track of, though Amy spends her every waking minute going through them, tracking them, checking they are safe, deleting incendiary stuff that isn't helping.

He should've known it couldn't last.

It's in the tiny, abandoned coms room at the studios he sees it, the message on the forum, buried in with a hundred others from that day: "I think we've been rumbled." Just that, no details, nothing. Jacob feels the beginnings of panic: the prickle under his arms, the heat creeping through his cheeks. He turns to Amy. 'Look at this.'

She bends over. 'Oh.'

'What d'you think it means?'

She sits down next to him, scrolls through some of the other messages. 'It's just random. Not an answer to anything.'

Jacob scratches the back of his neck. 'I don't know what to do.' He feels the panic bigger now, crawling through his body, crushing his chest. 'I don't—'

'Shh.' Amy puts her hand over his, presses it. 'Stop a moment. Let's just think.'

He runs his hand through his hair. 'Okay. Okay. It might be nothing, or it could be some kid in a training house getting caught on this forum. Damn it.'

Amy scrolls through some more. 'Yep. Nothing else here, only the usual stuff. Some groups are getting together next Saturday for a protest. They're brave. Some people here talking about breaking all the Think prisoners in the Centre out.'

His ears prick up. 'Any useful ideas?'

She sighs. 'Not really. Something about the tunnels under the Centre—'

'Tunnels?'

She looks closer. 'The old underground train system. There's a whole big network right under our feet.'

Jacob looks down at his feet, as if he can see them down there, these ancient tunnels, criss-crossing the Centre. 'Are there tunnels under the Think?'

'Not sure.'

Jacob ponders it, ignoring the other thing pounding at his head: *I think we've been rumbled I think we've been rumbled.*

Amy's phone beeps, and she looks at it then at Jacob. He can read her eyes. Not Gardener again, please not…

She opens the message and gasps.

'What is it? Who's it from?'

She shows him the screen:

> Mercia's sold you out. I thought you should know. The group is finished.

Oh no.

Amy looks at him, her eyes wide. '*Mercia.* I knew I couldn't trust her. Is this connected to that?' She points at the NCom screen.

'I don't know. But I need to get all this diverted quickly.'

'But what's to stop Mercia ratting on anything anywhere else?'

He pauses, his fingers hovering over the keys. 'I don't know. But it's not safe here anymore. Can you keep an eye on the corridors? I'll be a while.'

Mercia, he's thinking as his hands fly over the keys. Mercia. Something doesn't ring true. Who texted Amy? 'Is there any number on that message?' he shouts out to her.

She closes the door and sits back next to him. 'Nothing.'

'So it's like those other texts.'

She frowns. 'Those were threats, though. This is more of a warning.'

Jacob concentrates on the screen in front of him. He needs more time; he can't let this all collapse. Not now. They've come too far.

'Have you seen this one?' Amy's on her phone again, this time scrolling through the forum.

'Not another?'

'No. It's about a meet up. There are hundreds of people on this thread, Jacob! It's only been posted about an hour ago. Someone's talking about a location outside the Centre.'

He grabs the phone. 'I have to tell them not to spill it here. Wait.' He stabs at the phone, fingers falling over thumbs. 'I'm telling them to sit on it a while until I've sorted out this mess.'

He tries to concentrate, swiping away the sweat from his brow. He pins an announcement on the forum, telling everyone this will be closed down and certain admins will be given new details soon; if they wish to enter they must contact their area admins. He can't think of another way around it. Him and Amy won't be seeing them in person to give their leaders passkeys anymore. This way they may lose people, and they may still have snitches, but it feels safer. He uploads the backup he made on his phone back at Ashton to the server here so it's ready to go as soon as he closes the old one down. Just needs to sort out the new keyboard inputs…

It's taking so long.

'Wait... what's that?' Amy says, pointing at his screen. It's gone white. "Error 404" in small type. 'Who's doing that?'

'Someone's shut it down. Damn it, people won't know. Won't have seen the message.'

'NForce?'

'I hope not. This is a mess. I'm not good enough for this. What if they find the new one too?' He slams his hand against his forehead.

Amy hugs him. 'You're brilliant. None of us know what we're doing. We're all just muddling on.'

'How are people going to get back on now?'

'It'll spread again. Just send the new password or whatever to all the admins and get them to contact everyone they know.'

Jacob ponders. 'Even trying to send the message is dangerous. I've got their details, but—'

'Just try, I guess. I have faith in you.'

Jacob breathes out slowly as he checks the backup and sets it to go live from the *S Word* servers. This might be the stupidest thing he's ever done. 'I don't know why you have faith in me.'

'You're okay, you know,' she says, smiling at him, 'for a Productive.' She pokes her tongue out at him, and he laughs.

'Look, I don't think Mercia did this stuff.'

Amy scowls. 'You didn't have to live with her for nearly four years.'

'I know. I know. But I have a feeling.'

'You and your feelings.'

Amy

AFTER THE SHOW tonight she is more tired than usual; the whole thing is getting under her skin. When the judges led the audience in jeering at a young girl who had clearly been sent by her Trainers for "entertainment" purposes alone – she played a violin badly, the wail of it screeching through the auditorium and Amy's earpiece –

Amy nearly walked out there and then. What shambles was all this? She watched Lora closely, searching for more of the signs she'd started to see: not just in the increased amount of bruises and blemishes on her skin, but the telltale signs on her expression, the lines on her face, the loss of her sparkle. She looked thinner than ever tonight, on edge and argumentative, and Amy wondered if she might, finally, listen to them.

Jacob clicks the news on back in the flat, and they both freeze as the newsreader, Elva Anchor, speaks in the voice she reserves for the most serious occasions: 'Tonight a vile plot has been uncovered, right under our noses on the Newday net, but we can assure you it has been eradicated, and so will all those involved. The perpetrators are, as yet, unknown, but the Commander has announced that, in reaction to this and to the violent protests that continue throughout the nation, he will immediately form an elite branch of NForce specifically to address this issue. This elite group will be made up of the most highly trained officers and will begin action immediately, rounding up rebel and Unproductive groups and gathering intelligence on them. The Commander assures us that no stone will be left unturned, and, in a message to the nation earlier, said that any citizen who reports misdeeds and suspicions will be highly rewarded. Any resistance groups must now realise that they will be wiped out.'

Amy wanders over to the window and looks out over the rain-dashed city, at the new houses covering up ruins of ruins, some ruins still in evidence out on the edges, left to rot. In the distance, the Party HQ and Centre Think buildings, close to one another, dominate the still ravaged landscape. She pulls at her fingers and tries to hide from the images and memories rattling through her mind: the Subs Community, desecrated; Ashton, its new group already found and banned – and what of those in it? What will happen to them? – Carys, still in the Think, probably weak and beaten down after so long there now. Her parents, probably dead in the subdued airport camp. And now this new elite NForce, stronger than any of these fledgling groups, all ready to smash them down.

They don't have a chance.

16

THE RESISTANCE

Two weeks till Festival

'CAN YOU GET into the new forum?'

The man raises his eyebrows as Number Two scrolls through the blanked out page on her phone, her stomach tight with frustration. Nothing there but that 404 code. Is that Party? NForce? Someone else? If they've found the origins of the forum whoever started it could get in deep trouble any moment.

'I don't know where to look now,' he says. 'I think this was mostly led by trainees.'

She grits her teeth. 'We need to get back in.'

'We don't even know if it was up and running.'

'We caught that final message about the admins. We just have to find one of those.'

'Hmm,' he says. 'Was it helping us, though?'

'Knowing what they're all doing keeps us safe. We're not ready to join with them – whatever Arthur says—' she inclines her head to a man with messy hair and angry eyes, '—but we must know their activities. How they are organising themselves.'

'They are shambolic.'

'They were, but every week they're growing. In the last thread I saw before it went offline, they were planning to meet up in that camp near the Centre – a whole load of them, from what I could gather.'

He scratches his beard. 'They might have some good effect.'

She gets up and strides back and forth across the room. Everyone sits stock still, staring; the way they sit so rigidly, the way they look at her reminding her too much of… *no*. She won't go there. It's over. 'They could also sabotage our plans. What if they pull something at the arena too?'

The man shakes his head. 'I don't think they'll do that. Not with this new elite NForce thing.'

She scowls. 'Oh. That. They must feel threatened if they're pulling the big guns out.'

'Who d'you think started this all up?' a woman lost in the long shadows towards the back of the room asks. 'Where's it come from all of a sudden?'

'I have my suspicions,' Number Two says.

'It's not them,' the man says.

'Look at the timing: when did this all take off? What were Trader and Plumber doing? Come on. It's plain as day. What is it that Trader does so well, after all?'

The man says nothing, but she sees the quickly hidden light cross his eyes.

'They're putting on a good show, to be sure,' she says, smothering a tiny smile. 'But they don't mean a word of it.'

'Hmm.'

'Whoever started it,' she says, 'it's not going away. We just watch for now. Arthur, can you look into a way to get us back in the forum?'

Arthur, his fleshy body slumped so low in his chair it's a wonder he doesn't spill onto the floor, twists his mouth. 'Without Coder—'

She rolls her eyes. 'Yes. Without Coder. You need to step up now.' She looks round the room, at the people in the circle, some with faces set with determination and some with resignation. 'We all do.'

AMY

WHEN THE NEWS comes in, Amy's onstage at *The S Word*, going through the motions. A voice booms in her ear, 'You're getting boring. Amp it up.' She stands up straighter, injects something like enthusiasm into her voice, looks up to the autocue for the next lines. The stage lights blind her and she rubs her eyes, looks again.

She stumbles over the words. 'We're delighted to welcome a special guest on tonight's show.' She looks at Jacob; he doesn't look any more clued in than she is. Special guest? Surely not Anson again? She looks up at the lines scrolling on the screen in front of her. 'It's a great honour to welcome Cadman Showman back to *The S Word!*'

The roar of the crowd covers up her confusion. No one told them Cadman would be here. She gathers herself together. 'Cadman, welcome!'

He dances onto the stage as if he'd never left. She takes him in: clad in one of his most flamboyant outfits, a bright blue, too-tight jumpsuit with gold details at the collar and cuffs, he shows no sign of any legacy from the crossbow bolt; oh, except his arm movement – it's a little stiff. He raises one arm high, the other halfway. But other than that he seems unscathed, as larger than life as ever. Could this mean—?

Jacob takes up the commentary. 'As you all know, Cadman was the victim of hateful violence just weeks ago and has been recovering in hospital and at home since. Cadman, how does it feel to be here?'

Cadman grins, his teeth flashing whiter than white, but his eyes are more lined, Amy thinks. A grey kind of strain around his face she'd never noticed before. 'I'm good. I'm perfect! And I'm back!'

The audience scream and holler and bang the boards. Raulf Singer is up on his feet, bounding onto the stage to stand by Cadman's side. 'Cad! We've been half a show without you.' He side-eyes Jacob then, and Amy can't miss the smirk written across his face. 'Does this mean you're back with us now for good?'

Cadman mock-bows to him and then to the audience. 'It certainly does. I'm here and ready for this new season and I'm in love with what you're doing here. Of course, I'm very thankful to Oswall and Esla here.' He moves closer to Amy, pats her hand, gives her a ghost of his prior grin. 'But you'll all be delighted to hear that yes, I am back. From next week's show I will be your presenter once again and things will get back to how they should be.'

Amy scouts the crowd for their reaction. Some whoops, a lot of applause, but some of it muted too. Are all of them really pleased to see the back of them? And should she actually care? This means they are free, that they don't have to put on this sham of a show anymore. It means they can fight for the rebel cause without strings. It means she can stop feeling guilty about sending sick people to their deaths.

But deep inside she knows that guilt will never go away. She will always have this with her: for whatever reason she has done this, whatever justification she and Jacob have spun for themselves, she has been part of a killing regime. She has been implicit in murder. And because of that, she will never be the same.

She stutters and stumbles through the rest of the show, with Cadman sitting in pride of place on a chair brought out specially, next to the judges, watching her and Jacob almost like he's judging them himself. Jacob seems to have more energy than her; perhaps the knowledge this will soon be over has strengthened him where it's left her strangely weak. Why is it that only now the reality of what she has done is hitting her so hard? Even her body feels like it's draining of strength as she blunders her way through, as she puts on this final mask, as she shames a kid and sends a woman who is going blind to the Think. She feels the nausea rising, twirling and churning through her stomach and up into her gullet.

At the end of the show it's worse. The judges are on the stage, surrounding her and Jacob, showering them with compliments about what a great example they are, about how much they have been appreciated. 'What will you be doing now?' Raulf says to them, that strange glint still spiking his eyes. 'You'll be finishing your training, of course?'

Amy thinks about Principal's last words to them: 'I never want to see you again.' Could they go back now? Did she mean it? Do they even want to go back? She knows she doesn't, but doesn't see what else they can do. If they don't go back, they have nowhere else to go. Not unless they turn full on rebels at this point – but then would that mean all their hard work is undone? That they'll have nowhere to operate the forum from, no base of operations? That more Outsider camps will be targeted, that Carys's execution date will be brought forward? Amy doesn't think they'll do that now, but Anson's threat lies heavy on her. No. They must stay in the system, even if just for the next two weeks. They must keep playing the game.

Lora brings two huge, ostentatious bouquets of flowers to her and Jacob and presents them with a great outburst of applause and cheers from the crowd. She whispers in Amy's ear, 'I'll never forget what you did for me. Never.' Amy smiles at her, and it is her first real smile of the night; there is something about Lora. Something so fragile and broken, but still so pure. If only she would listen to them rather than her abuser. Will they see her again? Will they have another chance to save her from Anson?

ᴊACOB

ASHTON TRAINING HOUSE glows faded gold in the frail November sunshine. Leaves in all shades of autumn drape themselves across the long, tree-lined drive, and Jacob takes it all in. The beauty of it. He thinks about what it was like in the Before, as a school for kids with learning difficulties; something Newland doesn't even recognise (unless they are being branded Unproductive, of course).

Thinks about how Carys should be by his side now as their car crunches up the gravelled driveway, how she'd be lost in all the colours and start spouting poetry or some such. Will she ever be by his side again? Two weeks. Two weeks until that date, the one that makes his skin crawl, his stomach lurch into his mouth, makes him want to punch something again and again and again until his fists are bleeding.

Their welcome is muted, but he'd banked on that anyway. Knew Principal wouldn't be there for it, that she'd be mad they were even back. But there was nothing else for it: it was expected of them and expected of her, so no choice. But they have privileges now. This car is their own, given to them by Lora when they left, the small battered red car that has seen them through so much already. And with the car comes more freedom: border passes whenever they need. They're still expected to do that whole bullshit thing of being Newland patrons, still expected to visit other Compounds occasionally and hype them all up for Anson's ego. They must give a good reason to get passes and they'll be given them, just like that.

And then of course there's access to the Ashton NComs. They'll have to be more careful than ever – especially if Mercia really has sold them out and the group has dissolved – but he will try until his last breath. Now they're back there he will be free to use a different path for the forum.

It's not until later that evening they get the chance to figure out what's going on with the rebel group. Jacob spots Mercia at supper, avoiding his and Amy's gaze, and resolves to confront her afterwards in the common room. But it's busy in there; too many people around, too many of them in his face, pelting questions at him about who he thinks he is now – just 'cos he's already Productive and an ex *S Word* presenter, does he think he's better than them all now? He grits his teeth and smiles round at them all, saying nah, he's just the same old Boy T, and he'd prefer they call him that than Oswall, thanks. Of course, that gets some of them hooting that stupid name over and over, shoving it in his face. 'Oooh, Oswall, you're so important now.' 'Oooh, Oswall, you've had dinner with the Commander.' Oswall, Oswall, Oswall. He wants to tear the name to pieces and fling it into the fire.

He catches Mercia on the way to her Pod near curfew. She's walking along on her own; Boy L is still in the common room. Jacob grabs her arm and she turns, flinching; looks away from him. 'So it's true, then,' he says dully.

A flicker ripples across her face. 'I tried to keep it together.'

'But you sold us out.'

She looks up sharply. 'I didn't sell you out! What the hell are you on about?'

He searches her face. Her eyes are wide, guileless, confused. 'We heard…'

'Heard what?'

'Look, Amy got some text that you'd snitched and everything had broken up.'

She stops still, folds her arms tight. 'I. Did. Not.'

'So… the group?'

'This kid ratted us out. But it wasn't me.'

'Then why this text?'

'How should I know?'

He scratches his ear. 'And the group is done now?'

She shrugs. 'I tried to keep things going, but everyone's too scared. Might be different now you're back, but things are on alert here. Gardener stalks the corridors at night like some crazy wild man, goes into all the storerooms and old classrooms. There's nowhere to meet. And we don't know who we can trust. I've gone on the new forum, but some of us don't dare.'

'So who was it?'

'There's this third year girl, she's like a goody goody. Probably couldn't stand being part of something that challenged authority.'

'But that's the whole point!'

Mercia nods. 'Mmm. To be fair, she ratted the group but kept it anonymous. Didn't tell on Warden either. Told Principal she'd seen a group meeting and where they met, told her they were like Girl Clerk superfans or something. Principal threw out all these threats, demanded people come forward, but no one did. We don't dare meet though.'

'Why'd this kid even do that? Why not just walk away if she didn't like it?'

Mercia lifts her shoulders. 'Likes being in the Trainers' good books. Got a load of merit points.'

'So who sent the text?'

'Told you. No clue. It certainly wasn't me, and I'm not sure this kid would even have Amy's number. It's a bit weird.'

'Hmm.' He thinks about Gardener, everywhere in Ashton at all hours of the day and night, and figures he was right in the first place. He sent it. But if he did, how come he didn't tell Principal more? If he knew Mercia was part of the group, why didn't he shop her? Why not hand over him and Amy to the NForce? What's his game?

Amy comes out of the common room and bumps into them in the corridor outside. 'Oh,' she says, stepping back and looking at Mercia, her face falling.

'It wasn't her,' Jacob says, filling her in while Mercia stands there, fiddling with her hands, her face a mixture of anger and fear.

Amy looks uncertain. 'How do we know that's true?' she says in a low voice.

Mercia shakes her head. 'You don't, I guess.' She starts off towards the door to the outside and the Pods. 'You coming?'

Jacob's forgotten Amy will need to stay back in the Pod with Mercia and Aida. 'In a minute,' she says, and her voice is loaded with this grumpy sulkiness that isn't like her.

Jacob takes her arm as Mercia goes off. 'Amy, it wasn't her.'

'How d'you know?'

'I believe her. The text was from Gardener, playing some game with us. The group was almost caught, but it wasn't her. Just some kid.'

Amy shakes her head. 'I don't know.'

Jacob loses his cool. 'Look, you have to put that stuff with Mercia behind you if we're going to get through the next couple of weeks. We're going to need her. You have to move on.'

She huffs. 'Easy for you to say.'

He turns to her, drops her arm. 'Easy? Do you think any of this is easy? Was it easy for me that this system almost murdered my Baba? That they did murder my mother? Easy for me that my girlfriend is rotting in a Think cell and will be executed in two weeks' time?'

'She's my best friend too,' Amy says in a quieter voice, hanging her head. 'And I've had losses.'

He breathes in, breathes out. 'Yeah. We all have. That's the point. That's why holding onto old grudges isn't going to do any good. You'd do well to forgive Mercia, you know.'

'Forgive?' Amy screws up her forehead at him. 'How do you forgive someone who made your life a misery? Someone who got Carys thrown into the Think in the first place and started this whole thing off?'

'If she hadn't, where would we be? Still tiptoeing round the place, knowing some of the evil but not the whole picture? This way we have hundreds – no, thousands – of others now knowing the full extent of it and ready to fight. This way we can see an end in sight.'

'An end that involves the end of Carys,' she says, and Jacob sees tears filling her eyes.

'No. I don't accept that. Here's how I see it, though, with forgiveness. It's not about saying what the other person did was fine. Not about letting them off. It's more about letting yourself off from the bitterness of it. I've had to do some of that with my stuff, else I'd be exploding from the inside with all that hatred; I'd just be a whole pile of hate. No use to anyone.'

'Wait, you've forgiven the Party for your mum? Your grandfather?'

He rubs his forehead. 'I mean… it's not like saying hey, you did what you did and I'm cool with it. Not like that. More like hey, you are evil bastards but I'm not going to lose sleep squirming with it all anymore. Not gonna give you that power over me. It's sort of like bundling up the feelings and throwing them in a metal box, then chucking that box into the sea. The feelings are still there somewhere, but I'm not allowing them to mess with me anymore. Not letting them just consume me like they did. It's the only way I can carry on.'

She looks at him then, stares right into his eyes, sees the depths of him. Sees he only half believes what he says, that he means it about letting it go but still takes hold of it sometimes. Sees that sometimes the hate actually drives him and sometimes it kills him. He licks his dry lips, shoves the old thoughts away once again.

'I want to do that. A bit,' she says, 'and I don't want to, all at the same time. Does that make sense?'

'Yeah. You want rid of the bitterness, you don't want it to define you, but you also want to keep hold of the control in it all, right?'

She scuffs her feet. 'Hmm.'

'There's power in it,' Jacob says softly as they walk slowly towards the door. 'Forgiveness, I mean. There's a raw power about it I don't understand. A freedom I get the edges of and want to… I don't know, kind of jump into. We should give it more of a go, the two of us.'

'It'll get messy.'

'It already is.'

She pauses, her hand on the door handle. 'Is that how you forgive yourself, too?'

He stares at her.

'All that stuff we've done.'

He swallows. 'Don't know if I can do that.'

'So how do you get through the days?' she says.

He exhales slowly. 'Looking ahead. And looking to see if we can bring something good out of this unholy mess.'

'One step at a time. Listen, Jacob…' she stops, fiddles with the handle.

'Yeah?'

'Look, thanks. I never had friends, before you and Carys. Never knew what that meant. But you… you've been by my side for so long now. You… just thanks.' Her face flushes with red.

He steps closer and gives her a rough hug. 'Love ya too.'

She slaps him on the back. 'Don't get all touchy feely. Save that for Carys.'

'Oh, I will.'

She pushes the door open. 'I just hope she can forgive *us*. I think that's probably even bigger than all the stuff we're carrying.'

He nods. 'Maybe.'

Amy shelters her head from the driving rain and looks back at him as she splits off to her Pod. 'But even if she never forgives us, we will keep going. We will get Mercia, get Boy L, get the others, keep the forum running, find a way through.'

Jacob smiles through the rain. 'Night, Amy.'

'Night, Jacob Trader.'

17

CENTRE THINK

Ten days till Festival

CARYS

'HAVE WE GOT enough?' I say to Ava.

She's arranging something in the corner, hands working back and forth, her back turned to the rest of the people in the cell. 'Shh. He might hear.'

I glance behind me. 'He's right over there.'

She moves aside slightly. 'I couldn't do much.'

'It's beautiful,' I say. 'You are so talented. You made it look like—'

'Like something, anyway.' She flushes so deep red her face glows even in the shadows. 'It'll do, I guess.'

'More than. Come on.' I help her lift the creation and we walk with it towards Harry, the people between us parting, smiling.

Ava starts to sing. 'Happy birthday to you, happy birthday to you...'

It's a song I know a little, learned back in the bunker where people mattered and birthdays counted. I join in, wishing I could actually sing in tune. 'Happy birthday, dear Harry, happy birthday to you!'

He looks from me to Ava and back again, eyes pinched with confusion then lit with wonder. People crowd around him, ruffling his hair, patting his head, high fiving him, a chorus of 'Happy birthday, Harry' lifting the dank air and weaving some kind of magic through the cell. 'This is for you,' Ava says. 'It's not much. Sorry.'

Harry looks down at the plate, the rough-cut triangles of saved stale bread shaped into a cake-like circle, slices of cheese arranged across the top in zig-zag patterns to make up his name: *Harry*. 'You have to pretend there are candles,' I say. 'You make a wish and blow them out. Close your eyes and see the little flames lighting up the darkness. They are for you.'

He gazes up at me then back at his 'cake', his eyes filmy and dreamy. 'Make a wish?'

'That's what kids did on birthdays in the Before.'

'I'm not really a kid anymore.'

I bend closer, whisper in his ear, 'You can pretend to be. Just today.'

He screws his eyes tight-shut and hovers there a few moments, his mouth working, then, with eyes still closed, blows on the cake.

'You know what else they did?' I say.

'No,' he says, wiping his eyes with a grubby hand.

'They gave presents.'

'Presents? Like this?' He points to the cake.

'Like this, but this would have been actual cake, all rich and sweet and chocolatey. See the cheese on top? Pretend it's sweets.' I reach for a slice and give it to him. 'Feel the sweets melting in your mouth, like an explosion of sugar. Better than anything you ever got in training.'

Harry munches on the bread and cheese, his eyes so rapt I feel suddenly alive in them. 'I can taste the chocolate.'

'I know you can. And the jam too?'

He smiles; big, wide, his mouth full of dry bread. 'Yes. It's strawberry.'

'And you know what?' I say. 'It wasn't just cake you got. You got celebrated, see; just for being you. You got other presents.'

'Like what?'

I nod at Ava and another woman, Celia. 'Like this.'

Celia hands him a parcel of cloth wrapped in string. 'Open it.'

Harry pauses, turning the parcel in his hands. 'Open?'

'Presents used to be wrapped in brightly coloured paper,' I say. 'Kids would tear it off.'

He smiles, looks down at the rough parcel then tears at the string, rips apart the cloth, takes out the item; a ragged, dusty old tennis ball. He doesn't flinch for a minute. 'Thank you. Thank you.' He starts to throw and catch it, up and down, his wide brown eyes full of sparkle as they follow its movement.

I don't know where she got the ball, and it feels like nothing, but it feels like something too; something bigger than this cell can contain. It's something, and it matters, and it makes Harry happy.

Ava steps forward, presses another item into Harry's hands, this time wrapped in a sock. 'Sorry it's a bit stinky.'

Harry screws up his nose. 'Yuk.' But there's such a great big laugh in his yuk it fills the place with light.

'Open it then,' Ava says.

Harry sticks his hand into the sock, pulling another face. 'You should put this in the wash,' he says to Ava as he pulls something out. His face lights up. 'An NPhone?'

'It plays a couple of games,' Ava says, blushing again. 'Nothing else though. They took everything off. Even I can't get into anything on it. Sorry it's cracked.'

I nod at her, still awed that she persuaded one of the guards to give her an obsolete NPhone for a random kid's birthday.

Harry's face is one big grin as he thumbs through a menu. 'It's got that blocks game. And the one with frogs.'

Ava smiles. 'Yeah. Look, it might not last long, but the guard says he might charge it sometimes.'

Harry just looks at her, lost for words.

I grab his hand. 'See, if we could all give you presents we would. I'd give you the world. Give you a skateboard and a football and the book you were named for.'

He closes his eyes then, putting out his hand. 'Give me them then.'

I touch his outstretched hand softly, once then twice then another time. 'Here. And here. Happy birthday, Harry.'

And, as he stoops under the weight of all the gifts I want to give him, his light wraps me up for just this one little moment, and it feels a bit like the darkness is shattered into tiny pieces even while we are caged deep within it, and it feels a little bit like home.

18

THE OUTSIDE

One week till Festival

AMY

THE OUTSIDE NEVER looks any less barren. Amy closes her eyes, trying to picture it as it was in the Before: full of life and fading colour, the cold air carrying woody scents of autumn morphing into winter. Tries to feel it under her feet: the mulch of a thousand leaves of all the shades of red and umber, the crunch of horse chestnut cases. She tries to capture it all and imprint it on the landscape as they speed towards the Centre, but she can only see dead trees in twisted shapes, shells of burnt out buildings, acres of wasted wilderness.

The camp is north of the Centre and not accessible by road. Jacob draws the car to a stop on a broken street in an old ghost town and pulls out the hastily drawn map he printed out from the forum. 'There.' He points. 'About a mile that way.' Ahead of them, behind the street a half-dead forest trails off, with some signs of life that Amy takes as a sign.

She thinks about the invitation, opened only yesterday, a direct message to Jacob. 'Look at this,' he'd said, showing her the message, his eyes wide.

Dear Jacob, can you and Amy visit us at the reformed camp asap?

Amy had felt the prickling at her forehead. 'They know our real names.'

'I can't think who it could be. Who knows us?'

Amy had shaken her head. 'Someone from Ashton? Mercia?'

'Did she ever know our names, though?'

'Probably. We weren't exactly secretive back then.'

'Hmm,' he said. 'But she's here now, so how could she be inviting us to this camp?'

'I don't know.'

'And how does this person know 'Admin' is me, anyway? I'd kept this anonymous for a reason.'

Amy mused. 'Maybe it's a trap.'

'We have to go,' he'd said. 'Whoever this is. This could be the break we need to get help to spring Carys.'

'And how will we justify that?'

'Just say it's one of our patron things. Say we're going to the Centre for one of Anson's ego trips.'

Amy had smiled.

'I think there'll be a good few there,' Jacob says now.

'And it's an Outsider camp? That somehow survived?'

Jacob nods. 'It sounds like they're pretty clued in with tech stuff, like they know what's going on all over the place. They hooked up with some of these other groups through the forum.'

Amy smiles at him. 'You didn't need to worry about people finding the new one.'

'Hmm,' he says. 'I think we lost some.'

She knows he's balancing on the edge of anxiety all the time. Knows they might be found out any minute, shut down and worse. 'How come no one from the Party have managed to figure out it was you? Presumably they realised it came from Ashton.'

'Must've, to shut it down.' He mopes, dragging his feet on the rough path through the woods. The trees close around them, shutting out the world, most gnarled and yellowing, some in half-leaf, some dead and burned. 'I think I hid things okay, but who knows. It was a rush job.'

The trees open out onto more of the old town, bombed-out houses squatting forlornly against the darkening late-autumn sky. Sounds of activity float through to them: shouts, the clunk of wheels, the clop of horses. 'There,' Amy says, pointing ahead to a cluster of buildings, some in ruins, some more intact. People run in and out of a doorway in one of the largest, a great faded white building propped with stucco columns, half in ruins; some men lead a horse dragging a cart loaded with wood along a path to another building. 'Looks like they're camped out here.'

She stares ahead, watching for anything that might be a trap. Jacob strides forward. 'Come on.'

A small crowd is forming near the larger building. A mix of people, young and old – some obvious Outsiders, evident from their clothing, and a few trainees scattered through; Amy wonders how they got away from their training houses and Compounds. Then more than a few Productives, holding NPhones and eyeing Amy and Jacob as they approach.

'Who's in charge round here?' Amy says to a tall woman.

She motions inside. 'Look for Abs. Can't miss her.'

Amy stares around as they go through the doorway, its door long gone. It's a huge space, the remains of two sweeping stairways rising from the hall and meeting in the middle, all chipped carved marble and a few darkened ancient paintings of long-dead people from the Before still hanging on the walls. A gaping circular hole in the roof marks the spot a skylight must have once taken; it must be a beautiful, bright place in the sunlight.

'It was a museum,' a tiny woman in faded dungarees says to her, pointing at a plinth holding the remains of an old statue.

Amy nods. 'I've heard of them. My mother told me.'

The woman scowls. 'Another thing they took away. But we'll get it back.' She extends a hand. 'Abs.'

'Oh, hello,' Amy says. 'You're the boss round here?'

Abs laughs softly. 'No one's the boss. We mostly muck in together here. You must be Amy and Jacob.' She shakes their hands; Amy is surprised at the firmness of her grip. 'We've got a lot to discuss. Thanks for getting down here so quickly.'

'How'd you know our names and who we are?' Jacob says.

Abs gives him a steady look. 'You're more known than you think. Among us rebels, I mean. Come on, let's go and take the weight off your feet. I've got a few people gathered in the meeting room.' Without looking back she strides off quickly, leaving them following in her wake.

She leads them into one of the old museum chambers with shattered remains of display cases still standing in places, their contents long gone, signs and pictures still telling of what was once there. Amy wants to stop, to read each one, to drink it all in. Several people sit on battered, mismatched chairs in a circle, lounging and chatting among themselves. Amy glances around at them, then at Jacob, then pauses, looks more closely, startled. 'Jacob! Look!'

Coran Butler is sitting there, clad in one of his sharply-cut suits, smiling up at them like they're long lost family. 'Darlings!'

'*Coran?*' Amy starts towards him, her steps uncertain. Is this real? How is Coran Butler here?

Jacob grins back at him and salutes. 'Hey.'

Coran stands up, lunges in to give Amy a hug, and for a second it feels like she is safe again. 'Coran.'

'In the flesh,' he says. 'And this here—' he motions to the messy-haired man next to him with a flourish, '—is Ash. He's the gardener at Lora's.'

'Hello,' Amy says, not knowing where to put herself, what to do with herself, what on earth is going on here. Is this part of the trap?

'Ash has been… helpful, to me,' Coran says. 'He's helped me understand some things I was suspecting anyway. Since you all arrived, actually. I… I was a coward. I just shut it away and pretended, just like my poor dear Lora. But I've been thinking about it a lot, and Ash was in on all the stuff happening underground, as it were.' He smiles down at Ash. 'He's a dab hand with the technology, just like you, Jacob. May I call you Jacob?'

Jacob nods dumbly.

'How did you know about us?' Amy says.

He waves a hand. 'Ah, well, I'm more observant than you think. You dropped your names enough when you thought I wasn't around. I know Girl C is Carys, too.'

'But, I mean, how did you know we are… on this side?'

He gives a dramatic sniff. 'I'm not stupid, dear one. I knew you were pretending, just like I was. I knew you wouldn't abandon your friend. I… it was like a gradual process, for me, but I got there in the end.'

'So you were the one who messaged us to come here?' Jacob says.

'Nope, that wasn't me. Ash is on that forum thingy, but not me. I don't dare; my position is too precarious.'

'So who was it?'

He spreads his hands. 'Not a clue.'

'And Lora?' Amy says. 'Is she pretending too? Is she with us?'

Coran's face falls. 'Not at the moment, though it's my dearest wish, of course. I cannot talk with her about it. It's too fragile. But I… I pray she will see the light. That beast is hurting her more than ever, and there is nothing I can do.' His eyes fill with tears, and Ash pats his hand. 'I want to end that bully. That's why I'm here. Well, I mean, and everything else, of course. The injustice… I can't do this anymore.'

Amy rubs his shoulder. 'You okay?'

He smiles through tears. 'Mmm.'

'Do they know you're here? Have you left Lora?'

His eyes widen. 'No! No. I would never! No, we're here under a bit of cloak and dagger, aren't we, Ash?' He gives a small giggle. 'Told

Lora we were visiting the Southeastern Compound. I have a friend there.'

'You were brave to come here.'

'Stupid, maybe.'

Abs claps her hands at the front of the room. 'Can we come together for a while, please? Welcome to Jacob and Amy, whom some of you might know as Oswall Trader and Esla Plumber, but I'm guessing you don't go by those names in these circles?'

Amy shakes her head vehemently.

Abs checks a message on her phone. 'More incoming travellers. Tom, can you go and do the honours? Find them a place to stay.'

'Do you have room for everyone?' Jacob asks.

She shakes her head. 'Well… no. But we've got tents up in the fields at the back. No one ever comes this way. Quick potted history of us: we've been here for many years, and we have a few ex-Productives and even ex-Party here.'

'Ex-Party?' Amy says, wondering how that's possible.

Abs nods. 'Well… like me.'

Jacob frowns. 'You're Party?'

Abs smiles. 'I get that look a lot. But no, not now. It is possible to change, you know. I was brought up in Party circles, groomed all my childhood to be a member – well, you know, as much a member as a woman is allowed to be; I never knew different. I changed my name when I left my old life and my old self behind. I don't even like to say my old name now; it's not me. I have repented and these generous people have forgiven me, and it has been the making of me and the liberating of me.' She blushes pink a moment and folds her hands together. 'But I was talking about us. We're an old camp, and because we have good communications, we were able to avoid the destruction, to throw them off from this location. No one knows about us. Of course, this may change now.' She glances around, studying all the faces in the room. Amy senses a keen intelligence, an integrity she'd never have dreamed of with someone who was once Party. Is it really possible someone who was so evil could be on the side of good? All this woman once stood for is all that Amy fears, everything that broke her in two. Can she trust her?

Abs continues, 'Anyway. We seem to have gathered in a number of other groups, as well as some escapee trainees, and your forum has helped greatly with that, as have these Productives—' she points to Coran, Ash and a couple of others, '—as they've been able to link us in with others. There's another group, we think even bigger than us, but we don't know much about them. Call themselves the Resistance.'

'The Resistance?'

Abs grins. 'I know. But we hear they have strength behind them. Do you know anything of them? We'd love to be in touch.'

Amy shakes her head. 'Nothing.'

'Hmm. Well. You're here with us now, and we can share our plans.'

'You have plans?' Jacob says.

'Some. Half-formed. You want to break your friend Carys out of the Think?'

'Of course.'

Abs picks up a pen from the table in front of her and starts scribbling on a piece of paper. 'And we have quite a few associates in there with her we need to get out. Me and Tom – we have an old friend in there, Mason, very dear to us. I don't know if you heard any of the chatter, but we've been looking at the old underground rail system under the Centre.'

Amy nods. 'We saw something. Do you know anything about it? Is it under the Think?'

Abs pauses, pen mid-air. 'Right underneath. And the reason we know more now is this guy.' She gestures to Ash Gardener. 'Will you come and tell the group a bit about what you know?'

Ash gets up slowly; Amy notices he is beet-red. Coran gives him an encouraging smile. 'I… I only know all this because it goes back generations in my family,' he says with a slight stutter.

Abs beckons him forward. 'We're grateful. We know how risky this is for you and Coran. Tell us more.'

Ash picks up a leather satchel from underneath his chair and shuffles awkwardly to the front, pulling out a large roll of yellowed and cracked paper. He spreads it out with exaggerated care on the table and the others crowd around to look. Amy can hardly take it all in: it's an ancient map of some sort; all kinds of interconnected lines in different colours, criss-crossing one another, some with dead ends, some more circular, with hundreds of points with names attached. 'They're the old stations,' he says proudly, following her gaze. 'It was called the tube. My family worked on it as long back as we can trace, and they passed it all down. The knowledge. My great-great grandfather kept this map, although it was supposed to be burned with everything else. It was like a sort of secret game in our family, like we could all name these stations and the different lines. We did it on Festival days, me and my mother and father. It was like… I don't know. Just a home thing for me.' He's warming up now, the beet glow replaced with a kind of radiance. 'It wasn't something we could ever talk about, because the whole system was shut down, much of it buried, bricked up, burned, of course. But my grandfather and my father told me about secret ways down there that you could still get through; they used to have like these illicit card games down there for years with prohibition liquor and all sorts.' He stops, clears his throat, glances at Coran, who gives him a smiley nod. 'Anyway. You don't want my family history.'

'I love it, actually,' Abs says. 'It's good to hear of some kind of family joy in these times.'

Ash flushes red and avoids her gaze. 'There was a joy about it. It's like we all loved trains, like it was in our blood or something. It broke our hearts that they'd shut all the old national railway networks down and only operated poor local services in Compounds. So I found some of these entrances, when I left training; I messed around in there, exploring the old tunnels. Never found anyone else down there, though; the card games stopped in my father's youth, I think. It's like another world down there, you wouldn't believe it. It's… I don't know. Like super spooky but super homely for me at the same time. Probably doesn't make any sense.'

'Go on,' Abs prompts.

'Yeah. So, I've… well, me and Coran, we've been looking at the map. I know it off by heart, but it helps to have it here. This, here—' he points at one of the station names: "Bank", '—you can get in there, there's an open entrance, no one goes that way anyway. It's all ruins still. I know how to get in. And then here, see this river? The old Thames – well, you can go underneath that through these tunnels on the Northern Line, see here. And then this station, London Bridge – that's exactly where the Centre Think is. Its foundations go deep into its remains. And I'm pretty sure there's an old way through from that station to the Think basement. It's bricked up, but that's something we can deal with, yes?' He looks at Abs.

She gazes at him. 'Mmm. I'm not sure. It won't be easy. How'd you know about that blocked up entrance?'

He fiddles with his thumbs. 'It's just from all the exploring I've done. I like to walk there in the night sometimes, just me on my own, pretend there's no one else in the world. It's… a good place. And now I've shown Coran some of it. He doesn't like the dark though.'

Coran shivers. 'Why you go down there for fun I'll never know.'

Jacob leans forward, studies the map closer. 'So you're saying we can literally get into the Think through these tunnels, right?'

Ash nods. 'If you can break through that end, yes.'

Jacob pinches his nose. 'Okay. Okay. And then what? What's the plan once we break through? That is, if we don't get caught there and then in the basement?'

'The entrance is in the deepest service tunnels,' Abs says. 'Unlikely to be anyone there if we go at night.'

'And security cameras?'

'Not down there. I had a lot to do with the Think, when I… anyway. No, no guards, no cameras.' She grabs a clean bit of paper and starts drawing a rough plan. 'Here's the basement and the bit where we think the old tube entrance is. Above that you've got the Think level, still in the basement. Over that you've got the lobby and multiple floors of offices, suites for Compound staff and meeting rooms. It's the Centre council building, really; Party HQ is for the national stuff.'

'So we can get to the Think level. But that'll be heavily monitored, right?'

She sighs. 'Right.'

'If there are enough of us we could overpower them,' he says slowly. 'You have weapons here?'

'Not many. Some groups brought some they saved from the raids. We're making some, but they won't stand up to this elite NForce nonsense. Ones we have, we're saving them up for...' She trails off, gazing away into the corner of the room.

'For what?'

'For when we're ready to take on Newland.'

Amy watches her, sees the grim determination in the set of her chin and the lines on her face, sees the vestiges of the capable Party worker. This woman wants to start a revolution but knows they have little chance.

'Take on Newland?' Jacob says.

'The only way we're going to stop all this. We execute them like they execute everyone they deem worthless.'

Amy draws back, glancing at Jacob, at the frown-lines around his eyes. 'Execute?'

'One day. We must bide our time.' Abs puts her pen down, rubs her hands together. 'It's cold in here, and I'm hungry. Supper in the white room in ten, folks, Tom's on it.'

19

OUTSIDER CAMP

One week till Festival

JACOB

IT'S IN THE camp dining room where they see him.

Jacob spots him and doesn't recognise him at first; he's out of place here in this bashed up room that still carries shades of its former grandeur. He screws up his eyes, tries to remember. Where's he seen that guy? Oh, that's it! It's that kid with the curly hair who nearly mowed him down with a crossbow in that old crypt. (He doesn't want to think too much about that crypt.) The one from that tiny camp where they left Reia and the girls. Will, that was his name. 'Amy! Look!' He pulls her arm and she stiffens, stares at Will, stops stock still.

'Will?' Her voice is tiny.

'C'mon.' Jacob leads her over and gets the guy's attention.

He whirls round and then he's shining with this great big grin. 'You made it.'

'It was you?' Amy says, her voice a croak now. Is she into this dude?

'I sent the message, yes. I knew you set up the forum, or guessed it, anyway.'

'How?' Jacob says, suspicious.

'Just a hunch. I knew when you brought us Reia that you were okay. Later I knew that you weren't like they were saying on the news.'

'How'd you see the news?'

Will shifts from foot to foot with a small half-smile. 'I kind of got into the idea of it all after you came and shook up our little world. Reia and me, we found some old communications equipment in the ruined city, and she taught me some stuff she said some guy called Cory taught her.'

Cory. Jacob thinks about the man shuddering his last breath under a great weight of fractured stone under an angry red sky.

'So, well, we heard stuff. That's how I found the forum, in the end. Managed to get some old tablet from the Before juiced up and hooked into the Newday network. Turns out I wasn't half bad at that stuff. I met up with some other Outsiders after contacting them by radio and they told me about the forum, gave me the code. And I just knew it was you. I saw how you were desperate to get back to Carys.'

Amy stands awkwardly, twisting her hands together, like she doesn't know what to do with her body. Will goes to hug her and she goes all stiff, and Jacob gives himself a secret smile.

'And… your family? Are they here?' Jacob says.

Will drops his hands, steps away from Amy, his face as crimson as hers. 'They're still back home. My father wasn't a fan of me getting into all this, told me not to come, that he didn't want to see me again if I did.'

'Oh… um… sorry.'

Will shrugs. 'It's just Dad. But no, they're not a part of all this. My brother sort of wanted to, but he wanted to keep the peace with Dad too.'

'And Reia? The girls?'

Will's face brightens. 'Those little scamps. They've captured everyone's hearts, even Dad's. He can't do enough for that little Esther. My mum and dad have sort of adopted her; that kid has them round her little finger.'

'That's good. Reia's doing okay?'

'She's fine. Wanted to come, actually, but Hannah had a temperature and she stayed to nurse her. She adores those girls. Said she'll come down sometime soon, though.'

Jacob muses. 'They got a way of getting here?'

'Horses. Takes a long time, but it's all I've ever known. Don't even know how to drive these cars you all have.'

Amy shakes herself out of her silence. 'You have Shadow here?'

Will laughs. 'Yep. My old boy. Want to go say hi?'

She nods silently and goes off with him, her face lit up like Jacob's not seen it in weeks. It's hope on her face, and it grabs hold of him, too, wraps him up tight, warms him even with the cool of the evening breathing through windowless windows.

It's FREEZING COLD in the tent, and Jacob can't sleep. His mind is full of a hundred things, jostling against one another for space, keeping his limbs locked into an alert kind of stiffness; he can't relax. Seeing Will has thrown him back into the crypt in the old city, and he can't shake his grandfather's last words: "Search the old ways," he'd said to him. "The crossroads. The ancient paths." Jacob had promised he would. But what did he mean? What were the old ways, the crossroads, the ancient paths, and why are they so heavy in Jacob's mind now? He twists the words in his mind, tries to make sense of them, and shoves them away in frustration. How can he search the old ways when he doesn't know what the old ways are? But his Baba is there, his warm, rich voice streaming through his head, whispering the words, and Jacob feels it. The rush of love. The words are loaded with it, dripping in it, fortified by it. Baba's old ways are ways of love. But what does that mean? What are the crossroads, and which path should he choose? He gets the feeling the choice before him now is the biggest of his life; even bigger, perhaps, than his choice to play the game in the Newland system. He wrestles with it, squirms under the rough blanket, trying to get comfortable, to understand. But his confusion is as dark as the November sky outside.

A sudden noise. A rustling in the bushes behind the small city of tents where he and Amy have found a place to rest. Is it a wild animal? One of those packs of dogs you hear about here on the Outside? He sits bolt upright, glancing around the tent; about seven or eight others slumber in here, including Amy, fast asleep near Will in the corner. No one stirs.

Rustling again. Louder, this time; nearer. He pushes the blanket away and shivers, wrapping his arms around himself as he picks his way to the zipped entrance. Grabs his jacket, discarded on the ground nearby, and opens the tent as quietly as he can, sliding the zipper slowly, carefully upwards and then ducking out into the damp night. Light rain touches his face; the sky is clouded over, the moon hidden, the darkness complete out here where there are no streetlamps. He plucks his phone from his pocket, activates the torch app, shines it towards the back of the tents.

There. Movement. Not dogs; humans. More than one, there in the trees, scoping them out. He kills the torch, ducks down behind one of the tents, staring out at them. They are almost motionless.

Something gleams out at him as clouds release the moon for seconds, and he recognises it. A buckled belt. *NForce uniforms.* They are unmistakable.

The NForce are here.

What does he do? They have weapons, he can see that now, even from this far away. He creeps back to his tent, unzips it without any care now, shakes people awake. 'Shh. Shh. Wake up. NForce.' Panicked faces gaze up at him, white in his torchlight. 'Wake everyone up and get back to the museum as quickly as you can.'

He scrambles back through the opening, Amy and Will and the others on his tail, everyone creeping into other tents. Jacob glances back at the tree line and sees no one has moved. They are there, watching, weighing up. They must be able to see them all now, shuffling out of tents, some people making too much noise, some running off back towards the museum. But they don't move.

Jacob realises it too late: they are allowing them to get out of their tents and back to the camp buildings. They want them to. They want to pin everyone in one place and… and what? Mow them down? Bomb them? Jacob grabs Amy's arm. 'Wait. We need to spread out. Wait.' He shouts at some of the others, uncaring now about being heard. 'Stop. Spread out. Don't all go to the museum. I'll go there and warn Abs and the others.'

People scatter in all directions, panicking now and grabbing one another, ducking in and out of tents for possessions and weapons as he, Amy and Will sprint towards the ruined buildings, ghostly hulks looming at them through the damp murk.

That's when the first shots ring out.

Amy stops, gapes at him, eyes wide, Will grabbing her hand and yanking her away from the direction of the shots. Jacob sees someone go down near the tents, slammed in the back. No. No. Get to the museum. Get everyone there up and out. Get away from here. He pelts after Amy and Will, his pulse speeding at his throat, his legs weak with terror. This is real. Anson meant what he said. The elite NForce are here, and they are going to take out all these good people. How did they find them? Why are they always one step ahead? This is the end. His legs begin to shake, prickles of fear running through them as he forces them to work, to move, come on come on.

Abs and the others are already up. There's a great clamour in the foyer, people from the tents having rushed here and raised the alarm, folks dashing back and forth, gathering weapons, sticks, rudimentary spears from a near empty store cupboard. Jacob's gut falls harder; they are not prepared for this. Despite Abs's words about saving up weapons, turns out they're ill equipped. That her words were more about future hope than present reality. Jacob grabs a stick roughly honed to a pointed head, splinters poking at his flesh. 'Don't happen to have that crossbow of yours, do you?' he says to Will, trying to infuse a half-joke into his tone, but Will just shakes his head as he and Amy grab sticks. They are going to try and defend themselves against an army with automatic rifles… with sticks.

Abs is in the centre of the foyer, directing people around, but Jacob can see the fear written deep in the lines on her face even as she grits her teeth in a mask of bravery. 'There are too many of them,' he says to her. 'They'll be here any minute. What should we do?'

She closes her eyes, shakes her head. She doesn't know. No one knows.

'Get round the back,' she yells, sweeping her arms round the foyer at everyone. They stand there, frozen, then start to move, one by one, as Abs leads them out. Like ants against a wasps' nest.

Outside it is mayhem. Jacob can't see what's happening but sees the flash of automatic fire, hears the crashes of bodies hitting the ground, the screams of young trainees as they try to get out of the way. 'This way,' he bellows, collecting up a group of youngsters. 'Get in front of me.' He shepherds them between the two largest buildings, into a narrow space where a few others are gathered, eyes like saucers, trembling together. 'Wait here,' he says, and dashes out to collect more of them. Not that anywhere is safe.

He finds Coran and Ash outside the main doorway with some more kids, cowering against a partially collapsed wall, eyes wide with fear. Ash is shaking and wringing his hands, murmuring to himself; Coran stands next to him, his eyes pleading with Jacob.

'Can you take this lot round the back and look after everyone there?' Jacob says, pointing back. Coran's face falls into a kind of relief as he herds the kids with Ash and disappears behind the museum.

The elite NForce stride closer, ripped men in stiff uniforms in full control, mowing down anyone in their way. He hears harsh laughter, smells the acrid stench of fire and death, and feels the nausea in the pit of his belly. Where is Amy? Will? He shouts their names, but they are lost in the chaos.

Jacob grabs a kid as bullets slam into a young man in front of them, taking him down and spilling his blood wide over the wintering earth. No time to wait. No time to try to help. He pushes the girl in front of him and around to the alleyway and goes out for more. Sees Amy and Will off in the distance, huddled behind a broken-down shed, and others in scattered groups trying to take cover.

There are not enough of them.

The army advances.

Jacob skids to a stop as he feels eyes on him and finds himself staring directly at an NForce officer, recognition flashing over the man's face. 'You,' he says, pointing and hollering to his team leader. 'It's him from *The S Word*!'

His grim-faced commander steps out of the line and nearer to Jacob, levelling a rifle at him. 'Knew you were never for real.' He spits on the ground in front of him. 'I'll be rewarded for this.' He lifts the gun higher and Jacob spins, searching for cover, but there is none. Time slows down as the soldier steadies his hand. Jacob closes his eyes, the nausea in his throat now, burning the length of his body. Tries to collect himself, to find something. The ghost of his grandfather's words, somewhere deep in his soul. *Stand at the crossroads. Stand at the crossroads.*

He opens his eyes and squares up to the guy. 'Here I am.'

The man stops, stares at him, rifle steady, aimed at his heart. Looks at Jacob's makeshift spear and sneers. 'What were you going to do with that?'

Jacob says nothing. Out of the corner of his eye he sees movement. Amy? Don't come near, Amy, get out of here, please don't come here. Please not you. He twirls the words in his head like prayers and throws them at her. The man seems frozen, undecided; why?

Jacob hears the gunshot and flinches. This is it. This is it.

But nothing. He feels nothing. He looks down at himself, looks for the blood, for the hole in his chest, but there is nothing. His head spins as he looks up, looks at his killer, except he is not his killer because he has gone. He is on the floor, collapsed and his head shattered in a hundred pieces Jacob does not want to see. His world turns on its side as he gathers himself, spins round, sees them there. Crowds of people. More NForce? No. They are in Outsider garb, all ancient homespun clothes, and they are there behind him, with him, encircling him, and one of them has a shotgun, still pointed at the space the NForce man was taking up a second ago.

Bang.

Jacob is dizzy. The clouds are crashing into him, gathering him up in them, lifting him off his feet and slamming him to the ground. Was that it this time? Was he shot? He feels a blazing on his leg, a stickiness in his trousers, and his mind won't catch up; he is stuck somewhere in a fog. Where is Carys? Why isn't she next to him now? Baba is here, though. He's whispering soothing words. 'My dear boy. Jacob. My dear boy.' He sees his face, as dear as anything he ever knew, sees the depths of love in his eyes, reaching out to him and warming him, parting the fog, stopping the pain.

'Jacob.'

The word snaps him out of it, back to the battlefield, back to the sticky bloody darkness, back to the bodies on the ground all over, back to the large group of people near him, all now laying into NForce elite soldiers, some with weapons like their own, some with crossbows, some with sticks, some with hands. Why are there so many of them? His leg hurts. Amy is there next to him, tugging at his arm, Will pulling the other. 'Get up. It's okay. It's okay.' And behind them are more familiar faces. It's Will's brother, Matt, is that his name? Jacob can't remember. He is so tired. And is that their father, Stephen? No. It can't be. He's not here. He didn't want to be part of this. Jacob is dreaming, of course he is, because now Reia is there and she is magnificent, throwing spears and kick-fighting her way through a group of dazed NForce, but of course, that's just his dream, isn't it, because Baba is still here too, sort of, but he is leaving him now and Jacob doesn't want him to leave, he tries to catch his arm, to bring him back, but he's not there anymore and Amy is, and Reia is too, squatting on the ground next to him.

'That leg needs seeing to,' she says. 'Get him inside. He looks delirious.'

He stares up at the sky and thinks it looks like black ink all swirled up and dripping down on him. Something is wrong with his leg, but the blaze is too fiery to feel. He needs to close his eyes. Then everything will be fine, and Baba will be here.

❧

'GOING TO BE fine.'

'No bullet wound, he's just grazed, I think his head got bashed into by someone, passed out.'

The voices rouse him and he is here again, back in the museum, in the foyer, lying on a lumpy mattress, his jeans ripped open at the knee, his leg pulsating with pain. Amy's with him, and Coran and Ash, and Abs and Will, and Reia is here too. Reia is really here.

'You?' is the only word he can find.

Reia strokes his forehead. 'Shh. Yes.'

'B... but Hannah?'

The lines on her face all crease and meet together, then clear as she glances at Will. 'Oh. Yes. Hannah was a lot better, so I left her and the others with Sarah, and persuaded Stephen and Matt to bring a few of the others down. They've been realising we can't stay insulated from all this, and when Will left, Sarah got on side. Said we need to join up, to be a part of the answer. So here we are.'

He sits up, gazes around the room, the packed space. 'And all these others? Who...'

'We met up with a larger group on the way down. They were on their way here too. It's quite a meeting, isn't it? Looks like we were just in time.'

'The NForce?'

'Turned tail, for now. There were more of us than them, and they ran off spouting all kinds of threats. They'll be back soon, with more, or bombs. We must get moving.'

'Did you… kill some of them?'

'One or two. Damaged, mostly; some were shot. We managed to get some of their weapons. I know the original group here want to get some kind of mass revolution going.'

Jacob stares into her eyes, sees the pain there. 'Do you want that?'

She glances at Stephen, talking to a group of people, and at Will and Amy. 'I don't want evil to win anymore.'

'The ancient paths,' Jacob mumbles.

'What?'

'Oh, nothing. Something my grandfather said.'

'That's from the old holy book,' she says, her face falling further into pain. 'Back in our home. Gone now.'

'What, the ancient paths?'

'Yes. It was something about getting people to stand at the crossroads and choose the good ways. If I remember correctly, it said if they did that they would find rest for their souls.'

Jacob looks down at his leg. Rest for his soul? He tastes the edges of it for half a second and a yearning powers through his body. 'What are they, then? The good ways? Where do we go from here?'

Amy leans closer. 'I don't know if paying life for life is the way. I saw some of our side go down and I felt sick, then saw some young NForce cadet, barely out of training, saw him go down hard, saw this expression on his face, and I felt sick then too.'

Jacob looks at her, at the kindness at the heart of her; the face of the officer who nearly shot him is clear in his mind. He was young, too. 'We have to get real, though. We can't pretend that there won't be losses, that we won't have to make hard choices.'

Reia sits tall. 'The small hard choices will sit easier if we make the right turning on the big hard choice. There's a saying passed down from the Before, from a time injustice was rife: "Darkness cannot drive out darkness: Only light can do that. Hate cannot drive out hate: Only love can do that."'

Jacob swallows up the words, drinking them in and hiding them deep inside. 'But how? How will light drive out darkness when the only way ahead looks like hate?'

'We keep following the good ways,' Reia says softly. 'We amplify the unheard voices, we shed blood where we need and no further. Courage, Jacob. You have it already. You have it from your grandfather, you have it from your friends. Go walking ahead with it defining you instead of revenge, and see what happens.'

'And Carys?'

'I don't know what will happen. I cannot say. But we will walk strong, whatever, together.'

Jacob muses on her words as she cleans his wound and bandages his leg.

'Where now?' Amy says.

'Well, we can't go back to Ashton. I got well and truly clocked by that whole line of NForce. That's it for us now.'

She nods, and Jacob sees the mix on her face: relief and terror. 'So we stay with these folk. We go with them.' She glances up at Will. 'You'll stay too?'

Will grabs her hand. 'I'm by your side now. For good or bad.'

20

CENTRE THINK

One week till Festival

CARYS

M Y LEGS FEEL it most. A kind of jitter, a sense of anguish spreading through my joints and keeping me locked in somewhere inside of myself. In the cell people are impatient and angry with one another, with me, with the group who plot and laugh in the corner. There's desperation in the air, and it pushes me down when I try to get up.

I keep thinking of Boy Farmer's words: *There's this action plan to get you out of here.* Can I take hold of those words? Can those words save me now, here in the worst of times while we wait with each day creeping by slowly and so quickly at the same time? I repeat them to myself when everyone is asleep, whisper them out loud. I hug my knees to me and feel the bones sticking out. I stretch out my legs, kick out against the jitters. I need to keep moving. We have exercise times here now, three times a day; Ava leads us all in aerobic activities and the guards guffaw from outside the doors. Boy Farmer and Raza report that their cells are doing the same. People are fitter, grimmer, more determined; they will break out. I am sure of it.

But by then I will be gone.

'What plan?' The words come suddenly, hissed through the grate in the corner. *Raza.* 'Heard you whispering at yourself about an action plan. You mean ours? I don't think there's much more to sort...'

I move closer to the grille. 'A kid in the other cell told me there's this forum and they are planning to break us... me... out.'

Raza goes quiet.

'It's just talk though,' I say quietly. 'He didn't know details. The plan you have will work.'

'I don't want to do this without you, you do know that, right?' she whispers in a tone so low I barely hear.

I don't know how to reply.

'I just can't find another way.'

'I know,' I say. Then, to stop the march of ants up and down my body, I ask her, 'What will you do once you break out?'

'Oh, you know, eat some food, kill some professors.'

I smile.

'I'll make sure to get Lois and Alwin reunited with Amy.'

I shake my head, even though she can't see me. 'That's dangerous. She'd shop them.'

Raza pauses. 'I don't think she would. I remember how much she wanted to find them. Was desperate to. Don't forget that, Carys.'

I blow out my cheeks. 'Mmm.'

She shifts closer so her voice is almost at my ear. 'You've got to let this go.'

I draw back, surprised. 'You hate them too.'

'Yeah, but it's not eating me up.'

I pick at my fingernails, feeling the dull ache behind my eyes.

'It's making you different.'

'What do you mean?' I ask.

She sighs. 'Remember how you were on *The S Word* that time? It was like your energy filled the room, set it on fire. You had this whole passion thing going on, like a railing at injustice thing. You were so alive. It was awesome.'

'And?'

'Your hate is quenching it,' she says softly.

I laugh, and even I hear the ugliness of it. 'Who are you to talk about hate? You hate everybody and everything.'

She goes quiet, and I feel the squirm of shame wriggling through my chest. 'I… look, Raza, I didn't mean that.'

Silence.

I huddle over, drawing my blanket tighter around me, and try to erase her words from my head. *Your hate is quenching it.* I don't want to think on these words, on Raza's tone, on the hurt I just kicked at her. I have to hate them because I need the strength of it to keep me going in here, I need the coldness it pours through my body and the jagged edge it digs into my soul, because without it I would be gone altogether.

'Raza?' I hiss, but she says nothing. She has gone, left me.

Everyone leaves me.

A presence at my elbow, a light touch on my arm. Faltered words. 'I think she's right.'

I whip round at Ava, frown at her. 'You don't know me.'

I see the hurt on her face and wonder how many more people I can hurt tonight. Lois? Harry?

She doesn't move her hand. 'You need strength for the journey ahead.'

I laugh. 'What, the journey to my execution?'

She shakes her head. 'I still have faith in my group, and maybe yours, from what that kid said.'

I look away from her, not admitting I'd been repeating Boy Farmer's words to myself. Feel the shame crawling through me at my barbed words. Why does my temper always get me like this, my wounds always wound others? 'I'm sorry. I didn't mean that. You've been a good friend to me. I'm sorry.'

She squeezes my arm. 'It's okay.'

Why does she have to be so nice? I don't deserve her to be so nice. I deserve Raza, stewing in her cell, or Amy and Jacob, binning me off. I deserve to die in the Commander Lucan Arena on the fifth of December.

'It's just…' She pauses, studies my face, her deep blue eyes radiating kindness. 'Just that I know it's not who you are.'

I bite my tongue, stifle my need to fight back. Maybe I don't need to fight any more.

'They are your friends, and they won't abandon you,' Ava says, so softly the words are nearly erased by her breath.

I sit silently.

'Perhaps if you stop holding this feeling so tight – hate, abandonment, whatever – perhaps then you'll find some peace.'

I look up. Peace? What is peace?

Peace was when I opened my name stone. Peace was when I walked through a silky velvet night full of stars with Jacob by my side. Peace was the lake on Remembrance Night.

There's an ache cutting me deep inside, growing, gnawing at me. It's a yearning, a great wide-open longing. I feel the sobs pushing at the core of me, a huge big mix of emotions and memories; my parents, Jacob, Amy, Ashton, Aiden, Sim, all swelling up in a tidal wave, but I cannot cry. My body convulses but I cannot let it out. I lean against Ava Coder and she is shushing me, soothing me, and then Harry is with us too, his arm stretched around my shoulder. 'It's okay. It's okay,' they both keep saying.

In my deepest heart I embrace the longing and, for the first time, let some of the hatred slip through my fingers and drain out through the grate below me. A lightness powers through me, a shaky relief. I keep some of my bitterness back, bottle it up and stow it deep inside, but I let enough go to grab hold of something that smells a little bit like freedom, in this dingy, damp corner of darkness I have sat in for too many weeks. Enough to hold out my hands and catch a tiny piece of that feeling from Harry's birthday, to welcome a rush of warmth that infuses me with more strength and courage in these few broken minutes than in the hours and days of cold hate I'd so surrounded myself with.

Enough to remember I am still here and I am, somehow, somewhere, still loved.

21

THE CENTRE

Four days till Festival

AMY

THE QUIET IS unsettling on this deserted, long-dead street, and Amy shivers as she gazes out over the jagged skyline, at the skeletal frames of a hundred buildings and the rubble that lies all around her. This is the old part of the Centre; the bit no one ever talks about, north of the river where nothing has been touched. How small the Centre really is now, she realises; how tiny compared to this great ghostly sprawl. The barrier stands tall and curving not far away, cutting off even more of the once-great city. This area was scheduled for rebuilding once upon a time, Ash told them; back in the beginning when the Party's plans were bigger than they would ever be able to fulfil. They never even managed to clear it, so it faded into this cratered, hollow, forgotten land, the ground thick with mud and broken bricks and pools of stagnant water. It is a known eyesore to those nearby, to those who work in the towering Centre Think building on the other side of the river, and the wooden boarding all along the riverside with coiled wire strung along the top doesn't block the haunting view. But no one is allowed to mention it, Ash says.

Getting into the Centre itself was easier than Amy had feared. Turned out there were a few Centre Productives there at the museum. Some of them were taken down, now abandoned in the bloodbath of the field of tents outside, with no time to honour them, but there were enough left to stow away a few others from the community in their trunks; they sped down here before the authorities could get their act together and send calls out for her and Jacob's arrests. Others from the camp moved on elsewhere with horses and supplies, leaving as quickly as possible before the NForce closed in on them again, promising to leave messages on the forum and to reunite with everyone else later. Matt and Stephen left with them, taking Shadow and the horses they'd brought down, embracing Will with such tenderness that Amy longed for her own family with a new intensity.

A group of around a dozen are here tonight: her, Jacob, Will, Coran, Ash, Reia, Abs and Tom from the camp, and four or five other Centre Productives who wanted to help, some of whom have friends in the Centre Think. They hid out for a couple of days, healing and waiting for Ash's go ahead; they could only go at a time he could get away safely. Amy hopes they are enough and wishes again that more could have got through the barriers with them. They have few weapons between them, mainly armed with tools for breaking down walls. No one had guns to spare; most had been taken or destroyed in the attack or fled with soon after. Will has a crossbow, at least; Amy knows he can use it.

The landscape reminds Amy of the Birmingham ruins with its dead silence, its houses and office blocks slammed to the ground, its shells of burnt out, rusted cars, some crushed under the weight of fallen masonry. She shivers. It's a maze of twisted streets, the remains of what once was. Thank goodness for Ash, who seems to know his way around like he was born here. He shows them a way through the boarding and across the river over a barely intact old bridge far west of where they need to be, and leads them on a long, silent walk through the ruins, their torches dancing through the gloom. He points out ancient landmarks: 'That was once a great cathedral,' he says, motioning to several great chunks of dark grey stone near a couple of empty arches still standing, their fractured frames intricate and spectral in the moonlight.

'What's a cathedral?' Reia says.

'An old holy space.'

'How d'you know all this?' Jacob says.

Ash flushes, wrings his hands together. 'My family passed on a lot. None of them believed in Newland.' He smiles over at Coran. 'We like the old ways.'

Jacob nods. 'Me too.'

Ash points back towards the river where, in the distance, beyond many mangled, collapsed buildings, part of a bridge still stands, sad against the winter sky, its great concrete and steel girders twisted and lop-sided, most of it lying in ruins or lost under the water. 'And that there was London Bridge,' he says sadly. 'Most other bridges are completely gone.'

'So where do we get in?' Jacob says, hurrying him on.

'It's just up that way.' Ash points ahead and leads them forward, his shuffling gait unbalanced yet graceful as he weaves round fallen rock and countless debris: bricks, shards of wood, broken glass, scorched remains of trees. How does he know how to find things in this hellscape? 'Used to be a great big bank there,' he says, pointing to more destruction ahead as they pick their way through. 'I guess that's why this was called Bank Station.'

Amy spots half a battered old road sign lying amongst the wreckage and squats to try and read it. 'Three... no, Thread...'

'Threadneedle Street,' Ash says. 'It's a bit further on, though, down here. We're not far.' He ducks underneath the remains of a stone column, squatting low. 'Watch your heads.' Amy crouches and follows him through a narrow corridor of compressed stone, feeling as if it is closing in on her, as if it will squeeze her tight and take her breath at any moment. She exhales as they emerge into a larger space with more column remnants scattered around, fragments of stone carvings poking out here and there, half-covered with dust and long dead vegetation. 'This is it.'

The entrance doesn't really look like much of an entrance. Just more stone, twisted railings lying on the ground near a stairway descending into the earth, parts of an arch above with some remains of a sign, the lettering too faded to make out. Amy gazes down; all she can see is unknown depths. She doesn't want to do this. Doesn't want to go down there, to this unknown underground under the city, with tonnes of rock and soil above her head. She's taken back to the well at Ashton for a second, the tunnel they found inside it, how it pressed on her head, the panic in her stomach. Jacob grabs her hand; it is trembling. 'It's okay. You're okay.'

The staircase is narrow and steep with worn treads, partially collapsed. Amy follows Ash and Will down, stepping tentatively, her torch lighting the way in its quivering gleam, trying not to think about what's below. Ash leads them through a curved corridor to a larger area. 'It was the ticket hall,' he says, shining his torch around the gloomy, silent space; Amy sees the wistful light in his eyes reflected in her own beam. The twisted shapes of a row of ticket barriers loom through the murk like a line of ghost soldiers. 'We have to climb over these.'

She shivers, pulling her scarf tighter around her and huddling into her coat. 'Down here,' Ash says, pointing to a set of rusted escalators, frozen and stilled forever. A sign still hangs above, with some lettering Amy can just make out: 'N..th..n L.ne.' She tests her foot on the top step, trying to focus. One step at a time. Don't look down. Don't think too much.

'This station once had the most escalators out of every tube station,' Ash says, a note of pride in his voice. 'And hundreds of thousands of people came through here every day.'

Amy can't imagine it. She stares at the walls as she steps down the escalator, at the faded adverts, some of them torn down, some still speaking of life in a different time: of theatres and musicals and books. She tries to imagine herself surrounded here by thousands of people, bustling to and fro, going to work and school and all the places people were once allowed to go. The noise of them in her head wrestles so hard with the deadened silence she wobbles, nearly falls the last few steps.

Ash leads them through a maze of narrow, curving hallways with arched, defunct strip-light-lined roofs and faded, dirty cream tiles coating the walls with more battered pictures of lives once lived, and Amy pulls her arms tight around her. It is confined in here; too dark, too musty, too long, too cold, too dead. Remains of signs emerge from the gloom in their torchlight, giving a confusion of directions to long-past people. Ash laughs softly. 'My grandfather always used to say that even in the Before times people got lost in this station. It was a maze. Sixteen entrances and exits, it had. Rumour had it, he said, that people wandered these tunnels for years. Maybe they're still here now.'

Amy shivers. 'Why'd you have to say that?'

Will takes her hand. 'You okay?'

'It's sad down here. That's all.' But she likes the feel of his hand in hers, the warm presence of him near her.

They come to another set of escalators, and these are longer, descending into the very bowels of the earth, bare wires hanging down from the sharply sloped ceiling. 'I didn't know it'd be so far down,' Amy says. The only sound is the clattering of their feet on the rusted steps, parts of them decayed and fallen into fractured ruin. Down and down and down. The air grows slightly warmer, even more hushed. Amy wonders if she'll ever see the sun again. The pictures lining the walls give more glimpses of life in another world. One of them jars her, like it shouldn't fit here: a grimy photo of Lucan, the first Commander; an advert for the New Day Party: "Vote for James Hamlin." And, in smaller blue type underneath, "The Party for the People. Fed up of uncontrolled immigration and benefit scroungers? Tired of high taxes and workshy neighbours?

Bored of climate change myths and poor universal healthcare? Vote for us, the New Day Party, and we pledge to address these areas immediately."

They certainly did that, Amy thinks.

Near the bottom are one or two headed "Public Service Announcement", warning people that those rioting will be imprisoned. Another gives a warning about the Scourge, the cracked paper plain with faded black block capitals: "Masks are to be worn at all times. Keep apart by six feet. Stay home." Amy thinks about the book she read back in the bunker, how it described the Scourge sweeping through the population, most dead within a week, already weakened and depleted by the riots and the Party's campaign of destruction on the nation. This sign must have been a rush job; the very last one a surviving worker slotted into its place.

At the bottom Ash leads them through another narrow passageway. 'There's the northbound platform,' he says, pointing his torch, and Amy spots the hulk of an ancient train, a shell of it, burned out and forlorn in the darkness, windows blown out and doors gaping wide to reveal its charred innards. She shivers again. 'But it's blocked. We need the southbound,' Ash continues, leading them on.

On the platform they stand silently, shining torches around, at the huge, faded advertisements on the curved tunnel walls, at the metal seats that still, somehow, remain intact, at the remains of signs on the wall; a flaked red circle with a once-blue strip through the centre and white faded lettering: BANK. Amy gazes down into the tunnel, along the ruptured tracks, and, just for a second, a rush of warm air strokes her face. She blinks it away and shakes her head. She's making things up now.

'Let's go,' Ash says, jumping down onto the tracks and heading towards the southbound tunnel. The others follow slowly, carefully, picking over debris on the track, flashing their torches ahead. The walls are blackened, multiple rusted pipes running along the tunnel on both sides.

'I see why it was called the tube,' Abs says. 'Feels like we're in one.'

'There's a partial collapse up ahead,' Ash says. 'We'll need to squeeze through. Try not to worry, I've done it many times.'

Try not to worry? Amy will have nightmares about this for years. The space is barely enough to fit through sideways, and she scrabbles through, panic building, her heart fluttering, the darkness pressing in as much as the rubble. She breathes a sigh of relief on the other side and trudges on.

'We're under Monument now,' Ash says a few minutes on. Amy is thankful for his running commentary, for this strange knowledge that breaks the silent tension. 'We'll be under the river soon.'

She doesn't want to think about that.

'Is it far?' she says, as they make their way on. Damp seeps through the walls, green lines of mildew gleaming in the torch beams, the dank stench of it hanging fetid in the air. She pulls her coat tighter.

'Nearly there. We don't have to go back up at the other end,' Ash says. 'The tunnel's bricked up near the platform; the Think building's basements and foundations were filled deep into the earth, where the old escalators went up to the London Bridge concourse.' He grips his sledgehammer. 'We'll have some work to do… and, just to be clear, we don't know for certain the bricked-up wall will lead directly into the Think basement. It should do, near enough; my grandfather was involved in building it and had the original schematics. Always said one day he'd love to break through there… always loved his trains so much. I don't have those plans any more, sadly; they were lost when my father was a child.'

'What was up there before?' Jacob says, looking up, as if he can see through the immense mass of heavy, compressing earth.

'Some kind of news building, I believe, and other notable buildings nearby. All gone now, of course; that bit was fully cleared for the Centre Think and Party HQ further on.'

The narrow tunnel opens out to another silent platform area with more peeling adverts curving with the walls and a sign that says

'Way Out' hanging loosely from the ceiling along with several wires and broken pipes. Amy follows Ash as he clambers up to the platform, and her torch slips from her clammy fingers, skimming across the rails into a pool of darkness. She bends down to retrieve it and spots the edge of something soft, covered in filth and dust. She brushes some of the dirt away and stares at the item, abandoned there on the rails: a shabby teddy bear, one eye missing, a faded red bow tied around its neck and an old Union Flag motif stitched into its belly, blackened by muck now. She remembers seeing that flag on the videos of the riots they were force fed in Assembly every day. She picks it up, brushes it off some more. Thinks about the child who held this, perhaps who dropped it down the gap as she got off the train one day, a child who was murdered by the New Day Party. She tugs her backpack open and drops the toy in, moved so much her throat is one great lump.

She takes Will's hand and scrambles up to the platform then follows Ash and the others through to another passageway. The bricked-up wall looms ahead, bringing the tunnel to an abrupt end. They stand and gaze at the wall, coated with years of grunge and damp. 'That's really the Think, the other side of this?' Jacob says, eyes wide.

Ash nods. 'I'd swear on it. Pretty much.'

'Carys is so near,' Jacob says softly. He hands his torch to Coran and plucks a sledgehammer from the large tool bag slung over his shoulder.

Amy grabs the chisel and hammer from her own backpack and starts to chip at the mortar, already flaking and weakened in places. Will steps forward, motions to Ash to pass him his sledgehammer. 'I'm an old hand at this kind of stuff. Let me at it.' Coran stands behind Ash, his face white in the torchlight, looking about as terrified as Amy feels, and she goes to him, links arms, wraps herself up in the comfort of his presence.

Reia gets another sledgehammer, peels off her jacket and jumper, and powers in next to them. 'You boys could use some proper help, right?'

The three of them make light work of it, swinging their bodies as they grip the hammers with both hands, slamming them into the layers of brick over and over, until part of the wall crumbles into pieces at their feet. Dust chokes the air in great clouds and shards of brick fly at Amy's skin, clipping her cheek. Reia's muscular arms glisten with sweat as she crashes the hammer against the brick; she is stronger than Amy could ever have guessed. Before long a hole gapes at them, pitch darkness inside. Reia drops the hammer, brushes off her hands, peers through. Amy shines her torch over Reia's shoulder.

'Can't see much,' Reia says. 'Looks like another wall.'

She pokes her head through then climbs into the space. 'It's just plywood. This'll be easy.' Will clambers through with her, readies the sledgehammer. 'Wait. Let's see if we can pry this one apart. Keep it intact as we can, keep it quieter now too.'

Jacob digs into his bag and grabs a crowbar. 'Here.'

'Give it to me,' Reia says, and shoves the guys out of the way as she finds a gap in the plywood and drives in the crowbar, the veins in her temples standing proud as she grits her teeth, trying to get purchase and tugging at the wood. It comes reluctantly, screeching, but soon enough it peels away, leaving a small gap they can fit through. Reia peeps through. 'Well, it's definitely a building. A whole huge mess of pipework down here.'

'The Centre Think,' Ash says, his shoulders slumping as if he'd never really believed this was true, or possible. 'We made it.'

22

CENTRE THINK

Four days till Festival

CARYS

KNEW I couldn't trust the latest resident in my cell.

He got in last night, shoved in with some others, a strange grin on his face like he couldn't care less. He soon connected with the surly group in the corner and started whispering with them, flinging the occasional loaded glance over at me. Now, in the early hours, the group are still awake, talking in hushed voices like they're plotting.

I am not happy about these loose ends when we have just four days to go. Everything has to be right for the escape on Festival Day; everyone here must be on board. But how do I convince them? Nothing I say works. They sneer at me, telling me I'm a loon, that I should drown in all my conspiracies.

But still they don't tell the guards about the plan.

I weave my way over to them, plaster a friendly smile on my face as I extend my hand to the new guy. 'Hi. I'm Carys, um, Girl Clerk.'

He stares me down. 'I know.'

'And you are?'

He twists his lips. 'Never mind. I won't be here long, anyway.' He smiles at me then, a grin full of jagged yellow teeth. 'I know what they're doing.'

I stare at him. 'They?'

He folds his arms, beams round at the others, who seem a little anxious about his openness. 'I heard them planning.'

I feel a kick of frustration. 'Who? What plans?'

He laughs. 'They're trying to break us all out of here. Tonight.'

My heart skips a beat.

'I was in their camp, but I was fed up of it all. I'd been thinking of leaving for a while. The leadership's weak.' He sticks his chest out. 'I told the NForce about them.' Then he seems to deflate as he sighs. 'Still went and bloody got caught. They didn't listen. Will now, though, with what I know.'

'Who? What camp?' My palms are damp with sweat.

He shakes his head. 'Never mind.' He turns back to the others. 'Let's get out of here, then.'

I stumble back as he pushes past me, the small group following him as he goes to the door and pounds on it three times. 'Guards!' He looks back at me, a big smirk on his face. 'They won't have a chance anyway. Their plans were pathetic.'

I swallow, trying to get a grip on my thoughts. He is maddening; open and closed all at the same time. The others crowd round him, their brows creased in confusion.

The door slams open. 'What's this?' A tall, lanky guard stands there, hand on his gun at his belt, face dark with anger. The guard who gave Ava the old phone for Harry. 'You don't go banging like that in the middle of the night. Or ever.'

This new bloke squares up to him, though stands a foot shorter. 'I have a bargain to offer you.'

The guard scoffs. 'I don't take bargains. Get back in and shut the hell up.'

The man steps closer, so he's almost on the guard's foot. 'You'll want to hear this.'

'I doubt it.'

The man glances round at the others, who give tentative nods. 'If I tell you details about a break in attempt, will you set me and these good people free?'

The guard laughs out loud, then steps back, then looks harder at the man, scrutinising him. 'A break in attempt?'

'Here. Tonight. Now.'

The guard's face creases with uncertainty. 'Now?'

The man puffs his cheeks out. 'Yes. Now. I will tell you the details I know if you promise to set me and my friends here free.'

The guard scratches his cheek, pockmarked with acne. 'Let me talk to my superior.'

In minutes he is back, this time beckoning the guy out and slamming the cell door shut on everyone else, including the disgruntled group. The cell falls into uneasy silence as we wait.

And wait.

The man does not come back.

The group are twitchy, throwing glances at the door and at me, hissing in loud whispers at each other, shifting from one foot to another. 'He promised,' I hear one of them say. 'He's getting us out.'

'Doesn't look like it,' another says glumly.

I hear activity outside the cell and listen at the grille. Raised voices somewhere nearby, the clumping of loud footsteps in hobnailed boots, shouts from the stairwell.

And still nothing inside the cell.

The group grow more restless, more aggressive with one another, then, one by one, sink to the ground, resigned, splitting apart from one another, their faces heavy with gloom. I crouch next to one of the women. 'What was all that about?'

She scrapes her knuckles against the wall. 'I never thought he'd really come through. That was the others.' She stares pointedly round the room at one or two men from the group.

'Did he tell you anything about this… plan?'

She shakes her head. 'Not a lot. Said he'd get us out, said he saw we didn't deserve to be here, just like him. Huh.'

'Who is supposed to be breaking in here? And how?'

She shrugs. 'Some randoms from a camp somewhere, I think he said. Didn't say more about who. He was just boasting, the whole time, that he was clever and all that, listening in. Just a load of bluster if you ask me. Said they were tunnelling.'

'*Tunnelling?*'

'Yup. It's all too late now, though. He'll have told 'em what he knows, got his own pardon, forgotten about us.'

'He's a slime,' I say.

She stares at me then, right into my eyes, and I see the weariness around hers. 'Not sure if I believe 'em anymore.'

'You know the truth at heart,' I say gently.

'Hmm.'

I lean back against the wall, my body tight with tension, the mix of hope and fear at this news crashing into me and laying me flat out. Someone was coming. Is coming, maybe. Someone is coming, and the guards know.

Oh, God, I think. *Do something. Help.*

23

CENTRE THINK

Four days till Festival

JACOB

THE PATCHY CONCRETE hallway stretches ahead into gloom, the few working LED bulbs in bulkhead cage fittings casting strange shadows. The insulation on the pipes is peeling away, revealing tarnished copper with valves encrusted in layers of grime. A sharp hissing slices through the air, the heated steam curling in wisps as it climbs upwards. Jacob wonders how well-maintained this building really is, about the materials used to construct it in the first place.

They creep through the hallway, alert for any other movement, but no one's around. Jacob breathes in deeply, coughing at the musty warm damp in the air, relieved to leave behind the deathly quiet of the hushed, chilled tube tunnels. He shudders as he thinks of where they have been and where they now must go.

'What now?' he says to Ash, wishing they'd got further in their planning. But the days since the escape from the camp into the Centre have been spent on survival, with wanted posters and NCasts everywhere featuring him and Amy – "Newland's Traitors: Oswall and Esla, enemies of the state".

Ash points up a set of metal stairs, his finger trembling. 'So… the Think is the next floor up, but it'll be heavily guarded. I suggest we sneak past there and up to one of the office floors first, get our bearings, see if we can find a way of calling away the guards from there.'

Jacob shakes his head. 'We should take our chance right now and storm the guards in the Think. Element of surprise.'

'I don't think so,' Reia says. 'I don't want any of you shot. Ash's idea is best: we lure them away, maybe one at a time, grab their keys and go slowly.'

Jacob thinks. 'But there'll be cameras in the stairwells and in the offices, right?'

Ash purses his lips. 'They're all over the foyer, but I don't think they're in the offices; at least, when it was built, they didn't put them in then. I don't know about the stairwells. I doubt it. Why would they need them? They have the guards.'

Amy pulls a grim half-smile. 'If it's anything like the Midlands Think, there'll only be about two.'

'Sorry, it's not the same at all,' Ash says. 'It's running with guards here. I know this because I had a friend who worked here a while back. Sorry.' He looks beaten all of a sudden, his body all stooped, like he's got us here but now doesn't have a clue what to do.

Coran pats his arm. 'No need to be sorry. You're doing great.'

'Yeah,' Jacob says, 'you've been amazing. We'll find a way.'

They climb the stairs, keeping as quiet as they can. The doors at the top open into a narrow, dingy corridor, with doors at each end. 'Which way?' someone says.

Ash turns to the left. 'These back stairs should take us to the main stairwell. The other to the Think stairs, I believe, if nothing's been changed since the original layout.' He heaves in a breath. 'Come on.'

The narrow stairs are dimly lit, and Jacob tiptoes up, his hand damp with sweat on the chipped wooden railing. Ash pushes tentatively through a door at the top into a dim, red-bricked corridor with more doors leading off. He points back at a double door. 'That's the lobby. We don't want to go out there. And that's the main stairs down to the Think, that end—' he points to the other end of the corridor, '—but let's try one of these rooms. Quiet.'

They creep after him, Jacob's heart speeding: there are too many of them. They must be making some noise. He scans the ceiling for cameras but sees none. Were there any in the stairwell? Have they already been clocked? He thinks of Carys, so near now, and in his head he reaches for her, tells her everything is going to be okay, to hang on just a little while longer. He wants to break away and sprint down to the Think, to take on the guards himself, knock them all out and walk in to get her. He fights with himself, keeping his hands clasped tight around the handle of his bag. He will use these tools on those guards if he needs to...

'This one,' Ash whispers, finding an unlocked door and ducking in. Inside is a mess of workstations; a room that reminds Jacob of the Midlands Think offices where this all started. The group sneak in and Reia closes the door behind them.

Everyone's looking at Jacob. Why are they looking at him? Why do they think he has all the answers? He rubs the back of his neck, glancing around wildly at the NComs and other equipment in the room, most of them on standby with a Centre screensaver bouncing back and forth. Is he supposed to do something with these?

Amy's by his side. 'Can we find a way to call one of the guards up?'

'How do I know?'

Amy draws back, looks stung.

'Sorry. I just don't know what to do.'

It's Abs who gathers them together, sits them down at the stations, outlines a plan of sorts. Everyone is to see if they can get into one of these computers, and then they can see if they can find the details of the guards.

He wishes they had phones on them now. Ash and Coran insisted the fugitives all leave them behind at the camp; they might be tracked. They can't leave any trace of where they are. But if he had a phone, he could do this so much more quickly…

'I'm in,' Abs says, and he whirls round, staring at her screen. It's open, full of icons of different sorts: an admin screen.

'How on earth?' Jacob says, bending over her and beginning to scroll through some folders. 'Do you know the password or something?'

She gives him a half-smile. 'It's "centre-underscore-admin". I know how they work, sadly. Hit lucky on my fifth attempt.'

'Blimey, you're quick.'

'More like they're thick. I'll start on this one, you go there.' Abs waves at the next door station and takes over, tapping the keys quickly. He knows her camp had good communications and realises she is one of the reasons. He keys in the password to the machine at his station and digs in.

A clanking sound below: the metal stairs down in the basement?

Jacob ignores it and carries on. This stuff is tedious; it's low level administration, all bills and stationery orders and emails back and forth to each other about nothings. No secrets here, no clearance needed for higher levels. That kind of stuff must be elsewhere. This building is huge; he'd never find it. But that's not what they're here for anyway.

He slams his hands on the station. *Come on.*

'Look in that green icon there,' Abs says after a few minutes. 'It's a messaging app. There are guard's names here: Alfred Guard, Edwin Guard, a few more. Look. We can message one of them and keep trying until one answers. Right?'

Jacob nods, feeling a strange rise in his chest, a hot wave of jealousy, and then gets mad at himself. *Just because someone else can do this stuff and you're not the IT hero of all time.* He rolls his eyes at his own stupid self. 'Yep. Try that.'

Abs pauses, her hands on the keys. 'Wait.'

Jacob scoots nearer on his wheeled chair. 'What is it?'

The others come closer, abandoning their stations. She points to a string of messages on the app between Ida Admin and Edwin Guard. 'Read that.'

Jacob reads it out loud from the top of the page.

> EG: yeah it is too much down here.
>
> IA: Ill give u a back rub at home. Make u feel better
>
> EG: ooh, promises
>
> IA: now now. What u gonna do with them all anyway? Cant go on like this forever
>
> EG: hah. CA's sent us a plan. Day after festival they get done at the range, all of them at once. Live on NBC too.
>
> IA: no way
>
> EG: yeah. But don't tell anyone I said that lol.
>
> IA: haha as if

The string ends there. 'Someone's not been very discreet,' Reia says.

Amy cocks her head on one side. Her thinking face. 'But what does it mean? This is obviously about all the people in the Think.'

Coran leans his hands on the station, his face pale. 'The range is the place they shoot NForce deserters.'

'CA must be Commander Anson,' Amy says.

'They're going to shoot everyone from those cells on live TV?' Jacob says, incredulous for a moment then shaking his head. Of course they are. This is the Party. This is Anson.

'Then we must get them out now,' Abs says, her face hard with determination. 'I'm just trying this guard—'

A bang. Closer, this time, a clatter from the end of this corridor. From the lobby.

Damn.

'Stay quiet,' Ash hisses.

Voices now. Echoing through corridors, underneath them, above them. Feet stomping towards them—

'We have to go.' Amy grabs Jacob's arm, her face draining of colour. 'Now.'

He shakes her off. 'No. No. We must get Carys.' The others are on their feet, making for the door. 'No,' he says, desperately, whipping his head around to the screen as if that might have the answers. 'How about I see if I can get a fire alarm going—'

A soft touch on his hand, stilling his fingers. Reia. 'No time. We will be dead if we don't go now, and then we'll be no use to her at all. Get up, Jacob, and then we run.'

'We fight them. That's why we're here,' he says, grabbing the sledgehammer from his backpack.

The shouts are nearer. In their corridor now, outside their door. It's over.

Coran slams the door open and makes a run for it, tugging a shaking Ash along, the others crowding behind them, slamming into a guard just outside the room. The guard reacts quickly, pulling his gun, aiming it haphazardly. The bullet hits the wall behind Jacob's head. Will aims the crossbow quickly, fires, takes the guard down. Three more guards run towards them. 'Rush them,' Jacob yells, pelting headlong into one of them; the guy doubles over, winded. Abs and Tom start wielding sledgehammers around, but more guards dash into the hallway; more guards with weapons. Too many of them, too many guns. *How did they know?*

Reia pulls Jacob's arm. 'We have to run.'

'No. No.' He shrugs her off, slings his hammer, hits flesh, misses another bullet. Amy has his arm now, dragging him, screaming in his ear, but he can't leave. He can't.

Another guard shoots, catches Tom. He crashes to the ground, blood blooming too quickly from a wound in his head. Abs screams, tries to go to him, but Reia yanks her back and through the door to the basement stairs after the others. Abs fights, wrestles herself from Reia's grip and back through the doorway, flings herself down on the ground next to Tom, sobbing. Jacob reels back, another guard in his face, Amy catching his hand as she dives through the door; he shakes her off. Reia shoves the guard and pulls Abs up. 'Come on, sweetheart. Come on.' She drags her through and Jacob follows, hesitating in the doorway, turning to fight but faced with a large group advancing on them now from down the hall, their teeth bared, grim faces menacing.

'It's the Newland Traitors,' one of them says, his face darkly smug.

'Ha. Well, we'll be well rewarded then,' says another. 'Seen the price tag on their heads?'

Jacob despairs. No choice. He slams the door behind him and hurtles down the stairs, nearly tumbling headlong. Abs is in front of him, straining back, Reia hurrying her along. They're into the narrow corridor, through the doors to the basement stairs. More guards after them now. A crowd of them, through the door at the top, on the stairs, urgent shouts echoing down towards him; more shots.

'Back to the tunnel,' Ash shouts, his voice high with desperation. He shoves Coran on ahead of him and waits for the others. 'Hurry.'

Jacob throws a wild glance back and knows he is beaten. They can't get to Carys now. They needed more people, more weapons, more of a plan. The ache in his chest steals his breath as he tears along the basement hallway and squeezes through the plywood gap after Amy and the others.

All they can do now is run.

He pushes the wood back into place as best he can, but it won't be long until they find the gap and follow them through. At least they have Ash leading them so they won't get lost in the maze down here. They run together as a pack, through the narrow corridor, leaping down onto the track and taking off back up the tunnel, their torches dancing crazily through the darkness. 'Torches off,' Reia shouts from up ahead. 'Just keep running ahead; Ash knows where to go. Keep together, everyone.'

Running in the dark isn't ideal when the track beneath their feet is fractured in parts. Jacob feels the stab of jagged metal through his jeans and winces. He grabs hold of Amy's hand and sprints on, his breath coming in puffs of cold air.

They're in the tunnel. He can hear them, shouting at one another, can see faint lights way behind. Then the shots. One of them has an automatic weapon and fires ahead at them, a continuous burst of deafening cracks in quick succession exploding the heavy silence, spraying bullets into pipework, brickwork and tracks, disturbing dust and debris that have lain so still for more than a century. They skid around a curve in the tunnel, out of sight for just seconds.

This is it. They can't survive this. They made it all the way here and then—

'In here,' Ash hisses back at them and they clatter to a stop, the sound of screeching metal just about audible through the crack of gunfire behind. 'In quickly.' Jacob can't see what's happening but hands are on his arm, pulling him to the left, all of them moving as a mass and crowding through some kind of opening. Someone groans. Reia pulls a heavy door shut behind them; outside Jacob hears the guards slow as they take the curve in the tunnel.

'Did they see us?' Amy whispers into the darkness.

Where are they? He can't see a thing. The place is stuffy, the air musty and rank. The gunfire continues outside, muted now behind the solid door. They breathe fast, the sound of it too loud in this tiny space. Something tickles his neck. A cobweb? He shudders. What is this place?

'Shh,' someone whispers. 'Wait.'

Somebody groans again. Who is that?

They wait.

The guards have rushed past their hiding place, on into the tunnel, their voices fading out, in hot pursuit of nothing but ghosts. Jacob doesn't dare to breathe relief yet. 'Everyone okay?' Reia says softly.

A few mumbles of 'yeah', and still the groaning from the corner. Ash switches his torch on, and Jacob blinks then takes in the place, the room cast in great shadows, a hulk of some kind of ancient electrical equipment covered in dust and cobwebs taking up most of the space.

'These rooms are all over the place down here,' Ash says, and Jacob notices how he curls his hand by his side, how his voice is too high. 'Ventilation systems, signal control equipment, electrical stuff. The doors are pretty well hidden in the walls as it's so dark.'

'But you knew,' Coran says quietly.

Ash twists his mouth in a tiny smile. 'I know most of the ones in this stretch.'

'So now we wait,' Reia says.

Jacob slouches against a wall, closing his eyes, trying to get his pulse to slow down. What if they come back? They'll find them, surely?

'Let's hope that lot get lost down here,' Ash says, a note of mischief in his voice. 'Those tunnels back at Bank could send them haywire.'

'Help me.' It's the person who was groaning. Ash shines the torch around and it alights on her: Abs, on her knees on the dirt-packed floor, gasping, her face sickly white in the beam.

Reia is down with her quickly. 'Are you okay? Where is it?'

Abs points to her side and Ash concentrates the light there, showing the bullet wound, the blood flowing freely. 'I… I…' Abs stutters, a gurgling in her throat.

Reia takes her hand. 'I'm so sorry. Jacob, can you see anything in this room? Old first aid supplies? Anything in those cabinets?'

But there is nothing. A bundle of old cables, some rusted pliers and screwdrivers.

'P… put me out there,' Abs gasps.

'What?'

'I can… still help.'

Reia presses her hand into Abs's side, trying to stem the tide. 'We'll take you back. Get you better.'

'No. Tom's gone.' Jacob sees the tears on her cheeks, the grim determination in the set of her jaw. 'I can help... have to.'

Jacob feels a rush of pain and anger, wishing he'd taken time to know them more, to hear their story, that he hadn't had that stupid flash of jealousy at this remarkable woman's expertise. He crouches down next to her. 'You'll be okay.'

'Put me out there. I... I'll tell them you got away. Thought I was dead and left me.'

'But they'll take you to the Think.'

She pants, sweat pouring down her brow. 'So I'll tell them in there about this tunnel. Our friend is there. Mason. I want to see him, one last time. It gives them... a chance.'

Reia shakes her head. There is blood all over her hands.

'Please,' Abs whispers. 'It's too late for me anyway. Let me... let me do this one last thing. I've done so much evil... when I was Party... I need to do this.'

Reia looks at Jacob, at Amy, at the others. Nods her head slowly. 'Help me,' she says to Jacob, starting to lift Abs, so tenderly. Ash holds the door open; the dead silence is heavy out there. Jacob and Reia carry Abs a little way down the tunnel, back towards the Think, and lay her there on the tracks, lowering her petite frame carefully, gently. 'I'm so sorry,' Reia whispers, pushing damp strings of blonde hair from Abs's brow.

'Thank you,' Jacob says to her. 'And if you see Carys, please tell her I love her. Tell her I was coming for her.'

Reia says, 'And please, if you can, tell them about the plot to murder them all the day after Festival. Give them a reason to fight.'

Abs answers with her eyes, her voice swallowed in exhaustion.

As Jacob and Reia close themselves back into the service room, Jacob feels like the worst person in the world. He leans into Amy, feeling tears prick at his eyes. She pulls him closer and kisses his head. 'It's okay. It's okay.'

24

THE RESISTANCE

Three days till Festival

THE MAN PACES the room, raking his fingers through his hair. 'They were stupid. Stupid.'

The others look on, glancing at Number Two, waiting for her to speak. The room is chilled tonight, the winter air whistling through its cracked basement windows, and they huddle in hats and gloves, a new tension rumbling in the air.

It's nearly time.

'But they escaped,' Number Two says in a soothing voice most unlike her.

'Did they? No one's seen them since. Could've died down there.' The man scuffs a foot on the floor, back and forth, back and forth. 'Now all they'll have done is get the Party more riled up. There'll be more NForce at the stadium.'

Number Two breathes out slowly, closing her eyes. 'But we have a plan.'

He stops. Pins her with a glare. 'Do we? Do we really? We don't even have the helicopter yet.'

A small man with a wiry moustache pipes up from the shadows. 'We do, actually. The Glasgow camp have come through at last.

They've found an old helicopter in some deserted museum up there. Said it was in some basement and somehow left unscathed in the riots.'

Number One looks at him with suspicion lining his face. 'How old?'

The guy clears his throat. 'From the Before. It was old even then, they said, called a Sea King; was once in use by their military.'

Number One starts pacing again. 'And that's going to work? Have they got it in the air?'

The man hesitates. 'Not yet. But they will. We have someone getting a tanker of aviation fuel up there.'

'Sounds risky.'

'It is. But the driver is insider NForce. Knows what he's doing, can blag it well enough.'

'Good. And then they're sure they can get it going?'

The man nods. 'Luckily this model wasn't new enough in terms of Before tech to run fully on computer systems, so they can get it done manually. Chap from their camp is a pilot, ex NForce, and a bit uncertain as he's only flown brand new NForce stuff, of course, but reckons he'll work it out. One of the other guys up there is a bit of a geek about ancient aviation technology, so they should be fine. Said something about checking the oils in the gearboxes and the movement between engines and rotors.'

'Hmm. And what did they want for that? It's never for free with that lot, is it?'

The guy picks at the fingers of his gloves. 'We gave them the Northwestern stash.'

Number One frowns. 'That's a lot of weapons that we needed.'

'They said it was that or no Copter.'

He puffs out his cheeks, looks at Number Two. 'So we have it, but someone has to get it down here and then up there on the day. That pilot's happy with that?'

'Yup. He's a young chap, from what they said, but he's willing.'

'Hmm. And the bomb?'

She shivers, pulls her scarf tighter. 'The team at the Southeastern Compound are working on it.'

'It'll be ready?'

'I believe so.'

'Where'd they get all the parts?'

'From what we've heard someone on the inside managed to steal the explosive right out from one of the NForce bombs. Said they're just working out the signal and how to arm the thing, and they have the casing and other bits ready. Our contact down there said they were planning to fit a pressure switch so it'll explode on impact, and that way it gives our pilot just enough time to get the hell out of there.'

He sinks into a chair. 'This *is* going to work, isn't it?'

A low hum of agreement buzzes through the room. *Too non-committal.*

'We know all the Party staff will be there, and most Compound staff too,' Number Two says.

'How many altogether?'

'Got to be around thirty thousand in all in that place when it's full.'

'And the damage? How will it work?'

The guy with the moustache speaks up. 'The Southeastern contact says we can shove it right out of the helicopter. That Sea King has a side door that can be left open. Means we'll need a second body in the Copter, of course. If we navigate it properly, it'll wipe out the stand where the Commander's box is. And much more besides, but you can be sure it'll take them out.'

'How many besides?' he says, his face creased up in too many lines. 'How many will it take out?'

The woman shifts her eyes to the side. 'Thousands.'

He gets up again, strides to the back of the room, pushes his head against the coolness of the wall. Number Two watches, spotting the wetness at the corners of his eyes.

He turns around, goes back to the front, his tall frame slumped over. 'There will be so many trainees in there.'

'More now that they've got this whole *S Word* thing going on,' Number Two says glumly. 'It's a huge deal. They'll have the winners, of course, on the stage with the judges, performing for the Commander. But now they've said everyone in the winner's training house can attend.'

Number One kicks his foot at a chair. 'And all the trainees from the Centre Compound, as is usual at Festival.'

'Yup.'

'And the other rebels? Do we have intelligence of where they're at? Any of them be there?'

Number Two sighs. 'No doubt. We know the camp near the Centre was scattered the other day when the elites attacked; we think Trader and Plumber were there with them and somehow got themselves into the Centre shortly after. We don't know how organised they are down there, but we are hearing there are more and more of them; the forum is growing like wildfire.'

'We're back in?'

The tech man, Arthur, says, 'Only just yesterday. Took a while to find an admin who'd admit me. We missed all the stuff about the camp and the Think plan. All came to nothing anyway.'

Number One scratches his head. 'Mmm. Any more to share about that side of things, anyone?'

No one says anything.

'Okay. So we can probably expect quite a few rebels, if not more. Perhaps they're planning something, perhaps not. But we should be aware,' Number Two says.

Number One tugs a box from his pocket, lights up a cigarette, inhales slowly and puffs a trail of smoke out, closing his eyes and turning his face upwards. 'So they'll be caught in it all too.'

She shrugs. 'Collateral damage.'

'And the trainees – hundreds, no, thousands of them – they're collateral damage too?'

She presses her lips together. 'We always knew this, Ed. It's the way it is.'

He takes a few more drags of his cigarette, gazing at the cracked window high in the wall, the broken street just visible outside. 'Can we warn them on the forum?'

She shakes her head. 'Not a good idea. We don't know who's monitoring that. Someone let the cat out of the bag about everyone meeting at that camp, and look how that ended. A bloodbath, I heard.'

'But there must be a way.'

She gazes at him. 'Look. I feel as bad as you—'

'I doubt that.' He sniffs, looks away.

She looks down at her hands. 'I don't want innocent people to die. Especially trainees.'

'They're just kids,' he says. 'Why do we put this extra layer on? "Trainees", making out they're something more than children? We will be killing children. That's what it comes down to.'

She rubs her eye. 'Yes.'

'And you're okay with that.' He sweeps his hands round the room, taking everyone in. 'You're all okay with that?'

A mumbling ripples through the air. 'No one is okay with that,' Number Two says. 'You signed up for this too. You know we need to look at the big picture here. Think of the future. We're thinking of all the trainees... kids, if you like... in the rest of the nation; we're thinking of their future, of ours, of our future generations. We cannot allow our emotions to get in the way.'

'Ha.' He glares at her. 'Since when did you have emotions?'

She stares, stung, and he looks away.

'Think about our beginnings,' she says quietly. 'About Benedict and Sarah Clerk. How they risked everything for those files and got murdered for it. Now it's our turn to risk everything, and I'm afraid that means risking more lives for the greater good.'

He stubs out his cigarette violently on a plate nearby. 'So the greater good is to murder children.'

'Look, Ed. If you can't do this anymore, we'll understand. You've been a great leader, but we get it, okay? Go back home and back to your nice Productive life.'

His eyes are dark with hurt and rage. 'You think I want that?'

'No. I think you want what we all want. And I think you know this is the only way.'

He sits down then, sinks his head into his hands, allows the tense silence in the room to fold him up inside it.

'I know,' he says finally, raising his head and taking all the faces in; faces taut with worry and fear and sadness. 'I know.'

25

CENTRE THINK

Three days till Festival

CARYS

THE WOMAN IS so badly injured she can barely speak.

They shove her into the cell, taking no care with her, maybe even less than usual, pushing her so hard she collapses on the floor in front of me, a brittle heap in ancient blue dungarees. Ava crouches next to her, picking up her hand. 'Her pulse is weak. Hello? Are you okay?'

I kneel down next to them. The woman's face is ruined, her mouth and cheek yellow and purple with fresh bruises, and she holds her side, groaning. 'They hit you?' I say.

She gasps, sucking the air in. I wish it was fresher for her in here, not so loaded with the dank stench of captivity and despair. 'I... I... yes, a bit. Shot me.'

'Oh.' I check the wound in her side, difficult to make out in the low lighting. 'She's lost a lot of blood,' I murmur to Ava.

'You... you...' she pants, trailing off, her mouth twisting with pain.

'It's okay,' Ava says. 'Don't try to speak. Shh. Just rest now.'

She moves her head from side to side, great tears leaking from her eyes. 'Tom died.'

'I'm sorry,' Ava says. 'Was he your husband?'

'Partner.'

'They shot him too?'

She nods. 'Where is… where is… Mason? Mason?' She tries to sit herself up, to look round the cell. 'Mason!' she says louder, trying to push out the sound, but it is strangled, half-formed.

Ava gets up, shouts through the low hubbub, 'Is there a Mason in here?'

Nothing.

'I need him. Need Mason. Friend…'

'He's in the Think?' I say stupidly.

She nods. 'Captured. Must be… here.'

I have an idea. I go to the grate on Boy Farmer's side. No point whispering through, everyone is awake now. 'Hey! Anyone called Mason in there? Hey! Hey!'

A scuffling sound. 'No Mason in here.' It's Boy Farmer's voice. 'You okay in there?'

I dash to the other side and shout through, louder this time. 'Mason! Mason!'

This time it's Raza who replies. 'Carys? What are you saying? Stop shouting and tell me again.'

'Can you find out if there's someone called Mason in there?'

No reply. I wait, listening to the hum of rushed conversation, then, 'I'm Mason.' A low voice, but young.

'Good.' I turn to Ava. 'Can we move her closer?' Then, to the woman, 'Can you tell me your name?'

'Abs,' she gasps, holding her side, her eyes hollow with pain. 'Is he there?'

We move her gently to the corner, others helping, concerned for this stranger. 'She's here,' I say into the grate. 'Mason? You there? Your friend Abs is here.'

A short silence. 'Abs?'

Abs croaks, 'Oh, Mason…'

His voice is low, crumbling. 'Are you okay?'

'Tom is dead.'

A hush.

'Mason?' Abs says.

'I'm so sorry,' he says. 'What happened?'

'N… no time. Mason—'

'What's wrong?'

'She's hurt,' I say to him.

A shuffling, as if he's trying to get even closer to the grate. 'Abs, lovely, I'm so sorry. I wish I was there with you. I'm holding my hand out to you here, okay? I'm right here with you.'

'Mason.'

'Yes. I'm here.'

She turns her face to the side, as if she can feel his touch. 'You have to get out.'

'Shh. Shh. I know. We are trying.'

She closes her eyes. 'No. I mean you have to, soon. They… they're going to…'

'It's okay. Shh.'

'No.' Her voice is a tiny puff of breath. 'They're going to murder you all, Mason. We saw the message. At the firing range after Fes… Fest…' Her words falter away.

I look at Ava, see the shock in her eyes, then sense the rumble through the cell and through Raza's cell, too. I knew they'd murder everyone eventually, but so soon?

'Haf… haf to get out…'

Mason's voice reaches through to her. 'We will. We will. You just stay alive, darling. I'm here. I'm with you.'

She lays her head down again, spent, and Ava strokes her hair, stringy and damp. 'Are you… Carys?' she says to Ava, her eyes clouded with confusion.

'No, I am,' I say.

'You have to know—' She stops, her words a gurgle in her throat. 'To know…'

'Know what?' I say softly, bending my ear to her mouth.

'They came for you.'

'Who did? Who came?' My voice rises, and Ava shoots me a warning glance. I pull myself back. 'It's okay. Shh. It's okay.'

'Tunnel,' Abs says, her breath nearly smothering the word. 'You can all get out through the tunnels.'

'Where are they, darling?' Mason says through the grate.

She looks at me, at Ava, then lifts a trembling hand, covered in blood, her finger pointing at the ground. 'Down. Basement. Look for boarded up… door. Go through the tunnels.'

'The tunnels,' Ava says. 'Alright. Thank you. Rest, now.'

She strokes Abs's hand, but Abs shakes her head. 'No. Wait. Go up… platform. Bank. Escalators. Look… signs… way out. Don't go… right. Need… torch…' She croaks the words, pushes them out with all the strength she has, sending them on a wisp of weary breath. 'Over… machines.'

I look at Ava again and I can see her storing it all away in her head.

'Who came?' I say again, desperate for words I've longed to hear and yet pushed away the idea of. 'Abs?'

But her eyes are closing again, her mouth going slack around words that will not come.

'Mason,' Ava whispers, 'she's going.'

A choke through the grate. 'Abs, darling. You and Tom are like parents to me. I'm here. I'm here. Holding you tight now.'

Abs sucks in air, her body tensing then wilting, like everything is leaking out of her all over the cell floor, like she's wrapped up in her dear friend Mason's love at the end of all things, and then she's in Tom's arms, letting it all go, sagging into him.

'She's gone,' Ava says quietly, and Mason says nothing at all.

We cover Abs with one of the blankets, and my heart breaks all over again, for this unknown woman, yet another victim of this hideous regime.

For this brave woman who was with other people who tried to get me out of here. People who didn't succeed. People I don't dare think about, don't dare name, because hope is still too scary for me.

26

THE CENTRE

Two days till Festival

J ACOB

I N THE SILENT evening darkness Jacob drags himself through decaying ruins to the disused underpass where Ash will rendezvous with him, bringing them food. It's too dangerous to go by day and too dangerous to go in a group. He mooches as he walks, despair pressing a stoop on his back and a sluggishness to his legs.

They failed. They were so close, but they failed. He could sense her, just through a few walls, and he could almost smell the scent of her somewhere on the edges of hope; the scent he remembered so well from the bunker: a wild, outdoorsy tang, fresh straw from the horses she loved and the sweetness of summer berries, but he couldn't quite catch hold of it and was powerless to reach her.

And now their plans have run dry.

His only chance now is to get to her in the arena, somehow, in just two days' time. He will do it, if he has to die doing so. He thinks about the text Amy received back at the camp just before they fled, the same words as the last one and the one before that: "You will die with Girl Clerk." Maybe he will, and maybe he wants to, because he doesn't want to live without her.

The dark December night wraps itself around him, the bitter cold pinching his nose. He pulls his woollen hat further over his ears and hunches into his jacket. In the distance he can see the twinkling lights of the Centre Think and Party HQ. Ash knew a place far from the busy streets, out near the ruins and the barriers. It had been his grandfather's but had fallen into disrepair when he was taken to the Home and Ash's father moved further into the Centre. It is small, humble, shabby and weary, and Jacob prefers it a thousand times over his and Amy's ostentatious flat, their prize for selling out. It's a tight fit with him, Amy, Will and Reia, yet strangely empty now Abs and Tom are gone, leaving a gaping hole. Jacob thinks about Abs all the time, down there all alone in that dark, desolate tunnel under the earth, and half-hopes she died quietly there before they found her so she didn't have to go through more indignities.

He hopes to talk with Ash about options. With two days to go, they are narrowing all the time, and he feels the pressure of it on the back of his neck, the pain crawling down his spine. Maybe Ash will have another idea tonight. He has been brilliant, this second Mr Gardener, this good one, like a bright light in the deepest dark.

He slouches against the wall of the underpass, keeping his torch on a low beam. The walls are daubed with art over a century old, words and images and big wild colours the Party would never allow. It's not been touched since the riots; other areas took priority and so it fell into disuse, just like the rest of this area. Jacob's glad of it: the silence is his friend tonight, this unlit underpass a refuge.

He hears footsteps and searches the gloom for Ash, who shuffles down the steps awkwardly bearing two small shopping bags. 'Here,' he says, holding them out to Jacob. 'It's not much, but it'll tide you over the next couple of days until… well, until.'

Jacob takes the bags. 'Thanks, mate. Listen, about that…'

Ash hops from one foot to another, rubbing his hands together. 'Cold out.'

Jacob hears it in his voice. He has nothing. 'No further?'

Ash twists his hands, avoids Jacob's gaze. 'Sorry. Coran and I have been racking our brains. Coran even tried to approach Lora again, but she won't listen and he dare not say too much. All this has been a big strain on him… those tunnels, the chase…'

Jacob stares at his feet. 'I get it.'

'We'll keep trying, though. To the last.'

'I know you will.'

'I wish I… I wish it could be different. Wish the trains could've helped us more.' His eyes are big and sad in the shadows. 'Always been there for me before.'

'Maybe they'll still help the prisoners escape,' Jacob says, trying to inject some kind of optimism into his voice and failing.

'Anyway,' Ash says, glancing over his shoulder for a second, 'I see your forum is organising itself well for Festival Day.'

Jacob nods, thinking about the old NSlate Ash smuggled out to them to keep them in touch with everything. 'There are a lot coming down legally, like with work or training houses or whatever, and a whole huge crowd meeting outside somewhere to storm the barriers on the day.'

Ash raises his head. 'And they're planning to storm the arena too? Can they cause enough mayhem to get Carys free?'

Jacob scuffs a foot through gravelly dirt. 'I don't think so. Have you seen the setup they've got planned for her?'

'Yeah. It looks impossible to get into.'

'And it—' Jacob stops, presses a finger to his lips, gazes at the stairs in front of them. A sound. No, more than one, a regular beat, a clumping.

Footsteps.

Ash goes rigid. 'Get out of here. I'll just make like I was out for a run. *Go.*'

Jacob turns, grips the bags tight, flees for the exit at the other end.

Collides with two great big Productives.

In NForce uniforms.

He doesn't stop to think. He drops the bags, tins rolling all over the place, lays into the one on the left, punches him in the gut, but he barely flinches. He grabs Jacob's hands, wrenches them around his back, nods to the other guy who secures handcuffs round Jacob's wrists before he gets the chance to take a breath. The first one kicks him, hard, in his bad leg, and he flinches, pressing his lips together.

The officers laugh.

They turn him round, march him back towards the entrance steps, and his heart sinks like a great big brick: there's Ash, cuffed like him, another NForce officer gripping his arm.

And then another figure appears down the steps, walking carefully around Ash and his captor and planting himself in front of Jacob.

Gardener?

The first Gardener, the awful Gardener, the evil Gardener?

He should be back at Ashton, simpering up to Principal. How is he here? Why is he here?

His sharp teeth glint as he bares them at Jacob. 'At last. I've been waiting for this, Oswall. Although you're not really worthy of that name anymore, are you, *Boy T*?' He spits the last words with venom so sharp Jacob feels it like an arrow in his heart.

Gardener gazes around the shadowy space, shielding his eyes from bouncing torch beams. 'And your friend? Our esteemed Esla? Is she hiding somewhere? Because I will find her.'

'She's not here.' Jacob forces the words out, his throat aching with the effort of it.

Gardener narrows his eyes. 'Where is she?'

Jacob stares at the ground in front of him.

Gardener comes closer, gets right up in his face. 'I said where is she?'

Jacob shrugs. 'No idea.'

Gardener's breath is sour and fishy. 'You will tell me.'

Jacob raises his eyebrows.

Gardener kicks him in the same spot on his leg, and Jacob cries out. Ash is shaking behind Gardener, his face pale and drawn, his lips forming noiseless, panic-shaped words.

Gardener sneers at him. 'You'll give it up soon enough. I'm taking you to see the Commander.'

Jacob rolls his eyes.

Gardener glares at him. 'You won't be giving us that attitude when you know your fate.' He nods at the guards, his face a storm, and turns on his heel, strutting up the stairs and out of the underpass with them following, Jacob dragging his feet and slowing things down as much as he can. Not gonna make it easy for these creeps.

Jacob is forced into the back of one NForce NCV with Gardener, Ash in another. Gardener smirks as they weave through the ruins towards the city. 'I've been waiting for an opportunity like this.'

Jacob stares out of the window at the lights in the distance.

'I've been biding my time,' Gardener says. 'You think I didn't know about your little forum?'

Jacob whips his head round.

Gardener just sneers.

Jacob feels the confusion twisting in his head. 'So… when that kid ratted out the forum, you knew we were behind it… but didn't shop us then? I don't get it.' He doesn't want to give Gardener the satisfaction of watching him beg for details but can't help it.

'I was watching with interest. Waiting for the right moment. You got quite a thing going there, for just a little while.' Gardener smiles smugly; Jacob wants to punch him. He wonders if he doesn't know about the redirected forum, then, as he's not mentioned it. He's definitely not going to ask.

'You sent those texts to Amy?' he says.

'That was a bit of fun.'

'And… the poison farce in Principal's study?'

Gardener grins. 'I like to play games. Haven't you noticed?'

Jacob remembers the pointless car chase a few months ago. Yeah, it all figures.

Gardener wipes the grin, turning it to a snarl. 'You're very lucky I have such a robust immune system. Augusta was mad when you two turned up back there. I nearly offed you there and then, but knew I had to wait. To bide my time.'

'Whatever,' Jacob mumbles.

'I'm not thick, you know,' Gardener says, rattled. 'I know a lot more than you realise. Been on to you at most points.' He stops, sneers again. 'They're going to tell you that they will be executing you the day after Festival, along with the whole crowd of Think inmates.' He lowers his voice, glancing at the driver. 'But you'll be dead by then. I promise. As will your pathetic little girlfriends.'

Jacob feels the rage like a kick in his belly and bites it back, setting his chin sharp. 'Does Principal know all this?'

Gardener looks away for a moment, out of his window. 'I'm doing all this for her. She wanted rid of you three since all this started. She doesn't know you started the forum, because I'm waiting to tell her the whole story.' He smiles wide then, and his face lights up for a moment, the madness in his eyes morphing to something like love. Twisted, evil, narcissistic love, but still love; it's plain to Jacob. 'She's going to love me even more. Especially when I get my reward from the Commander. There's a price on you both, you know.'

Jacob puffs out his cheeks.

Gardener continues. 'It's all for her. I'm not telling her till it's all done. Then she'll see me for who I really am, Newland's hero who stopped Newland's traitors.'

'You're unhinged.'

Gardener twists his lips. 'I'm a hero for our nation. Augusta will see it and stop thinking about that defective baby of hers who takes up so much of her headspace.' His eyes shift to the side, narrowing with hate. 'It'll be all for me. Everything.' He gives Jacob a triumphant smirk.

'You don't even care about Sim?' Jacob says, the anger swirling up even more.

'Who the hell is that?'

'The kid you killed in cold blood, back in the Compound.'

'Ah. That little loser. Now, why would I care about Unproductive scum?'

Jacob feels the heat in his fists; uncontainable, burning him from the inside. *He will kill him.* He strains at the handcuffs, but they do not give. He channels the heat to his leg and kicks out at Gardener, his aim awkward in the confined space and barely touching him. Gardener laughs as the officer in the front passenger seat turns and aims his gun at Jacob's face.

'You don't want to know how we found you?' Gardener says, his tone mocking.

Jacob scowls. 'I don't care.'

'It was that weird train geek.' Gardener motions at the car in front, now pulling into Lora's street. *They're going to Lora's?* 'They've been monitoring him a while. He's been on the NForce radar, likes to talk too much about the old railways and how he wants them back. When they found you'd got through the old underground tunnels, they put further surveillance on him and realised he was acting abnormally. That odious little butler of Lora's along with him. Too much with him for my liking.' He turns to the side, spits, globs spattering on the window.

Jacob says nothing. Gardener likes the sound of his own voice too much.

'They found you all out. With my help, of course; my good friend at HQ keeps me in the loop. They realised how helpful I was to the Party and were kind enough to fill me in on the details and allow me to come along for the ride. And give me the reward, of course, seeing as I was the one who put two and two together.'

Did he really? Jacob wonders. He has clear delusions of grandeur. Will he actually get this reward? He spots a twitch in the driver's jaw; a sneer, perhaps, at Gardener?

They turn into Lora's sweeping drive, and Jacob gazes ahead at the white mansion coming into view, its long sash windows reflecting black in the pale moonlight. Familiar and malevolent. Why here? Why not the Think?

They don't want him near Carys. Of course.

'Why are you even here? Why aren't you at Ashton, anyway?' he says to Gardener, unable to keep the loathing out of his tone.

'Well, in case it escaped your notice, there's a very important country-wide event taking place the day after tomorrow. Augusta and I have been staying in a rather magnificent Centre hotel for the past few days. A well-earned holiday for us both. The Commander was kind enough to invite us to view the event from his box at the arena.' Gardener preens, sticking his chest out. 'It's very prestigious for us, but of course, only to be expected with the help we have offered all along in ensuring our nation continues to be the safe, pure place it should be.'

Jacob breathes out a long sigh.

The driver pulls the car to a stop and Jacob is half-dragged into the house, with the front door wide open and Coran standing in the hallway, pulling at his fingers, white as the sleet outside. Jacob's glad they haven't arrested him, at least; they must have no hard evidence on him yet. He can't imagine Ash will spill anything on Coran.

In their old den two people are waiting for him: one face full of fear and one full of gloating self-importance. Lora and Anson.

'Ah, Gardener, do come on in and show our guests in too,' Anson says, his voice like a knife in Jacob's gut. 'Our officers here can stand outside. No need for you to be in here, I think we can trust these good people not to do anything stupid, isn't that right, Lora my dear?'

Lora nods mutely. She's dressed in black tonight, a skintight catsuit with silver brocade details at the cuffs, jet-black eye make-up smeared round her face – left over from *The S Word* showing earlier, Jacob guesses; no doubt Lora gave a great performance, shedding big tears as always. He shudders, realising it must have been the show the winning trainee was announced at, with Cadman hyping everyone up in preparation for Festival, where the winning act will be live streamed around the nation as well as performed to tens of thousands in the arena. It could so easily have been him and Amy there on stage, still, make-believing in the hope it would get Carys free, and then he and Ash wouldn't be here now, at the mercy of Newland's highest authority and the deranged Gardener. At least Principal isn't here. At least he has that.

'And where is our darling Esla?' Anson says, an edge to his voice now, a steely spike in his glare at Gardener. There's no love lost between these two.

Gardener diverts the glare to Jacob. 'He won't say. But he will before I've finished with him.'

'Hmm. If nothing else, we can be sure she'll find her way into the arena, can't we?' Anson says, getting up from the sofa and pacing to the fireplace where he lays his hands flat on the mantel. 'Tenacious, that one. I trust her.'

Gardener shrivels. 'I'll find her before—'

'There is no need.' Anson's voice is iron-sharp. 'I'd like to surprise her on the day myself. Such excitement to look forward to, all in all. I just can't wait, can you?' He shoots this last barb at Jacob, who stares him down then looks away at the sheer hostility in his eyes.

Lora clears her throat. 'You're going to stay with me until Festival. Both of you.'

'Heavily guarded, of course,' Anson says.

'Naturally,' says Jacob.

Anson smiles thinly. 'We have armed elite NForce all over the place. Outside your room all night, by each exit, in the grounds. Don't even think of trying to pull one of your famous escape acts, because you'll be shot down immediately. Oh—' he stops, sneers, '— and, talking of shooting, you should know our plans. The day after Festival you will be taken to the range and executed along with all the prisoners in the Think. Live streamed, of course, and your part will be made much of. I will be there myself to oversee proceedings.'

Jacob glances at Gardener, who is gazing straight at him, his mouth curved in a chilling half-smile. He gives Jacob an exaggerated wink, and he thinks about his words in the car. *You'll be dead by then.*

'Why not just do away with us now?' Jacob says, tired.

Anson grins. 'Oh, I couldn't possibly have you miss your dear friend's… show. You will be a guest in my box at the arena. As for him—' he sweeps a hand at Ash, '—we have need of some of his information. My Party have realised some, er… shortcomings, in some of the old infrastructure. Young Mr Gardener here will tell us about every single existing underground tunnel, and we will fill them all in to make our city even safer.'

Gardener gives Ash a pointed stare, no doubt maddened by their shared surname.

Ash says nothing, but his eyes are dark with terror, and Jacob wonders just how Anson is planning to extract that information.

'But first, of course, he can join us at Festival, just like you, so he can pay homage to his Commander. It's so important everyone is given the opportunity to do that, don't you think?'

The silence falls heavy.

'But you will be comfortable,' Lora says eventually, 'while you're staying here.' Jacob looks at her, takes her in; her face still bears the telltale signs of bruising, her neck held stiff like she can't move it properly.

'Thanks,' he says, and thinks he means it, for her.

She smiles softly at him, her eyes bursting with something, quickly smothered as Anson grabs her hand and squeezes it so hard she winces. 'My girl here is always too kind,' he says, his voice laden with something like threat. He pins ice eyes on Jacob, his face creasing into one big ugly snarl, his fish lips peeling back as he bares his teeth. 'You should never have been in Newland in the first place,' he hisses, his thin veneer of polite joviality cracking in two.

Jacob tries to catch Lora's eye again, to urge her to help, to communicate everything without words, but she looks away, shoulders slumped, hand tight in Anson's clutch.

Ash sits on the sofa next to Jacob, stock still, tension gripping his body and his face in frozen stiffness. Jacob looks at him, tries to break through, to send vibes of reassurance, but he can't even do that for himself anymore.

He thinks about Amy, back at the house with Will and Reia. They must know by now something is wrong. He hopes she doesn't do something too stupid, too rash. Hopes she finds enough strength to make it through these darkest days, because he knows he hasn't got any left. Most of it deserted him back in the deep tunnels, and the rest now trickles through his fingers, spilling over Lora's plush cream carpet.

27

THE CENTRE

Two days till Festival

AMY

THE OLD HOUSE squats on a forgotten street, a place once built by the Party but long since abandoned in favour of the Centre's busier and wealthier districts. It's too near the ruins, Ash told them, on the wrong side of the river; no one wants to be associated with the past that speaks so loudly out here.

Amy and Will make dinner on an old portable gas stove with the last of their supplies as they wait for Jacob, while Reia sits in the shabby living room, blackout curtains pulled tight across the window, scribbling in a tatty notebook. Will drains the pasta carefully. 'How's it looking on the forum?'

She glances at the battered NSlate Ash gave them. 'Seems safe for now.'

'Good. Try not to let it get to you.'

She stirs the pot slowly. 'Mmm.'

'I know it's easy to say. I'm so sorry it hasn't worked out.' He leaves the pasta in the sink and steps over to her, puts a tentative hand on her shoulder. 'I still have this feeling we'll be okay.'

She grips the wooden spoon harder.

Reia wanders in, notebook in hand. 'Smells good.'

'Jacob's been a bit of a long time,' Amy says. 'We should wait for him, though.'

They sit at the flimsy kitchen table together in silence, waiting, as the food goes cold and Jacob does not return. Amy doesn't dare look at the others. She scrolls through the forum, checking the messages about the big meet near the Centre tomorrow night. There must be thousands on the thread, representing thousands more on their way down already, on horses, on foot, by car. She hopes they will be safe, that they will get through, that their plans will work out.

She shifts her body, rubbing at a crick in her neck. The food gets colder.

'We should eat,' Will says softly.

Amy shakes her head. 'We wait.'

Reia flicks through the pages of her notebook. 'I've thought about how we can get into the arena.'

Will looks up. 'How?'

'I've been mapping it here. See?' She shows him the creased page, marked with a rough map. 'See this goods entrance at the back? We try there.'

'It'll be guarded.'

'I think they'll have all their guards in and around the arena and on the main entrance. If we can sneak in there, no one will bat an eyelid once we're in. We'll be swallowed by the crowds. Especially if we wear hats and dark clothing.'

'We could try it,' Amy says. 'But let's see what Jacob says. He's convinced Ash will have some ideas. He and Coran might be able to sneak us in too.'

Will looks at her then at the doorway out to the hall. 'We should look for him.'

They bundle up and trail outside together, alert for any sound, thinking of Ash's warnings about walking out here in groups. They split off and walk the silent streets, but Jacob is nowhere.

Amy shivers, alone under a drizzle of sleet, poking into empty houses and wandering through alleys where old waste languishes in stinking piles. She walks all the way out to the half-ruined underpass, calling his name, softly at first then louder. 'Jacob! Jacob!' But he does not answer.

In the underpass she sees them. Tins on the ground. Split-open bags with food spilling out, a power pack nestled underneath; Ash replaces it every couple of days to keep the Slate charged.

But Jacob is not there with them.

Back at the house they flop together on the sofa in front of the fire, trying to get warm and forgetting all thoughts of hunger. 'He's not coming back, is he,' Amy says, and Will grasps her hand, his eyes giving her the answer.

Has she lost him too? Are the three of them separated forever now, never to see one another alive again? Is Jacob in the Think with Carys, or lying dead on a deserted street somewhere? And what about Ash? Did he make it back?

'Jacob and Carys were my first real friends,' she says eventually, cradling a mug of weak instant hot chocolate Reia has brought through. 'I don't think I realised until now how much Jacob means to me. How much I...' She breaks off, the tears cracking her voice. Will leans in, pulls her tight. 'He is... so very dear to me. He's funny and clever, and... my friend. My friend.'

'I know.' Will strokes a tear on her cheek. 'He's a good guy.'

'The best.'

'We'll find him,' Reia says, determination strong on her face. 'We'll get into the arena and get him and Carys out.'

Amy blinks at her through tears. 'I wish I could believe that.'

Reia stirs her hot chocolate. 'I think... I know we've all seen tragedy. But we've seen miracles, too. The miracle that got you out of the Think and the Midlands Compound. The miracle that brought you to us and that saved me and my girls when you joined us up with this amazing guy here and his family.' She nudges Will, and he smiles back at her; a gentle fondness running warm between them, something Amy finds creeping into her own body, her own tears, and thawing her out.

'We won't stop trying,' Will says. 'There are more of us than we can imagine. Reia's old crowd from her underground trainee rescue group. All the folk on the forum. All the Outsiders we don't even know about. And even this mysterious Resistance we've heard rumours of. You're not alone, Amy.'

'I had a dear friend back when I was working the rescues,' Reia says, hugging her mug tight to her chest. 'Never got to say goodbye to her when I had to flee. Often thought she would be there if there was ever a revolution. She was a bit like Jacob. Techy, I mean. She could break open any code; her brain was unbelievable, but she was brave, too. If there's a Resistance, she's with it, and if she's with it, they're with us. I know it.'

'What was her name?' Amy says.

'Ava. Ava Coder. I think she's out there, working all this. I think she'll come through.'

'I hope so.' Amy feels the warmth spread just a little more.

Reia places her drink on the table and takes Amy's hand. 'I often think about the camps back home, you know. The one back in the bunker and the one that has welcomed me like family now. I think about the simplicity, the sharing, the deep value at the heart of each person there. Such a contrast to the Productive narrative we were force fed. I think about the love at the centre of it all. And something in me refuses to let go of that, Amy. It's like some kind of force I know can't be stopped. Our days look dark, yes, and may get darker, but even in the camps things were never perfect.' She laughs. 'Oh, far from it. But still, I will not lose sight of hope.' She gets up, wanders to the window, parts the curtain a crack to gaze out at the night sky. 'Sleet's turning to snow. There's a world of beauty building out there.'

Amy and Will join her, cradling their drinks, staring out into the winter sky, lit by snow's strange inner light as flakes fall silently, resting on the windowpane just outside. Amy gazes at Reia's profile, her beauty and courage shining out of her, and thinks about how she never spoke much, back in the community, but when she did, it meant something. And it does now, too. Her words are not just insubstantial puffs of breath, lost forever. They are light and hope and meaning.

Amy touches her hand against the window and looks at the white world forming outside. 'It's so perfect,' she says.

28

THE CENTRE

One day till Festival

CARYS

'TIME TO SAY your goodbyes.'

They come for me a day too early. I thought they'd wait until the morning, that they'd fetch me in the early hours to get me out there to the stadium before everyone arrived. I thought I'd have more time.

The guard stares at me now, his hooded eyes devoid of emotion. 'If it were up to me, I'd have you out of here right now, but some round here seem to think you should have a chance to say goodbye to folk.' He throws a vindictive glare over his shoulder at another guard in the doorway, a younger one with a softer face; the one who hitched up blankets round the bathroom area. 'S'pose it can't harm. Not like it's going to buy you any time.' He cackles at that, and the young guard half-smiles with him.

My fingers start to prickle as panic thumps into me, stealing my breath. Ava is by my side, taking my arm. 'Breathe. Breathe. It's okay.'

Harry is here too, his serious face turned to mine, his eyes wide and brimming with tears. 'I don't want you to go.' I slump to the floor, trying to breathe along with Ava. Slowly. Slowly. Breathe. Breathe. Harry drapes himself over me, his face damp against mine. 'You can't go.'

I kiss his cheek. 'I know. I have to, sweetheart.' I pant out the words. Breathe. Breathe.

Ava crouches next to us. 'Shall I call the others?'

I nod. 'Please.'

'Come on.' She helps me crawl over to the grate in the corner, its rotten stink more palpable than ever today. I grimace and cover my nose. Ava shouts, 'Hey! Raza? Lois?'

Nothing.

There's a loud buzz of voices in there. Too loud. Ava yells this time, a full on bellow: 'RAZA!'

This time she hears us. 'What?' she shouts back, her voice as sour as ever. I want to take hold of that sour voice, to lean into it, to tell it she is my friend.

I can't get the words out. Ava speaks through the grate, quickly telling Raza what's happening. Raza goes quiet.

Then Lois's voice. Warm and tender, a voice I want to climb into, to sink through the wall into. 'Carys?'

'Lois.' I place my hand against the grate.

'They're here already?' Lois says. 'Alwin, come here, darling. Carys needs to go.'

I lay my head down on my hand, ignoring the stench, and listen to Alwin's deep, broken voice. 'Hello, Carys.'

'Hi.'

'I'm sorry I've not spoken to you much.' His words are soft, cracked.

'It's okay.'

'I want you to be alright.'

'I know.'

'I... I'm sorry.' I hear his body shifting, him clearing his throat. 'You... you're like a daughter to me and Lois. I hope you know that.'

I want to break, there on the filthy grate. I close my eyes and squeeze them, trying to picture the tears flowing through my fingers and into the drainage system, but they stay inside me still like a great big lump choking my throat. Harry strokes my matted hair.

'Carys,' Lois says. 'Thank you for being here with us. And those words Alwin said – it's what I think too.' She stops, coughs. 'I love you.'

I feel the words deep inside, like a feather stroking my face, like a warmth on my skin on a sunny day. I take hold of them and store them away, and more of my bottled-up hate drains into the gutter below me, gone forever. My body racks with dry sobs, and Harry still strokes my hair.

'Carys.' Raza now, her voice low and weary.

'Hey, Raza.'

'Hey.'

'You'll get them out, won't you?' I say.

'Yeah.'

'I need you to get them out.'

'I know.'

I press my hands to my forehead. 'I… I… thank you.'

'For what?' Her reply is as spiky as always, loaded with defence and defiance.

'You've been there for me. You rescued me back at *The S Word*. You… you are braver than you know.'

An indistinguishable sound floats through the grate.

'Raza?'

'Yeah?'

'Live well.'

The rest of the cell, and her cell too, is silent, held in waiting.

Then the guard strides over, wrenches my arm, lifts me too easily; my bones stick out at all angles, my body depleted. 'That's enough. Let's get you out of here.'

'Where am I going?' I feel like I am in a dream now; the room floats around me, like there are no anchor points left.

Then Harry is in front of the guard, pounding his little fists against the man's stomach, and it sucks my mind into a picture of Sim, in another cell in another time, his fists against another guard. I close my eyes, drink in the image of him. Take him with me too.

'You can't take her,' Harry is shouting. Ava takes his hand, whispers gently to him. He squirms against her. 'No. No. You can't go.' He wrenches himself from Ava's grip and grabs hold of the guard's arm. 'Take me too. Let me stay with her. Please.'

The guard shakes him off so violently he tumbles to the floor, but he's up in seconds, clinging onto me. 'Let me come with you.'

I wriggle free of the guard's clutch for a moment. 'Sweetheart. Stay with Ava. She'll keep you safe.'

'I want to be with you.'

'No.' I kiss his hair, so messy, so dear. 'I want to know you will be free. That you will live well.'

Harry weeps, burying his head in my chest, and the guard shoves him away and yanks my arm so hard it feels like it's wrenched from its socket. He pulls me out of the cell, and I don't even get a chance to look back. To say goodbye to Ava, my friend.

He drags me down the corridor to a small room at the end: a single cell with a pallet bed, toilet and sink, and a small plastic table with two chairs set opposite each other. It looks like luxury after weeks of sleeping on the floor in the dirt. I look at the guard. 'This is for me?'

He rolls his eyes. 'Someone wants you to have a comfortable last night for some reason.'

'Who?'

He doesn't reply. He backs out of the room and slams the door behind him, the key clunking in the lock.

It's not a comfortable bed, nothing like the bunks at the community or the bed at Lora's home, but it is a bed of my own, with a soft blanket and thin pillow. I curl up, pulling the blanket over my head, trying to shut out the world, to pretend I am free.

Then I get myself together and sit up, taking in the cell, searching every corner. I examine the bed, looking for loose screws, anything sharp I can use as a weapon. I study the plastic table and chairs, patting them down, feeling underneath. Nothing. There's no window. The toilet and sink are bolted to the wall and the bolts are unyielding. The red brick walls are bare, no loose mortar to pick at, no bricks to push away and reveal a secret tunnel.

Nothing.

I sink back against the stained pillow, thinking, trying to find something, some plan in the depths of me. My mind drifts to Jacob and Amy, and I wrench it back quickly. Instead I go over the plan for everyone else, tomorrow morning when most of the guards will have left, well after I have been taken, of course. Raza and Ava have it in hand, with Boy Farmer from the other cell taking charge in there. The group who wouldn't believe are in on it now, turned by the betrayal of the man who sold out whoever tried to rescue us. Everyone is ready. Readier than ever after Abs delivered the grim news about their future. The atmosphere has been tight with tension, the cell thick with fear and, just occasionally, hope. They made us watch *The S Word* last night, and I sat with Harry on one side and Ava on the other as a group from my old training house were declared the winners. Aida was in the group, standing proud and confident; something has changed in her. She has left Mercia's shadow, but not for the better. She is written over with envy and hate. Yet I felt for her then, wanted to scream at her, to tell her to stop all this, that Mercia is right. Cadman Showman made much of her and the band and told them that all Ashton Trainers and trainees would be joining them at the arena.

All Ashton will be there, in the flesh, watching me die.

Tomorrow morning Raza will lead a charge against the guards who bring breakfast, and the other cells will do the same. With little manpower left the guards will be overpowered and then every inmate will escape through the tunnels in the basement Abs told us about. Ava has mapped it in her head, remembered from Abs's patchy description. And then they will find their way to the Commander Lucan Arena, and they will storm their way in, and Ava will take Harry to safety far away.

Then, after that, I don't know what will happen. Raza wouldn't speak of ideas beyond that. I know how flimsy their plans are, and as I spin them in my head now I feel their fragility even more, see the cracks in them, see them shatter apart in my mind. See the prisoners mown down and shot. See the tunnels bombed, see Lois and Alwin and Raza and Ava and Harry buried under a great mass of earth. See them get to the arena but then fired on by elite NForce, shot to pieces outside the entrance.

I close my eyes and curl up tight. Try to hold Lois's words: *I love you.* I trace the letters on my name stone and think about someone else who loved me, but even that doesn't have the strength to save me now.

Later the door opens suddenly and a guard wheels in a trolley laden with plates and glasses and cutlery, with food in dishes on the bottom layer, and a bucket with two bottles of champagne on ice. He avoids my eye and covers the plastic table in a starched white tablecloth then lays out two place settings with matching napkins. I stare at him, my heart picking up its pace once again. What now?

That's when he walks in. Struts in, like it's his room, his place, his table, his prisoner.

Commander Anson.

He's dressed in an immaculate charcoal suit with a blue cravat at the neck, his silver hair slicked back, his eyes more ice-blue than ever under the harsh lighting of the one bulb that hangs bare from the ceiling. 'Well, Girl Clerk,' he says, rubbing his hands together and nodding back at the guard, who leaves the room, closing the door behind him, 'it's very good to see you.'

I swallow, shrinking back on the bed, pulling my knees to my chest.

'If you'd be so good as to come and sit with me.' He motions to the table, pulling out a chair, and then sits down the other side, spreading a napkin on his lap and pouring champagne into two crystal glasses. Is this a celebration? For him, I suppose. I drag myself reluctantly to the table and sit down, the chair screeching as it scrapes over the concrete floor.

He screws up his face. 'You stink.' And then he laughs.

I say nothing back.

He waves a hand. 'Ah, well. Now, before you get comfortable, I have a nice surprise for you. I thought you'd like to have your final meal together with me, but also thought you might like to dress up. So here.' He bends to the trolley and pulls out a garment bag. 'Your Ashton uniform. You will wear this for tonight and tomorrow.'

No. Not again. I thought I'd seen the last of this, back at Lois and Alwin's community when we disposed of it after I stumbled across the wasteland and into the old airport. 'Why?' I say, and he flinches dramatically.

'No need to take that rude tone. I'm spoiling you, after all. No other prisoners get a last night in a comfortable room. And a gourmet meal, at that. Your uniform will be a reminder to the nation of the price of treachery. Trainees must understand that actions bear consequences.' He lifts a dome from a large dish in the centre of the table. 'May I present your last meal.'

I glance at the steaming dish: the rare beef, the roast potatoes and succulent vegetables garnishing the plate all around it. Despite myself, my stomach churns. 'You get changed and I'll serve you,' Anson says, his voice as convivial as if he was wining and dining a Party member.

I try to change under the blanket, aware of Anson's unwavering gaze on me. Nowhere to hide. The blanket shifts all over the place and slides off as I slip out of my filthy, weeks-old jumper and T shirt.

Heat rushes to my cheeks and I yank the blanket back, cover my bony chest. 'The Think has not been kind to you,' Anson says softly, his eyes glinting as he watches. His thick mouth curves in a wet smile. 'This meal will cheer you up.'

I pull the uniform on quickly. The clothes hang loose on my thin frame, and I look down at them, hating them even if they are clean. The rough shirt, the grey pinafore, the blue cardigan with the Ashton crest. The black patent shoes with the white ankle socks. I feel like a child again, like a trainee with no idea of what is ahead of her. I shrink in these clothes and Anson sees it and it shows on his smug face.

I feel the ball of fury start to awaken. It's been dormant for a while, muted by captivity and despair. But it is there, a heat in the pit of my belly. I push it back down, try to quench it. How can it help me now?

Anson pulls something else out of a bag on the trolley. 'Here. Your hair needs brushing.' He passes me the brush and I look at it, weigh it in my hands, wonder if I can use it as a weapon. But it is plastic, soft and moulded, the bristles worn. 'Lora thought you might want it.'

I start to drag it through my hair, and the angry tangles stoke my rage as they pull and snag. I yank it harder, allowing the pain to take hold of me, the indignity to feed me. My hair is matted and filthy, knotted with weeks of grime. Long strands come loose with the brush, floating to the cell floor.

'There. That's better,' he says, appraising me and taking the brush back. 'Now. Come. Sit.' He extends his hand to mine, grips hold of me and pulls me to the table. 'Let's talk.'

Talk? What does he want to talk about? To gloat over me, maybe. To fix me with his lascivious gaze and enjoy my discomfort. To tell me that no one is coming for me now.

I wheeze and then cough. 'You are not well,' he says.

The fury is still there. A tiny white heat. 'Your jail doesn't help anyone who is sick.' I keep my voice measured, calm.

He smiles. 'Of course. Punishment must be of a certain nature, so people can understand their choices.'

'What, before they go to die?' It's out before I can contain it.

He takes a swig of champagne and the sparkling drops glisten on his lips and chin like diamonds. 'You're still trying to sell that old story?'

I pull at my fingers under the table. 'I guess I am.'

He picks up his fork and waves it at me. 'Eat. I've had this specially prepared for you.'

I look at the food on my plate and think about how I've dreamed of something like this for weeks now, locked half-starved in that cell, fed with stale bread and cheese that tastes like feet. I grab my fork and shovel a mouthful of potato into my mouth and it tastes so good. I close my eyes for a moment, blank out Anson and everything else in the room until it's just me and this plate of food. I take some beef and bite into it and its juices explode in my mouth.

'Good?' His voice is smarmy.

I open my eyes, and the room rushes back at me. 'It's okay.'

He laughs. 'I always did like you.' He grabs the bottle and refills his glass. 'Have a drink. You might as well taste a little of the best champagne Newland has to offer while you can.'

I pick up my glass, my hands trembling, and take a tiny sip. The bubbles dance on my tongue and I swallow more down, wanting more of the feel it gives me, the sudden rush after so long deprived.

He laughs again. 'I see you're in favour.'

I shrug.

He stabs at his beef and chews, his mouth open, and I look down at my own food, revolted. 'You know, you could have been something,' he says, his mouth still full of meat.

I chase some peas around my plate. My appetite is leaving as quickly as it arrived.

'You were such a good example, there, for a while, before your little performance. You had repented and saved my Lora. The nation was with you and for you.'

The peas skitter away from me.

'You always had a tenacity of spirit about you. I suppose that's why you did what you did, in the end. You disappointed me greatly, you know.' He lays his cutlery down and pins his gaze on me. It's like he can see right into my soul.

If he's looking for an apology, he isn't getting it.

'It's a shame that you need to be sacrificed for the greater good.' He slugs back his entire glass and fills it again quickly. His cheeks are flushing, the tip of his nose reddening. 'But of course it will be quite the spectacle. Have they shown you the box?'

'The box?'

'Your execution chamber. It's quite a design. It's been on NBC News, but I suppose they don't show you much of that in here.'

I grunt.

'I won't spoil it for you, then.' He stuffs a forkful of potato and carrot into his mouth.

I give up on my food and take another tiny sip of champagne.

'Your friends will be there, watching,' he says, his tone thick with glee now. 'They will be in my box with me, of course. They are very much looking forward to it.'

I stare at him, the disgust rising and mixing up with the fury and twisting into a new, sharper shape. 'I don't believe that.'

But do I?

'Hah. Well. You'll see. You'll have your own special screen in your box, you see. You'll see everything – and everyone – the camera sees. You'll be able to wave goodbye to your friends.'

I grip the stem of my glass hard.

'And of course, you will be allowed to watch the Festival Parade and the *S Word* performance before your grand finale. More friends of yours, I believe, are the winners of that. I didn't want you to miss out on any of it. It'll be quite a day.'

Red hot to white hot and rising.

Anson takes another dish from the trolley. 'Dessert.' He plonks the pavlova onto the table so hard some of the cream splatters his face. 'Oops!' he cackles, wiping it with his napkin. 'A little merry. Isn't this all lovely?' He scoops the mix into two bowls and shoves one at me. 'You didn't eat all your dinner up! Can't have been that starved in there, then, can you? Have this. My chef made it spesh… specially.' He digs his spoon in and slurps the pudding up, and I sit and watch him, repulsed. He chases it with another glass of champagne, then grabs the other bottle and slugs more into his glass. He raises it at me. 'To Girl C, my Newland Traitor.'

I stare down at my dessert. The nausea in my gut swirls up, choking me, and I push the bowl away.

'You really are the most ungrateful bitch.'

I flinch at the sudden venom in his voice. He grabs my bowl and shovels up the pudding in there too. 'Someone appreciates it.'

I dig my nails into my palms. I don't want to look at him. Don't want him in here. The fury is in my throat now, mixing with the nausea, surging into my mouth. 'You evil bastard,' I hiss, my words croaked out before they're properly formed.

He stands up and slams his chair back so it crashes to the floor. 'I'll enjoy watching you tomorrow.'

I get up too. Get into his face. 'I know what you are.'

He guffaws, his breath a stinking tide. 'Oh? And what would that be?'

'I know you kill without mercy. I know you don't care. I know you want everything for yourself. I know you hurt Lora. I know—'

He is gripping my throat, pressing in, his eyes bulging at me. 'I'm not the one going to die tomorrow.'

I claw at his fingers, my vision swaying. He presses in more. I feel blindly for something on the table below me. My champagne glass. I grab it, squeeze it till it shatters, feel the sharp sting, the hot blood. Bring it up and smack it into his face. He reels back, roaring, a jagged cut tearing at his cheek, blood pouring. I feel my strength return, the fury and the nausea and the hate and the love and the hope, all bundling together, all streaming through my body and out through my hands, and I'm on him again, wild and free, stabbing the broken glass at his eye.

Then I hear it: the clunk of the door, and the guard's on me quickly, tearing at my arms, yanking them around my back, cuffing me, shoving me onto the bed. 'Commander, I'm so sorry.' He takes Anson's arm and leads him out, shooting a glance back at me. What is it, written on this guard's face? Anger? Hatred? Or admiration? He hovers there a moment then slams the door closed, locking me in with the broken glass and the blood on my hands and the spent anger all over the floor.

PART III

WINTER FESTIVAL

29

THE ARENA

Festival Day

AMY

THE COMMANDER LUCAN Arena stands huge and imposing against the wide winter sky, multiple Newland flags soaring high from flagpoles bolted to the outside of the structure. Clouds hang in layers like great white sheets, and last night's snow has mulched to slush on the ground under so many thousands of feet. Around all the main entrances stand elite NForce officers with riot shields and automatic weapons slung over their shoulders. Amy, Reia and Will break off from the crowds and sneak around the back to the service entrances, where vans and lorries unload last-minute equipment.

Amy pulls her brand-new *S Word* cap lower. They found these in a quirky little shop on the outskirts of the city, Amy and Reia waiting outside while Will purchased them with cash Ash had given them. The wanted posters for Amy and Jacob are everywhere, though too late for Jacob now. The caps were a good enough disguise in the surging crowd, but won't protect them at the entrance where palms are scanned and verified.

'This is it,' Reia says, looking up from her notebook at a small gate leading to a short passage to a side door in the northern stand. 'Just got to get through here.' The gate is firmly padlocked.

'What about there?' Will points to a larger entrance further along, where delivery men haul various bits of musical kit through to the arena: drums, amps, guitars, keyboards.

'Too visible,' Reia says. 'I can pick this.' She fishes a small pouch out of her backpack and pulls out a small, flat, metal tool with a slight curve at one end, and a thinner, more jagged looking tool. She inserts the first one and moves it around slowly, her tongue stuck out in concentration, nodding at herself then gently nudging the second one in and jiggling it back and forth. Will and Amy look on anxiously, waiting for one of the delivery guys to look their way. It would only take one.

'Where'd you learn that?' Amy says.

'Had to use a lot of this kind of thing when I was working the rescues,' Reia mumbles. 'Oh. There.' There's a quiet click and the padlock snaps open.

They sneak through, pulling the gate closed behind them and tiptoeing even though the noise from the crowd inside is enough to drown anything out, and push slowly through the door into the stand. 'What now?' Amy says. 'All the seats must be ticketed, surely?'

'We go up to the back of the tiers. Always standing room there, and lots of people like to go there to stretch their legs and to go out to the refreshment stands anyway, so we won't look out of place.'

'You sure?'

Reia nods. 'We're here now.'

'And we can scope it all out from there. Work out how to get to Jacob and Carys, right?'

Reia hesitates. 'Right.'

Amy follows her up a long set of steep concrete stairs, past groups of people weaving through to blue plastic seats, laughing and calling to one another, many already drinking, all of them bundled up in winter gear, some with blankets shared between them. The wind whistles through the stand, stinging Amy's face.

At the top she turns round and wobbles. The tiered seating falls away too sharply below her, the main field a long way down. She sways forward, her stomach leaping into her mouth. Will takes hold of her arm. 'Lean on the wall. We'll be fine.' Others are up here with them, smoking and taking photos of the great sweeping arena. Amy takes it all in, knocked breathless by the scale of it all. The stands are swarming with people, all the way around in a massive oval. Huge NScreens hang at intervals, relaying scrolling news and clips of *The S Word* as well as close ups of people in the crowd. She hopes the cameras don't pick her face up.

One of the men nearby gives Reia a long, jeering glare, and Amy curls her fists by her side. *Keep it in. Don't be noticed.*

Fluttering bunting and flags are strung across the arena in every direction across a large circular staging area in the centre of the pitch where a band are setting up and techs in Festival uniform test microphones and audio equipment. To the right of the field stands a colossal bronze statue of Commander Lucan.

But it's not any of this that calls Amy's notice.

Suspended above the arena, straight above the stage, is a large, clear glass box hooked to the tallest tower crane Amy has ever seen. She's seen AI mockups of it on the news, of course, but in reality it is higher, bigger, stronger, more inaccessible than she'd ever imagined. She knows Carys is inside that box with her executioner.

She looks at Will then at Reia, despair crushing her body tight. 'There's no way.'

'No,' Reia says.

Will just squeezes her shoulder.

She slumps back against the wall, her mind scrambling in a fight with hopelessness. They made it here. They got in. Is it all for nothing? She scans the crowds for Jacob, hoping against hope he is alive and here, somehow. Too many faces. Too much noise, celebration, happiness in this place of evil and death. She scratches at a sore spot on her hand until it bleeds.

She looks up into the sky from under the lip of the stand, the cold biting at her face. She wants to shout at the sky, to get its attention, to make it do something. To crash down on the stadium and stop all this.

The first flakes of the day float slowly down over the crowd. She almost laughs. *Not quite what I meant.*

Suddenly a siren sounds through the arena and the screens go blank then cut to a harried NBC news presenter, out by the Centre border gates. 'The barrier has been breached. I repeat, the barrier has been breached. A crowd of thousands descended on the border gates just a while ago, mowing down our border guards without care and smashing up booths on the way through. They were last seen heading, en masse, in the direction of the Commander Lucan Arena. Please be prepared – they are armed and dangerous, violent Unproductive Outsiders – but I am assured there is no need to worry: the elite NForce are ready and waiting and they will be taken down and killed on sight.'

A hush through the stadium.

Amy stares in the direction of the main entrance, feeling her heart pushing at her chest. The forum. They made it. They are coming.

But how far will they get? Will they be able to break through in time to stop this whole charade? And how many will die trying? Amy presses her hands together. *Come on. Come on.*

People start to settle in their seats, munching on popcorn and chattering away. Amy notices many of them taking photos of the glass box on their phones, and feels sick. Will they post these on their NBook pages? #deathbox?

Then she hears the roar outside and the first shots, the crack-crack-crack of automatic fire, the more concentrated barrage of machine gun fire. The screens flicker with images of the front entrance, with the crowd surging, crossbows singing, people with bows and arrows and rough-hewn spears, the odd pistol and shotgun. The commentator starts to cackle. 'How far are these Unproductives going to get with those pathetic things?' The camera zooms in on rebels going down hard, blood everywhere, elite NForce standing in a line at the entrance with riot shields held out, arrows and bolts bouncing off harmlessly. The crowd seem to skid to a halt then slowly retreat as more of the front line fall. Amy can hear the loud voice through every speaker: 'Retreat or we will continue to fire.' She guesses they want to keep things as calm as possible so Festival can go ahead, and a full on battle won't do that.

The crowd of rebels are straggly and weary looking. Amy looks closely at those at the front and, with a jolt of recognition, spots Warden and Mercia, hand-in-hand, stumbling back with several others.

The loudspeakers squeal. 'Get back. Or we will continue to fire. You have one opportunity to retreat.'

Amy watches with a sinking heart as the crowd slowly draw back, away from the entrance, and regroup at a safe distance to stand, to watch, to wait. The NForce keep their shields high and their weapons primed.

They have no chance.

The audience is hushed as the cameras pan to bodies on the ground outside the entrance. Too many of them. Will squints as he peers at the screen, the lines on his brow all crumpled up, and Amy realises Matt might be out there, and Stephen, and others from his village. She grabs his hand.

Then the screens go blank again, and the lighting is dimmed before exploding into colour and a great dancing light show, the screen flashing with "Welcome to Winter Festival!" in time with a steady drumbeat; the band below are in place and ready. They break into song, a popular Newland classic, with Raulf Singer in prime place at the front of the stage, bellowing into his mic, whipping up the crowd to fever level. The crowd are relieved to leave the scenes of carnage behind, to know they are safe from the violent criminals outside, and they are on their feet, swaying and waving their hands and screaming along to the song.

Amy, Reia and Will watch in silence.

At the close of the song there's a burst of fireworks and the crowd go mad again, hollering and cheering and stamping their feet. The camera zooms in on two people on the stage in front of the band. Cadman Showman and Elva Anchor. Cadman dances to the beat, hyping the audience, his face wreathed in smiles. 'Ladies and gentlemen, welcome to a very special Winter Festival!' He claps along with all the people, who scream and whistle and whoop. 'I'm delighted to be able to be here with you today and introduce our first ever *S Word* Festival winners. But first, Elva, over to you for the first section.'

Elva Anchor steps forward, a diminutive figure in a white fur jacket and fur-lined boots. 'What a pleasure to welcome you all. We will start with Parade, of course, as usual, so please get in formation.'

Amy watches as thousands of uniformed Productives swarm onto the pitch. Most stay in their seats, ready to take part from there, because there are too many of them to form Parade lines, so those in uniform have been picked for the honour of lining the field: NForce officers, Party members in full regalia, council workers in special Festival garb, health workers and some Trainers and trainees too. The excitement in the air is palpable, like electricity running through a thousand wires at breakneck speed. They form straight lines in great blocks across the whole field, and still the snow continues to fall, turning muddy slush to a kind of luminous white around their feet. They are soon still, as if frozen in place, zoomed in images on the screens showing serious, inert faces all turned to the statue of Commander Lucan.

One drumbeat sounds, a dramatic crash in the heavy silence. 'First bow to Newland's first Commander, the saviour of our nation,' Elva Anchor says in a hushed, respectful voice. The blocks on the pitch bow as one, deeply, at the statue, crossing their arms over their bellies. They've rehearsed this, Amy thinks; it's too choreographed.

The audience are on their feet, bowing too, thirty thousand people bent low in mass silence.

Thirty thousand minus three.

Amy, Will and Reia stand as far into the shadows at the back as possible, hidden away, looking down on the tiers of hunched bodies in front of them, and they do not bow. They do not cross their arms over their bellies.

Amy searches the screens anxiously, afraid that at any moment one of the cameras will find them, these traitors, refusing to join in. She finds a smile playing on her lips as she imagines the crowd outside, standing tall, facing down the NForce, knowing that they will not shoot while this is going on. She joins hands with Will and Reia and with the others in her head, closing her eyes.

'And now to your Commander.' Elva Anchor's silky voice echoes through the stadium and the blocks in formation on the pitch turn to their left, immaculately in time with one another, and wait for the signal. It comes as the screen pans to Anson sitting in his box with Lora by his side, a champagne glass in his hand, which he slowly raises as the audience bow again. And, once again, Amy, Reia and Will stay stock still, their hands clasped.

Amy gazes at the screen, at Anson's face magnified by a hundred. His cheek is angry with a freshly stitched wound, another, shallower cut running close to his eye. Who did that? Next to him, Lora bows low with the others, and Amy wonders if she fought back at last. She hopes so. She searches her face too, but it's hard to make out, bent so low, her hair falling across her brow. Like Elva Anchor, she is dressed in fur, soft pink ear-muffs completing her look.

'And now we recite the canon.' Elva Anchor leads them and the familiar, hated words bounce through the arena, heartfelt and earnest and exuberant all at the same time. Amy, Reia and Will stand with lips buttoned and hands clasped tightly together. It has to be enough, Amy thinks. This tiny rebellion. If she does nothing else today, she will have done this, and it will be enough.

Anson stands up, a little unsteadily, Amy thinks. He raises his glass again and slugs it back then bellows into his clip mic, 'What a glorious sight. Now you will join me in the Newland Anthem. Raulf, lead us on.' Anson's voice is loud, with a slur at the edges. How much has he had to drink already?

Raulf and the band strike up the anthem and the crowd are ready for it. Belting it out at the top of their lungs. The arena resounds with it, thirty thousand voices lifted high in great waves, the power of it carrying the audience into rapture. Anson on the screen is standing, lifting both hands high and his face to the heavens, his eyes closed, thick lips curled in a self-satisfied smile.

But Amy, Reia and Will do not sing a note.

The camera sweeps now to those near Anson in his box. Amy flinches as she sees Gardener and Principal at the back of the box, both standing tall, mouths wide open as they sing. She recognises others: Party officials, the NForce chief from the Centre Think who nearly executed them back on that day months ago when they saved Lora, the other two *S Word* judges, Portia and Edwin. And then, as it pans along, she sees him.

Jacob.

He stands between two NForce officers at the edge of Anson's box, his hands behind his back, his mouth barely open as the anthem roars on. It looks like they have him cuffed back there. The camera zooms in on his face and it is blank, broken. Amy has seen him broken before, when Aiden died back in the Birmingham ruins, and when Carys was caught, but this is another level. It's like all the life has drained from him. It's like he's left the building and that is a shell of him. One of the guards pokes him in the side and he jumps, opening his mouth wider to join in the pretence. Amy wants to wave to him, to shout to him, to awaken him. To tell him she is here with him, at the end of all things. She bites on her tongue and stays quiet, and thinks her heart will not stay beating because it is breaking into tiny little slivers that cut through her chest and spill out onto the ground in front of her.

'I can't see Ash,' Will whispers.

Amy doesn't see Coran, either. He's not important enough to be in the Commander's box, after all. Was he arrested too? Are he and Ash in the Think now, with the hundreds of other rebels still crowded there?

The anthem comes to a close with more fireworks and a shower of silver confetti released from high in the stands, falling on thousands of heads, twirling and twisting with the snow. If Amy wasn't so wounded she would see a great beauty in it all.

Elva Anchor steps forward. 'Please stay in formation as you enjoy the Festival Parade.'

The audience, released from silence, clap and cheer as floats advance from one of the tunnels under the eastern stand and onto the track, a slow procession of them circling the people standing in formation. Amy remembers the floats at the Midlands Compound Parades, of course, but this is another scale. Some are trucks with open beds, mini-dramas played out as they go, recalling the riots and the fall of England; some horses pulling carts with costumed people dancing in their Scourge gear, skin made up with great festering wounds; some long limousines with actors hanging out of the sunroofs, arms stretched high, yelling over and over again, 'Glory to the Commander! Glory to the Commander!' The floats go on and on, a great parade of colour and creativity, a larger, flatbed lorry in the centre of them all featuring an actor playing Lucan, holding the Newland flag aloft, his head threw back.

And still, above it all, the glass box hangs motionless, snow gathering on top in great drifts.

30

THE ARENA

Festival Day

JACOB

O N THE SCREEN her face is white and scared. The camera in the glass box sweeps the space: the trolley she lies on, a thin figure in an Ashton uniform strapped down by leather harnesses; the executioner standing beside her, his mouth and nose covered by a black mask; the IV drip stand, the tube running to a cannula in her wrist. The audience falls into silence for a minute as they stare, calming after the great hype of Parade, and Jacob keeps his face still, blank, emotionless. He will not let the sobs that rumble at his chest fall out of him. He will not let his lips quiver. He will not give Anson the satisfaction. The guards on either side of him grip his arms tight, and his hands ache in their cuffs; he tries to stretch them out but waves of pain shoot up his wrists.

He closes his eyes, shutting the hideous images out, thinking about the past couple of days. Could he have done anything differently? Last night Coran came to his room, Lora persuading the guards to give him a minute. 'I don't have much time,' he'd said as he perched on the end of Jacob's bed, his hands trembling. 'I just wanted to… wanted to…'

Jacob had soothed him, telling him not to worry. 'Is Ash okay?' he asked him.

Coran's face darkened. 'They're keeping him in the cellar!' His voice was heavy with outrage. 'They won't let me in to see him. But he will be okay. He will be.' He picked at a hangnail, a mix of emotions skimming his face like clouds scudding across the sun. 'And so will you.'

Jacob thumped the pillow. 'I don't know.'

'I think Lora might be… thinking about things,' Coran said carefully. 'I can't say anything to her, of course. I can't possibly tell her of my involvement. But I know Lora. I know when she's thinking. I think she'll come round. I… I just can't quite trust her yet.'

'But will it be in time to save Carys?'

Coran just gazed at the floor.

Jacob scooted closer and sat on the end of the bed next to him. 'Can you do one thing for me?'

'Anything I can.'

'Only Amy is left free now. Can you make sure she stays free? Anson will be looking for her; he'll have his guards on it. Please see if you can keep her away from him. Can you do that?'

Coran stared at him. 'You think she'll be there?'

'I know she will.'

'I'll do my best—'

The door had opened then, the guard calling to Coran that his time was up. As Jacob watched him slink through the doorway, his shoulders slumped, he wished he had thanked him for his kindness and his courage.

He searches for him now in the crowd but can't see him, or Ash. Perhaps Ash is still in the cellar; perhaps he is already dead. Maybe they discovered Coran's treachery and murdered him too.

The screen still lingers on Carys, motionless on her deathbed, her hands curled into fists. He can't imagine how she must be feeling.

Elva Anchor skitters forward on the stage. 'We thought you'd appreciate this sneak preview of our finale.' She giggles. 'But of course, before all that, we have the rest of our Festival. Go and enjoy lunch now and return to your seats at two o'clock for our *S Word* special performance. The Newland state band will entertain you during your lunch break. Please be considerate of one another as you queue for refreshments. And remember: Power to the Strong! Justice to the Good!'

The crowd take up the chant, punching their fists in the air, and then the band strikes up below them, a more chilled tune, flat and tired in Jacob's opinion, with Raulf's rich bass echoing through the stadium. Jacob wonders where the forum crowd are now: still outside the entrance, waiting to be shot? Or have they withdrawn altogether, fled while they could? He wouldn't blame them.

He scours the crowd again, looking for Amy this time, but it's quickly a seething mass of people leaving their seats and streaming out to the refreshment stands outside. There's no way he could possibly spot her. He looks up at the box, scrutinising it from every angle, wondering how he could break in if he could possibly shake off these bloody guards. But it scuppers him at every turn, and he knows he is beaten.

'I'm glad you decided to accept my hospitality.' Anson is by his side, a champagne glass in hand, his breathing heavy and his face flushed. 'Are you enjoying your day?'

Jacob stares straight ahead. One of the guards pokes him in the arm, the force of it sending a wave of pain through him. He makes a noncommittal grunt.

'I'll have someone fetch you something to eat,' Anson says. 'Can't be neglecting my honoured guests. Perhaps you'd like to sit with your friends over there?'

Jacob follows his pointing finger. Gardener and Principal. 'No thanks.' He's sensed Gardener's glare on his back most of the morning already.

Anson laughs. 'Hmm. Well, I can't really blame you. They *are* tedious.'

Jacob scuffs a foot on the ground. Can he get to the bolts on this seat somehow? Can he strain his hands enough to loosen them?

'I'm sure you're looking forward to this afternoon's display most of all. As are we all.' Anson throws him another sickly smile and turns, wobbles down the steps towards Lora and his NForce entourage. Jacob hopes he slips and falls and splits more of his face open.

Nobody brings him food, but he doesn't care. He's not hungry. The guards stuff their faces with burgers each side of him, and he is nauseated by the smell. He tries to get a grip on a screw just underneath his seat at the back. Puts everything he can into loosening it. But it will not budge. Beads of sweat stand out on his forehead and he wants to slam his hands against the chair, the guards, the whole damn arena.

At two o'clock sharp the audience are called to sit quickly and quieten down. The band stop playing their fake folksy crap – sounds like the kind of tunes you hear in a supermarket, Jacob thinks – and stand silent, waiting. Portia, Lora and Edwin make their way down to the stage and join Raulf there on four huge purple chairs wheeled out during the lunch break. It's *The S Word*, Festival style. Jacob tastes acid on his tongue and spits, and one of the guards slaps his face hard. And he doesn't care anymore.

Cadman Showman is out there at the front, whipping up the crowd. 'Are you excited to be here? I said ARE YOU EXCITED TO BE HERE?' They respond to him, cheering louder and louder, the whole lot of them unhinged. Cadman shushes them down eventually, waving his hands up and down. 'I know you've all been waiting for this. You've been glued to *The S Word* more than ever for the past few weeks, haven't you?' He breaks off, waits for the applause to calm down. 'And on the show the other night we announced the winners, of course, and we are thrilled to have them – and their entire training house – here with us today. Ladies and gentlemen, please welcome the Ashton Crew!'

Jacob screws up his face as the crowd go wild again. The Ashton Crew? What kind of lame name is that? He wishes Amy were here next to him so they could exchange smirks.

A group of kids dance onto the stage, Aida leading them, dressed in matching outfits: baggy blue trousers and red silk waistcoats with an Ashton motif. They stand with Cadman, gaping wide at the huge crowd. One of the girls is shaking, Jacob notices.

Cadman bounds around the stage, his excitement level increasing with the crowd's. 'And of course, our honoured judges are here this afternoon to judge the performance. We know the Ashton Crew will be amazing, but how amazing? Our judges will give detailed feedback to make them even better!'

Jacob notices a section of the crowd opposite him, low in the stands, jumping up and down, shaking banners high and yelling louder than everyone else. He recognises Boy M there in the front, and more of his Podmates and classmates. There's Miss Trainer Three in the middle of them all, and more Trainers around the edges of the group. All of Ashton are there. No sign of Warden, Mercia, Lawyer or most of the others in the rebel group. Are they in the crowd outside? He didn't spot them on the screen, but he was mostly busy studying the glass box at the time.

'Now,' Cadman says, taking Aida's hand and leading her to the microphone at the front of the stage. 'Perform for the Commander. Pretend no one is here but him. Do it for his glory.'

Aida can sing, it turns out. Her voice is rich and melodic. It's a shame it doesn't match who she's become, Jacob thinks. He wonders if Amy is watching her too, right now, and thinking of how she bullied her in the Pod, how she dumped Mercia when she changed for the better. She leads her crew in a sweet melody swelling to an epic ballad, some of the other kids playing violins and an oboe, the state band backing them all up. The crowd lap it up, swaying along, raising hands in the air, some activating their torch app. Jacob just wants to hurl.

Snow continues to fall, only adding to the magical atmosphere. The lighting guys do a good job given it's still daylight, spotlighting Aida and casting blazing beams of silky reds and blues around the arena, highlighting the flakes falling softly on the band and the judges. Cadman sways at the side, waving his arms back and forth. Looks like a tosser.

Jacob sits through the judges' overdone praise, peppered with bits of advice and some criticism from Raulf: 'You need to train that voice more,' he says to Aida, who shrinks before him. 'You were flat at the high notes and screechy in parts.'

Cadman looks at Lora, waiting for her usual rebuttal, but she sits mutely, the camera so zoomed in on her face Jacob can see the snow gathering on her fake lashes. Portia chimes in, 'Bit harsh, Raulf. I thought she wasn't bad.'

'Me too,' Edwin says. 'In fact—' and he shoves his chair back and bounds onto the stage with Aida, flinging his arm round her shoulders, '—I thought she was magnificent. As were you all.' He sweeps his hand around the stage. 'I'd say we have the best group of Strivers we've ever seen on the show. Right, Lora?'

She seems to snap to focus, rubbing at her face. 'Oh, yes. They brought tears to my eyes.'

Jacob rolls his own eyes.

There's a commotion over to the right of him and he sees Anson himself, shoving through the gate from his box and stumbling down the steps towards the pitch then climbing up to the stage, tripping on one of the steps, an NForce guard at each arm keeping him upright. He strides to the front and stands with Edwin and Aida, takes Aida's hand and raises her arm high. 'This here—' he stops, puffing for breath, '—this here is an example of what Newland is all about. We have shown you today our future, our way forward, even in the midst of all this turmoil and aggression so unfairly thrown at us.' He moves closer to Aida and drops her arm, his own arm crawling round her waist and pulling her in tight. Jacob sees the expression on her face, the discomfort, and for a moment he feels for her. Remembers she's just a young girl, caught up in all of this. 'As you can see,' Anson continues, his 's' thicker than usual, 'we care greatly about the talent in our training houses, and from now on it will be showcased across the nation on a regular basis. These children here are our future. These talented, committed trainees. Here's to the Ashton Crew!'

The crowd are on their feet, roaring and stamping, and Jacob fiddles with the screw again. Is that a slight loosening? He gets a grip on it, his aching fingers slick with sweat.

'Now,' Anson says, letting go of Aida and shoving her none-too-gently back towards the rest of her band, 'now's the time for our grand finale. The moment we've all been waiting for. To help us all appreciate exactly why we are doing this, we've put a little film together. Enjoy.' He sweeps his arms wide, taking in the huge NScreens that dot the arena. The crowd fall to a quick silence, on the edges of their seats. Jacob hears a barely suppressed snicker from way behind him: Gardener.

It's Carys on the screen, back at *The S Word* on that fateful day, the clip filtered to a darker, distorted hue, giving her eyes an evil cast and her mouth a blood-red angry streak. Music plays in the background, discordant and jarring. Words come out of her mouth, but in a different order to what she said, ugly, spiky subtitles blinking in and out of focus across the screen. 'Commander Lucan was a sick, sadistic man.'

The audience take a sharp breath in.

'They are murderers. They are twisted. TWISTED.'

'You need forgiveness.'

'I will not bow to their will and do what they want.'

'The Party are SICK.'

'Productives are TWISTED.'

'The Party should be executed in the Think.'

'You should be ashamed of yourself.'

'Productives are Skivers.'

'All you trainees are weak and vicious.'

The phrases are stitched together seamlessly, but Jacob can hear the slight pauses and see the glitches on the film where the words have been turned around, interrupted. They've tried to disguise it with the filter, the darkness, the building music, but he knows. He knows they couldn't show the real film, because Carys's passion would move the crowd just as it did back at the studios.

The crowd stay hushed, staring up at the great screens, at the frozen image of Carys at the end, her face stuck in an ugly grimace. Anson steps closer to the mic. 'You see, we can't allow such blatant violence in our nation. Such heinous lies. Such betrayal and sheer hatred towards you, my dear Productives and trainees. Girl Clerk was a rebel even before this, when she tried to murder a fellow pupil at Ashton and then took part in an escape from the Midlands Compound, on the way committing treason by going into computer files and then lying to the nation about their contents, not to mention shooting her principal in the leg and causing lasting damage. After this little performance on *The S Word*, she continued to spout similar awful words, then sealed her fate by taking part in a murder attempt on our Cadman here—' Anson punches Cadman's arm and he tries not to flinch, '—and then running away and causing malicious damage by our border gates. She then teamed up with an Outsider group and plotted against us, but they were apprehended by our brilliant NForce here.'

He pauses for a moment as the crowd cheer for the NForce, pumping fists and chanting: 'N—Force! N—Force!'

'And you can all see what such treachery leads to. You can all see why we must punish Girl Clerk in this way this afternoon. Allow it to be a reminder to you of our Party's justice system: we do not allow injustice here in Newland.' He looks up at the glass box, and the scene changes again to Carys strapped onto the trolley, tears running down her face. 'Look how she cries now,' Anson yells into the mic, his voice booming around the arena. 'Look how she regrets everything she said and did. But it is too late! Now she will die. This is a positive thing, my dear people. A reminder of all we have come from and where we are going, a reminder that we, the Party, care enough about you all to make difficult decisions in order to keep peace in our nation and squash malicious lies at their roots. This is a great day.' He pauses, watches the crowd, throws a rancour-filled glare back Jacob's way. 'Please join once again with our Newland anthem, as we experience this moment together as a nation.'

The guards pull Jacob roughly to his feet and the screw scrapes his flesh as he lets go. He will not sing. Why should he sing now? Why should he even pretend? He presses his lips together, raises his head, watches as everyone else stretch out their arms towards Anson.

The anthem is slower, more thoughtful, Raulf Singer's deep bass reverberating round the stadium. Does everyone here mean it? Jacob scans faces, looks for signs of uncertainty, but all he can see is blankness now. The enthusiasm from Ashton's act has faded.

Anson steps forward as the song comes to a close, tripping slightly and giving a little giggle that echoes through the microphone and bounces round the arena. 'Now. Please sit and watch in silence as my colleague up there delivers this just and painless punishment, and think carefully on your own lives, your own actions, and your own future. Thank you.'

This time there is no applause, no cheering. The crowd sit quietly, hold themselves in hushed anticipation. Jacob watches helplessly, gripping the screw so hard it pierces his flesh. What's the point now? He doesn't care anymore. He doesn't want to watch this. The guards see him staring at his feet and grab hold of his face, forcing his chin up. 'You will watch,' one of them hisses in his ear.

Jacob lets the screw dig deep into his finger bed, allowing the stinging pain to cut through his body and his mind. In his head is a picture: Carys walking next to him on a velvet black night, her long hair flowing in the warm summer breeze, her grey eyes sparkling as she turns her face to his. He holds her there in his mind, but it is not enough to stop the sobs that come now, breaking their banks like a river in a storm, gushing out of him. 'I'm so sorry. I'm so sorry,' he croaks over and over and over, barely feeling the screw loosen and fall into his hands as he squeezes his fingers together so hard they are numb. On the screen the executioner holds an IV drip bag and a syringe, and slowly depresses the plunger, sending the contents into the bag that is connected to the tube that is connected to the port of the cannula in Carys's wrist.

The executioner looks directly into the camera for just a moment, his eyes empty against the starkness of his mask, and then he loosens the clamps on the IV tube.

And the poison starts to flow.

31

THE ARENA

Half an hour ago

CARYS

FROM MY GLASS prison the sweep of the arena below me looks like a whole world of freedom I will never now experience. People shuffle back and forth, a mass of colours, so small from up here, enjoying their lunch break like this is just a happy Festival day out for them. On the pitch the Commander Lucan statue stands tall and ominous, his carved bronze head almost on a level with my box. Soon it will be time for Ashton's performance, and then…

I try to talk to the executioner. When I was brought here I fought with everything I had, bucking and kicking and scratching, but none of it did any good. They strapped me down on this hard, cold metal trolley and left me with this man. He is not the person I want to spend my last minutes with. He refuses to talk back, his expression under his mask unreadable, his eyes blank. For a second I almost wish Anson was in here with me; at least he would engage with me, spar with me, make me feel like I am still a little bit alive.

I turn my neck and gaze down at the entrance area again. From here I can see outside to the crowd of rebels who are gathered some way from the gates, with NForce weapons trained on them. They are still and silent. I search their faces again, hoping against hope I will see some familiar faces: Raza. Lois. Alwin. But no one from my Think cell is there. The only faces I recognise – and still can't wrap my head around – are those of Mercia and Miss Warden. Earlier on the screens zoomed in to them and I couldn't take it in. How is it even possible they are there, out amidst the throng of Outsiders?

Where are the Think inmates? Did they not make it out? Did they get trapped down in those tunnels? My stomach drags tight at me. Is Harry safe?

I wish I'd tried harder with Raza. Been kinder to her. That I hadn't said those horrible words to her: '*You hate everybody and everything.*'

My wrist prickles where the needle was stabbed in without care, and my body aches with bruises from my final fight. I wonder if I am just in a dream. I look up; I am suspended from a tower crane way above the box, but it's harder to see now. Snow has settled on the glass, sealing me in even more, intricate crystal flakes resting just metres over my head. I want to reach up, to drag it in here with me, to embrace its frozen touch, to feel one last real thing.

I glance over at Anson's box again. See Principal and Gardener, there at the back, clinking champagne glasses, faces smug and red. Wish I didn't have to see them at all. I guess soon I won't. I idly slide my gaze over the box, taking in people I've seen before. The important Productives. Coran is not there with Lora; I guess he is not on Anson's exclusive list. I wish he was. His kind face would be a comfort to me.

I'm just closing my eyes when I snap my head round again. I saw something. Someone. There in the very corner of Anson's box, far away from the important people.

Jacob?

I strain my neck, feeling the leather bonds cutting into me. Try to see him closer. I can only see him in a blur, can't crane my neck around enough. It is him, though. I see it in his black hair, his tall, wiry frame, his shoulders so slumped now. His face is turned downwards.

My neck hurts. Is that an NForce officer next to him? And where is Amy? Maybe on his other side, which I just can't quite see? I wish I'd paid more attention to the screens earlier during the Parade; maybe I'd have seen them both more clearly. It shouldn't be a surprise to me that he is there, in the box; Anson told me they both would be, that they were eagerly anticipating it.

Yet there is something that doesn't feel right. Maybe it's the way he sits so slumped. I have a sudden memory of him on our Ashton trip to *The S Word* studios, such a long time ago now. How he'd slumped as far as he could in his seat, how his seething disapproval had bitten the air between us. How I'd been so convinced, then, that he was wrong, that I knew best.

I misjudged him then.

I feel a sudden sensation: a lightness, creeping through my limbs. Could I have been wrong this whole time? Have I been burrowing myself further into hating them when I should have trusted them?

His face is in my head. Bending over me in the Ashton Think, watching me open the name stone, a ripple of joy disturbing the dank air. 'Don't let them tell you who you are,' he'd said to me then. And that's when I'd realised I didn't have to be Girl C anymore. That I was Carys, and I was loved.

Have I forgotten that, in these desperate days? Have I let something else tell me who I am? Something that's told me I am abandoned, hated by the ones who loved me, betrayed? A narrative that has shrunk me down? I think of Raza's words the other day: *Your hate is quenching you.* And how Ava told me she could see beyond it, to who I really was, and how their words brought me a moment of such relief and then peace it carried me through. Is it time to let go of the rest of it?

Is it time to take back my trust in my two best friends?

I stretch my neck round and try to look at him again. The snow falls harder now; he sits under a confused white flurry, his body tight with tension. Why are his arms around his back? I look at the guard next to him again, and it falls into place. He is a prisoner.

As Cadman Showman and Elva Anchor bring the crowd back into place and introduce Aida's group, I allow the tears to fall. At last. They come silently, running down my cheeks in great rivulets, nothing and no one to mop them up, to comfort me. The executioner's eyes are ice. But my tears are not just sadness, they are not just despair; they are joy. I know, then, with everything inside me, that I was never betrayed. That Jacob and Amy were doing whatever they needed to do to survive and to help me survive.

I know who I am again.

As Aida sings, her warm voice rises up and cradles me for a moment. I relax back against my trolley, feeling the familiar weight of my name stone in my pocket, and wait.

32

THE RESISTANCE

Half an hour ago

THE MAN SHUFFLES from one foot to another as he stares at his TNSlate, at the choppy image of the ancient rust-grey helicopter. 'Thought you said this was all ready.'

The pilot thumbs back to a couple of guys lifting a long, narrow box into the cabin. 'Nearly done. Just making sure the bomb's in the right place for when we're ready to let go. The Southeastern took an age to get this thing out here.'

'When will you be ready to go?'

'In the next half hour or so.'

The man looks at his companion. 'Too late for Girl Clerk.'

She shakes her head. 'She'd be taken out with it anyway. We always knew that.'

He paces the room. 'Will we be in time to get to… everyone else? Surely it'll all finish after the… execution?'

The pilot's voice crackles through the poor connection. 'We'll be there.' The screen goes blank as he cuts out.

'They'll be celebrating in there all afternoon,' Number Two says. 'Don't worry.' But her voice is subdued, her hands quivering as she presses them together.

The man looks out of the window to the street outside, where the rebels from the forum are gathered in a huddled crowd, with the entrance to the stadium just ahead of them, NForce elite officers standing sturdy with weapons pointed. 'And them?' he says to Number Two.

'They should escape the worst of it. We can be thankful they didn't manage to break in.'

A pale woman brings in a tray with drinks and sandwiches. 'Will you be here long?'

The man smiles at her. 'We know it's been a big risk for you, and we're so grateful you've let us hide out here today. To be so near everything… it's a gift.'

She passes him a glass of water with a trembling hand. 'No more after this, that's what we agreed, right?'

He nods. 'Right.'

Only a half dozen of them are here in this modest Centre home today. Everyone else is scattered, most of them back in their own Compounds at their Festivals with the live link from here, some back at their main ops centre out on the Outside, and some of them in the arena itself, linked up to their coms and ready to flee at the right moment. Those are the ones who couldn't get out of it without giving themselves away.

The man watches the NScreen on his host's wall. The camera zooms in on Carys, in her glass box, and then pans around the arena again and comes to rest on Anson and Lora. He watches as it moves along the row to Boy Trader at the end, cuffed between two beefy NForce officers. How'd the stupid kid get himself in this latest mess? 'Anyone spot the other girl?'

Number Two nods. 'Saw her on the other side. With Reia, of all people, and some other kid, standing at the back.'

'Reia's alive?'

'I think it was her. Looks older, obviously. Surprised she wasn't getting hassle just for looking like she does.'

The man scowls. 'And now we're going to kill her, just as we've found her again.'

The woman just looks down.

He licks his dry lips. 'There's no other way?'

'You're still trying to turn back?'

He rubs his head, eyes glued on the screen. 'No. No. I don't know.'

Cadman Showman is doing some big pathetic act, leaping round the stage, introducing the kids who won the *S Word* thing. Ashton kids, they are. The man shudders as the camera pans to a whole bunch of them, cheering and yelling in the stands, waving Newland flags and jumping up and down. Hundreds of trainees there from Ashton, and thousands more dotted all over the arena, kids with their parents on Festival Day, the only time they get to see them. His heart is in his throat, choking it. He paces the room, slams his glass on the table.

His NSlate comes to life again with a connecting call. The pilot. 'Few last minute preps and we're ready. Will be waiting on your signal.'

'How long from take-off?' Number Two says.

'Twenty minutes or so.'

The man cannot settle. His legs are jittery, his hands trembling, his mouth dry. He knows this is the only way forward, but…

The Ashton kids are giving the crowd a good performance in there, standing on that huge round stage, bang underneath the glass box. The audience are swaying along, swept up in the whole thing, a whole load of puppets who have no idea what's coming.

So many kids.

The man paces again, counting in his head like it'll stop everything else, like he can crowd out the images. 'You're disturbing the air,' Number Two says, but her voice is different.

He stops. Faces her. Looks right into her eyes. 'You really up for this?'

She closes her eyes, looks away, fiddles with her glass. He can read the tension on her.

'I'm sorry I said that thing the other day. About you not having emotions.'

She looks up, surprised, her mouth wobbling.

'I don't think it's true,' he says.

She frowns. 'If you're just trying to butter me up, to get me to pull out of this thing—'

He puts up his hand. 'No. No. I know you won't do that. I just… I dunno. Felt like I should say something.'

She shrugs. 'Well, in that case, I forgive you.' But then she frowns, turns away, swallows down some water.

His NSlate buzzes again. 'Waiting on you,' the pilot says. The man looks at his face, blurry through the hazy connection. He's too young for this shit. Too young to murder children.

'Wait,' he says, glancing at all the faces in the room once again. 'Hold on.'

'It's time,' a man in the corner says, impatience heavy in the lines on his face. 'Tell him to go now.'

Number One gazes at the pilot's image. 'Not yet.'

On the big screen, the Ashton song is coming to a rousing close in a frenzied light show, and the crowd are on their feet, yelling and cheering, the arena a seething mass of excitement. Then the judges are doing their thing. That Raulf Singer can never help himself. Always has to be the bully.

He watches as Anson stumbles onto the stage, and smirks. 'So pissed.' Watches him as he blathers on and on about why they must do this and what Girl Clerk has done. Watches as they show this clearly doctored footage with her sounding off at the lot of them. He wants to join with her, to yell out all that stuff too, just as he did the first time.

He looks more closely at the screen, at the row of Ashton trainees in the stands, sitting silently now as they watch Anson spout on and on about treachery and just punishment. Sees a kid nearby who is so small she must barely be out of Infant House. The camera zooms right in on her little face, eagerness and certainty shining in her eyes as her tiny hands grip her flag. She turns her face to the sky and gazes in wonder at the snowflakes kissing her face.

Just a little kid.

Sees more of them now, scattered around the place, even smaller. Tiny children shifting on their seats, kids on their parents' shoulders. 'Oh God. Oh God,' he says, the words bowling out of him like a desperate plea. Number Two stands beside him, sees what he sees, exchanges a glance with him.

On the screen the crowd are standing, singing out the anthem once again, hands extended towards Anson on the stage. Are they quieter this time, or is he imagining it?

A scuffle in the corner. The impatient guy has snatched the NSlate. 'Go,' he shouts at the pilot, and kills the connection.

Number One wrenches the Slate back, stabs at it furiously. No connection. He's gone. 'Have to radio him.' He glares at the guy, who has the radio in his jacket.

The guy shakes his head. 'Too late. Won't connect now till it's done.'

Number One grabs him by the collar. 'We have to try, Dale.'

Dale shakes his head. 'No. We're just doing what we all agreed.' He glances round at the others. 'Right?'

They nod tentatively.

All apart from Number Two.

Time is frozen.

Number One sinks his head into his hands. 'It's not right.'

'You can't go back on it,' Dale says, squaring up to him. 'You promised.'

He looks at Number Two, sees the conflict in her eyes. Grabs her hand.

She gazes at him for a second. 'We could get them out,' she says, so quietly he can hardly hear.

He moves closer. 'You're with me?'

She stands taller, nods grimly. 'I can't... I can't... we have to try. We're too late for Girl Clerk, but we can try for others.'

He rakes his hands through his hair. 'If we try and warn the gate, they'll just shoot us down.'

'So we go in. We're still legal.'

The others are up on their feet, anger and fear bouncing round the room. 'Stop!' Dale yells as Number One shoves through the door and out into the hallway. 'Stop!'

Number Two starts after him.

'You're too late anyway,' Dale says. 'Helicopter's on its way.'

She turns, lunges at him, grabs the radio from the holster on his jacket. She tumbles out of the door, trips, and speeds after her colleague, who is halfway up the street, almost at the crowd of rebels. She picks up her pace, curses her high heels. Why'd she have to wear those? She always did try to look important. Imposing. And now all that is crashing down around her as she takes in the scale of the arena ahead. The reality of who is inside, and what they would actually be doing. It all sounded good in theory, but now…

'Stand by,' she screams into the radio as she runs, but all she gets is a crackle. It's en route now; maybe the pilot can't hear. Thousands of voices belting out the Newland anthem resound towards her. She runs faster, catching her friend as he arrives at the gates and palms the scanner. The guards look on with suspicion, but he's used to that, she knows.

'You shouldn't be so late,' a guard says, shouting over the roar of the crowd. The anthem has finished.

'Just got delayed with lunch,' Number One says, and the guard rolls his eyes.

They rush through a tunnel towards the pitch, batting aside a loose string of bunting.

And freeze.

The screens are back on Girl Clerk now, and her executioner, preparing the lethal injection. The crowd sit forwards, hushed, so many faces with eyes wide: some with expectation, some with fear, some with horror.

So many children.

Number One gazes up at the screen as the executioner injects the poison. Then he turns his head, looks at the Commander's box high up on his left, and sees him there, his head down, his shoulders shaking.

Number One feels something pushing at his chest. A great aching sob. He's too late for Girl Clerk now.

But maybe he can save Jacob.

33

THE ARENA

Half an hour ago

THE CRANE TOWERS high above Raza, its criss-cross steel work like a yellow lattice cliff side, sheer and imposing. She feels tiny as she stares up at it. Can't be that hard, she thinks. Just has to get up to that cab bit. Still has time.

Getting through the tunnels turned out to be the easy bit. It went more smoothly than even she'd imagined. They really did desert the Think en masse, the fools. The guards left were run down quickly, but the inmates took casualties. One of the guards panicked as soon as he sensed the tension in the air, started firing off his sidearm. They lost five of them right there, slammed to the ground before they knew it. Lois tried to stop to help, but Raza urged her on. 'No time.' They stormed the guards, stole their weapons and their NPhones, met up with everyone from the other cells, dived straight for the basement, knowing most of the staff left to man the building would be in and around the lobby. The woman from Carys's cell Raza had never yet seen face to face, Ava, found the entrance quickly and led them through down into these spooky old tunnels.

Raza wasn't into that bit. The torches from the NPhones worked well enough, but there were hundreds of them crowding in down there, kids as well, some of them sobbing. The darkness was like nothing she'd experienced before, like it was pressing on her head along with all the stuff she didn't want to think about between the tunnels and the ground way above them. Ava had that kid Harry by the hand, dragging him along. He kept screaming about getting Carys out, and Ava assured him, said they were on their way. They were slow, though. Raza was impatient; it was lunchtime before the guards brought food. Were they even going to make the arena on time? Because that was where they were going. They were marching on it. They were going to get in there, stop everything in its tracks, get Carys the hell out of there. None of them wanted to do anything else. Since Abs had told them about the Commander's plans, they had enough fire in their bellies to take the whole damn Party out.

Ava got them along the tracks, past these nightmare parts where the tunnel was almost fallen in and they had to squeeze through. Ava hesitated at some parts, round the next platform where a maze of tunnels led to who knows where, but she found a way out. Somehow. Up these ancient dead escalators, through narrow, eerie hallways, and up to the surface where the sudden brightness made Raza blink. After not seeing the outside world for too many weeks she reeled at the hugeness of the great white sky, took a great big gulp of the bitter cold air.

And then she ran. 'I'll meet you there,' she yelled to Lois, who held onto her hand too tight, like she cared about her. 'I'll see if I can do something up front.' Truth was she'd realised time was against them, that it was almost one already and they had to get back across the river then across the city to the arena. Half an hour's run for her, maybe, but longer for them. She had to do *something*.

Lois had kept hold of her hand a moment, squeezed it. 'Go,' she'd said softly, and then she'd drawn Raza in, hugged her tight, and just for a second Raza allowed herself to lean into her, let the unexpected power of the embrace stream through her body. Then she bolted, keeping the map of the Centre in her head and the Party HQ building in her sights, knowing the arena was just beyond it.

Finding a way across the river ate up minutes of precious time, so she just ran faster, her foot snagging against piles of rubble as she scampered across a half ruined bridge. Once on the other side the going was easier as she sprinted into the city, back past the Centre Think building, throwing it a gloating glare on her way.

As soon as the massive arena came into sight Raza took in the whole setup of the thing. She could see it all: the crane, its boom arm holding the glass box, the NForce strutting around the entrances, the motley crowd huddled up together some way away. She ran on, panting, making for an area past the entrance near the crane site where she could stay hidden while she got herself together, her heart lifting at the sight of the rebels then falling as she admitted to herself that they hadn't made it in, that they were standing under the threatened fire of a hundred weapons. That they'd most likely be gunned down as soon as this farce of a festival was over.

And so would her crowd, if they ever reached the place.

And now she stands here, getting her breath back, gazing up at the crane, an idea piling layers on itself in her mind. Looks like it's lunch hour right now, with people milling around the arena and outside by the food vans, all happy and festive. From here she can see one of the huge NScreens mounted near the top of the stands, the camera focused in on Anson and Lora then panning around to others in his box, quaffing champagne, their faces red and smug and pompous. Then it sweeps around the crowd, some in their seats, some on the move, some on the pitch dancing to the band in the snow. She wonders if her mother is there somewhere. Everyone is bundled up in their best winter coats, and Raza shivers as she glances down at her tattered clothes, the torn black jeans and jumper she's worn for weeks. She knows she looks out of place here: filthy and ragged. Smells even worse.

The crane is cemented to a large, level concrete slab surrounded by wire fencing with coiled wire strung along the top. The site is mostly deserted, some workmen in hard hats gathered near the gate at the other side, cradling steaming cardboard cups and munching burgers. A couple of NForce officers slouch idly against the front of the gate, joking with the workmen and taking swigs from what looks to Raza like cans of cheap cider. It's clear that the force of the Party's defence is concentrated around the stadium itself.

But even so, she can't just strut in through that gate and go straight up the ladders, get in the cab and take the whole thing over, can she? She doesn't have a clue how to operate a crane, but she'll work it out if only she can get to it. She looks up again; the scale of it is terrifying. It must be well over two hundred feet tall. She swallows, feeling the quiver in her hands, her feet. What is she thinking?

But she can't see another way. Her crowd won't arrive for a while, and Carys is in that box now, and in just half an hour or so she will be executed. The Commander made the exact time very clear on a Public Service Announcement during *The S Word* the other night. Raza hops from one foot to another to try to stave off the cold as she stares up at the screen, then at the crane, at the tiny cab so far up she can barely make out details, at the jib arm hanging motionless out over the arena. Her heartbeat picks up and she wrings her hands together as she scrutinises the area closely, plans it out, checks all possible ways forward. Wishes she'd kept that guard's gun, but knows it was right to leave it with Lois and Ava and the crowd.

On the screen, the camera is on Carys now, pinned to a metal trolley in her glass prison. She is frozen there, her wide grey eyes fixed on the ceiling above her, the image so jarring, such a contrast to the crowd's joyous revelry.

She knows, then, with a deep and strange warmth that surges right through her, that this is what she has to do.

She swallows, stills her mind, concentrates on each part of her body, letting the jitters drain away. She gives herself a little nod. She can see her path ahead: a dent in the metal fencing, way around the other side, far from the guards and the workmen. The path, pitted with gravel and chunks of stone, winds around the site until she reaches the battered panel. There. The dent is deep and weakened enough for her to shove at it until it moves away, squealing; the noise of the crowd keeps the guards at bay. She slips inside, snagging her arm on some wire, barely noticing the blood. The mast looms above her, taller yet now she's right underneath. Raza never did like heights. Even some of the bigger farming machinery back at the Community sent her weaving and wobbling.

She looks down at her hands and then wipes them on her jeans. Sweat and dirt all mingled. Looks back up at the screen again; this time it features the band, Raulf Singer crooning out lame Newland classics.

She slips through the open door of a metal cage propped around the mast structure, then clambers through the outer bars to the centre and faces up to the first ladder, its grey rungs sturdy and strong. Looks down; the crane is well cemented in its base. It's okay. She can do this. Flicks a glance back at the gate; the guards and the workmen are creased over, laughing at something. She's good. She clutches a rung above and places her feet on the first rung. It's fine. Starts climbing.

The rungs are cold and slightly clammy, the increasing snowfall not helping things. She climbs slowly, steadily, breathing in, out, in, out. Don't look down, Raza. Think about stuff. How Dr Chemist will get what's coming to him now you're out. How you'll find your mother, talk to her. How you'll say sorry to Carys for being such an arse sometimes.

One. Two. One. Two.

Her arms start to ache, and she's glad she started the strength sessions back in the Think. Some of them didn't want to bother, said what's the point, but she said they had to keep strong. Lois was brilliant, had these moves she taught them all, stretches and heart-strengthening exercises. Her muscles are trained, but will it be enough?

Gets to the first platform and hoists herself up onto its rusted grey mesh floor. Curls up for a moment there, panting hard, rubbing at her aching arms. The wind is stronger up here, rattling the entire mast, the platform creaking underneath her. She grips the bars and stands unsteadily, looking down the ladder below. A force slams into her, a wave of nausea. Come on, Raza. You've only done the first bit.

Then she sees them. The faces, turned towards her, their expressions unreadable from here but their body language obvious. Then moving towards the crane. The NForce guards. One of them bellowing into a radio.

Got to be quicker. She scrambles around and onto the next ladder and grips hold, the cold steel biting at her freezing hands. Wishes she had gloves. She climbs faster this time, only looking straight in front, at the next rung, at her feet, at her hands, at her feet, at her hands. One. Two. One. Two. She fights a sense of weightlessness as the outside world rushes at her, already too far below, the stadium ahead in her vision, that stupid statue leering at her. Dares to look up. Still such a long way. Will she be in time?

The band keep playing, the notes floating up to her, and she times her hands and feet with the rhythm. One. Two. Three. Four. Shouts below; she can't make them out. Won't look. She blocks out the world, thinks about the Community. The girls playing cards with her, accepting her, a broken, odd stranger. The Queen's deep, wordless understanding of her. The colours of Remembrance Night; deep indigos and violets dancing across the sky.

Keep going. Next platform. She clambers on, her arms and legs screaming at her. No time to stop.

Underneath, a gunshot.

The cab is in sight above, bigger now, a dirty grey rounded box, the huddled shape of the operator inside. So tiny and inconsequential when compared to the monolith it's attached to. Can she overpower him? Up, up, up. The rungs are hard on her hands. Cold and wet. The outside crowds in at her, drawing her eyes, a shiver running through her at the giant vista below, swathed in increasing snow. Flakes land on her nose and she wants to sneeze. Feels her cheeks going red raw, her fingers numb. Hold on, Raza.

At the Community there was a woman called Kate. When Raza first turned up there, battered and wounded, it was Kate who took her in. It was Kate who wrapped her in blankets, fed her soup, cuddled her close like a child. It was Kate who took time with her when others didn't because she was too prickly, and with her quiet, gentle presence, Raza found a home for the first time in her life.

Kate brought Raza books, later, from her husband Daniel's library, and with them the joy of imagination and wonder. She thinks of those stories now, of heroes of old who saved the world, of kids who fought against systems and dragons and found friendship on the way. Thinks of how, in some ways, those stories saved her, and they're saving her now, because there's no way this really is going to work, is there? She's in a story of her own, all arms and legs moving, moving, moving without thought, a story she is creating.

Up. Keep going. ·

There's a change in atmosphere from the arena stretched out ahead of her. She pauses on the ladder, clutching it so tight the whites of her knuckles stand proud. The crowd are stilled, back in their seats, tiny ants in a long wash of colour. She gazes at the screens, so small now from this height. There's Cadman Showman, prancing round the stage. She allows herself a tiny smile, recalling the last time she saw him on a stage and what she did.

And that band from Ashton now, their sugar-sweet melody floating up to her. She knows what that means.

It'll be Carys next.

Her trainers are rubbing her ankles from the sprint over here, and each step digs the blisters deeper, tearing at her flesh. Tendrils of her hair come loose from her plait and blow in her face, across her cracked lips, and she pushes them back with one hand. Thinks about the other night, when Lois sat braiding her hair, her hands so gentle. Told her she looked beautiful. She didn't believe her, but the cell felt a little bit warmer right in that moment.

The song goes on and on, the notes of it more and more distorted the higher she climbs, like she's hearing it underwater, somewhere far, far away. It climbs to a stirring finale, the lighting in the arena below a mass of writhing colours as the drummer beats out an extended ending.

She looks up. Not far now. One more ladder and she's at the cab.

She's so thirsty. She tips her head to the falling snow, allows it to stroke her lips. Down there the crowd roar, their voices lifting, wrapping around her, dragging at her eyes. The judges are on the screen, tiny, a haze from up here. Her stomach lurches as she looks down, her hands quivering on the wet rungs.

At the top she emerges onto a small platform, the cab tucked down at one side with the main jib extending way out into the distance over the stadium directly in front of her, the balance jib with its counterweight behind the cab. She grips the bars around the platform, swaying, the metal creaking below her feet. The wind whips at her hair, stings her face and her eyes. What now, Raza? What was the plan in all this?

The cab is right there. Just get inside, deal with the operator, start spamming those joysticks and buttons, cause some havoc. Get the box lowered. Stop this thing in its tracks, right now.

A shout below her. Two ladders down. Two NForce officers, scrambling up, grim faces red and damp, hair dishevelled under their blue caps.

She shifts her way around the narrow platform, gets closer to the cab entrance just below. Her hands are so tired, pains shooting up her wrists. She's not made for this. How does the operator do this every day?

Turns out, in the end, that the operator is a Party guy.

He looms large in the entrance, his fleshy body filling the space between Raza and the cab and, in his hands, an NForce grade handgun. Pointed at her.

His face is a smirk. 'Didn't think they'd have trained officers in this baby today? What'd you think you were gonna do up here, silly little girl?'

Raza wobbles. Clutches the railings; they are slippy with snow.

The guy glances down the ladder. 'Good to see my colleagues are on the ball. Now, time to get yourself back down.' He points down and she follows his motion. The ground undulates below her feet. She raises her head, stares at the jibs, the sky. Knows that going down means she'll die at the bottom, soon as she's out of their way and can't make a mess all over their platforms.

So there's just one way to go, then.

She eyes the main jib arm and the railing around the platform, then glances back at the guard, jeering in the doorway, holding his gun idly, then vaults over the bars, her arms screaming with the effort of it. Collapses on the narrow catwalk on the jib and flops there a moment, two moments, her pulse hammering at her throat, her heart a butterfly. Looks ahead down the jib towards the end, where it hangs over the arena, its narrow steel wire hoisting the glass box way below. How many feet? Two hundred? Three? No difference, really. Not from up here.

The guard cackles behind her. 'And where d'you think that's gonna get you?'

She glances back at him, sees the gun hanging loosely by his side, like there's no need to bother with that now there's a show here just for him and his mates. She drags herself to her feet, limbs aching. Brushes the snow from her hair, her face. Faces down the jib. The walkway is narrow, even narrower as it goes on, thin railings down both sides, not much else to keep anyone on the thing. The thick, faded yellow bars meet above her head in a kind of triangle shape, like a tent only without the cosy bit. She stands, reels, grips the railings.

Below her the world is white, the arena a circle of cotton wool with thousands of tiny flecks of colour. On the screens she can make out faces, far away, like they're on another planet. The Commander is there now, then some flickering images playing across the screens; she can't make them out. She stands frozen. Then the crowd are standing, singing the anthem. It's not the song she wanted to hear. Not now. She blanks out the words that fight their way up to her and steps forward, tentatively, slowly. Maybe she can find an object down here, throw it down on the box, shatter it apart. She saw where the executioner was before, bang in the middle of the box, bang under its hook, and Carys in the left corner on her trolley. If she can drop something… part of the pulley mechanism? Can she get to it, wrestle it off?

She glances down; wishes she hadn't. The world teeters beneath her feet, a thin mesh layer between it and them. The trolley and hook block are far out at the end, way under the jib. Not a chance in hell of getting those things free.

More shouts behind her. She inches her neck round; any movement could send her flying into infinity. The other guards are there, clambering over the railing. The one at the back exchanges harsh laughter with the operator. 'He's a chicken, this one.' He pushes at his colleague, who is green round the gills and slow to inch onto the walkway. 'Get a move on.'

The first officer falls on his knees on the catwalk, gripping at the mesh with his fingers. 'I can't,' he says, his words whipped by the wind.

His jeering colleague jumps on behind him and kicks him. 'Get yourself up. I can't get past you. Someone's gotta get her down. Don't want to be up here longer than we have to.' He glances down at the screen. 'We're missing the show.'

Raza inches forward again, the sound of the anthem a warped rhythm, clanging with her feet. The boom sways and she stops. Looks back. The guard won't move, his arms now hugging the walkway, his body bent double. The second officer looks back at the operator, shakes his head. 'Can't be doing with this.' He kicks him again. And again. 'Get out of my way.' The first guy's hands come loose from the walkway, his body convulsing with terror shakes.

Tries to grip the railings and his colleague shoves his hands away. 'Let me past.' Starts to squeeze by, but the first guard grabs hold of him. Clings onto his legs.

'Help me,' he says, his voice a thin cry, muffled by snow.

They both topple, the first guy clinging, fingers digging into flesh. Second guy curses, shakes his leg hard, clutches the railing. The first guy rolls to the side, grasping at clothes, at rails, then at air as he goes tumbling out into the white abyss below with a haunting shriek.

Raza reels back, her hands sticky with cold and sweat, grappling for the rails.

The second guard brushes himself off, throws a shrug back at the operator, who stands frozen behind him. 'Lucky this bit's not over the arena, right?'

The anthem is rousing to its finish below. Raza moves on. She's directly above Commander Lucan's ego-statue now, its bronze head a flat snow-tipped disc way below. Not far now till the end. The catwalk narrows further, its mesh floor barely a foot-width; Raza's balance is off. The wind rushes against her ears. The steel wire to the glass box is so thin; it looks rough, abrasive. Could she shimmy down? No. She can no way get to it.

The guard's footsteps, coming closer. Nearly on her now, making the jib wobble further. He plants his feet, holds the railing with one hand, raises his gun with the other. 'I'd shoot you now but don't want some poor sods down there getting all messed up with you landing on their heads. So you have one chance. Come back with me, now, and we can reason this all out.'

Reason it out? Like he did with his colleague?

She turns back and paces the few steps to the very end, where the jib ends in abrupt nothingness, the vast expanse of the sky and the earth laid out ahead, above, below. Grips the railings and slowly looks down.

The box is directly below her, its roof a confusion of shadows and snow. She rocks back, a wave of dizziness flooding her body. Hears the anthem's final flourish, a booming voice from the arena: Anson proclaiming Carys's moment. This is it.

The world slows down, the whiteness of it all swirling and twirling until it fills her mind with choking fog. The tiny people in the stadium seem to raise up towards her, faces upturned. Her mother is there, right beside her. One Festival Day she told her mother she hated Pre-training, she didn't want to be there, 'cos all the other kids thought she was an oddball. But Mother didn't step in, didn't hug her. Told her she should try harder to be like them, then she'd fit in, then she'd be happy.

Her face washes away with the snow. It's Carys there now, and Raza's chest fills with a warm glow, like she's suddenly found a fireplace to huddle by. She's bound to Carys, she realises then, in life and in death. One above, one below, a thin wire stretched between them. The glass might hurt Carys. Might kill her. But they're both going to die anyway, so she must try.

Dr Chemist pushes through her fog and she reels back, the railing a damp, cold presence hanging onto her by a thread. She was going to kill him. It was all she'd been about, these last months; the only thing that mattered. But his face is mushy now. Like it's draining down a plughole, like it no longer matters. She can let go of him at last. He doesn't have that power over her anymore, not now, not in this wide, wild moment. She feels lighter, like she could take off now like a bird and soar away into the great white heavens.

Somewhere in her mind she hears a song. A sweet, high voice. Who is it? It's not from the arena, which nestles silently in the grip of Anson's speech. The words come clear and wrap themselves around her.

I see you all around
In dreams of morning you'll be found

Her song from Remembrance Night. But not her voice. It's like a bell ringing somewhere deep and high all at the same time.

I hear now as you sing
Your voice streaming through the wind

Is her daughter calling? Or is it the snow, falling on her upturned face, sparkling on her red-raw hands?

She blinks, takes in the trembling world under her feet, the guard almost on her, leering down at her. She will not give him the satisfaction. Won't bend to the Party's will and go quietly, only to be murdered as soon as it's convenient for them. She turns her face away from him, blanks him out, takes in the view instead. The hugeness, the wildness of it draws her closer, strokes her soul. She glances down one more time in the direction of the rebel group by the entrance. Wishes she could've known whether the others made it here, whether they got free.

Everything will be okay. She knows that now, with a blaze of certainty that pierces her heart and breaks her in two. It's all she can do now. It's what she has to do. She takes her hands off the railings, one by one, stands tall against the driving snow, raises her face and her arms high. Screams out to the sky, one last time, 'You'd better save her.' The song murmurs through her mind, its plaintive notes building, and she breathes out once, so softly.

And then she drops.

34

THE ARENA

Now

Amy

Amy senses the stirring in the crowd before she hears the voice.

It's Cadman Showman, his hand against his heart. 'Stop. Wait.'

On the screen the executioner stands stony still as the IV mix begins to enter Carys's body, his expression giving nothing away.

The crowd murmur, pushing at one another, some of them gesturing up at the box. No, further up. Into the sky. 'Look up there,' someone hisses. Amy, Reia and Will gaze up, moving forwards from under the lip at the rear of the stand to see more.

On the stage, Commander Anson stands stock still, fists curled by his side. Cadman is next to him, shielding his eyes as he gapes at the sky. 'Who's that up there?' he says, his voice loud and booming in the microphone.

Amy watches as the screens pan up, and up, and up some more, focusing and unfocusing as the zoom lens struggles to find its object. 'There,' Will whispers to her, pointing. A hazy figure comes into view, poised right on the edge of the crane arm, way above the glass box.

The camera zooms in further, and Reia gasps. 'It's Raza!'

Amy stares closer. Sees the dark hair, the ragged black clothes so stark against the driving snow, the determined face.

'She was in the Think,' Reia says slowly. 'Means she somehow broke out.'

'The tunnels. Abs,' Amy says, a spark of something igniting in her chest.

Reia stares up at Raza, her dark skin pooling to grey. 'What is she doing?'

Cadman gives a nervous laugh in Anson's direction. 'Looks like we have an uninvited guest.'

Anson scowls and says nothing.

The crowd hover in anxious silence, watching. On the screen a guard appears close behind her, wobbling, a gun quivering in his hand. Amy feels a prickle of sweat under her arms. Even the sight on screen makes her sway and wobble, and the tiers of seats below rush up at her, dizzying her head.

She grasps Will's hand and stares at the screen. Raza's eyes glisten; is that just the snow? Something on her face is strange. Radiant, perhaps? She shuffles forwards, closer to the edge of the jib.

Reia grips Amy's arm. '*No.*'

Raza is taking her hand off the rails. Then her other. Raising them to the sky. On the screen the snow falls on her upturned face. She opens her mouth wide, shouts something, and the guard behind her reels backwards.

'No,' Reia says again, the word a tiny puff of breath.

Amy's world turns to slow motion as Raza tumbles forwards, arms outstretched. Amy thinks for a moment she is like a bird, soaring and free. She drops dart-straight, and the camera cannot keep up with her, but the crowd see her anyway, falling, falling, and then smashing into the glass box, shattering its roof to pieces, shards of glass flying everywhere and spraying out over the pitch like a million icicles.

Silence.

The crowd sit frozen and Amy's arm hurts with the strength of Reia's grip.

The camera catches up with itself and zooms to the box. Amy strains to see, but it's chaos in there, with glass and snow everywhere, an upturned trolley, something lying inert on the floor. Two – no, three somethings, buried in debris, a drip stand on its side over one of them, a ripped out cannula still attached to its dangling tube.

Amy gasps, her heartbeat speeding faster. Searches the scene closer, looking for details but not wanting to see them at the same time.

She makes out one of the faces, a torn black mask stretched over it. The executioner is down, still, and, collapsed on top of him, her body twisted and broken, is Raza. Amy feels sick. The blood…

Reia loosens her fingers from Amy's arm. 'Look there.' She points to the trolley. To the body still half-strapped to it. 'She's moving.'

A pale, bony hand feebly grasps at one of the straps, pulling at it. The camera zooms further in, and a blotchy image of Carys's face looms on the screen, and the crowd gasp as one. She has her head turned to the side, and she is retching.

The audience seem to suddenly catch up with themselves and with the situation. Some are on their feet, roaring, and some even cheering. Why are they cheering? Amy's head is slow. Cheering that Raza is dead or that Carys is alive? The stands erupt then, mayhem gripping the entire stadium, with people shouting at one another, tearing down to the stage, kids screaming, trainees bellowing at their Trainers.

Amy pauses for a moment, thinking of the promise she made to herself just a little while ago. That her actions today would make a difference, even in the tiniest way. And now she can extend that out. Now is the time. The spark bursts into flame. She grabs hold of Reia's and Will's hands, then pulls them forward, propelling herself down the steep, narrow concrete steps, down and down, through the surging crowd, down to the barriers. She vaults over, sees Reia and Will right behind her, urging her on. Rushes onto the pitch, pushes between two of the floats left there from earlier, runs across the expanse to the middle and then up the steps to the stage. She doesn't care what she is doing anymore. She's spent long enough in hiding, long enough pretending to be someone she's not. She barges straight into a shell-shocked Cadman and grabs the mic, then she pauses, raises it to her lips, gazes out at the turbulent crowd, at the others storming the field.

She looks up for a moment, right above her head; she can't see through the sturdy base of the shattered glass box. She takes a deep breath, then she pushes the words from deep inside, so loud they break through the chaos and bring the crowd into silence.

'I was known as Esla, the truth teller,' she begins, and Will and Reia are at her back, their hands on her shoulders. In the corner of her eye she spots Anson, looking on cynically, arms crossed. 'But my real name is Amy Plumber.'

The crowd shifts, stares. Amy sees her own face magnified back at her on all the screens around the arena.

'Esla was not a truth teller, but Amy is. I was cowardly once. I left my best friend alone to die. I… was trying to help. But I couldn't, in the end. In the end it was another dear friend…' she stops, shudders, '…Raza, who showed us the truth. She has brought everything down. She spoke to us louder than words could ever manage.'

Anson sidles nearer, his gait unsteady.

She shifts to the side. 'Because what Carys said originally on *The S Word* was the truth. And you all know it.'

Someone whoops and someone else roars. A kid near the front in the stand behind her hollers, 'Go, Amy!' Who is that? Is that an Ashton kid?

'So now you have a choice,' Amy bellows. 'All of you. Are you going to carry on like this? Or are you going to stand with me?'

The crowd fall hushed.

Then chaos breaks out. Kids are up on their seats, hollering, stamping up and down. Trainers have flails out, whipping them, shouting, but still they stand tall. More and more of them. Some of them with their parents, standing alone, tiny figures with arms raised high. More people storm the pitch, the stage, some swarming up towards the Commander's box.

Then Anson is next to her. Breathing down her neck; great rancid fumes laden with alcohol. 'I knew my girl would be here,' he says, glancing back at Lora, who sits still on her purple judge throne, pale and shaking. 'Told you, didn't I?' He glares up into his box then, and Amy follows his gaze to Gardener, who stands leering, his gaze a spike in her gut even from so far away.

Anson snaps his fingers at his security detail. 'Arrest her.'

Amy turns. Runs. Doesn't leave a second for them. Aware of Reia and Will, streaming close behind, she bolts for the stand ahead, where the Commander's box sits high up, full of Productives raising fists. As she runs she notices another commotion; more people running from another direction, a tunnel leading from the entrance. Vaguely familiar. No time to look. Others are running with her. She sprints on, her legs light with new strength. Hears a shot behind her, then Anson's voice bellowing, 'Don't shoot. I want her alive.' She vaults the fence then slams herself onto the ground and crawls into one of the rows of people, keeping her head low, some of them patting her on the back as she goes. Reia and Will are hidden somewhere behind. Way above her, Gardener sneers down, rising from his seat and beginning to make his way through the box towards Jacob, who still sits surrounded by guards. Amy scrambles up a tier, and another, some hands helping her, some slapping her down.

She will keep going until every tiny drop of this new, justice-raged strength has drained out of her.

35

THE ARENA

Now

ᴊACOB

T HE SCREW HAS torn a chunk out of his hand. He feels it now, gaping raw, burning at him as he tries to make sense of what he's just seen. He grips the screw in his other hand, staring up at the screen, drinking it in, trying to see more of Carys. Did she move? He's sure she moved.

Amy's on her way up here. He's seen her down there, way below him, somewhere in the tiers below Anson's box. What the heck is she doing? She's going to get shot. NForce are everywhere, training weapons on the crowd, shots ringing out as people get into fights. Jacob shuffles on his seat, desperate to get free. The screw is too large to pick the handcuffs. He doesn't know what his emotions are right now; doesn't have time to think about that. The guards flanking him sit up straight, hands on guns, tension tight in the set of their shoulders.

He can't let hope in. There are too many elites, too many Party members, too many loyal Productives. The rebels outside never made it in, and there aren't enough to challenge the NForce, even though the place is going wild. Maybe people are turning, he thinks; he hopes. Maybe Amy's message got through. He throws a glance back at Principal and Gardener; Gardener, who is out of his seat and shoving people out of the way, looks like he's been punched by a large lemon, and Principal sits frozen, staring at the screen.

Carys. She is there and she is alive. But Raza...

There's a jagged rock lodged in his throat, and he wants to weep and laugh all at the same time.

So much chaos. Movement all around him. But in the Commander's box, people are still, tense, disapproving. Somewhere way behind him two kids are locked in a screaming match. People are running everywhere: to the stage, through the tunnels to the exits, up and down the stairs on every stand. It's like a kind of madness has taken hold of the whole place and is shaking it to and fro.

'Jacob!'

The shout is harsh. Loud. Familiar. Who the—

Two people are pushing their way up through the crowds towards him, hurdling the enclosure round the box then shouldering through a bunch of totally wasted Productives who laugh and cheer as they boulder through. Jacob stares. Leans forward. Stares more. It couldn't be—?

'Jacob.'

It's his father. Edlin Trader, here in the flesh, when he should be at the Midlands Compound Festival. And... who is that just on his tail? Tall, formidable, familiar... *what?*

Miss Trainer One?

Is he in some kind of dream? That's it. This whole thing. It's a dream he's made up to get through the trauma of losing Carys. That whole bonkers thing with Raza and the crane, this arena erupting, Amy on the stage, and now his pops and Trainer One of all people, laying into the guard on his right, knocking him flat out. Jacob closes his eyes. He'll wake up soon.

'Jacob, get the hell up.'

He snaps his eyes open. 'Father? What are you—'

Edlin shakes his head. 'No time. You gotta get out of here.' He bends close to Jacob's ear, hisses, 'There's a bomb.'

Jacob can't think straight. His mind is befuddled, trying to make sense of it all. He frowns at his father and side-eyes Trainer One. 'What's *she* doing here?'

Edlin is scrabbling through the guard's pockets. 'Here.' He has his keys. But the other guard is on them, wresting them from Edlin's fingers, trying to balance his handgun in his other hand. Jacob smashes his body into him as hard as he can, but the guard takes the gun and thumps it against his head, then into Edlin's arm. Then Trainer One is up in the guard's face, and Jacob sees it in her hand: An NDart. She's injected the guy in two seconds flat, and he slumps in his chair, his eyes closing.

'C'mon.' Edlin grabs Jacob's arm and pulls him forward then shoves a key into his cuffs and frees him. Jacob twists his hands round and round, trying to get some feeling back. He keeps the screw tight in one, just in case.

Trainer One turns to Edlin. 'Ed, come on. We can't wait any longer.'

Edlin shades his eyes as he stares up at the sky. 'I know. But if we can get Amy—'

'We must go. I can hear the Copter already.'

Edlin runs a hand over his beard; it is dripping with sweat. 'Try the radio again.'

Trainer One shakes her head. 'Nothing.'

Jacob is reeling. 'Anyone want to tell me what's going on?'

Edlin glances at him. 'No time. Get up. Hurry.' He yanks at Jacob's arm. 'Follow us through. Now.'

But Jacob will not go without Amy. The crowd in the tiers below the box is seething, and he can't see her, but he's not going to leave now. And he's definitely not going to leave without Carys. She's up there, alive, and he has to get to her.

His father's words rattle in his head: *There's a bomb.*

'Come on,' Trainer One bellows, right in his face.

He stares at her. 'Why would I listen to *you*?'

She steps back, and he swears he sees something in her eyes. Regret? Nah. Can't be. 'We'll explain later,' she says.

'You go,' Jacob says. 'I'll follow as soon as I've got Amy and Carys.'

His father's face is creased with desperation. 'You're a stubborn fool.'

'Takes one to know one.'

Edlin grabs his arm again and pulls at it. 'You have to come.'

Jacob shrugs him off. 'Don't have to do anything. I'm waiting for my friends.'

Edlin seems to slump before him, the fight draining out of him in front of Jacob's eyes. 'Then I'm helping.'

Trainer One's face is as pale as the falling snow. 'You can't.'

Edlin touches her arm, and Jacob notices a strange intimacy in it. 'You keep trying the radio. Get the pilot to abort. I'll be out asap. Okay?'

She stares at him, the lines on her brow creasing into little peaks above her nose. 'Ed—'

'Go.'

She takes one last long look at him, then glances at Jacob, nods, and takes off back down towards the edge of the box, yelling into the radio. Jacob sees it before his father does: the NForce guard, advancing on her from behind, his gun pointed straight at the back of her head. Jacob shoves Edlin aside and dives after them, smashes the screw into the guard's neck just as he shoots; the bullet goes wide. Trainer One turns, staggers, the guard falling flat on his face on some drunk baying Productive's lap. Trainer One locks eyes with Jacob for a moment and something passes between them. He can't grab hold of it, can't reconcile the Trainer One he knows with whatever the hell is happening here. She gives him a slow nod, a thanks, and then turns, vaults the fence, bolts off down the steps, stumbling in these stupid high heels she's wearing.

Edlin lays a hand on his shoulder. 'Thank you.'

Jacob wriggles his hand away. 'Yeah. Well. Are you going to tell me anything?'

'Look. There aren't enough of us in here to challenge the NForce. And the bomb—' He hisses the last word, glancing up at the sky, where a dot approaches somewhere east of the arena.

'I don't care.' Jacob starts to make his way down the box, searching the crowd for Amy.

'We've got people doing their best out there,' Edlin says, eyes scouting the arena.

'Who's "we"? What people?'

His father looks right at him. 'The Resistance.'

Jacob stares. His father has been working with the mysterious Resistance? And Trainer One?

'We really do need to get out,' Edlin says, quieter now, as if calming things down will persuade him.

'You're going to bomb the arena. The Resistance.' Jacob sees it all now.

'Something had to be done. All these Party members… all these oppressors… we have to get rid of them, Jacob.'

Jacob realises it for the first time. 'You're calling me Jacob.'

'I… yes.'

Jacob swallows. 'You're taking out the whole arena?'

'Most of this side. Look… I wanted to stop it.'

Jacob puffs his cheeks out. 'Yeah.'

'I tried. But it's done, see. We can't stop it now. Please, son. Please come with me now.'

'And the rebels outside from the forum? They could get hurt too. Did you think of them?' Jacob says, feeling the heat curling in his chest. 'Did you think of the trainees in here?'

Edlin takes his arm. 'I'm trying. Come on.'

That's when he feels it. A heavy thump on his neck, choking him, pressing him forward. Who is—? He grabs for his father, but Edlin is out cold on the floor, a wound on his cheek. Jacob lurches, nauseous. Is he okay? He bends down, finds his father's pulse; strong.

And then someone hits him again.

He staggers back. His assailant is round in front of him now, just near the front edge of the box, which extends out over the steep tiers underneath.

Gardener.

Of course it's Gardener.

He's been waiting for him all day, in some ways. His promise stalking him: *You will die with Girl Clerk.* And now he's here to fulfil it, and Jacob has no strength left to fight. He kicks out at him and Gardener crashes his fist into his face, his eyes blazing with madness. 'You didn't think I'd forget, did you?'

Jacob still has the screw, bloodied from the guard's neck. He gets a tight grip on it and brings it slamming into Gardener's face. Misses as Gardener ducks, laughing. 'Think I'm stupid?' Gardener grabs his wrist, twists; the screw goes tumbling to the ground. How did Gardener get so strong? Jacob staggers, his back right against the barrier. He turns his face, sees the sheer drop below down to the lower tiers, his stomach churning at the sight. Gardener comes closer, gets him in a bear hug then shoves him back against the barrier, which creaks and dents as Jacob's body smacks into it. He bends double, winded.

Gardener has a gun in his hand. 'I've waited so long for this.' His sharp ferret teeth are bared in an ugly grin and Jacob wants to lunge at him, to shatter them all apart in his mouth. But the gun is on him. And Gardener means it. His finger is on the trigger, squeezing—

Crash. What the—

Someone's there. Principal? No, she's still in her seat above, still frozen, glaring down at them. Someone has rushed in like a little ball of fire and slammed their body into Gardener's back.

Amy.

And there, near the top of the box, scrambling to follow her, Will. And Reia.

Gardener whips round, shoves the gun in her face now. His grin widens. 'Ah! Two for one. This was my dearest wish!' He grabs her arm, pushes her back against Jacob.

But he didn't reckon on this superhuman strength she seems to have suddenly got hold of. She bares her teeth at him, shrieks in his face, and goes flying at him, head-butting his neck, grabbing his arm, twisting him round. Jacob is still winded; he can't get his breath. The world is fading at the edges, black dots dancing in his vision. Is it just more dream? Gardener has his gun up again, going for Jacob; this time he shoots. Misses again. Pulls up the gun quick, finger on the trigger—

Amy grabs Gardener's thinning hair. Pulls hard. Grabs his coat, his scarf, shoves him so hard back against the barrier it bends and squeals and one of its panels goes flying back down into the crowd below. Amy keeps shoving, her face a mask of fierce rage, trying to wrest the gun, but he pulls away from her, goes lurching backwards through the gaping hole in the barrier.

Jacob can see it registering on his face as he goes. The realisation. The horror. He falls, and Jacob hears the thump below, the crack of Gardener's head on one of the tiered seats, the silence.

Then Reia and Will are on them. 'Let's go.' They help Jacob up; the air puffs from his lungs in tiny wheezes.

'My... pops.' He points to Edlin, squirming on the ground.

Reia nods. 'On it.' She helps Edlin up. He groans, and she mops his bloody cheek with her sleeve. 'Amy. Come on.'

Amy stands frozen by the gap, looking down at Gardener's twisted body. Jacob takes her hand. 'Come... on. Bomb.'

Edlin and Reia start towards the gate at the left side of the box, and Will helps Amy and Jacob. Way above them the Copter circles, its whumping blades slicing through the mayhem in the arena. Edlin starts to hurry. 'Come on. Come on.'

Below them, Anson is still on the stage, staring up at the glass box, weaving and wobbling as two NForce guards prop him up. In their box, people start to move, a sudden atmosphere of tension cutting through drunken stupors and pulling people to their feet. A mass of them now, shoving one another out of the way, shouting and kicking and clambering over seats and barriers.

Down in the arena, elite NForce are everywhere, gunning people down, never mind whether friend or foe now. Jacob heaves himself down the steps, glancing up at the box. He has to get up that crane. But on the pitch thousands of people scrabble for the tunnels, trying to escape the incessant fire. Jacob's heart is exploding, his breath still seized by Gardener's iron shove.

The elites are organising themselves, surrounding the pitch, weapons trained inwards, a growing circle of them. The arena starts to calm, people to freeze. The helicopter thumps above. Jacob sees Trainer One dash through a tunnel, slipping from the clutch of an officer. One of them is on the stage, pushing aside a stunned Cadman Showman, bellowing into the mic. 'You are surrounded. Now, return to your seats, or we will continue to fire.'

Edlin glances up wildly. Pushes his hands through his hair. 'We have to get out.'

People are giving up. Making their way back into the stands, crouching under their seats. The elites are strengthening in every moment. Out of the corner of his eye, Jacob sees more guards hustling Anson, Lora and the other judges off the stage and towards the exit tunnel.

The officer on stage waits for silence to fall, then says, 'Oswall Trader and Esla Plumber, you are fugitives from the law, and I give permission to anyone nearby to apprehend or shoot you.'

Amy pulls down this hideous *S Word* cap she's wearing and looks down at the ground. Jacob feels exposed, out here on the pitch, and he's right to feel like that. Some dude with a Commander Lucan scarf comes bowling up to him, grabs him by his collar. 'I got one! I got one!' He starts tugging Jacob over to a nearby elite officer. Jacob kicks out at him, trips him, sends him flying, but the officer is on him now—

A roar outside. No, in the tunnel. Coming closer. A great, mighty roar and a wave of NForce lurching back as a tightly packed crowd come rushing through, shouting, waving and chanting their slogan: 'Power to the Weak! Justice for All!' Again and again and again, more and more of them.

The rebels. Warden's there, and Mercia, and – oh, Boy Lawyer, behind them.

But more now. There are more of them here, powering through, streaming onto the pitch. More than the crowd that got locked outside. Some of these look emaciated and pale but stand tall anyway. One woman is chasing a messy-haired kid who looks a bit familiar, grabbing him by the hand. 'Harry! Told you not to go in!'

Reia gasps. Stares. Breathes out a word. 'A… Ava?'

The woman turns at her name, breaks into a huge grin, drags the boy over. 'Reia!' She hugs her tight, and Jacob sees the imprints of tears on her face, specked by dirt. Then she spots Jacob's father. 'Ed!'

'How are you here?' Reia says, but the crowd is too big, the noise bigger, and they're all caught up in it, waves and waves streaming in. Some going down under bullets, some diving for the NForce officers, taking them down. The audience are alive again, on their feet, scrambling down to the pitch. More and more of them take up the chant: 'Power to the Weak. Justice for All!' and Jacob thinks the words sound like a long-ago summer day.

The tide has turned.

But the helicopter hovers above, lower now, nearer, its blades casting long shadows over the churned-up slush.

36

THE ARENA

Now

THE RESISTANCE

ANNE TRAINER ONE pushes through the tunnel, screeching into the radio. 'Do you read? Do you read?' The handset just throws static back at her. She throws a glance over her shoulder, looking for him. She's been a pain to him, she knows that; cold, mean, sullen. It's how everyone has always expected her to act, after all. Even when she was a child, back in pre-training, they called her the Ice Queen. But with Edlin she wants to be different. She feels softer around him, somehow, more alive than before. He'd better get himself out of that carnage in there.

She rubs her back where the guard hit her. Thinks of young Jacob, his bravery, and the way she used to treat him. Bellows into the radio again: 'Anyone? Pilot?'

Out by the entrance more Resistance folk hover at the edges along with thousands of people who've made it out, some of them sprinting off down the street, some huddling in groups, gazing at the other, bigger crowd, the one going the other way, breaking through the barriers and storming into the arena. Rebels from the forum and now a whole load of very dishevelled and determined looking folk, some of whom she recognises.

She sees her former colleague, Miss Warden, near the front with some of the Ashton youngsters. How did she not know Warden was on their side? They could have teamed up. Maybe even been friends…

She becomes aware of another sound. Oh, just the helicopter, dead above. Wait… no. That's not theirs, that's a brand new NForce military Copter with all its bells and whistles. Their Sea King hovers over the other side of the arena, its rust-streaked metal fuselage dirt-grey against the white sky. This is not good. She stabs the button again. 'Abort. Abort. Do you read?'

The pilot they sent is too young. She knew that, really, but chose to blank it out. He's just a kid, barely older than some trainees. He might be trained with NForce, but he doesn't have years of experience to draw on in a catastrophic situation like this. She shields her eyes as she stares at the sky. Come on. Answer.

A crackle. 'Ed?'

She presses the handset to her lips. 'It's Anne. You've got to abort.'

More crackling. '… ready.'

'No. No. The Commander has gone. I repeat, the Commander has gone. It's chaos in there, and a whole crowd of rebel groups have just stormed the place. A load from the Think too. Some of our people. Abort. Did you hear me?'

His voice is so achingly young. '… can't hear you. I'm going in.'

'No! No!' But the thing just crackles at her.

She clutches the radio tight, watching as their Sea King circles around the crane at the far end, then as the NForce Copter goes after it. 'No. Listen. Get out!' she yells, but the pilot doesn't hear. Why are their communications so bad? If they hadn't lost so much in the destroyed camps…

She feels so helpless. She knows she made a snap decision, going back on their plans like this, but she also knows it was the right thing to do. But it looks like they're just too late. And now she'll lose Ed, too, just when—

The Copters are too close.

Crackles. 'What… advise… Mayday!'

Then nothing.

She watches, pacing, the radio sticky in her sweat-slicked hands. What is the pilot doing? He's so young. He's panicking. Trying to wrest the machine back round, out of the arena. Too near that crane. The NForce Copter goes after him. But he's losing control. Anne can only imagine what he's feeling up there: the confusion, the chaos below, the snow on his windshield, the NForce on his tail. The Sea King seems to stall, to shiver in mid-air, and the NForce are too close.

They crash into one another with a great bang, and the Sea King starts spiralling, its tail section catching the crane near the top then slamming once again into the NForce machine.

They both go up in a thunderous fireball.

The bomb.

Anne runs her hand over her hair. *Too young. Too young.* She sprints back through the tunnel. The NForce Copter is still over the stadium, its blades whumping, slower, slower as it tumbles, great fiery debris raining on the crowd on the pitch, now a huge mass of people: NForce, Productives, rebels. They scramble out of its path, retreating up to the stands, the whole place in chaos. It crashes near the stage, its fuel tank rupturing into another huge explosion, digging a crater in the pitch.

That's when the fireworks start.

Anne stares. A whole lot of them, all going off at once, an array of colours sparkling against the snow-and-fire sky. The crash must've set them off. People turn, watch, scream, run. NForce guards pile out of the tunnel, getting out of there, no longer caring, and no one is shooting any more. The rebels stay on the pitch, watch the show, roar the chant.

Anne gets her head together, looking for their Sea King. It's gone down the other side, near the crane. Then she sees it: the crane is shifting, squealing, leaning, leaning some more. Its cab is on fire. Damn it. 'Move out of the way!' she screams in the direction of the crowd, but they've already seen it. The main jib, under extreme stress as the whole structure shudders, starts to detach from the mast, slowly, creakingly descending, the glass box hanging at an awkward angle. Anne rushes for the stage, bellows at the last two members of the band who still sit there, frozen, 'Get away from here. The box is coming down.' They snap into action, abandon their instruments, head for the tunnels. Everyone else is long gone – Elva Anchor, Cadman Showman, the sound and light crew – all deserted. Anne wipes sweat from her forehead and watches the great crane slowly, haltingly buckle, its weakened mast smashing into the western stand.

The jib's rust-yellow frame wails, twisting and tearing itself away from the main structure as its connections fail, slowly, painfully, the shattered glass box suspended not twenty-five metres from the ground now. Anne wills it on. *Slowly. Slowly, now. Hang on a little longer.*

She sees Jacob and Reia and Edlin making for the other side of the stage and goes after them. Is it possible they could get the wretched girl out, after all this? The arm tilts further, the box plummeting several feet as another part of its lattice frame tears away at the top; Anne's stomach plummets along with it. She can just see inside it now but can't make a whole lot out; it's one huge mess in there. The jib lurches, taking Commander Lucan's bronze head clean off its body. For a moment, Anne almost laughs. She catches up with the others and they watch in horrified fascination as the steel wire securing the box to the crane's hook starts to fray and then snap under intolerable pressure, pitching the box straight at the stage. It crashes down, showering glass in every direction, then the rest of the jib follows, narrowly missing the box and slamming into the track where floats stand abandoned and now flattened. The once-great central mast of the crane leans precariously against the arena's western stand, the Sea King's rotors tangled in its cold embrace.

37

THE ARENA

Now

Amy

AMY CLAMBERS OVER the remains of a smashed up drum kit, following Jacob to the box now standing wrecked on the stage, its glass exterior jagged and broken. He's making for the door, although it's not really a door anymore.

'Careful,' Amy says, pointing at a shard of glass too near his arm. But he pushes through, knocking it away with his bare hands, already bruised and bloody.

She picks her way over more broken instruments and other debris to the doorway. The box is huge from here, its sturdy steel posts still giving it structure. Amy's pulse thumps against her throat as she ducks through under more broken glass and takes in the grim scene. Glass everywhere. The floor is soaking wet, coated in melted snow and something else. Blood. Amy turns away from the sight of it and focuses her eyes on Jacob, who scrabbles at the straps still tethering Carys to the trolley.

'C'mon, Carys,' he says softly. 'Wake up.'

Amy goes closer and grabs her hand. 'Carys!'

Her face is grey-white, her body bruised and dirty in a torn Ashton uniform. Amy bends closer to her and brushes a tangled string of dark blonde hair from her forehead.

Carys opens her eyes.

She looks at Jacob. Then looks at Amy. Her face creases. 'W... where...'

'Shh,' Jacob says. 'You're okay. We're getting you out of here and we'll find you a doctor.'

Carys turns to the side. Vomits all over Jacob's trainers. 'Sh... shorry.'

He grins. 'You can clean it up later.' He moves closer and kisses her dirt-streaked cheek. 'Thought I'd lost you,' he whispers.

Amy watches her in wonder. How can this be true? How is this really happening? The events of the last half-hour gallop through her mind at top speed, leaving her reeling. She can't get a grip on anything. Gardener... she killed him? Jacob's dad, here and working with the Resistance? And was that Trainer One she saw with him? She shakes her head, tries to clear it, to climb into this moment. *Carys is alive.*

Somehow, all three of them are back together, here in a smashed-up glass room.

She glances over her shoulder, out at the surging crowd on the pitch and in the stands. It's a lot emptier than before, but there are still thousands of people here, and they are coming together in one chant: 'Power to the Weak. Justice for All.' Above them, the screens are blank, cut dead soon after Raza fell and Amy gave her little speech.

Raza.

Amy doesn't want to see, but she needs to look after her now. To make her warm. She stumbles over to the inert body in the centre, still draped over the executioner. 'Help me,' she says to Jacob, and they roll her away gently. Her face is strangely serene, only her twisted body evidence of the fall. Amy whispers in soothing tones as she lies her out on the floor, smoothing her matted black hair. 'We need a blanket,' she says. But there's nothing in this room to cover her.

In the doorway Will and Reia hover with Edlin Trader, heads bowed. Amy wants to curl up here, right now on this killing ground, to push out the sea of emotion that swirls in her belly.

Jacob's father steps in quietly and lifts Raza in his arms, wrapping her in his coat. 'We won't leave her here. Jacob, Amy, you can help Carys, yes?'

Amy nods mutely and takes Carys's arm as Jacob takes the other, helping her onto her feet. She grunts as her legs wobble under her. 'D… dizzy.' She slumps against Jacob, her body going limp.

'She's okay. She's passed out,' Jacob says, lifting her into his arms. 'Let's get her out of here.'

Back on the pitch the crowd fall to silence as their ragged little procession makes its way through. Amy scouts anxiously for NForce, but they've all gone. She cradles her injured hand, trying not to think about Gardener's face as he fell, the crack of his head on the seat below. She's not sorry he's dead, so why is she even thinking about him? She remembers the leer on his face back in the Ashton Think when Principal commanded her and Jacob to strip. Thinks about how he liked to get close to her, to breathe on her, to creep around her. How he toyed with them, mowing them down in his car, trying to poison them, sending threatening texts.

Then she sees his face again as he falls, hears the crack of his head. Knows that another little piece of her is broken.

The crowd on the pitch thickens as more people pour down from the stands. The remains of the Copter still smoulder behind her, the crane's mast squealing as it shifts and falters against the stand. Reia's friend who escaped from the Think, Ava, her name was, Amy thinks, comes rushing towards them, the boy in tow, shouting, 'Carys! Carys!' But Carys is blotto, slumped in Jacob's arms.

Ava turns, walks alongside Amy, studies her face. 'You're Amy.'

Amy nods slowly, uncomfortable. 'Y… yeah…'

Ava blushes. 'Yeah. It's just…' She trails off, scans the crowd, a big grin on her face. 'I need to find someone. Be right back.'

Amy walks on, aware of a small hand creeping into hers. She looks down at the kid's face and remembers who he is. Boy House, the kid they sent to the Think for disturbing the crowd at *The S Word.* 'I knew you were good,' he says to her, his serious brown eyes fixed on hers. 'Always kept saying to Carys you were good.'

She looks back at him, stores this away with the rest of it all. Is she, though? Is she good? She hears the crack again. His head on the seat…

Outside the arena she can breathe again. The crowd is thinner out here, groups huddled together against the increasing snowfall. Edlin Trader takes Raza off towards the crane site. 'I'll lay her with some others who sacrificed themselves today,' he says over his shoulder, and for a moment Amy sees Aiden in him. 'I'll be gentle. We'll come back for them soon. Give them a proper burial. I'll meet you back here in a while.'

Amy's chest aches so much she wonders if it might splinter into tiny pieces. She bends over, suddenly unable to breathe, unable to stop the sobs that threaten to rupture her in two. Feels the tears streaming down her cheeks. Not now, she thinks. There's no sign of any NForce, but they still need to get to safety. She bats away her tears, angry at them, at herself, but feeling the lightness of joy somewhere within them too, its sparkles swallowing up some of the darkness. Jacob leans Carys against a wall and puts his hand on Amy's shoulder. 'You okay?'

She smiles through her tears. 'I don't know.'

'Nor me.' He crouches next to Carys, wraps his jacket around her.

'What now?' Amy says.

'I… I think we should wait for my father. His group might have some plans. Though…' he turns his head back to the arena, sighs, '… if they are more bombs, I don't want any part of it.'

'No.' Amy curls herself up next to them both, pulling her scarf tight. It's so cold, she realises. She can't feel her feet.

She hears a hoarse whisper. A hesitant voice, breaking through the group milling round next to them. 'Amy.'

The voice isn't real. Maybe Amy passed out too; maybe it all got too big for her in there.

'Amy.'

It's a voice from her dreams. A voice that loved her, that soothed her when she was afraid, embraced her when she was sad. She looks up slowly, doubtfully, trying to see through the haze of tears. She sees her shape there, right in front of her, shimmering and real all at the same time.

'Mum?'

Dad's there too, right next to her, thinner, greyer, but still Dad, still so very loved. Amy's on her feet, diving at them, the sparkles of her tears raining in a hundred different directions. She falls into her mother's embrace and nothing else matters anymore. She is here. Dad is here. This moment she dreamed of for so long. 'Where… why…' she gasps, hugging them again and again and again.

Mum strokes her hair. 'You've grown so much. So beautiful.'

Her dad kisses her cheek. 'I never believed them on that *S Word*.'

Amy hugs him. 'I know. I know.' She doesn't know how to process this moment so she falls into it, laughing, crying, hugging till her bones ache. Reia's friend, Ava, and the boy watch from next to them, laughing along.

Her mum spots Carys on the ground with Jacob. 'She needs help?'

Amy nods. 'Think there's poison in her system. But we don't know where to go now. They're going to be out for us everywhere. It's not like we'll be able to get out at the barrier.'

Her mum crouches with Carys and Jacob, taking up Carys's wrist. 'Her pulse is good. She's been sick?'

'Yeah.'

'Good. Good. She may be able to sleep it off.' She looks at Jacob. 'Where can we go? Tell you one thing, I'm never going back to that Think.'

Jacob shakes his head. 'I don't know. I don't know what to do now.' He cradles Carys in his arms.

'Come with us.'

Amy whips her head around, widens her eyes in disbelief. Another sight for sore eyes. 'Coran!'

Coran looks tussled and hassled, as if he's been in a fight or two. By his side is Ash, and another guy… in an NForce uniform.

Amy steps backwards.

'It's okay,' Ash says. 'Alfred here is with us.'

Amy studies the guy. He has loosened his uniform at the neck and taken his cap off. 'You sure?'

Ash smiles. 'He's been turning for a while, and your little speech kind of finished him, right, Alf?'

Alfred looks uncomfortable, but nods. 'I couldn't be doing with the whole thing anymore. What you said… it got a lot of people. Trust me. And when they showed that mess of a video of Girl Clerk there, folk got turned by that too, even though the fools were trying to indoctrinate us all further.' He laughs. 'I'm not the only one from my quarters who's thinking this way. I assure you.'

'So how did you get free?' Jacob says to Ash.

Ash hops from one foot to the other, his face red. 'Alfred was one of my guards, and Coran took out the other. Should've seen him.'

Amy is not sure what to think. Can they trust this guy? Can they ever trust any NForce or Party people?

She thinks about Abs. Perhaps it really is possible for people to change.

Coran steps forward, takes Amy's hand, gestures at Carys. 'Bring her to Lora's.'

'But that's no way safe!'

'She's at the Commander's mansion for now. But even if she comes back, she's not going to shop you, darling. She's in pieces.

Come on. We'll get you back through the streets. We have an armed guard, after all.' He glances at her parents. 'Room for whoever needs it.'

Jacob grins at him. 'I always knew you'd come through for us, Coran.'

38

THE CENTRE

Half an hour later

JACOB

JACOB'S FEET HURT as he drags through the Centre with the mass of rebels, Resistance and Think escapees. All of them united in one purpose. 'We're marching on Party HQ,' his father had told him, back at the arena. 'We can't let it go now we've come this far. We must bring them down. Burn the whole lot of them if we have to.'

Jacob had just wanted to go back to Lora's with Carys and the others. He couldn't take his eyes off her now he'd got her back. She was pale, emaciated and filthy, but more beautiful than ever.

'You go,' Amy had said softly. 'They need you.'

How could they need him? What difference could he make? Sure, there was a part of him that wanted to march with them now, take the whole lot down, but the thought of it wasn't as sweet as he'd once imagined.

Reia and Will had agreed. 'We're with you,' Reia said. 'This crowd needs direction so things don't go even more down the pan.'

Amy had gone off with Coran, Ash and the guard, who Jacob hoped was sincere, and a few others – Amy's parents, the kid from *The S Word*, and a few more kids and sick-looking prisoners. And, of course, Carys, still in and out of consciousness. Jacob felt torn in two. What if he'd just got her back only to go and get himself arrested or killed?

But, as Amy and the others encouraged him to go, his grandfather's words rattled round his mind once again: *Stand at the crossroads.* Was this his crossroads? What would it really mean, in the heat of these adrenaline-packed moments?

He looks down at his feet now and thinks about the path ahead. Nearby, his father leads the crowd with Trainer One and a few others who must be Resistance, and Reia and her friend Ava are just behind. Will has disappeared; gone off to look for his dad and his brother, somewhere in the surging crowd. Has it got bigger along the way? They seem to be gaining people at every step, and Jacob has no idea who he can trust anymore. It all feels surreal as they march on in silence, grim, determined, wounded.

Ava catches up with them, turns to Edlin. 'When did you lot get into this whole bomb thing? Before I was arrested we were talking peaceful revolution, not full-scale murder.'

Jacob's father seems to shrink even as he walks. 'It just seemed like an opportunity we couldn't pass up. At the time, I mean. Peaceful protest was never going to work, let's face it. All those Party heads and NForce together… seemed like a gift.'

Ava frowns. 'Guessing it was Arthur and Dale who pushed that one forward.'

Edlin scratches his neck. 'I was… on board for it. For a long time.'

'Wasn't just you,' Trainer One says.

'Was only when we realised the scale of it… I mean, all those kids…' Edlin says quietly.

Jacob steps closer. 'So you were willing to blow everyone up. Including Carys. Including me.'

His father says nothing.

Jacob breathes out a long puff of frozen air. Why is he surprised his father is like that? It's not like he's ever been much of a dad to him. He thinks of his riches, his big, opulent home in the posh bit of the Midlands Compound, then his mind flashes to the weapons stash his father showed him and Amy all those months ago when they were planning to break into the Think. He had a whole arsenal thing going on there. Jacob had been kind of disgusted, kind of impressed at the time, but he'd never really taken any time to think about why Edlin had all that stuff. He'd spun some crap about wanting to be well defended or something; same went for that secret room he has up there. But now it all makes sense.

'You think I'm impressed with you for all this?' he says to his father.

Edlin gazes straight ahead, shoving his hands into his pockets. 'No.'

Jacob rolls his eyes.

'I did what I had to do,' Edlin says.

'Why'd you never tell me? How long has this all been going on, anyway?'

Edlin sighs. 'Look, I have a lot to tell you. But maybe now's—'

'No. Tell me now. You owe me that much.' Jacob looks at the massive Party HQ building up ahead, its mirrored facade throwing the snow back at the sky.

'I didn't want to risk you getting hurt,' Edlin says.

'So you pretended you were… what? Like some super loyal Party minion all these years?' Jacob wants to spit on the ground.

'Look. I've been in this for the long haul. You wanted to know, so… yeah. I've been heading this up for about sixteen years now. Since Benedict—'

'Benedict? Benedict Clerk?'

'Carys's father – and her mother – were involved. They were kind of our founders, actually. It was Benedict who got me on this path.' Edlin clears his throat. 'He was… a very dear friend to me.'

'And you never thought you could trust me with any of this stuff.'

'I always loved you.'

Jacob feels the heat rising through his chest. 'Some way of showing it.'

'I know. I know. I just… I always wanted to protect you.'

'And Baba? Did he know too?'

'I think he might have suspected something, but I wanted to keep him safe, so I never said anything.'

Jacob folds his arms tighter around himself, shivering; he left his jacket with Carys. At least Baba wasn't keeping it from him. At least he has that.

'I know I got stuff wrong,' Edlin says.

'You think all this makes up for years of treating me so bad? You hit me. Ignored me. Half the time you weren't even around on Festival days. Did you even care?'

Edlin turns to him, stops for a moment, people bumping into him from behind. 'You don't know how much.'

'Yeah. You're right. I don't.'

'I… I'm sorry.'

Jacob turns away, keeps walking, fights back the tears. He snaps his head back around. 'Why'd you keep all that money, then, if you were into all this stuff? If you didn't actually believe in Newland? All those riches, when people are starving?'

'It was to keep up the facade. I was in a good position to co-ordinate things, with the Party behind me rather than on my back. You can see that, right?'

Jacob's throat aches really bad all of a sudden. 'Maybe. But…' he stops, swallows, '… you let them take Baba to the Think. When you knew damn well what was going on. A… and my mother, too. How do you think I could ever forgive you for that?'

Edlin looks at his feet. 'I… my hands were tied. I was horrified, both times, more than I can possibly say. Your mother… she was in this too. We were fast friends, all of us, me, your mum, Benedict and Sarah.'

'I thought Carys's mother was called Ora?'

'Oh, that was her Productive name, all right. But she kept Sarah for Benedict and all of us. Said it was who she really was. She was the best of us. The bravest.'

Jacob stores this away to tell Carys sometime. She'll love that.

'I wish I'd been able to stop them going to the Think,' Edlin says, and Jacob hears the crack in his voice. It's like he's seeing the real Edlin, for the first time ever, and he doesn't know what to do with it. 'When your mother got depressed, and they said she had to go to the Home... we both knew, of course. But I couldn't stop it.' He sinks his head into his hands. 'I couldn't stop it, and it's the biggest regret of my life.'

Jacob stares at him. Remembers how he didn't rat him and Amy out when he found them in his secret room. How he helped them. Sees the truth in his eyes, the long wounds of time reflected there. 'B... but you didn't seem to care, when Baba—'

'Oh, I did. I was keeping it all in. It wasn't easy, Jacob. I just couldn't... show anything. To keep you safe.'

'That's why you never let me bring Carys home for Festival.'

Edlin nods slowly. 'I knew who she was, of course. But I could never say anything.'

Jacob scrubs the tears away, irritated. 'So why'd you never call me by my name?'

Edlin exhales slowly, his breath a mist on the wind. 'I wanted to. I just... I could never be seen to be against the Party narrative, in any way at all. I... look. I screwed up. I know that. Knew it all along. Do you...' he turns to Jacob, touches him tentatively on the arm, '... think you might ever forgive me?'

Jacob can't find words, so he walks on mutely, trying to contain all the emotions. How is it that he can feel desperately sad and elated all together?

Trainer One turns to him. 'Your father has helped lots of people, you know.'

'Really.'

She blinks. 'Yes. We've not just been plotting away. We've been actively at work in getting people out of sticky situations and growing the movement.'

Jacob scowls. 'And you've been a part of this all along too?'

She nods.

'Then why were you always so vile to us trainees?'

She flushes. 'It was the same with me. The facade thing.'

'And the facade included bullying children.'

'I couldn't be seen to be different,' she says. 'I had to toe the line – more than any other Trainer there, so as not to fall under suspicion. So I guess…' she pauses, casting her gaze to the sky, '… I guess I overcompensated somewhat. With the strictness.'

'You're telling me.'

'I tried to be better. Did you not notice, as the years went by? Tried to advocate for trainees. I never used the flail myself, did I?'

Jacob thinks about it. About the amount of times he was flailed in that dismal Think. 'I guess not.'

'I left in the end. I couldn't do it anymore. It was… a heavy price, I was paying in there.'

Jacob bristles. 'And you don't think that price was heavy for us? I remember you screaming at Amy and Carys. Picking on Carys because she has difficulties with reading and writing. You were hideous when she was ill that time. What was all that about?'

She has the grace to look down at her feet. 'Like I said. Keeping up a pretence.'

'And you're not sorry for it?'

She pauses. 'Every day.'

He shakes his head. 'I don't know what to say to you. How to be.'

'It's okay.'

'Was anyone else there in on it, then? Not Principal, surely?'

She laughs. 'Not a chance. She was the reason I had to go full on dragon lady. She was suspicious of everyone. Her and that rat Gardener.'

'He's dead.'

Trainer One stares at him. 'What?'

'He went for me, back in the arena. Had a little accident for his trouble.'

'Oh. Oh, well, I can't say I'm going to miss him.'

Jacob smiles then, and they exchange something between them; something new. He thinks back to certain incidents at Ashton, seeing them with new eyes. Remembers something Carys told him later on, about when she'd been ill in Warden's sick bay. She'd overheard Trainer One trying to persuade Principal not to write Carys off as Unproductive there and then. Jacob had thought, back then, it was just so she could torment her some more, but now he knows different. Seeing her, and his father, in a new way is mind-bending, exhausting, frustrating, exhilarating. He tramps on, one foot after the other, the Party HQ building looming nearer and nearer.

It hits him then. His father and Trainer One stepped in at the last minute to save him and others. Doesn't make it right, what they planned, but they made a decision. They took a path. So what's the path ahead, now, for all of them? For all these bruised and battered people? There's a fight going on inside him, and it's not just about how to act with his father and Trainer One. It's bigger than that. It's a fight between what he wants and what is right. He's standing at Baba's crossroads.

'Do we want to be like them?' he says to his father, in tones so soft Edlin barely hears.

'What d'you mean?'

Jacob edges closer to him. 'The New Day Party began this whole thing with mass genocide. You know that, right?'

Edlin nods.

'Their narrative has always been killing. Mercilessly, gleefully. Justice has never been their thing.'

'Yup.'

'So we… I mean, you, the Resistance, but all of us here, actually – we could be starting something new here. But do we want to be like them? Do we want to go in that building right now and just kill, one after the other, till they're all slaughtered?'

He's asking himself as much as Edlin. Part of him does want that. Part of him is desperate for revenge, to go in there and slay without mercy. It's a part infused with strength, and it wrestles with something else in his mind. With the world he wants to see.

His dad trudges on, saying nothing.

'I don't want to be bad,' Jacob says. He thinks about the guard with Ash, the one who changed his mind. About Abs, who was ex-Party. About that NForce kid who got shot down at the camp, barely older than himself. Then he remembers Reia's words, back at the camp. *The small hard choices will sit easier if we make the right turning on the big hard choice.*

'You're not. Sometimes things must be taken down to be built up again,' Edlin says. 'Sometimes there isn't another way.'

'But you chose another way, back in the arena.'

'It doesn't mean I'm suddenly good. Far from it.' Edlin stares off into the distance, his eyes dark with pain. 'I thought I was good, see, doing all this. But then I saw all those children… saw you…'

Reia comes closer. 'We all have shades of good and bad. It's the actions we take that matter. I'm with Jacob. I think we have a chance to build better. I say we go in now, we get hold of them, march them all down to the Think. There are enough of us, and most of them will have scattered anyway.'

'And then?' Edlin says slowly.

'Then we do justice. Whatever that looks like.'

Edlin grits his teeth. 'They deserve to die.'

Reia shakes her head. 'They deserve to be punished. Don't you think life imprisonment would be better? Not just to stop the killing, though I think that is right, but also to actually punish. To keep them stewing in their own mess.'

'It was about innocents in the arena,' Edlin says. 'These people are not innocent.'

'No. They are not. But neither are you. Neither am I. This isn't about that, Ed. It's about mercy. It's about dignity. Humanity. We can choose to be who we want to be, right now.'

Jacob looks at her. 'Yeah. And it's like… then we're not stooping to their level. And how we go forward from now, how we treat people. All people. No more of this Productive and Unproductive nonsense.'

Reia smiles. 'Right.'

'I think they're right,' Trainer One says quietly, and Jacob stares at her. How could his words have this much power, when the fight is in himself as well? 'We go forward together. Let's get everyone stopping here, Ed. Get the crowd focused, like we're going to need to do in the days ahead. It's not like we have the weapons, anyway.'

Edlin frowns. 'I don't know what to do anymore.'

Reia steps forward, breaks through the ranks at the front, turns, spreading her arms. Her voice is crystal clear, breaking through the din. 'Wait.'

Somehow, in some miraculous way Jacob can't get a hold on, this unrelenting tide of rebels comes veering to a stop, there and then, to listen to this astonishing powerhouse of a woman.

PART IV

The After

39

THE CENTRE

One day after Festival

ℭARYS

T HE FIRST THING I become aware of is the gnawing hunger deep in my belly. I sit up, rub my head, blink. Where am I? Glimmers of the night before flicker through my mind. The pain. The sickness. Not knowing where I was, who I was, what was happening.

The bed is soft, the sheets cotton, long blue velvet curtains at the window. Lora's house? How am I here?

Someone's with me. An Amy-shaped lump, snuggled under the duvet, dark hair poking out in tufts, flat out. I want to hug her, to say I'm sorry for everything, but I need some time. Some quiet. I look down at my body, still clad in the hated Ashton uniform, at the bones standing out on my wrists, my hair hanging in filthy strings in front of my face, and everything comes back to me in a heady rush. The glass box. The executioner. Jacob, on the screen, cuffed by a guard.

And Raza.

It was only on the screen in my box I saw her. Standing tall, graceful, resolute, on the tip of that crane. Then falling.

And that's when things went black.

I knew, though. I knew when I woke up in the box, heard the chaos outside, the explosions, felt my whole body jar when the box slammed to the ground. I knew what Raza had done.

I am alive because of Raza, and I don't know what to do with that.

I stumble out of bed and straight into the shower, desperate to wash the whole thing away, like it will cleanse my inside as well. My mind reels, more flashes of the day before taunting me. Did I see Ava, out there outside the arena, or was that just my dizzy head? But I know Raza made it out, so maybe the others did, after all.

I find some old comfy clothes of Lora's laid out in the bathroom. I slip them on and glance at the clock on my bedside table. It's only five am, but I can't wait any longer. I tiptoe out of my room, leaving Amy still gently snoring away, and down Lora's sweeping staircase into the darkened kitchen. Is it safe in here? Are there NForce outside, waiting to take me back to the Think? I can't go back there, to the darkness, to the stench, to the desperation.

I make toast and coffee and sit at Lora's island, alone in the gloomy silence. I think of the last meal I had, not that I ate much of that; think of Anson's face leering above me, gloating. Where is he now?

'Since when were you an early bird?'

I whip my head around, my heart suddenly plunging into my stomach, my palms sweating. It's him. I saw him yesterday, in glimmers and bursts; saw him leaning over me in the box, lifting me into his arms, but now I see his face. His loved, loved face. I don't know what to do. My arms and legs are all tangled up. Do I go to him? Will my face betray the way I doubted him? Hated him, even, for so long? The sweat from my palms is on my forehead now. On my face, glowing, warming—

'Come here.' He's over before I can get off the stool, hugging me, kissing me all over my face. I can't find words for him, not in this moment, but that's okay.

'How are you feeling?' he says eventually, letting me up for air.

'I don't know. I was hungry, so...' I wave at the remains of my toast.

'You're okay, then.'

'I guess.' I don't really know what okay means. Not anymore. 'Who's here? What's happened? Are we safe?'

He smiles, pulls up a stool next to me, pinches a crust. 'Amy's here. And her parents, and a few others. Reia and Ava, too.'

'Ava?' Something warm bursts in my chest. 'And Harry?'

'Oh, the kid? Yep.'

'Wait. Did you say Reia?' I screw up my face, thinking. 'The Queen, right? Ava told me her name, back in the Think. She made it out of the bunker?'

Jacob strokes a strand of hair from my face. 'She and four of the girls. Hannah, Ella, Emma, Esther.'

I feel the mix fall heavy on me: the joy and the crush. 'Raza would be so happy.'

Jacob kisses my forehead. 'I know, love. Listen... I... I'm so sorry. That I didn't stand with you.'

I pick at some toast crumbs.

He shifts awkwardly, his mouth twisting, forming words that won't come. 'So... after we got you out, yesterday, the crowd marched on Party HQ.'

I stare at him. 'There were enough of them? Did... did they make it?'

He picks at his nails. 'We took some losses. But a whole lot of that elite NForce had already scarpered, along with like half the Party workers. We caught some left there and took them to the Think.'

'There are Party members in the Think?' I want to dance round the kitchen. To cheer. 'And... the Commander?'

Jacob shakes his head. 'We've all been out most of the night. Went to his mansion after storming HQ and the Think, but he wasn't there.'

'Lora?'

'Found her shivering in the kitchen. Couldn't get anything out of her. Reia and Ava brought her back here, tucked her into bed; she was like a little kid, they said.'

I lace my hands round my mug. 'So he's still out there.'

'My father's still looking, with some others from his group. Anson has supporters everywhere, though.'

'Wait. Your father?'

He grins. 'Oh, yeah. You didn't know. Turns out he's with the Resistance. Leads it, actually.'

I study his face. Can't tell whether he's proud or disgusted.

'We could've burned HQ down,' he says.

'But you didn't.'

'No. Reia turned out to be an incredible leader. Should've known it. She got us whipped into shape. Did this whole speech thing about how only light can cast out darkness. Some of us weren't sure, some wanted to storm in there, take the lot of them out. Even me, a bit. But Reia led us in, and it all just happened, you know? Messy, but different to what we expected. We've just got to decide what to do from now.'

'But… the rest of them. If they've scattered, they'll be back, they'll release them.'

'We… my father and his group I mean… have people there. In Party HQ and in the Think. The Resistance turned out to be a pretty big outfit – they've basically taken over HQ – and along with the whole forum movement, and your lot from the Think, it looks like we have a chance at something.'

'You *were* behind that forum,' I say, thinking about Boy Farmer in the Think, and how I'd refused to believe even the possibility that Jacob and Amy had done this. I breathe out slowly. 'So… it was you? In the tunnels, with Abs?'

Jacob's eyes are dark with sadness. 'I'm glad she made it through to you. She didn't give you my message?'

'She told us about the plans for all the inmates. Wait – that was going to be today!' I sit up straighter. 'Are they all safe?'

He shrugs. 'Some didn't make it at HQ or back at the arena. But yeah, most of them. My father's got them all in Party suites at HQ. Living it up in style.'

I hope Boy Farmer made it. One day I'll meet him. Give him a great big hug. 'They deserve it. But listen – what message? Abs was… very poorly. She died soon after. Her friend was with her, kind of. It's a long story.'

He takes my hand. 'We'll have all the time in the world soon. I asked Abs to tell you that I'd come for you. Tried, anyway.'

I see the world of pain written across his face. He looks older, somehow, like he's seen too many things. I squeeze his hand back. Sit there, letting the early morning silence drape us, for long, consoling moments.

'So, I'm to call you Oswall now, right?' I wink at him.

He cups my face in his hands. Stares right into my soul. 'I never want to hear that word again. A… and there was something else I asked Abs to tell you. That… that I love you.' Then he kisses me again, and it's like all the stuff that's unsaid between us hovers less fiercely, all the barriers we still need to cross loom less large.

He flicks on the NScreen above the island. A very flustered-looking Elva Anchor is standing a way away from Party HQ, hair whipping in the wind, throwing continual glances over her shoulder. She falters over her words, pressing an earpiece to her ear. 'And now we are hearing of more riots in the Northern Compound and the Glasgow Compound. Party officials' homes and Thinks are being targeted. Prisoners have been broken out and left to bring more violence to our streets.' She stops, listens, frowning. 'We are… happy to assure you that the Commander is safe and well, and will soon be leading the nation as always. The… the Party asks that all good Newlanders stand firm against these atrocities and come together to restore order. Do not bow to the rebels.' She glances down at her notepad, its pages flipping in the wind. 'Our NForce will continue to search for the three fugitives at the centre of all of this and bring them to justice. We will—'

I see people behind her. A growing crowd, with hastily crafted banners and flags. Not Newland flags. Are they... Union Flags? I think that's what they were called, the old Before flags. They are a swirl of glorious colour against the grey sky. Red, white, blue. Some of them trail streams of bunting in every colour of the rainbow, and the crowd surround Elva and her crew, chanting our slogan and singing something I can't make out. Yet they don't touch her. They part as she shoulders her way out, her face fallen in on itself, the camera following shakily. The newscast cuts out abruptly.

'So what now?' I say to Jacob.

'Let's get the pieces of ourselves back together first,' he says, grinning, and then catches me up in his arms again.

I'M IN THE den with Jacob when Amy comes in with Ava and Harry. 'I have a young man here who was desperate to see you,' she says, and Harry runs forward, sinks into the sofa next to me.

I take in his face, the freedom of him, and my heart swells so large it might burst to pieces. 'It's good to see you.'

'Ava got us through the tunnels. I didn't like them. They were dark.'

I cuddle him close. 'And you're here.'

He slumps against my shoulder. 'I'm hungry.'

'Coran's cooking us a big breakfast feast,' I say, nodding in the direction of the kitchen, tantalising aromas floating through. 'Sausages, bacon, pancakes... everything you can think of.' My mouth waters even as I say it; the toast barely filled a corner.

Harry's hair is as messy as always. I rumple my hand through it, grateful beyond words he is here. My mind flits to another boy his age I loved in another place, another time, who wasn't so lucky, and I hold Harry tight.

Ava crouches down with us, takes my hand. 'You've been so brave.'

Don't say that, I think. Don't say that, or I will start crying again, and I've already cried out all the tears in the world. And it's not me who was the brave one, anyway. I look at Ava, stare into her eyes, and know she's thinking of her, too.

'You found Lois and Alwin, then,' I say to Amy.

She beams so wide the whole room is brighter. 'Couldn't believe it when I saw them at the arena.'

'I've got so much to tell you about them. About the whole thing,' I say, longing to spring up, to hug her. But I can't shake off how I stopped trusting her, how she must see it written across my face.

'I know. Me too.' She comes closer and takes my hands, then kneels next to me, buries her face in my neck. 'I was so afraid—'

I kiss her hair. Allow this moment to wrap us both up together. 'I know.'

Lois comes in, clad in a white cloth dressing gown, ruffling her hair. Alwin follows closely, always slightly in her shadow, and I think he looks a little bit less broken than before. I take in the whole room and realise all the people I love most in the whole world are right here. I want to stay in this moment, to climb into it and keep it, to stop the world from turning.

Lois folds me into her arms. 'Dear Carys.'

Out of the corner of my eye I see Amy, looking on, a mixture of emotions flicking across her face. Is it that I got to be with her parents before she did? I don't blame her for feeling funny about that. But she smiles then, and her eyes are sparkling just like her mother's. Amy always was the one to show me how to bring kindness into darkness.

Lois takes my hand and leads me to a smaller sofa near the window, away from the others. 'I have something for you.'

I sit down next to her. 'You do?'

She digs into the pocket of her dressing gown. 'It's from… Raza.'

My body goes cold. 'Raza?'

She presses a scruffy piece of paper into my hands. 'She asked me to give this to you, if ever she couldn't… get back to you.'

'What… what is it?'

'She wrote it in the Think. One of the guys had a stub of pencil the guards didn't find.'

'Oh.'

She strokes my arm gently. 'Take your time.'

I look down at the paper. I don't want to open it. Don't want to see her words, not without her here with me. I long for her sour, broody presence, the way she never lets me get away with any nonsense, the way she's never anything but real. The way she's the bravest person I ever knew.

I close my eyes tight, blinking away the tears. How are there any left in me? I rub my hands over my face and then take up the note, creased and torn, turning it over in my hands. I unfold it slowly and the words swim into view, the pencil marks as spiky and sharp as Raza herself.

> Dear Carys,
>
> Just in case you're wondering, this isn't some sickly love note or something.

I look up at Lois, exchange a tiny smile. *Raza.*

> It's just in case I go and buy it or something stupid like that. I mean, we all probably will, so this is written in some kind of hope that everything will be okay and you'll all live happily ever after.
>
> I'll admit you got on my nerves at first back in the Community. You were actually annoying as hell. But you grew on me. I know I was a pain, but I thought you were okay in the end. Remember that dawn after Remembrance Night? I'd spilled my guts about my little Carys, and I thought you might just, I don't know, think worse of me or something. But you were just

there, and I felt a little bit less alone from then on. This is gonna sound weird, but it was like we were linked. Maybe cos of your name and my baby girl. I don't know. But on that morning, it was like the most beautiful dawn I ever saw, and it was like I could hope again, and that was kind of cos of you.

Thanks for being here all these weeks. You and Lois kept away the darkness. Stopped loneliness from crushing me. All those whispers through the grate, all those mad plans we've made in the dark hours. I hope they work out.

Love,

Your friend,

Raza xxx

40

THE CENTRE

Two weeks after Festival

AMY

THE STUDIO IS transformed. It's like a world of magic: fairy lights strung all around, tall firs and spruces dragged in from outside, decorated with more lights, snow spray and shiny paper chains they've spent hours cutting and pasting together, the screen draped with long strings of multicoloured beads and balloons. Amy stands on the stage, gazing around at it all. She thinks of the books that inspired it, back in Daniel's library, now buried underground with him – *A Christmas Carol*, *The Lion, the Witch and the Wardrobe* – and how she longs for them again.

Carys and Jacob stand with her, one on each side, waiting together in a moment of stillness before it begins. The last ever *S Word*. But it won't be like any other *S Word* in the history of Newland.

The audience will be here soon. Amy doesn't know how many will come – if any at all. Tickets have been thrown open on the forum, which is now a fully-fledged website, out there on their brand new nationwide network. Ava and Jacob and a team of other tech people from the Resistance have worked all hours for the last couple of weeks, bringing down the Newday net. Jacob's even been talking about how one day soon they'll hook back into the world's internet, and Amy can't even imagine what that will be like. It's like the biggest doors she can imagine, opening up ahead of her, a blaze of light radiating through, beckoning her into the great unknown.

Will people come? She knows the forum is huge now, but what about the people who weren't part of it all, the regular Newlanders, those who supported the Party? She thinks of the chaos of the last two weeks. Riots breaking out everywhere. Mutinies in training houses, kids walking out and joining their parents at home. NForce officers deserting in droves and disappearing. The Resistance taking over Party HQ and council offices throughout the Compounds. Some remain in the grip of the Party, but they are fewer and fewer and must know their days are numbered. She sighs, thinking about how much of a mess it all is, how much is still to be done, how much violence she has seen on the streets.

Getting *The S Word* team on side turned out to be easy. Cadman Showman has disappeared, but many of the stage staff knew and liked Jacob and Amy, and after the experience at Festival and the chaos since were more than ready to hand it over to them for this one final show. Resistance people have already taken over most of NBC. With Coran on side as well they are ready, dressed up to the nines and set to go live in just half an hour.

'They're opening the doors,' Jacob says, shading his eyes against the lights in the auditorium. Amy watches, twisting her hands together, as a trickle of what looks like trainees filter in, slowly, silently. Then more. Then a group of Productives – *no, stop calling them that* – and… is that Miss Warden there, with Mercia and Boy L and a big crowd of others? Mercia spots them and runs to the stage, waving, and more pile in behind her, pouring in now, more and more of them, folk of every age. Some she recognises from the Resistance, some from the camp where they met Abs. The atmosphere is charged with electricity as they take their seats.

It's full in minutes, and still they come, standing round the edges, squatting in the aisles. Amy watches, awestruck, a whole mash of emotions bouncing round her mind. Faces are open, hopeful, excited; some fearful, some, maybe, angry. Amy looks at Carys: she stands still, her hands quivering slightly, her eyes wide. 'Let's take a minute backstage,' Amy says, taking her hand and leading her out.

In their old studio lounge they perch together on the ancient horsehair sofa. 'It doesn't feel real,' Jacob says.

'Ha, it's just another workday for you, right?' Carys says, poking him in the side.

'Funny. Look. Are you both okay? Both ready?'

'As I'll ever be,' Amy says.

Carys smiles softly. 'Sort of.'

Coran bustles in with a sound guy. 'Time to get you sorted.' Coran fusses round them, straightening collars and smoothing hair, while the guy gets their radio mics fitted up.

'Is everyone here?' Amy says to Coran.

He smiles. 'Everyone who needs to be.'

Carys sniffs. 'Apart from Anson.'

'They'll find him,' Jacob says.

One of the stage crew pokes her head around the door. 'Five minutes.'

Amy feels the leap of nerves, the butterflies in her belly. She's done this enough times, but this is different. This is real. She waits just a moment more, letting the others go ahead, and closes her eyes. It's okay. It's okay.

As they run onto the stage the audience are up on their feet, cheering, whistling, clapping. Amy is glad she will never have to do this again after tonight. She gazes at the four empty judges' chairs and swallows.

Jacob steps forward, grins wide at the crowd, waits for them to fall into silence. 'My name is Jacob Trader,' he says. 'You once knew me as Boy T, then Oswall—' he screws up his face as he says this, and the audience laugh, '—but I am, and have always been, Jacob.'

It's Amy's turn. 'And, as I think a few of you might have picked up the other day at Festival, my name is Amy Plumber.' More laughter, eager faces, Mercia in the front, whooping her name. 'I have never been, and never will be, Esla.'

Carys steps forward tentatively. 'My name is Carys Clerk. And I promise not to do what I did last time I was on this stage.'

This time the laughter is louder, deeper; they are with her. With all of them. Amy relaxes just a little bit. She pins her gaze on the back of the hall, where a whole group of media people are huddled together with cameras and Slates. 'You may have noticed a change in decor in here,' she says, and the crowd cheer again. She feels the smile pulling at her lips, the joy sparking inside. 'In the Before, in December they used to celebrate something called Christmas. We don't know a whole lot about it, only some stuff from books we got hold of. But we do know it was a celebration of light in the darkness. Of goodness over evil. They sang and feasted, and… oh, so much we have to discover. People gave each other gifts and reminded each other of how much they were loved. The Party took all of that away.' She pauses, her eyes roaming the crowd. 'So now, tonight, we are starting a new tradition. Or reclaiming an old one, really. From now on, we will celebrate together every year. As one of the books I read said, "A Merry Christmas to us all!"'

The screen flashes up with the words, illuminated by thousands of sparkly lights, and the audience roar, stamping their feet. Amy spots a small kid a couple of rows back, her face filled with wonder, and she stores it away inside herself for later, thinks about how this Christmas thing holds deeper, stranger power than she'd imagined.

Jacob steps forward. 'You might be wondering what the show is going to look like tonight.' He pauses while the audience laugh again. 'A little bit different. We'll have some great entertainment for you, of course; we have a choir and a dance troupe who never got a chance to perform on the show because they were known as Unproductives. Outsiders. That will be a little bit later.'

He stops, takes a deep breath. 'This show used to be about judgement. About separating out the so-called Strivers and Skivers, and shaming those who weren't seen to try hard enough. So we're going to bring you judgement tonight, but not quite as you remember it. This time it will be a choice between justice and injustice. This time the Party will begin to face their crimes.'

The crowd are hushed, hanging on his every word. There's barely a shuffle of feet or a cough.

'So, everyone, please welcome our four judges!'

The silence stays, everyone suddenly frozen. Amy watches as the double doors in the screen glide open and the four judges process in, with none of their usual style. Lora is pale and drawn, her gaze on the floor ahead of her. Portia and Edwin just look amused, and Raulf looks like he's got so much rage cooped up he might burst any moment. It took some doing to get them here, most of it Coran's and Lora's.

Carys walks over to them as they sit down, Raulf slumping in his chair like he'd rather be anywhere else. 'You spent a lot of years giving out judgements on normal working people,' she says, her words poised, ominous. 'And now you know the truth of what happened to those people because of what you did.'

Raulf snorts; the others say nothing.

'So tonight we're going to welcome some of your beloved Productives to the stage. Do come on through, folks.'

A motley group of people shuffle onto the stage, all of them cuffed. Amy knows who they are. One of them is the chief of NForce here in the Centre, the one who once tried to kill them. Another is the nurse who injected them in the Think, and another two are from Anson's cabinet, the minister for health and the minister for education. With them are two Resistance police, a brand new law enforcement group just beginning to recruit, one of them the ex-NForce guy from the arena. The crowd remain hushed.

'We have a few... representatives here tonight,' Carys says. 'They represent the Party, and those who have committed serial atrocities over years in full knowledge of the truth. We felt it important that our judges should make some decisions on these lives, just as they have done for so many others.'

This time the crowd start to clap, slowly and then gaining in volume.

Jacob steps forward. 'But we don't want to spend too much time on this. We have more important things for tonight. Now, judges, please watch the screen and judge these stories on the merit that you see.'

Raulf crosses his arms, scowling, as the screen lights with an image of the first man, the NForce chief. Instead of showing his story, though, the screen scrolls with a long list of names, superimposed over his face. One after the other after the other. Some of them don't even have names: Boy Baker. Girl Banker. Girl Retail. The list goes on and on.

Jacob pauses as it comes to an end. 'These were the people Chief Officer here deemed Unproductive and sent to the Home or the Think.' He lets that sink in, and the chief stands there, his face blank, the only tension in the set of his jaw.

As Jacob repeats this tableau for each of the prisoners on the stage, Amy notices Lora's ravaged face. Lora is no stranger to shedding tears on *The S Word*, but these are different. These are real. She stares up at the screen, taking in each name, her mouth quivering. Amy thinks about how Jacob and Ava Coder have spent so long digging up all these names. As each one scrolls up the screen she tries to picture them, to hold them in her mind for just one little moment.

'These people might have been forgotten by the Party,' Carys says, 'but not by us. Please take a moment to bow your heads and think of them.'

The audience bend their heads in silence. Raulf stays in the same position, slumped, a smirk twisting his mouth.

Jacob turns to the judges. 'So, what's the verdict? Do you have anything to say?'

They sit frozen, staring up at him.

It's Raulf who breaks the silence. 'I don't know what I'm doing here. None of this is my fault. Of course these people should be punished. Executed. Of course they deserve it. It's the Commander who is at fault for all of this, not me. I've always been one for proper justice. But I didn't know about any of this, so...' He trails off, twirls his chair and spreads his arms to the audience, makes a confused, pouty face, waiting for their usual adulation. But they do not give it.

'Okay. So it's a No from Raulf,' Jacob says, and the large 'SKIVER' above Raulf's name over the screen lights up with a harsh buzz.

Raulf sits up straighter. 'Wait... what? I didn't say anything about Skivers.'

'You proclaimed that they should be executed. And that's what you've done every time you have judged someone to be a Skiver.'

Raulf snickers, his face pulling in on itself in a mock-frown. 'Nonsense. The Skivers were shameful to Newland and deserved their time in the Think, which is all we did on this show, I can assure you.'

Jacob laughs harshly. 'Portia? Edwin? Anything to add?'

Portia sits there detached, her chin held high. 'I didn't ask to be here.'

'But you are an *S Word* judge,' Carys says.

Portia waves her off as if she's an annoying gnat. 'I don't condone these people's crimes, if that's what you're asking.'

Jacob smiles grimly. 'Good. Skiver for Portia, then.' He ignores her snort and moves on to Edwin. 'And you?'

'I... I...' Edwin stumbles over his words. 'I don't want to execute anybody.'

'So they are Strivers?'

'No! No. I don't... I mean, they are wrong, of course—'

Jacob nods. 'So three Skivers. Now Lora.'

Lora stands up, and Amy sees the tears still fresh on her cheeks. She feels for her then, thinks about how Lora has been largely absent the last two weeks, locked away in her room, only allowing Coran in. But she's never once asked them to leave. 'I'm sorry I was ever a part of this,' she says, her voice cracking. 'I'm so, so sorry.' She bends her head, rubs her eyes. 'I didn't want to believe it for so long. I was blind, stupid. But now… I see what you're doing. I don't like it, but I get it. Of course, I say these people have committed grievous crimes. But so have I. So have you.' She sweeps her hands round to the other judges, who tut and cackle at her, then turns to the audience. 'Please… forgive me.'

Nobody moves. Jacob lets the silence fall for a few moments, then the screen lights up again, this time with more names: reams and reams of them, scrolling up. In the background, music plays quietly; a gentle piano melody. 'As you have judged these people, so we too remember those *you* have sent to the Think,' Jacob says to the judges. 'These names are those you deemed Skivers. Those you sentenced to death.'

Lora gasps and crumples to the floor, sobbing, but the others sit cross-armed, stony-faced. It's only Edwin who Amy notices has a slight edge to his expression, a tremor around the lips.

'So what are you saying?' Raulf says eventually, a sulk in his tone. 'You're going to, what, kill us? Like this scum here?' He waves his hand at the prisoners, who shrink back, faces a mix of terror and scorn. Lora sniffles, still curled on the floor.

'Before anything else, we'd like you all to watch a video,' Amy says, stepping forward and helping Lora into her seat. 'Guards, please take the prisoners away.'

She waits while the officers hustle the four disgruntled Productives off the stage.

'Girls, Reia, would you please join us now?'

Reia walks in from the wings, regal and beautiful, in a black jumpsuit and biker boots, her piercings glinting under the lights. The four girls follow, hand in hand; Hannah, Esther, Emma and Ella, all in simple white dresses with bare feet, their hair caught up in red-flowered braids on top of their heads. The audience clap politely, confused by the change.

'Please welcome our first act of the night: The Subs,' Amy says, and the applause warms up. 'These guys are what was once known as Outsiders, and they lived in a community where love wrote the rules. Sadly, that community was destroyed, or "subdued"—' she curls her fingers into quotes as she says this, '—as it was always put on the news. They have a special song to share with you all, and we would like to share some images with that song.'

The four girls stand in place, on tiptoe, heads bent, two on either side of the stage, and Reia stands in the centre by a microphone, lit now by a single spotlight. 'Please honour with us these people whose lives were ripped away by this cruel regime. I am going to sing a song written by one of our community.'

Reia's voice is rich and deep, carrying the plaintive, soaring notes of Raza's song into all the corners of the auditorium:

I see you all around
In dreams of morning you'll be found...

Amy is taken back to that strangely beautiful dawn when Raza sang as they launched paper candle-boats on the rippling water and remembered.

The screen flicks on behind Reia and images start to roll. Benedict and Sarah Clerk are first, their names and dates of birth and death blazed in large capitals across the screen. Ava and Jacob found all these pictures, too, deep in old files. More Resistance workers fade into the screen, then Jacob's mother, Eda Coder. It was only recently Jacob's father had told her what his mother once worked as, and Jacob had wept in his arms.

Amy feels the tears prick the back of her eyes as Reia's rich voice wraps itself around the pictures: Girl S, who never got her own name, sent to the Home because she was too sick to be Productive. Sim, his red hair tumbling over mischievous eyes in an old training house photo. Aiden Driver, Jacob's beloved grandfather; Amy hears the choke at the back of Jacob's throat. Cory, from the Subs Community, and Esther's mother, and more from their little bunker.

Then Lewis. Her big brother, her soul-child, larger than life up there on the screen, his easy grin lighting up the picture, the laugh-creases hugging his dark brown eyes. Amy wants to reach out, to touch him, to find him there with her. She hears a quiet sob from the front row and locks eyes with her mother.

He fades out to more pictures. Losers from *The S Word* – Audrey Retail, Garrett House. More Resistance, Outsiders, trainees from the forum who were taken down at the camp. Abs and Tom. The audience sit transfixed, the song soaring, the girls still standing, heads bowed as Reia sings of loss and hope.

Amy knows what the last image will be. Jacob's found an old picture from her training house, and it doesn't really look like her, but Amy sees her there in the eyes, the stubborn set of the chin.

Carys stands nearby, softly crying, and Amy takes her hand. The girls raise their heads, one by one, and turn to the screen then bow deeply as Reia brings the song to a close.

But now I see you in the stars
See you shining through the dark...

The lights fall into darkness and the audience stays silent, and Jacob, Amy and Carys gaze up at the screen where Raza's image remains, the words "Raza. 15th October N103 – 5th December N121" frozen in place.

A scrape in the audience. Someone standing from their seat – Mercia? She raises both arms slowly, and then Warden stands with her, clasps hands, raises her own. One by one people stand, grasp hands, raise them together, lift their heads, eyes on the screen. Amy's throat is a great big lump as she takes in the sight of them, the rapt silence in the room as Reia's last notes fly away. The little girls catch on, raise their own arms, joining with Reia in the centre of the stage, and Carys links hands with Amy and Jacob and they stand tall, and it is dazzling, and it is everything.

'Well, this is all very pretty.'

The booming voice comes from the wings, and Amy knows it. It's cold in here suddenly, the chill coiling through the air like a thousand snakes crawling through the auditorium. He struts onto the stage, a small group of NForce officers surrounding him.

'And now it's time to bow to your Commander,' he says.

41

THE CENTRE

Two weeks after Festival

CARYS

IT'S LIKE HE sucks all the joy out of the room. All the Christmas sparkle, the memory of Reia's poignant melody: all dimmed, muted, spoiled. I don't want to look at him. I'd hoped never to see him again, but something in me knew he'd always be there, that I'd always be looking over my shoulder. He stands tall in his Commander's garb, ornamental gold epaulettes gleaming against his shoulders, many medals dragging at his blue blazer.

I glance at the officers surrounding him. Their faces are hard to read. Some of them are rigid with determination, but others hover with uncertainty. At the edges of the stage, armed Resistance police creep into place, surrounding the group. I wonder how he got in, but then I remember how many people round here still worship him.

Anson repeats his line. 'I said, and now it's time to bow to your Commander.'

But no one takes any notice this time, either. The crowd stand solid, chins raised, hands still joined and lifted at Raza on the screen, a wholly opposite stance to what he requires. I watch his face closely as he takes in the truth that these people are not going to bow to him. Watch as the lines on his brow quake and deepen, as his thick lips part, his teeth grit together, his eyes narrow.

'You. Will. Bow.' It is a roar, this time, and still they stand, upright and tall and glorious. I drink them in, breathe in this moment, feel the warm embrace of Amy's and Jacob's hands in mine.

Anson turns to the judges. 'Get up and bow to your Commander.'

But they do not. Not even Raulf, who still sits slouched, his arms crossed, his feet sticking straight out in front of him.

Anson's face is red-hot, his coiffed silver hair quivering as his rage storms through his body. I want to laugh all of a sudden.

'I am appointed by the Illumen,' he bellows, and his words echo around the auditorium, bouncing back as if the walls themselves want no part of them. 'I am your Commander. Now bow to me.'

Not a flicker.

He glares at the producer. 'Get your team to play the anthem. Now.'

The producer does not move.

The NForce officers around him stand awkwardly, as if they feel like they are taking up too much space. 'Make them,' he yells in their faces. 'Shoot them.'

But the Resistance police step closer, their own weapons trained, and the NForce look to me the weakest I've ever seen them. Anson shoves at one of them and he jumps, grabs his gun from his holster and aims haphazardly at the judges. The shot is a crack in the silence, and Edwin Runner slumps over, sliding out of his chair. Portia gasps and Lora cries out. A Resistance guy is on the shooter in seconds, disarming him, the others hovering close, eyes pinned on the rest of the NForce guards, who stand in frozen shock. Anson bellows at them as if he cannot see a threat; it's like his narcissism makes his head so full of himself he can't see beyond it. Why did he come here tonight? Is his ego so huge that he was convinced we'd all drop everything, bow to him like we were all waiting for him, like nothing's changed? 'Make them!' he yells again, and his poxy detail shiver in their shoes.

Reia ushers the girls behind her. 'No more of this.' Her voice is loud, authoritative, and Anson starts to shrink. His shoulders slump, his belly sticks out, his stiff uniform trousers crease at the knees as they start to buckle. He smooths himself down, glares at Reia, strides over to Lora and drags her from her chair. 'You will bow to me. You, at least.'

Lora just stands limp in his clutch, head down; I see her lips pressed together, a tiny quiver rumbling through her cheeks. I feel the old anger rising, a ball of fire in my belly.

Anson barks, 'You belong to me.'

Lora says nothing.

Anson raises his hand. Brings it down on her face, a resounding crack through the heavy stillness. I can't do this anymore. Can't bear to see Lora so reduced by him. I tear away from Jacob and Amy and go bowling into him just as he aims another punch at Lora's shoulder. He skids back, shoving Lora over, grabs hold of me by the straps of my dress, laughs in my face; the alcohol is strong on his breath. '*You*. It's always been you, hasn't it? You've always been the one to bring everything crashing down.' He curls his lip at me, his eyes pinpricks of ice. Out of the corner of my eye I see his security guys and the Resistance police facing off at each other, weapons raised. By the judges' seats, Portia crouches with Edwin, stroking his forehead, crying softly.

'Yeah. Yeah I have,' I say, and slap Anson flush on the cheek, right over the wound I gave him two weeks ago. He staggers back, his hand on his cut, teeth bared so wide his gums show angry and purple. Jacob's with me now, fists clenched at his sides, and Amy on my other side. I think of the last time I exploded in this place, and how they weren't there for me then, or at least that was how I felt. This time it's different. This time they are by my side, and I feel the strength radiating from them.

Lora scrambles up from the floor, her face flushed, veins in her temples straining as she pushes him full force into one of his guys. 'I never belonged to you,' she hisses, her voice dripping with disgust, and then she turns to the audience. 'He beat me. He hit me again and again and I took it because he was my Commander. He's nothing but a sadistic bully. But I don't have to do that anymore. I don't have to.'

This breaks the audience's trance, and they begin to cheer Lora on, clapping their hands high above their heads. They are reclaiming the nation's sweetheart, their voices rising in a chant for her. 'Lora! Lora!' Portia and Raulf are silent, their faces suddenly broken down, finished. Edwin is curled on the ground, too still.

'Now go,' Reia says coldly to Anson, nodding to the Resistance police. 'I think you'll find the Think very comfortable. That's what you always used to say to people, wasn't it?'

Anson snarls at her, beckoning frantically to his own guards. They scramble for their weapons, their faces jagged with the breach between loyalty and fear. Anson turns back to me, spittle flying as he shouts, 'You will bow to me. You all will. You'll see. Newland will collapse without me. I am appointed by the Illumen.'

I want to rush him, to strike him, to kill him right here. I wrench myself together, looking at him, Amy's hand on the small of my back. He's pitiful now, shrinking before me as his guards surround him, his ice eyes fading to mud-grey, his medals suddenly too big for him. 'I was under your noses all the time,' he boasts, but even his voice is fading. 'Hiding right out near Party HQ.' He twists his mouth into a sneer, but his lips are trembling, unable to hold it there; his lips slump like dead slugs. One of his guards grabs his arm and starts hustling him away. He wrenches himself free. 'Shoot them all.' His guards glance at one another wildly, then at the Resistance officers, then at the silent crowd. They know they are outnumbered. And the Resistance keep their weapons steady, too aware of all the innocent people packed tightly into the studio. No one is shooting here. The guard who seems in charge pulls Anson away, and this time he allows himself to be led, his body sagging between two of them, his head bent, hurrying off the stage and away into the maze of passages I once belted through to escape myself. The Resistance officers dive after them, and that's when I hear the burst of gunfire backstage; too much of it.

I stand there and stare at the stage exit, my insides in turmoil. I'm with Jacob and the Resistance in what we've all decided, but I still hope one of those bullets found Anson. I know, deep inside, that somehow he'll slink away again; know he still has too many supporters out there. Maybe he'll always be somewhere in the shadows, waiting. But I know too, with everything within me, that his words are not true. That I will never bow to him again. And that his shame, in here now, in front of a live audience of thousands and hundreds of thousands across the nation, has to be enough.

But I am not sure it ever will be.

42

THE CENTRE

Two months after Festival

AMY

A T THE BORDER gates the great screen hangs loose, its twin from the other side already torn down and ripped apart. The crowd outside the barrier watches NBC replaying the scenes at *The S Word* once more. A great cheer rises as Lora stands up to Anson, and then again as Reia and Jacob stand together at the front of the stage, proclaiming that all those now incarcerated in the Think and all Party workers apprehended from now on will be subject to the Newland Trials, which will take place in an international court of law; Edlin Trader has more fingers in more pies than any of them ever imagined. The camera zooms in on Raulf, sitting straighter now, his face a map of confusion. 'It was your way to execute without trial,' Reia says to him, her voice sharp enough to cut him in two. 'Your way to commit mass murder, right from the start of this wretched regime. We do not consent to the New Day way.'

The audience cheer, both on the screen and here now on the plains outside the barrier; thousands of them are gathered, as far as the eye can see, and via live link thousands of others all over the nation, gathered around their Compound barriers. They come armed with serious kit: sledgehammers, a crawler crane complete with a wrecking ball, bulldozers, all waiting for Reia to give the go-ahead.

Amy gazes at the people near her, drinking them in; she still can't get her head around the fact they are all here, with her now. Her parents. Carys, standing with Jacob, Harry and Ava. Will, with his parents and brother, Matt. The girls from the bunker, barely able to contain their energy, hanging on Reia's every word. Coran, Ash and Lora.

She turns to a light touch on her arm, a whisper. 'Hey.' It's Mercia, with Boy L on her tail, except he's Luke now, and Miss Warden a little way behind.

Amy pauses for just a second, then hugs her tight. 'Sorry I doubted you.'

'It's understandable. Sorry for all the times… and… your hair—'

'Yeah.'

Mercia smiles at her then, and she notices for the first time the beauty and strength of her. Amy hugs her again. 'We must sit down. Swap stories. Is Aida here?'

Mercia's face falls. 'She didn't agree. She's back at Ashton, with the Party hangers-on there.'

'Principal still ruling the roost?'

'Of course. The Resistance are on her tail, though, building a case against her.'

'And you? What will you do?'

Mercia smiles shyly at Luke. 'We've joined up with a project back in the Midlands Compound. It's a centre for sick and elderly people. Lizzie… I mean, Miss Warden… she's like the manager. Always was good with people who were suffering.'

Amy grins. 'But not like the Home, right?'

'Ha. Never again. You should come and visit, Amy. You won't believe what it's like. What we've done in a short time… what we're going to do. We have more centres springing up all over the nation – not just in Compounds. We call ourselves the Hope Project.'

'I've heard. Can't be easy, though, with the riots and the protests from the Party side now too.'

Mercia nods. 'Let's say we're up against it. There are more of us every day, though. So... how about you? What now for you and these guys?'

'We're at Lora's for now while we get ourselves together. Jacob is working in IT for the Resistance now, with Ava here. He's kind of working for his dad, though he won't admit it.' Amy laughs, casting a glance over at Edlin Trader and Anne Trainer One, standing apart from the others, laughing together so hard it's like they're choking in joy. 'I'm just helping co-ordinate stuff for now, but I'm thinking about medicine.'

Mercia smiles. 'All those books you used to read in the Pod. I thought you were such a geek.' She flushes.

Amy smiles. 'I own that. It's all I've ever wanted to do, and now we have access to all the information in the world, or will very soon, it's never felt more exciting.'

'And Carys?'

Amy looks over at her, deep in conversation with young Harry. 'She wants to work with kids. She's got this whole thing about finding families for kids who don't have them and helping kids who struggle with education.'

'Get her to come and visit us,' Mercia says. 'We have so many branches now, and we're looking at centres for kids as well as older people.'

'She's on it. She's already got something going in Lora's mansion, with Coran.' She gestures over at Coran then, smiling at his happiness; he is in his element here, carefree in a blingy red suit, with Lora and Ash beside him. Lora, who is now the first minister for health.

Just then Reia's microphone squeals as she raises it to her lips. 'I want to thank you for coming out today, in such large numbers too. You are all amazing!'

As the crowd cheer, Amy gazes at Reia, their new leader – their prime minister, some are calling her now; she shouted down any mention of her being a Commander – a regal, poised woman with so much dignity it shines from her. The early spring sunshine gleams at her back, lighting her face, her shaven head, her deep brown eyes.

'Are you ready to tear down some walls?' she yells, and the crowd go wild, hollering and screaming and whistling, some of them flying flags and banners. On the huge screen, NBC flicks between different Compounds, their own excited applause joining with theirs until it's one mighty roar. Will grabs Amy's hands and starts spinning her around and around until her head goes dizzy and she laughs so much she wonders how this much joy can be possible.

Reia laughs, the deep waves of it echoing through the microphone. 'You know it won't be easy. You know some Compounds are still closed, still ruled with an iron fist. There are pro-Party factions in the open Compounds, a resistance to our Resistance, if you like. And, of course the ex-Commander is still at large…' the crowd boo and hiss, '… and so we must be vigilant. But we will work for freedom wherever we can, and knowing you are all with us gives us even more strength, when there are still dark days ahead.' She waits as the crowd applaud. 'All I ask is that we keep choosing justice and mercy instead of hate. That we walk the good paths.' She winks at Jacob. 'As you know, we're working at the former Party HQ to establish a new government – in days ahead, of course, as we journey back to democracy, you will all be free to vote for your leaders. For now, please be assured we are working for your good.' Her voice rises as she stands taller. 'Every person in our nation is of equal value. Every child will be given a name and raised in their family, and brothers and sisters will be born once again. There will be no more divisions of Productives and Unproductives, or Strivers and Skivers, or Newlanders and Outsiders. And there will be no more Home.'

The crowd is one big party, with its cheers and banners and balloons and, somewhere further back, a full on brass band playing a tune I've never heard, so unlike the Newland anthem: celebration streams through the air.

'Once upon a time,' Reia continues, 'this land valued freedom, but not just that. We valued the outcast, the oppressed, the marginalised. Oh, I'm fully aware this wasn't always the case. I've seen some of the history now; I know some of it is just as bad as what we've experienced here. But I've also seen enough history to know that there is always hope. That there will always be good, and light, and love, and that if we keep seeking those things then maybe we can make our nation just a little bit better. Even in our darkest days here, that hope broke through, with three youngsters in a training house and countless others working behind the scenes for so many years to bring this thing down. And so, now is the time to really bring this thing down. This is the day when Newland will fall. Are you ready, Britain? Are you ready?'

Amy is caught up in the shouting, singing, dancing crowd, jumping up and down with Will as the band play louder, faster, the drummer rolling out a fast-paced rhythm. Then they're surging forward as one, taking their sledgehammers to the barrier and slamming, crashing, cheering, bulldozers piling in, earth flying everywhere. Amy watches as a large crack fractures the concrete from top to bottom, right near the border gates; the sound of it is an explosion of liberty and she dances with Will, then with Jacob, with Carys, with Emma and Ella, twirling and whirling until she's flushed with exhaustion.

On the screen scenes from all over the nation play out: barriers smashed down, border gates burned, parties in full flow. Kids are everywhere, not a training uniform in sight; they hold hands with parents who swing them into the air again and again.

As Amy watches, the screen flickers, like it's cutting out, then another scene fuzzes into focus, and she can't understand what she's seeing. Around her, people down tools and stare. It's a huge crowd of people on a beach, holding a massive banner aloft. Amy tries to read the words, frowning: "Bon retour, Grande Bretagne!" Then, underneath, the words "Welcome back Britain, love from France!" The scene changes quickly, now to another crowd on another beach with another banner: "¡Bienvenido de nuevo, Gran Bretaña!" "Welcome back Britain, love from Spain!" Then more and more scenes of more and more countries, a mass of pixellated faces smiling at them, and Amy's heart swells at the glorious diversity displayed before her. Nearby, a bunch of kids dance on fallen concrete chunks, joining hands in an extending circle and skipping round and round, and still the scenes play out, still the nations of the world break an enforced silence of over a century.

Carys sidles up next to her and takes her arm, leaning her head against Amy's shoulder. 'It feels like a dream, right?'

'I keep waiting to wake up.'

'I just wish everyone was on board.'

Amy nods. 'I think we can only go forward. One day at a time, to do what we can do in that moment. We'll probably mess up, but having the freedom to mess up is huge, right?'

Carys cuddles in further. 'Mmm. Did I ever tell you, Amy, you're my bestest friend?'

'You been on the celebration champagne already?'

She laughs. 'I don't think I'll ever be able to touch that stuff. It'll always be Anson's face I see.'

Amy shudders. 'Don't say that name.'

'I guess we'll always be looking over our shoulders.'

'Mmm. But we don't have to let him have any power over us anymore. He's done. Forget him.'

Carys smiles. 'I'm trying. Hey… what's that noise?'

Amy looks up into the pale February sky, where a buzz – no, a roar – draws closer, closer, closer still. 'Is it a storm?'

'I don't—' Carys stops, eyes widening, as something hurtles through the sky above. More than something. A whole formation of them, trailing long billows of smoke in red, white, blue; aeroplanes, Amy realises. Fast as lightning, noisy as thunder, a sight she's never seen before. They whip upside down, fly over again, somersaulting and tumbling and climbing high, and Carys gasps, her mouth falling wide open.

Ash comes to stand with them, his face aglow with joy. 'My great-grandfather told my father about these. There used to be air shows, in the Before, with this kind of display. Must be one of those countries organised it for us.'

Coran grins. 'You're a plane nerd as well as a train one.'

'Yup. Good thing I'm the new transport minister.'

They watch the show, transfixed, the screen alive with crowds of people cheering. In front of Amy, the cracks widen as more and more of the barriers fall, great concrete chunks scattering the ground everywhere she can see. In between some small stone debris nearby a tiny white snowdrop fights its way through a crack. It's like the land is being redeemed, she thinks, like it's springing into life where there was none, being bought back at such a great price but with so much hope ahead it cannot be contained: in her mind, in the barriers, in the ground itself.

EPILOGUE

Ten months later

ℂARYS

T HE SEA IS strangely still tonight, waves lapping peacefully at the shore, where a light dusting of snow rests on winter-damp sand. In the distance I spot a large cargo ship sailing into harbour and marvel at the sight; it is still all so new. I stand and gaze out at the world beyond, a world I'd never dreamed of.

The cold is sharp, its frozen fingers coiling through my gloves and scarf. I rub my hands together and shiver, and Jacob moves closer, his arm around my shoulder. I look again at the endless line of people standing in a long row up and down the beach, on the very edge of the shore, the silence falling softly among us. All around me are everyone I need. Jacob one side, Amy the other, others who have been with us on our journey close by.

On the makeshift screens set up at intervals along the beach, Reia fades into view, holding a candle. 'Welcome to Remembrance Night,' she says. Standing with her on the screen are Hannah and Esther one side and Emma and Ella the other, their faces lit up with their own candles. 'When all your candles are lit, please step forward together and whisper your names.'

We wait quietly as volunteers walk along the line with tapers and candle lanterns. They are made of willow and shaped like a bird in flight. I cradle mine, thinking about freedom and what it has all cost, and what it continues to cost, and how it is still all worth it. I think of Sim's Place, the new family we have established at Lora's old home. Kids who have lost parents to the Think and the Home. Kids who never knew any home but their training houses. We have ten of them there with us now – Coran, turns out, is a natural director, and Reia, though insanely busy, is the best mum in the world, according to the children. Harry, Hannah, Ella and Emma are with us; Esther has been adopted by Stephen and Sarah. I think of the five more Sim's Place projects now going across the nation, with plans for more, and for one moment my mind takes me back to a young girl on her first night at Ashton, quivering under Principal's glare, lost without knowing how much,

The screen flicks over to other beaches and lakes around the nation, where people hold up their lanterns high as they go forward into the shallows. So many people with so many names to remember.

There are names I don't want to remember, too. Names that still haunt me; some still out there somewhere, some gone altogether. Anson. Principal. Gardener. I bundle them all up in my mind and fling them far out into the deep black sea.

The candles are a thousand lights in a flickering line, tiny sparks that together dispel the darkness. I feel a gentle rumble under my feet as people move forward, the soft splash of the waves the kind of quiet that restores your soul. I wade into the sea and hold my own lantern high, and in its flame I see my parents, Benedict and Sarah Clerk, and they are smiling at me. I see Sim, I see Aiden, I see Abs, and then I see Raza, and she makes the flame shiver and blink, and I think, *how like Raza.*

I set my lantern on the sea and whisper the names, and they are a vapour on the wind, and they echo up and down the line, like they are reluctant to leave. The boats bob on the water, scattered in different directions, some drawn far away, some hovering close nearby.

As Reia sings Raza's song once again, I link hands with Jacob and Amy, breathing the music and knowing it will never leave me. We wade in further together, the ice-cold water lapping over our knees and stealing our breath, and stand in our own line of three, gazing out at the far horizon where dawn begins to paint the sky and wake up a new day. The bird-boats drift out to sea, the lights fading slowly, and the darkness drapes us like a big warm velvet cloak.

THE END

ABOUT THE AUTHOR

E.M. Carter is an award-winning author, poet and editor who can't get enough of words. She is the author of the Newland Trilogy (*Repression Ground*, *Rebellion Ground* and *Redemption Ground*) as well as a writer of several non-fiction books.

Liz was poet in residence for Wellington in Shropshire 2022/2023 and a finalist in the Woman Alive Reader's Choice award 2019. For other writers, she offers a freelance service editing, formatting and designing book covers and interiors. Liz likes to spend her days clad in fairtrade turquoise dresses trying not to eat chocolate and is proud to be a grammar pedant.

For updates and more, visit emcarter.carterclan.me.uk and sign up to her newsletter.

If you've enjoyed *Redemption Ground*, Liz would very much appreciate it if you could leave a review on Amazon or Goodreads. Thank you so much!

ACKNOWLEDGEMENTS

Writing this trilogy while living with my own disability has been a long adventure all of its own, and I want to thank a few people in particular. First of all, you, the readers – thank you for taking a chance on a new author and seeing the story of Carys, Amy and Jacob through to its ending; I hope you enjoyed their company as much as I loved writing them! I'd love you to leave a short review or rating if you liked the books – it really does help!

Thanks to all at Resolute Books. What a team! It's been such a privilege to get to know so many talented authors and to work with you through this process. Special thanks go to Paul Trembling, Sarah Nicholson and Claire Dunn, my peer reviewers; your wisdom and encouragement have shaped this series in such great ways, and your support has been incredible.

Thank you to my ARC team – I massively appreciate each and every one of you.

Finally, thanks to all my friends and family, and especially to my favourites, Tim, Tabby and Nathaniel, always my first readers and always cheering me – and my characters – on. You never let me give up on this thing, and I love you more than I can ever express.

About Resolute Books

We are an independent press representing a consortium of experienced authors, professional editors and talented designers producing engaging and inspiring books of the highest quality for readers everywhere. We produce books in a number of genres including historical fiction, crime suspense, young adult dystopia, memoir, Cold War thrillers, poetry, and even Jane Austen fan fiction!

Find out more at resolutebooks.co.uk

for the joy of reading

9 781915 981356